waltzing through flaws

waltzing through flaws

paula sharp

BLOOMSBURY

First published in Great Britain 2001

Copyright © 2000 by Paula Sharp

The moral right of the author has been asserted

Bloomsbury Publishing Plc, 38 Soho Square, London W1D 3HB

A CIP catalogue record for this book is available from the British Library

ISBN 0 7475 5290 8

10 9 8 7 6 5 4 3 2 1

Printed in Great Britain by Clays Limited, St Ives plc

This book is dedicated to Ross,
and to the memory of Joyce Edna Simmons Sharp.

ACKNOWLEDGMENTS

Grateful acknowledgment is made to Jennifer Barth for being such a brilliant, wonderful editor; without her, this book surely would have died gasping on the sand. I am also thankful to Peternelle van Arsdale for her editorial contributions to the manuscript in its last stages; to Alison Lowenstein for her graceful handling of the book in all its stages; and to Gina Maccoby, for continuing to be such a stellar agent. I wish to thank Margaret Diehl, Ross Eatman, and Lesley Sharp for reading and criticizing the manuscript; Rosemary Sharp for information on Mayan glyphs; Uncle John and Dr. Gagliuso for information on cataracts and retinal disorders; Julio, for his method of counting to twenty, jokes, and question about pigeons; Jesse, for his monologue on translation; and Charles for his opinion about God.

CONTENTS

the mother

by Gwendolyn Brooks

Abortions will not let you forget.
You remember the children you got that you did not get,
The damp small pulps with a little or with no hair,
The singers and workers that never handled the air.
You will never neglect or beat
Them, or silence or buy with a sweet.
You will never wind up the sucking-thumb
Or scuttle off ghosts that come.
You will never leave them, controlling your luscious sigh,
Return for a snack of them with gobbling mother-eye.

I have heard in the voices of the wind the voices of my dim
        killed children.
I have contracted. I have eased
My dim dears at the breasts they could never suck.
I have said, Sweets, if I sinned, if I seized
Your luck
And your lives from your unfinished reach,
If I stole your births and your names,
Your straight baby tears and your games,
Your stilted or lovely loves, your tumults, your marriages,
        aches, and your deaths,
If I poisoned the beginnings of your breaths,
Believe that even in my deliberateness I was not deliberate.
Though why should I whine,
Whine that the crime was other than mine?—
Since anyhow you are dead.
Or rather, or instead,
You were never made.
But that too, I am afraid,
Is faulty: oh, what shall I say, how is the truth to be said?
You were born, you had body, you died.
It is just that you never giggled or planned or cried.

Believe me, I loved you all.
Believe me, I knew you, though faintly, and I loved, I loved you
All.

"God is an idea thought up by the devil to make people fight and kill each other, and start religious wars," my uncle F. X. told Isabel Flood.

Isabel had sailed up the front steps to our porch, where we sat drinking iced tea. She carried a religious leaflet with **ABORTION IS FIRST DEGREE MURDER** printed in bold letters at the top, and now she drew her hand back, as if F. X.'s arm had changed into a snake. In her other hand she held a puzzle—she always did—not a jigsaw puzzle, but the metal three-dimensional kind that you work to see if you can extricate one bent tangle from another.

F. X. offered Isabel an iced tea. It was May 15 of 1977, and forty-eight degrees in Stein, New York, but my mother and F. X. were from Louisiana, and my mother insisted on iced tea beginning in May every year, out of spite, she said, for "New York's vicious climate." From our position on the top step, my sister and I could hear our mother shouting at our future step-father, David Slattery, "You can go to hell! Sneaking around behind my back!" Her bedroom window was open, and I thought that not only Isabel Flood, but the entire block could hear her. The house was in an uproar. My mother had locked herself in her room, and David had been standing outside her door for half the morning, repeating in a restrained, patient voice, "Marguerite, I'll just wait until you're ready to talk sense."

Isabel's hand tightened on her metal puzzle; you could hear it, a faint jangling in the lower air. She tilted her chin toward our front door and said, "I see I'm intruding on family business. I'll come back to talk to Mr. Slattery later." Isabel declined the iced tea and descended our steps. Her expression was hard to place—it did not reveal the forbearance or moral condescension you might have expected from a churchy person. It was a complicated look, half-hungry and half-knowledgeable. She had come to the house to speak with David about watching my sister and me for the that summer. Isabel turned at the bottom of the steps to look up at the bedroom window, deposited her leaflet in her brocade pocketbook, and walked quickly up the street, her hand still worrying the metal puzzle parts. She was in her mid-thirties and tall, with a foxy, pointed face, and that day she had twisted her yellowish hair into a small whirlpool over her neck nape. She wore a long cotton dress, and an anachronistic hat.

After Isabel left, David headed down the stairs from our mother's bedroom. He returned to the front porch and told my uncle, "F. X., the devil himself couldn't get your sister to open that door."

F. X. laughed. "Just sit down," he said. "She'll cool off."

David sat down. He looked exhausted. F. X. poured him a glass of iced tea and said, "Let me have a whack at it." He headed inside and up the stairs, bellowing a song:

> *"If you get to heaven*
> *before I do*
> *just bore a hole*
> *and pull me through."*

My mother stopped the song at her bedroom door.

"For God's sake," she demanded. "Don't sing that awful thing."

David told my sister and me, "Mahalia and Penny, I need to talk to you about something very difficult."

He looked at us each in turn, straight in the eye. He was a prematurely gray man with a weathered face and a mustache divided on the right by a scar. He had worked for fifteen years as a parole officer in Stein, and perhaps that was what first attracted him to our mother—he was drawn to people who strayed. He broke his news to us with a terse solemnity, as if offering us the terms of our release: "Your mother and I have decided to go away for part of the summer. I have a problem that I need to tackle."

Mahalia and I were impressed by David's valor; we knew the problem wasn't his. It was our mother's—she was drinking too much—and David was taking her away so that he could devote himself to getting her cured, and spare us from having to watch. It was our mother, and not David, whom I sometimes woke to find curled at the foot of my covers, as if she had been unable to navigate her way back from the hall bathroom to her own dreams. And it was our mother, and not David, who had driven onto the ice of Stein Lake, where F. X. had had to retrieve her. And it was our mother who had bumped into the rear of a stationary police car two days before, and then proposed to the officer who tried to ticket her.

"We're displaced persons," my mother had told him. "We belong in New Orleans, but fate brought us to Stein, and we absolutely in no way imaginable belong here." My mother often called us "displaced persons." She had a flair for melodrama that surfaced occasionally, and which she felt would have been tolerated and even appreciated if she had stayed in the South where she was raised, and had not been "dragged to the edge of nowhere" by my father two years after my sister, Mahalia, was born.

My family's melodramas found no harbor in Stein, which was a small town, inward-looking, near the Canadian border and just beyond the American pale, shouldered up against Stein Correctional Facility. Many people who do not live in New York imagine the state as an urban place, consisting of New York City and an undefined periphery; even some Manhattanites think of it that way. But I think of New York State for the most part as an expanse of small communities whose male population is employed largely by New York's penal system. Stein Correctional Facility towers over its town, an expansive building made of red brick and cement, surrounded by concrete walls ten feet thick and thirty feet high, with turrets on each corner. These walls are in turn encircled by a series of cyclone fences festooned with concertina wire.

"They have to make the walls high and sturdy," my mother told us whenever we drove by, "to make sure we Daigles can't get in." In the thirties, after the prison was erected, white box houses were built in a neat grid nearby, for prison personnel to live in. This side of Stein still has the look of a company town. All of its streets lead to the prison, and the houses seem to huddle around the prison grounds for warmth. By the time we moved there, this area had become Stein's central residential section. On the northern edge of town was the Stein School for the Blind, where my father was director before his death, and on the eastern end was the Stein Motor Inn, where people visiting loved ones at the prison spent the night. A small icy lake snuggles against the west side of Stein, and ten miles away, beyond the lake, the foothills of the Adirondacks rise, a barrier to whatever lies beyond. The outlying land on all other sides is an expanse of winter-beaten ground, planted principally with horseradish.

"Horseradish is Stein's idea of lively food," my mother once told us, reminding us in the next sentence of the spicy jambalayas her own mother had made, the turkeys stuffed with crab and liver and whole okra and hot peppers. She wanted us "never to give in to the horseradish way of life of people who live in cold northern places." In the face of the dour, tight-lipped saleswoman in the town's only women's clothing store, my mother was exuberant and talkative. "I look like a cat in heat," she would say, as she tried on a new lipstick at the narrow cosmetics counter. Or "I want a dress that's so tight, it looks like it's wearing me." Back in the days when they still got along, my mother had once made herself and Mahalia matching green silk nightgowns with green feather boas stitched to the necklines. She and my sister had danced around our front yard in those costumes, singing the "Tennessee Waltz."

The men of Stein and its outlying areas, who were for the most part taciturn and restrained, often reacted to my mother as if she were a rare animal they might be interested in hunting—attractive but also potentially dangerous. On the night my mother proposed to the police officer, she told him a long tale about her exile in Stein, and her words spilled around him, vivacious and articulate and curlicued: Her stories always meandered and circled backward, relishing themselves and the absurdity of all sorrow. When she finished, the officer tore up her ticket and handed her a cup of coffee.

This was in the years before anyone we knew would have used the word "alcoholism" unself-consciously, before the mystery of drunkenness had been resolved by the dry psychology of addiction. To me, liquor was a thing in itself: It had its own vital place on earth, like crocodiles, hurricanes, and stony ravines that led downward to dark waters. I never doubted alcohol's right to citizenship in our world. It was a question of territory, that was all: whether liquor would give you space to live or not.

After David made his announcement that he would be taking my mother away for part of the summer, neither my sister nor I questioned him further, or let him know that we saw through him. We humored him; we were grateful for his interest in helping my mother overcome liquor. Mahalia and I were fifteen and eight, respectively, and that year she was usually silent around adult males, and generally prone to brooding. I myself already knew far more about my family's summer plans than David had chosen to reveal to us, because I had cornered my uncle F. X. that morning to ask him why my mother had locked David out of her room. By then, F. X. had been staying with us for two weeks and had become my source of most of the vital information other adults would not furnish.

My mother's brother, F. X. Molineaux, was a reporter by nature and profession. Earlier that year, he had lost his job with a Louisiana paper because
he had changed facts in news stories, making up details and inserting bits
of his own experiences. The last piece he had written, which had cost him
his employment, was as follows:

> **Baton Rouge physician Porter T. Fuller was disabled for nine years
> by cataracts, which eventually left him blind and unable to practice.
> On Friday, he underwent a new surgical technique for removal of
> cataracts, which has fully restored his vision. Dr. Fuller proclaimed:
> "It's a shock to see how everything and everyone looks, after living
> so long in such comforting darkness. There have been moments when
> I wished my vision had not been restored. This is especially true in
> the case of the governor of Louisiana. Last night, I saw him on tele-
> vision for the first time and was distressed to learn that he is just as
> ugly as he is stupid."**

In fact, Dr. Porter T. Fuller was a prominent surgeon who had never suffered
from vision problems, and he had contributed to the governor's electoral
campaign. He contacted the newspaper in an uproar, demanding corrections
and retractions. But the story had not been entirely fabricated; it simply
belonged to F. X. himself. F. X. had lost his vision in his early teens and
remained functionally blind for over a dozen years, into his late twenties.
He had met my father at a Louisiana school for the blind where he taught
music and history before accepting his appointment as director of the Stein
School for the Blind. F. X. had introduced my father to my mother, "without
realizing," my mother liked to tell us, "what a stunning physical specimen
your father was." F. X.'s vision had been restored by cataract surgery in the
late sixties, and through later experimental procedures that repaired damage
to his retinas. Afterward he proclaimed that the cataracts that had developed
in his boyhood were like "masks of blindness" that kept him in a "murky
no-man's-land, on the border of sight and darkness, beyond the wildernesses
of both worlds."

Following Dr. Fuller's protests, the newspaper had turned up countless
irregularities in F. X.'s recent stories: He had reported on a flood that "rav-
aged and ransacked" a small Louisiana town, where many of our relatives
lived, and which proved upon further investigation never to have been
under water at all; he had written an article on a murderer, Owen Schenk,
who had discovered the cure for porcine encephalitis while caring for pigs
in a prison stockyard, and the prison now reported no inmate by that

name; and F. X. had composed a story from whole cloth about a Port Arthur man who could play twelve instruments at once while riding a tractor, "the tuba curled around his waist like a beauty contestant's sash, his bare feet changing the gears, a trumpet fastened to his left arm with a piece of duct tape."

Three and a half months after he got fired, F. X. sat on our living room couch and told us, "Reality was making me too gloomy." He was a massive man, six feet five inches tall and weighing around two hundred eighty pounds. He had my mother's olive coloring and furious dark red hair, and a thick mustache. My mother had told me that in his days of blindness, F. X. had wielded his cane with a jarring delicacy; its long, graceful feeler moving to and fro before his great bulk, his red hair flaring like pure light above the darkness that cloaked him. He believed that his blindness had aided his career in journalism. He said that it coaxed people to open up to him, because blindness made a man of formidable size less threatening, and because people illogically assumed that their words would be heard less acutely and recorded less pithily by a man who could not see. But since his surgery, F. X. had come to feel weighed down by facts. As a blind man he had felt a career change too impractical, "but now that I've grown more used to seeing," he told us, "I want to be a dog sled driver or an astronaut or an archaeologist unearthing tombs. Something more daring." Before joining us in Stein, F. X. had spent half the winter applying for jobs and sending away for applications forms for medical school, the Navy and Air Force, and various graduate schools; he would eventually become a renowned archaeologist who deciphered Mayan glyphs. He would later call 1977 "the year of my unsettlement and your mother's settling down."

During the time F. X. visited us while contemplating his change in careers, he had become well aware of my mother's habits. When I asked him early in the morning of May 15 why my mother and David were fighting, F. X., with a reporter's alacrity to divulge, provided me with the facts David later so discreetly withheld. I remember F. X. began, "You can only get so wet, and then you have to wring yourself out like a mop, lie in a hot place, and let the dry seep back into you." F. X. explained that he and David had conspired, once and for all, to help my mother stop drinking and "return to her former steadiness." My mother was going to accomplish this by going off to a convalescent home for drinking women of Louisiana, run by an order of Catholic sisters, and called The Place, whose precise location I still do not know. (Even now, I sometimes think of The Place as a kind of dry-cleaning factory where they sent you in wrinkled and you came out pressed and bleached.) David had arranged to take a leave of absence from his job in order to stay nearby The Place, and after that his plan was to make my mother walk the Appalachian Trail with him and F. X., from Georgia to New York, in order to keep her away from liquor stores as long as possible. F. X. was going to meet up with David in Louisiana in ten days, and stay there with him to assure that my mother would not bolt too soon. The Place would not hold residents against their will after their tenth day, and F. X. and David both believed it would take two people struggling with my mother to hold her there, and to persuade her to keep to the Appalachian Trail afterward.

————

While F. X. argued with my mother upstairs, and David sat with us on the porch, Mahalia said disdainfully, "I hope you survive the summer, David." My sister fingered a small mustard seed set in a glass teardrop that hung from a slender chain around her neck; Isabel Flood had given it to her. "I don't think I could be alone with Mama right now for fifteen minutes."

"Don't talk that way," I told her. If David hadn't been there, I would have hit her. I found her statement blasphemous. I did not want my mother to go away for so long.

Mahalia and I listened to F. X.'s voice rise at the end of the hall, and my mother's sailing above it. F. X. shouted, "You're not drinking it anymore. You're drowning in it!" My mother answered, "All men know how to do is take over! I will not be *rescued!*" and then later we heard her voice capsize, subdued, spilling something with the names "Mahalia" and "Isabel" in it, and F. X.'s unintelligible rush of answers.

David explained to Mahalia and me that our mother would be gone through August, and that he and F. X. would be leaving us in the care of Isabel Flood, who would cook all our meals and communicate with him and F. X. about how we were. David had met Isabel before, and he knew that Mahalia liked her, but neither he nor my mother nor F. X. was fully aware of how long or regularly Mahalia had been visiting Isabel by then.

At the time David sought to hire her, the adults thought of Isabel principally as a woman who lived on our street, supported herself in the neighborhood by baby-sitting, and kept a note posted in the entryway of Stein Grocery that read:

ISABEL FLOOD.
EXPERIENCED, MATURE WOMAN.
WILL WATCH ANY CHILD.
LONG AND SHORT TERM.

For a while she had watched Nicholas Groot, a neighbor's son whom my mother described as "the kind of boy who will grow up to murder both his parents." We had seen him once, dragging a pile of his mother's dresses onto the front lawn, where he poured black house paint on them.

David and F. X. had not conferred with my mother before deciding to pay Isabel to stay with Mahalia and me. My mother was not especially drawn to Isabel. She boarded in a ramshackle gray house one block from ours and often came to our door with religious pamphlets like the Jehovah's Witnesses, although she took pains to clarify that she was not one of them. My mother once told me she thought Isabel was "an empty shell of a person, with her nose glued to a Bible." My mother called her, with fantastic irony, "Princess Isabel," and alternately, "Lon Chaney."

When I asked F. X. who Lon Chaney was, he answered, "He was the actor who made the Mummy a household word and the Phantom of the Opera famous, but your mother doesn't mean that Miss Flood literally resembles Lon Chaney. Your mother uses the name as a term of art, to capture the state of Miss Flood's soul and personality. She is the kind of woman who would be considered pretty if you saw her lying dead, in a coffin, improved with red lipstick. It's only when the personality inside her animates her to move that you begin to think otherwise."

Despite this view of Isabel, on the morning of May 15, 1977, F. X. strove to convince my mother to let Isabel stay with us for the summer. David had persuaded him that Isabel would be "a reliable watchdog" for Mahalia and me. I, at least, needed watching—I was not well behaved. My teachers at school frequently telephoned my mother to discuss me. They called me hyperactive and that year my third grade teacher, Mrs. Fury, had once told my mother that "Penny has a piece missing. It's that piece other people call a conscience."

After forty minutes of wrangling, F. X. returned downstairs to the porch and sent David back up. F. X. reported to Mahalia and me that my mother had finally conceded to the general summer plan when he talked with her about the Appalachian Trail, because she saw the wisdom in traveling far enough into real wilderness that she would not run into temptations made attractive by her own inner wilderness. She, David, and F. X. had heard of AA, but my mother did not think it would work for her because, F. X. explained, "She's afraid that all those other people's tales of woe would send her back to the bottle. Her sense of despair is already adequate. And it's not as if she doesn't know what's driven her to drink."

We all knew why she drank, even my sister and I: My mother liked the way liquor felt, the way it coursed through her blood like a fast race horse and then leapt the wall of her brain into a pitch ravine of unconsciousness. Her own mother had drunk too much and had died at the age of thirty-six, driving a staggering car down a highway into a muddy bayou outside New Iberia three years after her husband abandoned her. My mother had been eighteen then, and F. X. sixteen. Everyone in my mother's family drank. When I visited them in Louisiana during school vacations, I never saw a Molineaux without a fat glass of Wild Turkey in one hand. (Even F. X. drank. It just hadn't caught up with him yet, the way it had with my mother. In 1977, he had allowed liquor to grab hold of only a few fibers of his vast personality, where it clung for dear life.) Years after that summer, my mother told us that she had awakened one morning when she was thirty-seven and found she needed a little whisky to start the day. She understood that she had undergone a kind of change of life overnight, slid into a new personal chemistry that required alcohol the way a car needs gasoline to run. After her first sip, she knew something in her had altered abruptly. The feeling, she said, was as definite as knowing you were gravely ill, or that you were pregnant.

———

After my mother finished speaking with David in hushed murmurs above us, she asked him to deliver us to her bedroom. When we entered, she sat leaning against her dark headboard, a blue pillow behind her. Her arms rested gracefully on the worn blue knees of her nightgown, looking like driftwood. She appeared hung over. Shadows ringed her eyes, and her hands shook a little. The shaking must have bothered her. Her hands were pretty, long and deft. When sober, she could paint miniature landscapes on the sides of china cups, fix dripping faucets, rewire the frayed circuitry of secondhand appliances, and repair old dressers by wetting and rewarping the skewed tongue-in-groove corners, as if her fingers held their own memory and intelligence. She made many of the clothes she wore, and our party dresses, by examining styles in stores and then drawing and cutting the patterns herself and running them off on the sewing machine. She distrusted the workmanship of fancy name brands and gloated charmingly over the straightness of her seams, her perfect lapels and cuffs, acting amazed when they turned out well. She liked discovering mysterious orders and solutions in a universe that she believed was essentially chaotic and indifferent to us. Even the smallest reliable event struck her as humorous, as if reliability were a trick played on life. When she showed me how to tie my shoes, she did not teach me the conventional way, but advised me to wrap the second lace twice around the first in a captain's knot. She laughed and claimed that "this sailor's knot is so much stronger than a double knot, it will never slip back into a string flapping next to your shoe"—and she was right, it never did.

My mother's occasional faith in the physical world contrasted starkly with her view of humanity. "There is no limit to human possibility" was her favorite expression, and the peopled world she painted for us was inhabited by woeful adults who encountered sudden reversals and upheavals. There, leering, wolfish bosses were blackmailed by young secretaries "straight out of convent school"; a straitlaced wife drove her husband to "a racy nightlife in the striptease bar where he would be arrested"; a Baptist minister made off with his church coffer in order to enter into wedlock "with a woman twice his size, a great Brahma bull of a woman"; blind men like our uncle F. X. suddenly regained their sight after "needless years of learning Braille" while children were "crippled beyond redemption in Catholic school wrestling tournaments." When my mother had told me the year before about how babies were conceived and born, she had laughed with me and Mahalia at the idea of a man being at the mercy of an appendage between his legs, which my mother described as "bigger than a salt shaker but smaller than a sugar shaker"—but she had stopped us short by saying, "I'm glad you girls can laugh now because when you're grown you'll find yourselves doing crying gyrations over it all."

That May morning of 1977, shaken by the conflicting seductions of liquor and her own heart, my mother looked at us both hard, as if trying to find the right and wrong of what would happen mirrored in our faces. I thought she seemed sad to be leaving, but also as though she had forgotten we were still there.

"It looks like I've grown to be too much for myself to handle," she said.

I sat on the foot of her bed. When I was eight, I was in love with my mother, and to me she was more beautiful than any other woman—unlike Mahalia, I had no doubts about why David wanted to be near her. My mother had hair the impossible dark red of a Persian carpet, and peacock-green eyes, and olive skin that darkened in the hollows of her wrists and under her eyebrows, like the bruised shadows in the throats of moonflowers. My sister had the same wiry red hair coiling back from the same widow's peak, the same eyes and coloring and, as she stood before my mother now, was almost as tall at fifteen as she would be when grown—exactly five feet six, like my mother. But Mahalia wore her body differently—she made me think of pictures I had seen of desert wanderers in National Geographic, with burnt olive skin and scorched hair, and hooded eyes flat from looking at too much distance and stark light.

My sister glared defiantly at my mother, impossible to cajole; she seemed intent on holding to her word and refusing to talk with my mother for even fifteen minutes. I did not feel defiant. I felt curious as I watched them, sensing Mahalia's difference from me. Her desire to have an effect on the world, to shape it to some inner sense of rightness she had, left me baffled. My sister wanted the mere fact of us to cure my mother and stop her in her tracks, to make her be the way she had once been. It would seem odd to me now that I never felt the same as Mahalia, were it not that I remember so clearly how off-kilter I felt as a child, how reckless, prey to my impulses and sudden lightning patterns of thought. On many days, I could no more control my actions than a ball thrown through the air, and so it never occurred to me to expect my mother to control hers. I accepted people unquestioningly on their own terms, and what I experienced in moments when I might have summed up circumstances was a suspension of understanding, an anticipation that if I waited long enough, all of life would be revealed in a way that justified everything.

Mahalia crossed her arms and gave my mother that look that people who are relatively steady emotionally often direct toward people whose interiors are raging hurricanes of feeling: a piercing look that seemed to go right through my mother and come out the other side without having seen a thing, without having noted the anxieties and desperate unnamed griefs and longings tangling and spooling in darkness.

"Mahalia," my mother said. My sister frowned, disapproving in advance of whatever my mother had to say. "I know you think you're too good to go astray. But sometimes when a girl's your age, things can catch her unawares, especially when she thinks she's safe. I still have to warn you to be careful around boys who can get you in trouble." ("A brazen hussy in the making," my mother used to call Mahalia, fondly, before my mother's drinking came between them. "A mermaid without a tail," a "step-back-gentlemen-and-look-what's-coming-this-way kind of woman," and once Mahalia's favorite, a "man-killer with eyes you could die for.")

"I'm not the one who's in trouble," Mahalia answered.

My mother sighed. She turned to me and said, "Penny, don't forget to brush your hair while I'm gone. Right now it looks like grass trampled by a wild animal." I smiled. "You know other people like things to be neat, not messy like me. I'm too much for them, and why should I expect anything different? I'm too much for myself."

Mahalia glanced in the mirror on my mother's dresser, majestically wrathful, searching for a nod of agreement from her own reflection. I thought Joan of Arc must have looked the same way when she argued. Although I behaved badly at school, and could slip easily into wildness and meanness, my fleeting, tumultuous angers lacked Mahalia's passionate intensity, and my face could not hold the force of moral conviction in the commanding way that hers did. Mine was a little girl's face, and I was small for my age, not yet four feet tall, still built like a boy, slippery and quick. My hair was no color at all, a common brown, always braided in a rope down my back, my hands were square with bitten nails, my eyes a flat, dark brown. I never looked in the mirror, and I prided myself on this fact: I kept track of the days (211) since I had last seen my own face.

My mother concluded, "Mahalia, I know that relations between us have become strained. And I'm sorry. I'm sure we'll all look back at this period of our lives and have a good laugh."

"No we won't," Mahalia said. "We won't ever laugh about it."

My mother told me, "Don't fidget yourself to death, Penny. You can go now if you want." Out of the corner of my eye, I saw my own reflection flicker darkly beside Mahalia's, and I looked away.

I ran down the stairs and through our long hallway until I reached the backyard. Five minutes later, I heard the upstairs door slam, Mahalia descending the stairs, and the screen door shut as loud as a gunshot behind her. (Doors were always slamming in our house). Then she whirled and vanished into our narrow side yard.

I assumed she was headed up our street to Isabel Flood's house. There, Mahalia would find Isabel propped up in her mustard-colored armchair, a Bible or religious pamphlet in her lap, a single lamp dangling over her with its beam pointing at the book like the sword of truth itself. Mahalia could look over Isabel's shoulder and see not just words on paper, but my mother, as clearly silhouetted as a cardboard doll held up before a lightbulb: My mother was a soul gone astray, dark as the devil.

I sat on the cold back steps, where brown stalks of overwintered ferns nestled against my feet and shins: Goose pimples covered my forearms as I thought about my mother's leavetaking. I knew she was wrong to believe that Mahalia's feelings would change with time. Even mine would not, although they were different from Mahalia's—my mother's imminent departure filled me with uneasiness. I felt, superstitiously, that she might never return from The Place. They would see she was incurable, but charming, and keep her forever. I knew I was lucky in the parent that life had bestowed on me. Someone more solid, more even-tempered, would not have understood or tolerated me. A mother like my teacher, Mrs. Fury, I reasoned, would have me locked up.

I tried to hold my mother in my inner vision, to burn her into a permanent memory. I closed my eyes until I felt the roundness of the olive from my mother's martini in my mouth, the sophisticated stink of vermouth, the way it curled around my tongue, the soft flesh of the pimento center. My mother could play tricks of memory, sleight of mind in which whole nights and days disappeared. Around her, incidents that shaped Mahalia and me fell into a doped, sweet forgetfulness. My mother, for example, had no clear memory of proposing to the police officer, or even of her first meeting with Isabel Flood.

The following morning, we watched from the sidewalk as David and my mother drove away. My mother waved good-bye and David looked ahead. My sister turned her back on the departing car and set off for Isabel Flood's. F. X.'s hand tickled the back of my neck. He stood beside me frowning, the sun glinting off his fiery hair, his eyes closed as if he were savoring a familiar darkness.

PART ONE

ARGUERITE

Catholics

F. X. and my mother grew up in Franklin, Louisiana, just south of New Orleans, until they moved to the city in my mother's late teens so that F. X. could attend blind school there. Here is their favorite piece of family history: Their grandmother was widowed early with several children and remarried a Protestant, a man named Carl Casburgue who proved to be a decent husband and kind stepfather. When he lay dying ten years later from malaria, his wife sent for a priest to come to Franklin's outskirts and administer extreme unction. The priest refused, naturally, because Carl was a Protestant. But my great-grandmother was beyond reason with grief. She wanted a guarantee that if she ever strove to make it to heaven, Carl would be there too. "And so my uncles," F. X. would say, "rode to the rectory on a pair of mules and dragged the priest out of bed at gunpoint, and tied him to one of the mules and carried him back to where Carl lay dying. They made the priest say extreme unction with a gun muzzle pressed to his head."

My mother and F. X. loved this story. They could not mention their step-grandfather's death without falling off their chairs laughing. By the time I was eight years old, I had heard the tale so many times that I could conjure the spectacle in my mind's eye as vividly as if I had participated in it only moments before: I could feel the black metal in my great-uncle's hand pressing against the priest's temple, hear the muck sucking at the mules' feet as they loped through darkness, mark the priest's consternation as he ushered a man toward heaven whom he believed did not deserve it.

Our family's attitude toward religion explains in part why Isabel Flood, the only religious zealot I have ever known well, was able to lead Mahalia onto a narrow path, before landing herself in jail. Both Mahalia and I were raised to view God with a kind of naive skepticism. No one had told Mahalia that religion, once it entered the blood, could be a rage-red feeling, full of light; that goodness could blaze through you hotter than hell; that whirlwind voices could seize your throat and pour through you, talking in tongues; or that God Himself could act and command people in ways so crazy and irrational that my mother might seem calm and well-reasoned in comparison.

When people asked what religion we were, we had been raised to answer, "Seventh-generation lapsed Louisiana Catholics." My mother said that she sent us to Catholic school not to make us Catholic, but because she wanted us to understand firsthand why it was impossible to follow the church's teachings. When my sister returned from her first day of kindergarten at All Saints Elementary and asked whether we were baptized, my mother said, "Just tell them you are, but I'll tie a rock to my head and I'll drown myself in the Mississippi before I let anyone throw holy water on you." When Mahalia asked why, my mother gave varying, inconsistent answers. She told us that our father had been the kind of Holy Roller who believed people should not be baptized until they were old enough to comprehend the significance of full-immersion baptism. She told us, alternately, that she had wanted to baptize Mahalia, but that the priest had not shown up for the christening. This, she felt, was a kind of holy retribution for the priest, who had been forced to perform a ceremony by our family two generations before. She told us, in addition, that we were not baptized on principle because she thought it was "wrong to belong to anything exclusive, especially heaven."

Given my mother's hostility toward religion, it was remarkable that she had married my father, Joseph Daigle, an observant Baptist who never missed Sunday services and expected her to attend with him. I do not know how he handled her views on religion, or whether my mother's beliefs simply changed or reverted after his death, out of bitterness or heartache or a desire to bury any ties to his religion with him. My father died of a heart attack shortly after I was born, when Mahalia was seven. I have no recollections of him. When I was very young, my mother did not speak of him, except to say once that she believed she "might have loved him too much." Her marriage to my father was the only interval in her adult life when she had stopped working and trusted herself fully to another person's care.

My father's death only a few years after he relocated her to Stein was especially terrible for my mother, who had no older relatives to turn to.

Once, when I was grown, she told me, "So many people close to me disappeared when I was young—I lost my father and mother before I was twenty, and so when my husband died, I thought I made people vanish." As a child, I saw my mother's life as a vast black river under a black night: She had no guide, no handhold extended from a boat, nothing but the movement forward. No map, no compass, no mother or father to row her into womanhood, no husband to call to across the dark water of her middle age. My mother's early womanhood required tremendous strength and independence. She turned down a college scholarship in order to care for F. X., and worked as a secretary to pay for his education at blind school, and later to cover the expense of a reader to help him through Tulane. By the time F. X. had his first journalism job and offered to send her "to Radcliffe or Newcomb, anywhere your heart could desire," my mother had met my father, who, she said, "married me and packed me off to Antarctica, New York, and I considered myself lucky at the time." After Mahalia was born, my mother lost herself in housewifery for seven years. When Mahalia was four, my mother miscarried a boy in mid-pregnancy, and subsequently decided to go back to school at a local New York college to get a business degree. However, my father discouraged her; she abandoned plans to further her education and remained a homemaker until my birth three years later. "Married women were not supposed to work in those days," my mother once told us evenly, without betraying strong passions on the subject.

My mother held together for many years following my father's death. After the funeral, she found employment at minimum wage as a secretary for a lawyer in Dannemora. The lawyer's name was Mr. Snook; and F. X. always referred to him teasingly as "Mr. Snook, with whom your mother did not have an affair." After nine months, my mother changed jobs and went to work for a different lawyer, in Plattsburgh, who paid his legal secretaries better but required her to come in on occasional Saturdays. His name was Parker Barks, and most of his business was drawing up wills and parceling out estates. My mother called him "the Graverobber" because, she said, "he makes his living stealing from the dead." However, he allowed her to leave each afternoon at four-thirty, so that she could arrive home an hour after us, as long as she took with her any typing that had to be completed for morning deadlines. He gave her a telephone with a speaker button, through which he would dictate legal documents in a sepulchral voice Mahalia and I liked to imitate. (*"Mrs. Stickley's will clearly expresses the intent to leave her sons nothing and to donate her entire estate to the children's museum."*)

My mother's life must have been hard, in those years. She must have been lonely, and it must have been exhausting, caring for two small children and

working for a man whom she thought of as the Graverobber. I remember
that when I was in early elementary school, she would come home from the
office, prepare us dinner, and then work one or two more hours after my
bedtime, typing up dictation she had taken in shorthand. To this day, I find
the pounding noise of typewriter keys comforting. My mother typed one
hundred words a minute and could take shorthand faster than anyone I've
ever known. She taught Mahalia and me shorthand in elementary school,
and I saw it as a private language that bound my mother and sister and me
together. No one at All Saints wrote shorthand. For years, I enjoyed con-
founding my classmates and teachers by taking notes in that mysterious
writing that looked like the flights of swallows or the runes of a mystical,
feminine society.

In the morning when we awoke, my mother's typewriter was already going, as she finished odd assignments. By seven, when we got up, she would
have large breakfasts on the table: tomato juice spiced with Tabasco sauce;
sausage and biscuits; grits F. X. sent from Louisiana; and scrambled eggs with
tomatoes and hot peppers. I remember feeling keenly the dogged heroism of
my mother's life, her competence and energy, and believing that the world
was something that could be mastered easily, reduced to shorthand, scrolled
into a typewriter, and retyped to correctness.

————

You might ask how a woman like Isabel Flood first insinuated herself into a
family like ours. Complicated as she was, her method was straightforward—
she slipped in through one of those holes that can develop in families—
"waltzed in through my flaws," my mother would later reconstruct. But to
me, her point of entry was located slightly differently; it tore open the love
between my mother and sister, which was special and peculiar and vulner-
able, because my mother and sister were so fundamentally different from
each other. My sister was a self-conscious, orderly, and well-behaved person;
even as a child, I often had the sense that only my mother's jitterbugging
energy and wild bouts of humor could have lured Mahalia into the dance
of life. No one but my mother could overcome Mahalia's quirky and outlandish terrors of small, unpredictable things. My sister, although generally
self-possessed, was—unlike me—afraid of lightning and thunder, and actually trembled when she heard them. She would go stark still with fear at
the sight of a snarling dog or a rat snake or someone's else's broken arm after
they fell out of a tree. She could not stomach late-night movies that involved
vampires emerging in murky rooms, or poisonous spiders climbing onto the
pillow of a sleeping man. She was also terrified of routine trips to the dentist

or to the doctor. Mahalia had always been frightened beyond reason of shots—she would turn dead white with fear at the sight of a needle, and stand frozen outside our pediatrician Dr. Epstein's office, refusing to enter, until my mother found the words to coax her inside.

When we had received our German measles shots the summer before I started third grade, my mother had taken Mahalia by the elbow in the doctor's hallway and told her, "I'll sing a silly song and you concentrate on saying it to yourself to the end—don't even pause when you feel the shot, just keep saying the words." My mother had leaned forward and whispered into Mahalia's ear a nursery rhyme my mother customarily changed to make us giggle:

> "I had a little sister
> Her name was Penny Daigle
> I put her in the bathtub
> To see what she would finagle.
> She traded the water for whisky
> She traded her washcloth for liver,
> She tried to sail the bathtub
> down the Mississippi River.
> She drank up all the whisky
> And ate up all the soap
> She tried to eat the bathtub
> But it wouldn't fit her throat.
> 'Measles' said the doctor.
> 'Rabies!' said the nurse.
> 'Nothing!' said the lady
> with the alligator purse."

Mahalia had mouthed the words nervously and allowed herself to be led inside the doctor's office; she remained standing to the end, her eyes closed, and then passed out right in my mother's arms, ghost-pale and limp, while my mother cradled her shoulders and head, smiling down at her as if she were the Christ child.

My mother and Mahalia, unlike as they were, at times fit together perfectly because my mother was so good in unavoidable crises, in those moments that embarrassed Mahalia with the drama they wrenched from her. Six months before, when Mahalia had gotten her first period, she had sat on her bed, wringing her hands and crying, "I can't bear it! I can't believe we have to go through this every single month! Every month for the rest of our lives!" My mother had kneeled in front of her, and asked with mock astonishment, "Would you rather have a *PENIS?*" We had all dissolved into raucous, ribald laughter.

Before the year of Isabel's appearance, my mother sometimes induced Mahalia to shed her school uniform, draw on my mother's silk bathrobe, and spend hours at my mother's dresser mirror as they preened and tittered at one another, trying on intoxicating perfumes and outrageously colored lipsticks.

Shortly after I started third grade, our home altered. I do not know why my mother's life first began to spiral downward and lose its center, whether some special event marked a turning point in her existence. She was a private person, although it often took people years to discover this, because she was generally warm and talkative and listened to scandals with a pleasurable sense of irony and with what I now see was a rare disinclination to be judgmental. It was impossible to get facts from her that she did not want to reveal. I asked my mother one day when I was in elementary school, "What made you decide to marry Daddy?" I had meant the question harmlessly, wondering how women reached the point where they threw themselves away and surrendered their souls and very names to men.

"That's *my life*," my mother answered. Not yours." My mother used this phrase to mean, simply, that people should mind their own business, that they would never have enough facts to sum up a person unless they were that person. In my early twenties, I once ventured to ask my mother why our lives took such a turn for the worse when I was eight. "Your lives took a bad turn because mine did," she answered. She added infuriatingly, "As to why mine did, that's *my life*."

Perhaps she mourned a lost lover we never knew about, or perhaps she had financial worries that she kept from us. She might have been falling apart all along, gradually, and finally collapsed like an old house, under the pressure of constant housework and child care and a full-time job. Perhaps she felt unbearably unfulfilled; she was intelligent and well-read but had never held a job more interesting than secretarial work. Or perhaps it was just the liquor itself, working independently with its own exuberant will.

The first night my mother did not come home by dinnertime, Mahalia and I were frantic with worry. I had just turned eight. It was a Saturday in October when the Graverobber had asked my mother to work until late afternoon. We waited until long past dark, and then, in a period of six hours, Mahalia called the Graverobber's office a dozen times and let the phone ring on and on when no one answered. We did not even think to make supper that first night; we were that helpless and frazzled. We waited at the front window and watched every passing car, leaning toward its promising tilt and deceleration at our corner, and then slumping with disappointment as its tires whooshed by. At one point, we put on our coats and sat on our front steps until we froze, as if by baring ourselves to the elements we might make clear the seriousness of our claim.

Snow lay on the ground and the sky above us was what F. X. called "Bright Night," words he had once heard used to describe blindness, the grayish yellow of a cloudy night sky reflecting snow. (He differed with the description. He said that for him, blindness never sat still. It radiated sudden fluorescences of blackened color, with yellows flashes at the periphery.)

This is when our initial personal encounter with Isabel Flood occurred. She appeared first under a corner streetlight about a block away. The light fell on her mustard-colored hood as she entered a circle of illumination, and then she disappeared into a hollow of darkness, and reappeared as an ochre shadowiness growing larger with each step. When she was about a half block from us, I could make out her thin legs picking carefully over snowy patches on the sidewalk. She slowed down a little when she saw us, and then looked away until she was right before us.

She stopped a foot from Mahalia and asked, "Did your parents lock you out?"

"Why would they lock us out?" I answered.

Isabel removed her hood. Her hair was in pigtails, which struck me as odd for an adult, but in the darkness it was hard to guess her age. Her hand rustled in her pocket, and I heard the ringing of metal on metal. I was surprised she had spoken to us. Most adults in Stein would have been reluctant to pry into our lives; they would have left us alone, or maybe nodded to us.

"It's late and cold to be out here," Isabel said.

Mahalia groped for a response that would not embarrass us. "We came outside to look at the stars," she said finally.

Isabel tilted her head back and stared up at the starless heavens. "That's peculiar," she answered.

She lingered a moment longer, I guessed to see if we had anything further to reveal. Then she said, "I live there, in that red brick house on the corner. Bottom floor." She continued on, and we watched her until the darkness swallowed her. A minute later, the interior downstairs light of a corner house turned on and remained on.

"I'm freezing," Mahalia told me. I followed her inside to the living room couch, where we sat, huddled and quiet, until Mahalia fell asleep curled up on the cushions.

Our house was shaped like a shoe box downstairs: The front hall, living room, and kitchen were all one area, divided on one side by a dusty upright piano that had been my father's, and on the other only by the kitchen table. You could race through our front door and living room with your eyes closed, and without knocking over any furniture, and exit still running through our kitchen door into the backyard. The yard was a small rectangle that abutted a swampy patch of woods, and the kitchen's back door was ponderous carved oak, as if the builder had planned it as an entrance for what might surprise us one day from the wild tangle behind our house. From the armchair where I sat after Mahalia fell asleep, the woods looked frenzied, jerking back and forth like entranced ghostly dancers under the moonlight.

Once during the night, I rose to get a bottle of Coca-Cola from the refrigerator. Out the kitchen's side window I saw the lights on in Isabel Flood's house. I thought I glimpsed her face, a yellowish gray oval pressed to her window and staring toward our house; I wasn't sure. I walked upstairs and fell asleep on my bed.

I awoke to the sound of my mother making Sunday breakfast. I pounded on the bathroom door but Mahalia would not let me in. (She had started locking the door and taking morning showers, which struck me as grown-up and affected.) I walked downstairs to the kitchen, wearing my wrinkled school uniform from the Friday before—my mother usually did laundry on Saturdays, but that weekend, my play clothes lay damp in the washing machine.

"Eat for the two of us, honey," my mother said. "I feel like a poisoned dog." She lay plates of eggs and grits, biscuits and ham on the table. She did not eat anything. She sat down opposite me, her hand curled around a mug of hot tea, something I had never seen her drink before. She liked hot coffee with chicory in it. She did not say anything more, which was unusual for her. When my sister came downstairs, dressed in cleaned, ironed clothes, her hair pulled back in a French knot, my mother told her to serve herself from the stove.

Mahalia stopped on the last step, looking hurt and baffled. "Where were you?" she asked.

My mother did not answer. She rose to get Mahalia's breakfast herself and set it on the table. Mahalia sat down. She took a few bites, and then asked again, "Where did you go?"

"I wasn't anywhere," my mother said. She put an extra spoonful of sugar in her tea and handed me a biscuit.

The telephone rang. "Penny, will you answer it?" my mother asked. "I don't want to speak to anyone who calls." When I picked up the phone, the Graverobber was on the other end.

"I must speak with your mother immediately," he said—his voice echoed loudly in the kitchen, as if he were sitting right at our table, because the telephone's speaker attachment had been left on; my mother liked to talk through the speaker to her friends or F. X. while she stood at the stove and cooked. The Graverobber's voice sounded strange to me, a little unhinged for a grown-up's. My mother sighed, took the phone, and turned off the speaker.

"I'm sorry," she told the Graverobber. "The work will just have to wait. Penny's sick, and I can't leave her with a baby-sitter when she's like this. I'll come in early Monday morning." She hung up, saying, "There is no limit to human possibility. Girls, I don't feel well. I'm going back to bed." She carried her tea upstairs to her bedroom, adding under her breath, "Fucking asshole."

Mahalia turned bright red, as if my mother had slapped her—my mother had never used such language in our presence. She had called the Graverobber other things before: a Warthog from Hell, and Grabbyhands, and a Slime-necked Old Toad. And my mother, especially when she was with F. X., sometimes used religious curses, swearwords that grappled with the Blessed Virgin (The Blessed, Bony Sex-Starved Virgin) and the Holy Spirit (The Great Holy Moly), and even Jesus Christ (Old Skull and Crossbones). Nevertheless, there were scatological words and derogatory names for women and sex generally (words I personally relished) that she believed were crude and unimaginative, offensive and beneath her. And now she had pronounced two of them, one after the other, and in the morning.

Mahalia raced up the stairs, passing my mother, and slammed our bedroom door in disapproval.

I climbed the stairs after my mother disappeared inside her room. I opened our bedroom door and decided to slam it a hundred times, to test the hinges: F. X. had once told me that the test of a good door was that "you can slam it through the generations."

Mahalia surprised me from behind, grabbing my elbow and saying, "Penny? Penny, what are you doing? Are you trying to drive me crazy? You'll wake up Mama, and I need to do my homework!"

My sister had spread out a pile of books on her bed. She sat down on her bedspread, hunched over a folder, and began writing notes for a science report. Open beside her was a huge, yellowed botany book, *Ferns of North America*, that had once been our father's: It smelled like moss and dust and cigar smoke. All along the back and side of our house were fern gardens, which my father had started before his death and which Mahalia tended diligently and even zealously: There were Sensitive Ferns, Rattlesnake Ferns and Adder's Tongue, Marginal Woodferns and Cliffbrakes, Lady Ferns and one rare Male Fern. By late summer, extravagant Ostrich Ferns reached halfway across our walk and tickled our shins when we stepped through the backyard. Even during the winter, my sister kept a large terrarium in our room containing a miniature forest of Lipferns and a Maidenhair Spleenwort first propagated by my father, which was now sixteen years old—an impressive testament to Mahalia's ability to take care of things. The forest struggled toward the lavender glow of grow lights behind her now as she studied. Beside the terrarium was a dish of small cellophane packets in which Mahalia had wrapped summer fern fronds, so that they would wither and shed their spores in an infinitely fine dust she intended to plant in the spring.

I leaned over her shoulder and read:

1. Woodferns like root-welcoming kinds of rocks. Because of their light roots, they do not take away moisture from the plants around them.
2. Some ferns have not changed for 500 million years. Page 412: "The origin of life is shrouded in mystery."
3. Page 289: "The greedy Sensitive and Hayscented ferns have no place in a small garden."
4. In rich soil a clump of Lady Ferns may increase growth to the point of needing restraint.
5. To transplant an Osmunda Fern, use a strong butcher knife and cut a neat circle around it.
6. Sterilize the soil with boiling water before planting spores in containers. Keep them covered and only give them a little air at a time.

My sister placed her hand over the page and said, "Penny, you're distracting me. You should do your own homework."

I fled downstairs to play outside. I felt indifferent on the best of days about Mrs. Fury's assignments, and recently she had proposed what she called "my personal newfangled theory that children should start learning languages in third grade, and French above all because it's the most cosmopolitan language." Every morning, she made us sing "Frere Jacques," and she gave us lists of French vocabulary words to memorize. Later we would have to stand up in class and use them, not in the middle of French sentences, but in

English ones: "My *chat* meows," "I like to read *livres*." I knew enough to understand that Mrs. Fury wanted to change us into something we were not—something any sane, healthy child would laugh himself sick over. On Friday, she had made me stand in the hall because I resisted her.

I had told the class, "Chitty-*chat*. In English that means, 'Would you like to buy some lipstick?' " The children behind me giggled, and I continued, "And in Russian, it means, 'Do you have a toothpick?' " The children laughed louder, and I stood up in my seat and carried on, "And in dog, it means, 'Woof! Woof!' In German it means—" I gave a loud Bronx cheer.

"Penny!" Mrs. Fury had interrupted. "Why do you disrupt everything? Why do you intentionally interfere with my class every second of the day?"

Pushing Mrs. Fury from my thoughts, I wandered to the yard beside our own, where a German shepherd usually lay tied to an enormous oak. He growled at me: I howled back at him, setting him into a frenzy of barking. I grabbed a branch of the tree that touched ground just out of his reach, and he leapt upward frantically, his mouth open as if he hoped for me to fall in. He barked until I climbed so high that he gave up and resettled in a hollow he had dug for himself in the dirt. I unsettled a flock of grackles, who scattered upward over the tree, angry and cackling, a black noise. Feeling elated, I sat in a crook at the top, where the limbs were barely larger than my wrist.

I often perched up there, looking down on the town. From my tree, I could see our street, the neighborhood behind our house, and in the other direction, most of the rest of Stein, which appeared absurdly small and orderly, its grid of houses ending abruptly on three sides in horseradish fields, the prison its dense center. I knew everything that happened on our block— I knew that the woman across the street sunbathed nude on her widow's walk during the summer, and that her husband had once kissed their babysitter beside the attic window, and that our next-door neighbor had once kicked his dog. I had once seen an armed robber race from the town liquor store and hide behind a parked car a block away, gun in hand, invisible to the police who ran in and out of the store's electric doors searching for him. I saw him scratch his head with the muzzle of his pistol. Watched from a bird's-eye view, adults would do outlandish things because they believed they were unobserved—who really thinks God is spying down on them?

On Sunday while my mother lay in bed, I saw a truck slow down beside the curb while a grown-up in the passenger seat overturned a bag of trash onto the road. I watched a woman emerge from a house four blocks down, calling someone's name; a teenage boy lay on top of a van parked in her driveway, smoking a cigarette and staring at the sky while she walked by him, still calling, and peered up and down the street. I saw a collie overturn a garbage can, and a man urinate in the parking lot behind the florist's, and two boys empty a can of rocks into the slit of the post office mailbox on our corner.

When I climbed down from my tree and returned home, my mother was still in her bedroom. She slept through lunch and then dinner. Around ten o'clock that night, Mahalia opened two cans of tuna for us, which we ate straight from the tin.

On Monday morning, my mother did not get out of bed. We waited for her until five minutes before school started and left without eating. My mother did not keep cereal around the house. She believed it was an un-healthy substitute for a real breakfast. Under my coat, I wore the same shirt and jumper I had worn home on Friday and used as play clothes all weekend.

As we walked toward school, Isabel Flood emerged on her front steps ahead of us. She carried a sheath of pink pamphlets in her mittened hands. I crossed the street, avoiding her instinctively. She waved to us. Mahalia raised her hand in a half-gesture.

I closed my eyes and eased forward feeling my way with my feet, some-thing that always irritated Mahalia. My mother had once told us how F. X. had begun to walk more quickly as a child when his vision dimmed, "as if racing his blindness to wherever he wanted to go." He memorized the roots and dips in the road outside his house, the laughs and raging voices of neighbors and slaps of their screen doors, the nuances in the barks of dogs on his block, until by the time sightlessness had descended completely on him, "he had a map of our entire world in his head, and it took us a full two weeks before we realized he could no longer see anything, not even a pin-point of ground." What finally tipped off the family was F. X. reading the eye chart perfectly when the doctor tested him. "F. X. hollered out the letters like a person with twenty-twenty vision," my mother explained. "He had memorized the eye chart. He always had such a boisterous mind." When his family decided to enroll him in a school for the blind, F. X. had said, "The only reason you're sending me there is to teach me to be blind." This state-ment still made my mother chuckle: It embodied perfectly the rueful irony with which she and her brother both saw the world.

And so, when Isabel accosted us again by crossing our path at the corner, and stopped Mahalia to say, "Off to school?" I answered, "I'm just going there to learn how to be in school."

Isabel squinted at me and said, "Open your eyes and button your coat—it's chilly and the sidewalks are icy," and then she turned the corner and was gone.

Mahalia never acted up in school—she was earnest and hardworking, and had she been in my grade, I might have disliked her for being one of those demoralizing girls who received hundreds on all her tests and enjoyed friendly relationships with her teachers. However, that Monday, Mahalia's history teacher brought her to the principal's office during last period. When she walked in, I was already sitting in the office. I had been there all day—I was usually there. I was unable to pay attention in school, or to stay in my seat, and during the fall Mrs. Fury sent me to the principal, Sister Geraldine, almost every day.

Sister Geraldine was in her late fifties, short and wiry, and did not wear her wimple in the office—she kept it in her desk drawer and put it on when she wanted to awe outsiders. She had exuberant gray hair, like Einstein's, and a long, slender gambler's nose. She passed the hours at her desk adding up numbers in ledger books and writing letters to wealthier parishes asking them to donate money to All Saints. In those days, All Saints was run by the Sisters of Charity and charged nominal tuition; my mother paid fifty dollars each month for the two of us.

"Penny," Sister Geraldine told me once, "this is how to ask rich people for money. Don't beat around a bush. Just say, 'You're rich. Give me money. I need it.'" My mother laughed when I repeated this to her. She told me she could easily picture Sister Geraldine sitting down among wealthy church patrons from Plattsburgh or Albany, "cowing them with that I-could-drink-you-under-the-table look of hers."

Early in the year, Sister Geraldine had installed a child's desk beside hers for me alone. "You're driving one of our best lay teachers into premature retirement," she told me. "You're the second worst-behaved student this school has ever had." I asked her who had been the worst. She smiled, as if evil amused her. She visited Stein Correctional Facility every Saturday, and I imagined that she had seen men at their wickedest. On some days, Sister Geraldine would lean over and tickle me.

The day Mahalia appeared at the principal's office, Mrs. Fury had brought me there after early morning recess because she caught me doing flips on the playground, something Mrs. Fury had outlawed. I would jump into the air until I was upside down, perfectly perpendicular to the ground, my head inches from the asphalt, my arms folded behind me as if straitjacketed.

"I'm not going to be responsible for your death," Mrs. Fury told me as she dragged me down the hall. "You've frightened every child in the class." I knew this wasn't true. I was the only third grader who could do flips, and the other children admired them because they were so dangerous. As we approached Sister Geraldine's office, I saw Mrs. Fury's face in the large mirror at the head of the school hall: She looked as angry as a child.

She stopped and pointed me toward the mirror, holding my head in the vice of her hands. "Penny," she said. "I want you to see who your own worst enemy is." I closed my eyes and turned my head sideways for extra protection. This was when I first resolved not to look in the mirror again until I was an adult. I thought I could meet the challenge of remembering to avert my eyes whenever Mrs. Fury led me past the school mirror on the way to the office. I recalled F. X. telling me that the oddest thing about regaining his sight was peering into a mirror for the first time in a dozen years. "I had expected to see a boy and instead I found a monstrous green-eyed adult."

"Fine, don't look," Mrs. Fury said, exasperated.

Mrs. Fury left me at Sister Geraldine's door, stepped inside the office and announced to her that I lacked "any rudimentary sense" of right and wrong. "Penny Daigle may be smart," Mrs. Fury said dismissively, as if this fact were of no concern to her—a teacher. "But a lot of good it's going to do anyone. At first I thought Penny was just hyperactive, because she doesn't act like an eight-year-old girl—she acts like one of the badly behaved boys, or a first grader. But now I sometimes wonder if it's deeper. Maybe it's something organic, something she can't help. Do you think it's possible that someone can be born without a sense of right and wrong, the way people can be born color-blind or with an inoperative limb?" Her monologue stopped there because Mrs. Fury saw me listening. She frowned in that way adults save exclusively for children—with that exaggerated expression that is a parody of condemnation. She was in her late thirties, wore a blond wig, and was thin, with a nose so upturned that it appeared almost tipless, which made me think, against my will, of a skull.

Sister Geraldine told her, "It's part of our work to take care of lost lambs." She stepped outside her office and said, "Penny, take this note downstairs to the school nurse and then come straight back."

I would never know how Sister Geraldine responded to Mrs. Fury. I was interested in Sister Geraldine's reply, because I saw she was far more sensible than my teacher. I tried answering Mrs. Fury's question myself. Because my mother liked to say people were capable of anything, I believed it was pos- sible I was missing the very piece Mrs. Fury wanted me to have. I savored the thought that there might be something special, a little monstrous, about me. That year, I did things no other girl in the third grade would have. I bit a button off a sixth grader's jumper during recess. I kicked the fourth grade's volleyball onto the road so that an oil truck ran over it. I leapt from the top bar of the jungle gym—immediately after Mrs. Fury told us always to climb down carefully—and dislocated my shoulder. When called on in reading group, I sometimes memorized my paragraph while the other children took their turns, and then when mine came, I would read out loud with my eyes closed. Or sometimes, I read my sentences backward. Mrs. Fury would pretend I hadn't. She tried to choose her battles with me carefully, but sometimes, when I antagonized her enough, she would make statements like, "Do you do these things to torment yourself, to ostracize yourself among your own kind?" and "Satan rebelled against God, Penny, and now here you are, rebelling against me." Once Mrs. Fury even said, "Are you above the rules, like a criminal? Do you have a criminal mind?"

I disliked her intensely, and unlike the other children in the classroom, I lacked all ability to conceal my feelings. Any emotion, joy or anger or the thrill of risk, would carry me away, and I would watch myself as if from a dizzying height, with a calm elation, while I ripped out all of the pages of my spelling workbook, one by one, and stacked them on top of the empty cover. At such times, I was profoundly happy; I felt impossibly close to things, as if I were breathing down the neck of the world.

When Mrs. Fury sent me to the office, Sister Geraldine gave me punishments that were laborious and time-consuming. She frequently asked me to copy a page from a large *Webster's* dictionary, with all the diacritical marks intact; or she would give me a multiplication problem of impossible size, twenty by twenty digits. She was amused by the fact that I could write shorthand, and on some days she would command me to translate a chapter of the New Testament into shorthand. On other days, she would require me to diagram every sentence in a chapter of the Old Testament, or tell me to copy instructive phrases containing underlined vocabulary words. Thus, I might spend all day by her side, like a court clerk, writing two hundred times:

I will not pretend to be inebriated when Mrs. Fury teaches history, and fall to the floor.

I will not adhere my books to each other with white glue.

I will not draw pictures of Mrs. Fury, portraying her as a cadaverous individual who sleeps in a casket.

I will not draw derogatory pictures of Father Peter, depicting him as a woman.

When I brought these punishments home for my mother to sign, she would often laugh outright, so that I received the impression that they were a shared amusement between her and Sister Geraldine. Nevertheless, the assignments had some effect on me. As I sat down to begin them, I could feel that jittery chaos whirl through me that arose whenever I was forced to sit still. I jiggled my knee in my seat; I jumped up from my desk and wrote standing up, without realizing that I was doing it; I chewed on my pencil until the yellow paint flaked off, leaving only the gnawed brown surface and the feel of graphite on my teeth. But eventually, the rhythm of the work would pull me in, and I would grow relentlessly methodical and finish my assignment. When I was done, Sister Geraldine would let me read science-fiction books she kept on the shelf beside her desk: *The Illustrated Man*, *Planet of the Fire Ants*, *Nights of the Unborn*, and others that were too hard for me, with Christian themes and names like *That Hideous Strength*. Most of the books had vocabularies well beyond my comprehension, but I understood a few of them well enough to get lost in their worlds, in battles fought against monsters who made the worst human evil seem paltry. Sister Geraldine appeared to read nothing else—I thought she privately savored the idea of worlds beyond the influence of Rome, beyond the edges of the earth.

When I returned from taking Sister Geraldine's note to the nurse, Mrs. Fury was telling her, "I want to discuss putting Penny on Ritalin." I knew what Ritalin was—it was the medicine an energetic fifth-grade girl named Persis Boards took every day at lunchtime after she was suspended for throwing the school's fire alarm.

Sister Geraldine appraised me, looking down her gambler's nose, and answered, "If Penny were having trouble with her schoolwork, it would be different, but she reads and spells like an eighth grader. She's the only eight-year-old I've ever known who can read and write shorthand! I think that's remarkable. Ritalin doesn't cure everything, in any case—" Sister Geraldine closed the door again, leaving me outside. I heard Mrs. Fury mention my mother. The words she used were muffled behind the wall. They sounded like "Mrs. Daigle doesn't know sticks from sticks!"—nonsense spoken with a mean, insinuating tone.

Outside the window, a few autumn leaves clung frantically to an old maple in the school's front yard. My mother did not like the fall; it was emblematic of her displacement from a culture and climate she had been born to: southern Louisiana with its ripe, exuberant air, its melodramatic bayous full of mustached catfish and snapping turtles and water moccasins like black ink dropped in water. The fact that when I looked at leaves in fall, I felt the same sense of estrangement, although I had visited Louisiana only a few times, impresses me now with how much I viewed life vicariously through my mother.

Mahalia crossed the lawn under the maple tree, right in front of the window, escorted by Mr. Molinari, the tenth-grade history teacher. He had a look of formal unhappiness I was well acquainted with; he frowned for the purpose of signaling that a wrong had occurred. Mahalia's dark red hair stretched out behind her like a banner. Even at that moment of ignominy, she looked like a heretic sure of her position, and Mr. Molinari like a cruel, petty official from one of All Saints' biblical school plays. I wondered if I were misreading the situation. The idea that Mahalia could be in trouble seemed incredible to me even as Mr. Molinari ushered her up the steps to the door of the principal's office.

Mr. Molinari directed Mahalia, "You wait right there, young lady." He bumped into Mrs. Fury, who departed without looking at me. He stepped into Sister Geraldine's office and told her, "I will have to talk with you privately."

When Mr. Molinari closed Sister Geraldine's door, Mahalia wiped her face so that I could not see her tears. I tried to catch her attention, and smirked in solidarity, but she pretended not to notice. She looked through the window at the trees as if she ached for them, for their wasted dry leaves rattling in the bleak wind.

"Mahalia!" I asked. "How come you're here?"

"Why are *you* here?" she answered. A flush crept over her cheeks and took refuge in the roots of her hair. She was the only one in the family who blushed, and it fascinated me. Because her face had my mother's olive cast, Mahalia's features seemed to darken instead of redden. They turned the deep color of sherry.

"I'm here because I'm a lost lamb!" I cried. "A little lost lamb!"

"Don't talk so loud, Penny!" Mahalia whispered. She turned her back to me. Her calves and ankles were long and slender like my mother's, deerlike. Even standing there looking paralyzed, Mahalia seemed graceful, almost womanly, and she was mysterious to me. I could never predict or understand the workings of her thoughts. Why did she care so much if she wasn't perfectly behaved?

Sister Geraldine emerged from her office and said, "Mr. Molinari tells me you were impolite to him, Mahalia." She paused, studied me, and said,

"Penny, I want you to take this paper with you to Mrs. Fury's room, and copy this sentence two hundred times." Sister Geraldine wrote on the top of a blank sheet:

I will not contravene Mrs. Fury's edicts concerning perilous flips.

I took Sister Geraldine's sentence and ran down the hall toward the third grade, but I stopped when I heard Mrs. Fury's voice. It rose like a siren that wakes you up at midnight: She was scolding some other child. I turned and climbed up the stairs to the second floor, where the upper grades were kept. I entered Mr. Molinari's classroom. A teacher's aide stood instructing the tenth grade. "Sister Geraldine sent me here to do this," I told her, holding out my paper. The aide read it and indicated that I should sit down at a desk in the fourth row; she never guessed that I was expected back in the third grade. Tenth graders who misbehaved were sometimes sent to the lower grades, which was thought to be humiliating, and third graders were sometimes sent to the upper grades, which was thought to be sobering.

As I copied my sentences, I wondered if there were children who simply weren't made for school. What if in some future world parents had to decide which children should go to school and which shouldn't? Those who weren't fit to educate would be trained for jobs no good person would want, but that someone had to do: We would be asked to hold up the banks of other planets, or be placed on rockets and encouraged to loot the spaceships of alien enemies. Or we would be the first people to start life in other galaxies: We would be wild, we would eat with our hands like the first humans on earth. I would be good at eating with my hands, at not caring if I never washed, at singing wordless songs in front of fires.

A tenth-grade girl I had never seen before passed me a note that said, *Mahalia called Mr. Molinari an asshole. She wrote* MR. MOLINARI IS AN ASSHOLE, ASSHOLE, ASSHOLE *on her paper in shorthand, and Mr. Molinari made her read it to the class.*

I personally used far worse words than this on a daily basis. My classmate Joel Renaud and I had a list of twenty-seven curses we had culled from adults, which I kept in a cigar box under my bed, and which included phrases as inspired as "Christ in black holy hell," and "piss-poor" and "pissing drunk," and "lower than snakeshit," and "Mary, Bloody Udder of us," which Joel and I found sublimely ridiculous, the funniest of all. However, for Mahalia, directing profanity at a teacher was as extreme as it might have been for me to burn down my own house. I sat in my tenth-grade seat until the end of the last period, longing to learn what Mr. Molinari had done to merit such a curse from Mahalia, to move her to try on just a little bit of badness like a girl sampling perfumes on her mother's dresser. The idea that Mahalia and I might be in cahoots and ridicule our teachers' wrath together elated me; I thought that she might understand me better and never turn on me the scornful look she now directed so often at our mother.

When the bell rang, there was a general search for me. My mother had been summoned to the school to discuss Mahalia and had not found me in the third grade. Mrs. Fury was beside herself when she learned I had escaped upstairs. Her voice strained and anxious, she appeared with my mother and Mahalia at Mr. Molinari's doorway.

"Penny's not manageable," Mrs. Fury told my mother. "I think she needs to be examined by a psychologist. Have you heard of Ritalin?"

My mother squinted, as if her eyes bothered her, or as if she were trying to see me in a skewed way. When she spoke, her sentences shimmied around Mrs. Fury's tired, chaperoning words, and I sensed my teacher's dissatisfaction. "I'm sorry Penny makes your life such a living nightmare, Mrs. Fury," my mother said. "You got her at a bad age. She'll calm down in a couple of years. Most of the children in my family start off like wild animals, but we run out of energy and behave once life weighs us down. Except Mahalia— Mahalia takes after her father's family." She added, "Except today." Facing Mahalia, my mother tried to arrange her expression into a look of reproof, but seemed to give up in the middle. "I'll speak to you later," she told my sister. "Penny, Sister Geraldine wants you in the office tomorrow morning." As if continuing her admonishments, my mother turned back to my teacher and concluded, "Mrs. Fury, it's difficult for me to be called away from work at three o'clock. I'm sorry, but I have to be leaving."

We followed my mother out of the school and down the street toward our Oldsmobile. She walked hurriedly and did not chastise either Mahalia or me further. In the front yard of the house near our car, a woman and her daughter kneeled, planting bulbs in a car tire painted blue. They made me feel sad and anxious. At my house, we had a better tire—it was much larger, a tractor tire that sat in our backyard. The past spring, I had spotted it on the edge of town, and because it had been too large to fit in the car, my mother had helped me roll the tire down Main Street, at my request. She had worn a green dress with a bare back, tied at the neck, and high-heeled sandals, and she had not cared when people stared at us. The last two blocks, she had let me climb into the tire and whirl around inside until I fell out. Afterward, she had poured black dirt into it from a burlap sack, and then sat at my side, instructing me as I tucked squares of petunias into the soil. The tire lay in our backyard all summer. From up high in my tree, it looked like a wild purple eye; when the air stirred, it transformed into a lush violet mouth gobbling down the wind.

My mother struggled with the Oldsmobile door, so that the woman kneeling in her yard looked up at her oddly. Mahalia avoided catching the woman's eye and climbed into the front seat beside my mother, glancing at her furtively as we headed down the road.

"Mahalia," my mother asked, "what happened in Mr. Molinari's class that made you feel called upon to write that note?"

Mahalia turned away from my mother and did not answer.

When we reached Main Street, my mother said, "Here we are—displaced persons on the edge of nowhere." In 1976, Stein was still far enough from anywhere that it had never been caught in the outstretched arms of centralized businesses such as Long John Silver's and the Gap. Its Main Street consisted of a small women's apparel store called The Closet; a grocery store; a florist that stayed open all hours but usually stocked only chrysanthemums and a pale array of dyed carnations; two of the town's six taverns; and an Esso station that sold coffee, children's coonskin caps for $3.00, and bright orange hunting apparel. I half-closed my eyes to make the street dim and turn into a dark river. Tall forms, gray sails, approached us: I opened my eyes and saw three uniformed prison guards sauntering toward us. Two boys from the blind school walked behind them, canes outstretched and marking time so perfectly in tandem that they must have intended it for their amusement. They passed Luther Canon, who owned all the property in town that was worth owning, including Stein Grocery Store, but whose wife and children had left him years earlier. My mother had once taken us to the Stein Tavern for lunch, and he had called me "Captain" and catapulted peanuts from his spoon into a glass stationed to the right of the cash register. Now, whenever I saw him, he walked in an edgy way, almost sidelong, like a man who is balancing on a wall only he can see.

"Mama, you missed our turn," Mahalia said.

My mother continued to the end of Main Street. Five blocks from our house, she pulled suddenly onto a side road. She opened the car's front door without turning off the ignition, got out hurriedly, and threw up behind a building. When she was done, she returned to the car and wiped her face with a Kleenex. Her hands were trembling.

"Can you girls walk home from here?" she asked. "I have to hurry back to work." We slid out of the car and watched her drive off.

Mahalia stood rigid on the sidewalk, her arms crossed and her hands clasping her sides. Her expression was one of such profound embarrassment edged with pain, that I put my hand on her shoulder. She wrenched away from me and headed toward our street. She walked exactly like my mother, and watching her, I experienced a displaced fear, as if I were watching my own mother leave me behind. I ran to catch up with her. As I reached her, I heard her say, under her breath, "I'll never forgive her! I'll never forgive her!" But I did not believe she meant it.

A man on the sidewalk turned to stare at Mahalia when she passed him. He catcalled something to her. She pretended not to hear and hurried on. She did not turn once to look at me until she reached the house, flung open the door, and slammed it shut behind us. Then she said, furiously, "I'm going to kill Mama! I'm going to kill her!" She fled up the stairs and locked herself in the bathroom.

––––––––

My mother made a symbolic effort to punish Mahalia, although my mother's heart was not in it—all of us knew that, of the three of us, Mahalia needed the least correcting. My mother told me, "I wonder what that poor Mr. Molinari did to make your sister get herself in trouble. Imagine how a homely old water moccasin like him feels when he learns a pretty girl like Mahalia has ridiculed him." My mother told my sister, "You're too old to be acting like Penny," and ordered Mahalia to cook every night for two weeks. My mother must have considered this a light penalty, just enough to memorialize the rare event of Mahalia acting disrespectfully toward a teacher; my sister generally enjoyed cooking. However, this was in fact the worst discipline my mother could have chosen, because it only strengthened Mahalia's fear that our family was coming unglued. My mother, even on the nights she came home late from work, kept a neat house and customarily made us elaborate dinners. She was the kind of cook who put meat in a marinade in the morning, so that it was tender at night; when she served us fruit, she placed a decorative leaf of lettuce under it; every year she canned her own hot pepper sauce in mason jars, and a morning announcement that we would have barbecued ribs for supper kept me hungry all day.

When the two weeks ended, my mother complimented Mahalia's cooking efforts, telling her, "You're a natural chef because you have a timer in your head that lets you finish the meat and rice at the same time. Cooking is all juggling." My mother then asked Mahalia if she would be willing to continue making dinner, for just herself and me, on Wednesdays. My mother explained that Wednesdays would be her "nights off," when we should expect her to come home after our bedtimes, and when she would trust us to finish our homework and get to bed on time.

My mother's request must have irked Mahalia unbearably—my mother seemed to have forgotten that cooking, after all, had been characterized as a punishment, and that now Mahalia had fulfilled her sentence and had a right to be freed. The continuing Wednesday dinners seemed to both extend her punishment and rob it of any significance. Thereafter, when she made meals, Mahalia banged the pans loudly on the stove and wore a look of pure outrage. Once, as she peered into a pot, I heard her say, "*She* needs to go waltzing around some bar and I don't matter at all!" Steam collected on my sister's face like dew; she turned toward me and scowled, as if I were the cause of her heartache.

Mahalia and I never discussed it, but we knew that Wednesday nights were the time my mother had decided to set aside for drinking. I think my mother was trying to rein herself in; she must have felt that it would be better for us if she compartmentalized her life in this way, so that on the other days of the week we could rely on her. Perhaps having Wednesday to look forward to was the only way she could survive the rest of the week.

On Wednesday nights, my mother would return home around eleven or midnight. On such nights, she was gay and talkative and I learned more about her during that period than I had up until then. The nature of my mother's confidences strikes me as peculiar now. She did not, as many intoxicated people are prone to do, dwell on her suffering and relate past heartaches with great energy. Instead, her revelations were incidental, factual, commonplace.

She would tiptoe into our room and lean over us to see if we were asleep (I never was—I was a chronic insomniac), and then perch on my bed or Mahalia's and talk. "Do you know what I did to Mr. Snook before I quit at his office?" my mother asked after midnight one Wednesday. She swayed slightly, as if the bed were a swerving car. "I had to pick up some dry-cleaned suits for him, and when I arrived at the office, I took them into the women's bathroom, and I ripped out all the seams in every crotch, one by one, with a pair of nail scissors. About two inches up the front and two up the back. So that he wouldn't notice when he put them on, but would see his own undergarments when he sat down in a judge's chambers. He wouldn't even understand how it happened. Men are in the dark about anything related to sewing." She revealed that the Graverobber was a terrible speller and barely knew how to punctuate a sentence, but that she "never corrected a single mangled word" when she typed up handwritten letters he told her to send out. "I leave them just as they are, as a warning to those poor people who have hired him."

Once my mother lay in bed beside me and closed her eyes for so long that I was afraid she had fallen asleep. Finally, she said, "According to F. X., the blackness of night and blindness are similar. Sometimes I try to imagine what it must have been like for him when he first lost his sight. The year before he finished blind school, he said the school's director told his class that the color which blind people really see is a blankness, a failure to understand color, not blackness, and F. X. disagreed with him: He said he saw a 'swampy darkness and flashes of light like lightening bugs flickering in blue mud.' The director told him that proved he was not a true blind person, and F. X. told him he was an idiot, and the director suspended him. He threatened to expel F. X., and I had to go to the school and beg them to let him back in. He had to finish the year there before colleges would accept him. I was only nineteen years old myself at the time. The director told me he would reverse the suspension if he could touch my hair. So I stood there, while the director ran his hands through my hair, saying, 'It's wine-colored, it's wine-colored.' After that, F. X. called him 'King Hair.' "

On another night, my mother told me that she had read novels when she had attended Baptist church with my father. She had a leather-jacketed Bible with the pages cut out, which she had ordered in the mail from a catalog called *Lady of the Night*. The Bible was made to conceal a sizable whisky flask, but she fit paperbacks inside. She sat behind the congregation, in the last pew, where no one could see over her shoulder. "I liked Mary Renault: *The King Must Die*, *The Bull from the Sea*, *The Persian Boy*. You wouldn't believe those books," she told me. "They're supposed to be historical novels, but I think my whole generation of gawking, church-cheated wives learned about life outside the missionary position from them." She concluded, "The problem with people who are too good is that they drive everyone around them into a state of secrecy. Look at any high-and-mighty person and you'll see all the people around him weaseling in and out of cave holes all their lives just to find a way to enjoy the darkness." I nodded, wishing I understood what she was talking about. She fell asleep on the edge of my bed so that I held myself awake all night, afraid that I accidentally would push her off.

My mother and I accommodated ourselves to this Wednesday arrangement, which was like living with two people, one who was private and evasive, and a second one who was intimate in a pleasant, conspiratorial way. At times, I was uncertain which one I liked more. I was unsure exactly how Mahalia felt. She would act exasperated when my mother appeared at the door and refuse to say hello to her, but I knew Mahalia kept herself awake until my mother's return. I suspected that my sister feigned sleep, and that she listened to my mother's stories with her eyes closed.

On Thursday mornings, we would drag ourselves out of bed, and our mother would serve us breakfast as if nothing out of the ordinary had happened on the evenings before. Her recollection of what she told us on those nights was spotty. Years later, I would inadvertently reveal something about her past that she had told me on one of those Wednesdays, and she would answer, "How in heaven could you possibly know that? You're as chock-full of secrets as a priest in a confessional." My mother, notably, did not go to confession: She claimed the priests of her childhood were "predatory gossips," and once told me, "They'd ask you in a snaky, sexy voice, 'So *what have you been up to?*' " My mother made her voice lascivious and raspy when she said this, so that I laughed devilishly with her, although the priest who haunted All Saints, Father Flahrety, was a taciturn old man who wheezed and waved at us with a gesture that looked half like a blessing, and half as if he were holding out his hand to catch himself before he fell.

On Thursdays when I walked to school, brimming with my mother's stories, I was unusually quiet—Mahalia's tacit command not to discuss my mother's antics on Wednesday nights robbed me of the desire to talk about anything at all. Thursday was usually the day I behaved the best in class, because I was too dizzy with sleeplessness to cause much trouble.

By late November, my mother's Wednesday nights pushed Mahalia right into Isabel Flood's arms. On Wednesday evenings, my sister would fix me something simple for dinner, baked chicken or hamburger or minute steak with rice and beans, and then she would wash the pots, wipe her hands on her apron, slip out the back, and walk up the street to Isabel's house. The look on my sister's face on such occasions was a mixture of sorrow and determination. Just once, I followed Mahalia. I threw my dinner in the garbage. (I always did on Wednesday nights—I never ate what Mahalia prepared, but instead consumed bowl after bowl of Cheerios, which my mother had begun serving occasionally at breakfast and which I loved.) I waited until Mahalia was about a block away, and then I grabbed my jacket and followed her. Mahalia knocked on Isabel's door, but instead of inviting her in, Isabel stepped outside. She and Mahalia struck off together down the dark road. Under the streetlights, the snow sparkled as it were full of unmined diamonds. I could not imagine where my sister could be going, and as I followed her, a tumultuous curiosity rocked my heart.

Chapter Two

The Unborn

For many years after the events of this story, I continued to bury myself in science-fiction books. As a young woman, I admired completely the ability of those writers to construct universes from whole cloth, to invent not just character and plot, but every exotic detail of their separate realities—beings that read our most private thoughts like newspapers; man-made machines who rose up against us with the outrage of mistreated children; languages that invented themselves like mouths chewing the delectable black silence between solar systems: *Manthrox, Wrode of Throth, Mlixer, Farkoptamoil.* Religion is not so different from that in this country, once you escape the restraining arms of doctrine. Any man or woman may open the Bible, spy in it interpretations recommended by no one else, and speak directly to God without intervention of priest or preacher. God will answer: *This is your world as I've made it.* But who knows what form that world might take?

The Wednesday night that I first followed Isabel Flood and Mahalia through the darkness, I felt as if I were about to witness something forbidden, as if I were hot on the trail of two thieves. They walked half a mile and never noticed me shadowing them. The path they left in the unshoveled snow was so narrow that they seemed to have stepped in each other's footprints. In places their trail was almost too thin to see; I ran into icy patches that tauntingly pulled themselves out from under me, and high mounds of whiteness that stopped me dead. Finally, I moved over into the road, with its wider blackened wheel tracks. When I approached the streetlights, my shadow lengthened to an impossible stature and then shrank until my body disappeared in a chasm of light, and I asked myself, *What if my shadow is the true picture of who I am, and watching it more important than looking in a mirror?*

Isabel and Mahalia turned onto the gravel driveway of a low rectangular cinder-block building with a sign in front that read:

WHAT IF YOUR MOTHER
HAD BELIEVED IN ABORTION?

I had never heard the word "abortion," and I did not know that Isabel and Mahalia had entered a church until I stood on the top step and a woman behind me addressed a man by the door as Reverend Bender. He looked nothing like a minister: He had a bulldog face and a crew cut, and he was dressed in a dark gray suit and a white wrinkleless shirt with an ordinary collar rather than a minister's collar. A miniscule sparkling pin shaped like a cross held his tie in place.

"You must be Katie," he said to me. "Stein Evangelical is glad to have you at Wednesday night prayer meeting."

I smiled shyly, the way I thought a girl named Katie might, and I edged by him. I saw Mahalia and Isabel seated in a row of wooden chairs at the front of the church. A group of women stood beside them, cackling to each other. They all wore hats; one had a red hat shaped like a fireplug and the rest wore shapeless winter hats pulled down low over their ears.

One woman told the lady with the red hat, "Myra, we'd hoped to see Nicky here today."

She answered, "He hasn't been arraigned yet." I recognized her as the mother of Nicky Groot, the boy my mother said would grow up to murder both his parents. Mrs. Groot sat down beside Mahalia and Isabel.

The church had no organ. In front of the choir, an elderly woman with a crooked back and a cough bent over an upright piano. No cross adorned the wall above the choir, and there were no pews or floor cushions on which to kneel. I sat in the back behind a large man, so that Mahalia would not see me if she turned around.

The only church I had entered before had been Catholic. I had studied the same lessons as any other parochial schoolgirl, and skimmed through the catechism, and rarely thought about God at all. He didn't seem to need it. He was so established in His power, so obviously there before me and sure to endure after me. Stein Evangelical's God was different—He seemed as if He needed to stir up our attention and drink us like whisky, or He might evaporate into thin air, leaving us to the chaos we had invited. And Reverend Bender did not act like the priests at All Saints Church, who led the Mass from a high dais. He wandered around and through his congregation, touching a few people on their heads. I was afraid he might lay his large palm on my head. He stopped beside me, brushing my knee, and leaned over my chair until I worried he would inhale the air I breathed.

"Do we know what death is?" he asked quietly.

I thought I must have misheard him, but then he circled halfway up the middle aisle and repeated, in a loud voice, "Do we know what death is?" He gazed toward the people in the front rows; they swiveled in their seats. Mrs. Groot's fireplug hat turned and she looked backward, her mouth parted with a mournful expression. I leaned sideways to hide myself better from Mahalia.

Reverend Bender answered himself: "We all know what death is!"

He strolled forward, rubbing his chin with his hand, and continued, "We don't have to die to know. It's the end—you close your eyes, it's the darkness of sleep, you fall away and. . .you're gone! It's as if you've never been. And an unborn child? An unborn child has no soul that will rise into heaven. He's like a struck match—for a moment, there he is, the flare of life, and then darkness."

Reverend Bender paced to the front of the congregation with his back to us all. He pulled a kitchen match from his pocket, held it above his head, and struck it on his thumbnail. It flared above him; we watched its small solitary flicker; he blew it out; a hush seized the room. He looked over his shoulder, his bulldog face grinning, as if he were trying to spy how many of us he had fooled. He retraced his steps, running backward to the end of the aisle until he arrived again at the rear of the church. We all turned to watch.

"That's what people who don't have faith think about death," he told us. "And that's what people who don't have faith think about the unborn." Reverend Bender shook his head and grimaced as if he found such disbelief troubling.

"Last night I had a frightening dream," he announced, wandering back up the aisle to the front of the church. "I dreamed that all the unwanted unborn children, all the castaway children, were imprisoned at Stein Correctional Facility, that they leapt its walls and spilled out onto the land. What could such a dream mean?"

A look of consternation slowly crossed Reverend Bender's bulldog face, and then, he lifted his head and said, "I awoke. And I thought of the unborn children who await us, who will walk here among us, cherishing this world the way we do, and I thanked God I was awake and still had time to do his work. Here. I thought of those who long to cast away our unborn children while their little hands and hearts and brains are forming, and I was dum-founded."

Reverend Bender held out his own hands and stared at them as if the sight of them astonished him. He stopped speaking briefly to pull a wooden chair from the edge of the platform where an unused podium stood; he sat down, his jaw set, his forehead wrinkled with annoyance.

He remained there until I felt so restless I thought I would die if I had to stay a second longer in my seat. How much could a person say, I wondered, about people who hadn't even been born yet? If my mother had been there, she would have explained to me why Reverend Bender chose to talk about unborn children—she loved giving me advance warnings and translating facts into words I understood, during adult events I attended impatiently. When the plots or dialogue of a movie submerged into the mysteries of adulthood, she would say, "That woman is so jealous she's fit to be tied—always avoid jealous women as if they're copperheads," or "Widows in Greece aren't allowed to have open romances—cover your eyes, Penny, they're going to stone her to death and I don't want you to see it," or "It would be awful for a girl like that to have to marry a rich old stiff like him." But without my mother there, I could not make heads or tails of Reverend Bender's sermon.

He rose from his chair, strode along the narrow aisle on my side of the congregation, and again stopped next to me. His hands hovered at my eye level, and then he rested them on my head.

"What if you had never been born?" he asked in a gravelly voice that seemed to cause the very foundations of the church to rumble, and made me want to cover my ears. "What if you had never seen the light of day? What if—what if you were nothing at all? Just a little piece of nothingness in the void?" He surveyed the congregation, waiting for us all to consider his question and find our individual answers to it. I squirmed under his hands.

He removed them from my head and walked back to the front of the room where he reassumed the podium. "How can the most hardened soul not care about a child who hasn't even tasted the pleasure of breathing air? Because *you* care, don't you?"

"Oh yes," a woman sitting behind Mahalia said. Mahalia and Isabel, and Mrs. Groot in her fireplug hat, had turned halfway in their seats, and were watching the minister. I was surprised that Mahalia could listen so atten-tively to Reverend Bender's sermon. On the holidays when we attended Mass at school, she always sat in her class's pew, looking stonily ahead.

Reverend Bender continued, "Do you think Jesus scoffs at conception?

Does He turn His back on children in the womb? Does He form their bodies, but not their souls? Does He half-make them, forgetting the more important half? Does He fill a seed with knowledge of how to grow leaves, stems, and petals, but not give a human infant knowledge of Christ?"

The woman behind Mahalia said "Amen," again, and then a low moan rose to my left. I looked down my row and saw a girl no older than Mahalia. The girl's face was buried in her hands; she moaned again and a sky-blue hat fell from her head to the floor.

"Behold the lilies of the field. They toil not. Neither do they sow."

"Amen," the girl repeated. She moaned again. I looked back toward Mahalia, but my view of her was blocked by the woman behind her, who was now standing up, saying, "That's right! That's right!"

"That's right! That's right!" the girl in my row echoed. I felt intensely uncomfortable. She breathed in quick intakes of air, like a sobbing child.

"But even Solomon in all his Glory—"

The young man seated to my left groaned, drowning out the rest of the words. He had the same yellow beard, red cheeks, and startled expression of Saint Paul in the print over Sister Geraldine's desk, which depicted him fallen from his spotted horse, lying on the ground, his mouth wide and eyes fastened in alarm on something only he could see in the overhead darkness. I felt panicky. I pulled my feet up on my chair and felt my chest beat against my knees, my blood jangling. I covered my ears.

The woman beside me tapped my leg and pointed at the floor; she wanted me to take my feet off my chair. The young man jumped up, so that his groans rained down on my head, and he spoke a language I had never heard: *Murdo morn, morny morn!* I unstopped my ears and looked up at him; he did not seem to see me; his eyes were watching some inward horizon.

"Does God fail to protect the budding lives of unborn children because they do not toil or sow?"

"JEES"—the young man's voice rose high above me, and I steeled myself—"-US! JESUS."

The girl at the end of my row pulled herself to her feet, grasping the chair back in front of her, and swaying as if drunk. She crooned, "Oh Lord, oh lord, oh *low, low, low!*" She reminded me of a yowling cat. Her pocketbook fell to the floor, and its contents scattered and spilled across my foot. I looked down and saw a compact, a nail file, mascara, and a package of Kleenex.

"*Low! Low! Morny morn!*" she shouted.

More voices rose, more deafening than the cries of children on a playground. I felt as if the adults had lost their minds, and I leaned forward and tried to catch Mahalia's eye. I was seized by a fear that she might be yowling alongside them, and I still could not see her over the heads of the adults standing up in front of me. The shouting continued until I felt as if the church floor under me was rocking, while Reverend Bender's bulldozer voice plowed it under. The young woman in my row grew louder, repeating *morny morn, morny morn, morny morn.*

"Now honey, now honey," someone behind me answered. I looked up— Isabel Flood was taking the girl by the arm, pushing her gently down into her seat and offering her a Dixie cup of water.

"You've just drifted a long ways from us, but you're coming back," Isabel told her. Isabel retrieved the girl's blue hat from the floor. A man with a jagged beard held the girl's other elbow. She was pale, almost blue, and her blue eyes had a glassy, unseeing look. Isabel glanced once, quickly, at me; our eyes met. At the front of the church, the choir began to sing:

> *I see the sights that dazzle, the tempting sounds I hear;*
> *My foes are ever near me, around me and within—*

I bolted. I slipped by the knees of the woman on my right, ran down the aisle past the swaying congregation, and fled out the front door.

I turned once to look back at the church, but no one was watching me. Reverend Bender stood solemnly to the side of the choir, without singing, and the door swung closed. As I ran back to the house, I said aloud, under my breath, *"Morny morn, morny morn!"* Reverend Bender's image fixed in my mind, this man who could make grown-ups jump from their seats and caterwaul. They were crazy, all of them.

———

I thought Mahalia might have seen me escape from the church. I tore off my clothes, pulled on my nightgown, and slipped into bed. When I heard the downstairs door open, I prepared myself for Mahalia's accusatory anger. Instead she stole quietly into the room and crawled under her covers without taking her clothes off first. She rustled under the sheets, changing into her pajamas. Nowadays, she would not undress in front of me, even in the dark. My mother had warned me with unusual sternness not to make fun of my sister for this.

"Penny?" Mahalia whispered.

"Yes?"

"Is Mama home yet?"

"No," I answered. I waited for Mahalia to question me about my appearance at the church. Was it possible Isabel Flood had not mentioned seeing me?

"Where did you go?" I asked Mahalia.

"I just went for a walk," she answered.

I knew that other older girls got in trouble for sneaking out of their houses at night to meet boys. I almost asked Mahalia, perversely, "Were you with a boy?" but I stopped myself. I wondered if Mahalia actually knew I had followed her, but was pretending she did not in order to save herself embarrassment, or to avoid a talk that would destroy the secrecy of this new part of her life.

"Penny?" Mahalia asked. "Where do you think Mama is on Wednesdays? Do you think she goes somewhere where people from town can see her?"

"I don't know," I answered.

I was surprised that Mahalia would have such a worry. I had been the object of talk among teachers most of my life, but it had never bothered me much; perhaps because, until she began to complain later that Isabel "snooped around our home," I never sensed that my mother feared town opinion. Perhaps the only thing about Stein my mother praised was that people there did not seem to gossip much, as they had in Franklin, Louisiana, where she had grown up. She liked to say that in the town of her birth, "Everybody sized you up and decided who you were years before you were even born. Whenever you met someone, you had to try to figure out what lies they had already heard about you, and live up to them." (According to my mother, her family was referred to as "that crazy woman whose husband ran off when he learned his son was going blind, and that wild little girl.") Stein, by contrast, was a cold place, buried under snow most of the year. Freezing winds careened around corners like drunk drivers; it was not the kind of town where people stopped to talk idly in the street. During the summer, people basically kept to winter habits. If they ran into one another outside, they exchanged nods. Possibly the presence of a prison in the vicinity made the small evils of people's day-to-day existence loom less large. I never felt that people were interested in our private lives; although a few, our neighbors and school officials, must have known much more about us than they would ever reveal.

Perhaps, paradoxically, the privacy of my mother's drinking made it seem all the more shameful to Mahalia. If more people had talked about us, if things had been out in the open, she might have felt her burden less. I never would be certain what tortured Mahalia more—her efforts to conceal my mother's behavior, or a more desperate wish that someone, anyone, from outside our family would intervene, and help us all. I don't think my mother ever guessed how continually Mahalia steeled herself against what she saw as our family's humiliation. If the phone rang after six o'clock, my sister would not answer it. She did not want to have to explain why my mother was not there. The year before, teenage girls from Mahalia's class had come over on weekdays and weekends to study with her or whisper behind our closed bedroom door; now, Mahalia never invited her classmates home. Once, when a friend rang our bell and knocked while our mother was sleeping on the living room sofa, Mahalia wrestled me into the armchair and pinned me there with her knees on my arms, her hand over my mouth, until the knocking stopped.

————

In December, after the lake froze, I felt hemmed in with the earth; there was never enough time to do anything before dark fell and I was expected home. During the longer days of spring, I had spent almost every afternoon walking along Stein Lake, which was a mile from our house. I looked for fire newts—skittery, flame-colored animals that appeared briefly and then vanished utterly. On other days, I skipped stones for hours: They kissed the water; the water held each one like a wafer balanced in its mouth; the black lake devoured them all as if they never were. Or I whiled away afternoons carrying rocks to build dams across a small stream leading to Stein Lake, in order to watch them burst and erode until they left no trace. In late spring, I had discovered a larger stream at the lake's far end that narrowed as it neared its mouth and plunged over a series of eight-foot falls into buckets of pools. You could climb to the top of a low cliff, leap with an inner tube into the stream below, and barely miss hitting your head on rocks. The tube magically followed an invisible thread of current, shot high into the air, and fell precisely between two jutting boulders into a tunnel of icy white water. I occasionally wandered to the stream in December; there, the white water waited, restrained against its will, its wild leaping frozen in midair.

One afternoon after school, I walked partway home with my classmate Joel Renaud. I played mostly with boys—girls' mothers rarely had me over. The mothers of boys, on the other hand, were less likely to view me as too out-of-control.

Joel and I headed toward the lake. He stopped when we were halfway there, leaned toward me conspiratorially, and said, "I have a new joke." He was the largest boy in the class, had huge hands and apologetic hazel eyes, and in middle school would accidentally break the wrestling coach's leg. He asked me, "What did the fish say before he ran into the wall?" He waited for my answer and then yelled, "DAMN!" We both doubled over laughing.

We ran to a patch of woods bordering the lake and tossed rocks at the same tree. The stones made a sound like *clock* against the trunk.

That day in school, Mrs. Fury had asked us, "If you were our ambassador to France, what one thing would you give France from the United States?" She had ignored me when I had answered, *"English!"* Now, I asked Joel, "If you were traveling through outer space and you landed on a foreign planet, and they had nothing there at all—no airplanes or cars or houses or anything we have—and you could give them two things from earth, what would you give them?"

Joel stopped throwing rocks for a moment. He looked at me, as if he took my question very seriously. He considered the moon, a pale squashed egg balanced on the dusky horizon. He looked above it, into space.

"I'd give them a fly," he said. "And then I'd give them a flyswatter."

He turned back to the tree and threw another rock. He barely smiled; we knew how funny we were. We continued to throw rocks through the darkening sky until one disappeared, hushed, as if the dusk had caught it in a mitt of air. Finally, Joel told me he had to go home.

"Won't your parents get mad if you stay out late?" he asked.

I shook my head. I told myself that it was Wednesday; I could do what I wanted.

He eyed me enviously. He threw a rock straight up in the air. We covered our heads with our hands; it came down several yards away. I picked it up and put it in my jumper pocket.

After Joel headed home, I walked on toward the lake. There were several vehicles in the park that abutted Stein Lake: a yellow truck with a coonhound inside that leapt out of the cab, raced in a circle around me, and leapt back in; a white station wagon containing teenagers smoking cigarettes and drinking beer; an empty blue Volkswagen bus painted with psychedelic graffiti; and last of all a dark green Oldsmobile that I took a moment to recognize. I saw the black cutout of a monster I had taped to the window for Halloween and realized that the woman in the front seat was my mother. I approached our car from the left side. My mother sat by herself with the motor idling. The car radio played faintly, as if from far away, and she tapped on the window glass with her knuckles and moved her lips, singing to herself. I circled our car, wondering whether I should knock on my mother's window or yank open the door on the passenger's side and surprise her. I decided to climb on top of the car; I crawled onto the back fender, pulled myself on the roof, slid forward on my stomach to the front, and looked at her, upside down, my hair falling over the windshield.

My mother recoiled from me. Her expression frightened me, because she seemed so genuinely afraid. She started to the side and raised one arm in front of her, and then, suddenly, she laughed. I pressed my nose against the windshield, and she opened the door.

"Penny!" she said. "You looked like a banshee! You scared me half to death!"

I climbed down, and she hugged me and asked, "What are you doing out here? It's too late for you to be at the lake. Does Mahalia know where you are? Did she walk you home?"

"No," I said.

"Don't come out here after dark anymore." My mother pulled me inside onto her lap, then shut the door. She turned off the radio and scolded me a little longer. I leaned into her, happy, soaking up the tones of her voice, which were rich and melodious and lively. She had the heat on high, and the car was warm and comfortable. We stared at the blue lid of ice clamping down the lake.

"Do you like this lake too?" my mother asked. "I try to stop here every day, just for a few minutes, on my way to work or on the way home. It gives me time to—to pull my pieces back together." She laughed, suddenly—a bark of a laugh that stopped itself in the middle.

She pressed her face against the back of my head and said, "Your hair is going to end up the exact same color as your father's. Chocolate. What would he have thought about that? You don't act a thing like him. It's as if your looks and Mahalia's got crossed up. You're pure Molineaux." I loved the idea of my hair being the color of chocolate. I leaned back and sighed, sinking into my mother, thinking I would gladly have fought anyone for her, that I would have killed for her if necessary.

As if reading my thoughts, my mother said, "Your father was principled, like Mahalia. And what about you, Penny? Are you old enough to be principled?" She laughed again. "Maybe not, but you're loyal. Is that the same thing? Maybe it is." She rambled on. She pulled me close against her and said, "My wild barbarian." She concluded, "Penny, whatever you do when you grow up, make sure you have children. Nothing else in your life will be more—more luscious. I hope you have a little girl just like you, because you would get a kick out of a daughter like yourself."

We gazed at the lake a while longer, while the sky deepened to a brilliant violet. I could have wrapped myself in that sky like a king's robe. My mother said, "Your father once drove onto the lake, right here, on New Years' Eve.

He said if Jesus could walk on water, he could drive on it. He took me by surprise! It was the only reckless thing I ever saw him do. He drove out about twenty feet and kissed me, and then drove back." I waited for her to go on—it was so rare for my mother to talk about herself so early in the evening, and she had never volunteered such information about my father. "I wonder," she said, "what your father would have thought, if he had known that three years later I'd be working as a secretary in Dannemora. But what man in the prime of life ever imagined the world after his own—" She let whatever thought she had been after scamper away. "Do you know, Penny, that one of the secretaries at the courthouse and I once snuck over here after work and went skinny-dipping? We parked by some trees and swam all the way out to that island there." My mother pointed toward a small hillock of land at the center of the lake. In the winter, it was a white hump with a scattering of stripped trees. "We stayed there until after dark. We soaked up the sun until there was nothing left of it. When we swam back, there wasn't even a moon above us. It was like swimming through air—we couldn't see the water, and we just guessed where the shore was. I tried to figure the exact place in the lake where your father had driven out to kiss me, but I must have been way off, because when we two secretaries touched bottom, we were on the wrong side of the beach. We had to race like two naked lunatics all the way around until we found the car. Later, we called our bosses and told them we'd both gotten food poisoning eating bad potato salad at a restaurant. We almost giggled ourselves to death taking turns on the phone. It's a miracle we didn't drown or choke on our own snickers." I wished that I had been with them, skipping along the shore like a naked lunatic. I imagined my feet touching a darkness like wet sand, lapped by the separate wilder darkness of the water.

The twilight grew murkier, and the ice glowed faintly before us, the lake's ghost. My mother slid me off her lap and turned on the ignition. We drove home on a back road, two blocks from Main Street. There, we saw two men thrashing on the sidewalk, caught in a net of light cast by the streetlamps in front of the Esso station. A woman, her face twisted with the effort of whatever she was yelling, was trying to pull the smaller man off the other. On the curb behind them was a second woman with two little boys clinging to her like sailors lashed to a mast in a storm.

As we neared the group of people, I recognized the second woman as Isabel Flood. She was dressed oddly, with a triangular skirt that fell to her ankles, and a helmetlike cloth hat. The smaller man broke away from the other woman's arms and stumbled backward. The two little boys with Isabel Flood maneuvered behind her. She held up one hand before her in a theatrical manner, high in the air, and shouted something. The man backed away and leapt into a truck. I wondered what Isabel Flood could have said to produce such a reaction. The truck darted in front of our car, barely missing us.

My mother stepped on the brake and said, "Penny, evening falls a lot sooner this time of year. You have to make a point of walking straight home from now on. Straight along Main Street, without going to the lake. All kinds of strange fish ghoul around in Stein after dark. In spring, it's different—there are lots of regular people out by the lake, and it's safer. Just play in our neighborhood until then, okay?"

I sighed as loud as I could, and she said, "I'm serious. Did you hear what I said?"

"Yeah, Mama," I told her. There was a slight rebellious note in my voice—I hadn't intended it: It was just there.

All of the lights were on in our house, as if Mahalia had been searching for us in every room. Mahalia opened the front door before we were halfway across the yard.

"You know better than to let Penny walk home by herself, Mahalia," my mother said as she stepped inside. "What were you thinking? Who knows what sort of character might spot a little girl walking by herself at night? A child out after dark looks uncared for."

Mahalia answered, "Penny was supposed to stay after school. I waited for her, but she slipped outside when her teacher wasn't watching!"

"You should have gone looking for her."

"Where were you?" Mahalia answered.

I could not bear to see them fighting, and I was sorry I had made Mahalia get in trouble. "I climbed out the school's bathroom window while Mrs. Fury was waiting for me," I said. "I didn't think I'd fit, but I squeezed through it like a snake."

My mother sat down on the couch, pressing her eyes with her fingers. "All right, Mahalia," she said. "But you know how Penny is. You can't just go through the motions. You have to think a step ahead of her."

"What about you!" Mahalia answered. "Am I supposed to figure you out and keep after you every day after school too?"

My mother looked at Mahalia wearily. "No, you aren't, Little Miss. I'm smart enough to figure myself out." Mahalia bristled at the epithet "Little Miss"; my mother used it when she thought we were acting too grown up for our age.

My mother poured herself a glass of tomato juice from the refrigerator. "I'm so bone tired all the time," she said. "Every morning I feel like I'm rising up out of my own grave, and every night I feel too exhausted to even die."

"I'm tired too," Mahalia snapped. She carried her books upstairs to our bedroom and slammed the door.

———

By January my mother's Wednesday nights spilled into Thursdays and even Fridays, so that Mahalia began to cook for the two of us several nights each week. Finally my mother let down her reserve and began to bring liquor home.

In the ensuing weeks, my mother became more careless, thinner, otherly: I would come home from school to find nothing on the refrigerator's large top shelf except a bottle of orange juice that she mixed with her gin. Mahalia and I ate bacon and eggs off paper plates for dinner, sitting in front of the television, which I liked. I threw off my school uniform when I came home and left it where it lay—on the floor or the piano or coffee table. No one told me to pick it up. I never thought to sweep or dust or vacuum, and it amazed me how quickly the house cluttered itself. Mail and school notices, magazines and grocery store advertisements piled up on the piano bench and counters and chairs. One afternoon Mahalia pushed the clutter indiscriminately into a garbage bag and dragged it outside saying, "If *she* doesn't care what's in the mail, why should I?" Unsorted laundry sat in heaps on the kitchen table for two weeks until Mahalia put it away. I lost the blue sweater that matched my school uniforms, and found it days later, frozen stiff like a dead cat, in a mud slick behind our back steps.

About six weeks after the night I followed Isabel and Mahalia to church, the doorbell rang too early in the evening for our mother to be home. Mahalia ignored it; she was standing beside her terrarium, shaking the reddish dust from one of her cellophane fern spore packets into a mason jar she had half-filled with peat moss and soil. She had boiled the soil the night before to assure its sterility; as soon as she emptied the fern spore dust into the jar, she clamped it shut to avoid contaminating her sample. She labeled the jar: OSMUNDA FERNS.

I slipped past her and headed down the stairs. She followed me and asked, "What are you doing Penny?"

"Getting the door," I told her.

She grabbed my shoulder at the bottom of the stairs and said, "We can't let anyone in! We can't let them know how we live!"

I could see her in the rectangular mirror that hung in the front hall, that odd reflected space that seemed to be behind the actual wall, the place where we could view each other but not ourselves. Mahalia looked anguished, her hands drawn to her mouth. Before her I saw the living room in disarray, my schoolbooks littering the floor, the week's papers toppled on the kitchen table over our last night's dishes, one of my mother's stockings from the night before draped like a slender fainting woman over the back of the arm chair, and suddenly, as I looked away, I pictured us as Mahalia must have: me in my slip and dirty kneesocks, looking uncared for, my mother drunk and unsteady, my sister wretched, ashamed. I was astonished. I had never thought to judge us—I loved us all.

Mahalia said, "Come up to the bedroom so they can't hear us. Just let them ring." She rushed back upstairs.

A folded pink pamphlet slipped halfway through the mail slot and stuck there. The person on the other side tugged the paper back, tried again to push it into our house, and then jerked it so that it caught and tore. It disappeared, and then a second paper, unfolded this time, slipped halfway through, dangling over the doormat. I stepped forward and took it. The paper declared:

WE MUST CHOOSE SIDES!

Underneath was a picture of a bassinet, but instead of an infant, a skull with crossbones protruded from the baby quilts inside. On the adjoining page were the words:

HOLOCAUSTS
PAST AND PRESENT

We hear a lot of talk about the Holocaust—what about infant genocide? Abortionists say: "A woman can do whatsoever she will with her own body." If you believe this, then I'm afraid that your ignorance blinds you. Shall we stand unmoved while Herod's slaughter of the innocents is renewed in our land, or shall we fight tooth and claw? Can't we draw the line at baby torture?

All the vocabulary I had learned from my hours in Sister Geraldine's office did not enable me to make sense of these words.

The doorbell rang again. "No one in here but us chickens!" I called.

But I was curious; I could not keep from opening the door. When I turned the handle, Isabel Flood peered into the living room, tall and thin, her straight yellowish hair pinned back at her temples with dime-store barrettes, her eyes light brown and narrow-set in her small, foxy face.

"—Flood," she said. She held a sheath of pamphlets, and when she extended another one I took it from her. "Isabel Flood from Stein Evangelical."

"My mother isn't home," I told her.

"I know," Isabel answered. "You can give her our literature when she comes back. Could I come in for just a moment?" I watched the toe of Isabel's shoe slide between the door and the door frame. Her feet were long and narrow. Her shoe-shadow rose and lapped like a long tongue across the lintel. Her shoe was mustard-colored with a paisley design. It looked like a cotton slipper, too thin for such a cold, snowy time of year.

"I don't just talk to grown-ups," Isabel said. "I talk with girls too." She entered and searched for a place to sit down. Isabel removed my mother's stocking from the armchair and perched there, taking in the room. She took off her coat; a small yellow tam teetered on her head, but she did not remove it. She withdrew from her pocket a metal puzzle and worked its parts absently without looking at them. The puzzle had one thumb-sized flat piece and a second piece like a twisted letter A. They looked impossible to unhook from one another.

"I have a rule," Isabel told me, "that it's not enough to take a puzzle apart—you have to figure out how to put it back together too." She placed the puzzle on the table and pushed it slightly toward me, but I left it where it was.

"Mahalia!" I yelled. "Someone's here to see you!"

Mahalia opened the upstairs door, and I anticipated how mad she would be as she descended toward me. Her face appeared, wrathful, but when she saw Isabel, it transformed—Mahalia took the last step looking tentative but relieved.

"Penny!" she said. "Why didn't you tell me who it was!" Then, remembering she had never openly acknowledged her relationship with Isabel, Mahalia asked her formally, "Would you like coffee or tea or anything?"

"I carry my own tea, but I like a hot cup of water to put it in," Isabel answered. She opened her brocade bag and dropped her pamphlets inside.

Behind her, Mahalia frantically pushed clothes off the kitchen table into a pile on one of the chairs. She filled the kettle and stacked dirty cups and saucers in the sink. She sponged off the counter. The phone rang and she did not reach for it until the fifth ring, when she lifted up the receiver and put it down quickly so that the ringing stopped.

Isabel picked up a family photograph on our coffee table: F. X. had taken the picture the summer before, and in it, my mother and Mahalia stood in the front yard, wearing their green silk nightgowns. They had traced black lines around their eyes like Cleopatra and wore dark lipstick. I stood in front of them, also wearing lipstick, and dressed in leopard-spotted pajamas, with long Ostrich Fern fronds stuck in my waistband like the costume of an exotic dancer.

Isabel noticed me watching her; she set down the photograph and studied Mahalia as she stooped and scrubbed at a spot on the kitchen floor. "I'm here to invite young people to our winter indoor picnic at Stein Evangelical Church," Isabel said. "Twice each year we try to invite outsiders to the church. Because it's too cold to hold our gathering outside, we call it 'the indoor picnic.'" She turned to me and asked, "What's your name, honey?"

"My name is *Hookamamey*!" I answered.

"Did you make up that name yourself?" Isabel asked.

I shrugged my shoulders.

"That's Penny," Mahalia said.

"When will your mother be home?" Isabel asked.

"I don't have the wildest idea," I answered.

"I guess anytime now," Mahalia said.

The phone rang again, once, and Mahalia picked up the receiver a second time and returned it to its cradle. She pressed a button on the front that turned off the ringer.

I crawled onto the back of the armchair. Isabel told me, "Get down from there. You'll set the chair off balance and it will fall backward on you." I stayed where I was. She stood, took me by the elbows, and seated me properly. She picked my school uniform off the floor; wrinkles criss-crossed its black-watch plaid.

"Do you attend the Catholic School?" she asked, examining the uniform as if she only now surmised that we attended parochial school. This seemed curious to me, because surely she had seen us walking by her house before, clad in our All Saints jumpers. (I often felt around Isabel, in the beginning, that she did not make connections immediately, or that she pretended not to, so that she could fish around in her own lake of silence and abruptly pull out an idea as if it surprised her to find it lying there, gasping in her net.)

"We're seventh generation lapsed Louisiana—" I began, but Mahalia cut me off.

"We're not really Catholic," Mahalia said. "Our father was a Baptist." I thought Mahalia was trying to placate Isabel in some way I did not understand. "We go to All Saints, but we were never confirmed or anything."

Beside my sister, an orange rectangular light on the front of the tele-phone flashed mutely beside the turned-off ringer button; there was another call. Mahalia again lifted the phone's receiver and replaced it; the light turned off.

"You don't have to be Catholic to attend All Saints?" Isabel asked.

"No, lots of the kids who go there aren't Catholic," Mahalia answered.

"I wasn't aware of that," Isabel said.

I thought of what Isabel could not divine: my uncles hollering into the wet night, the priest bouncing as he felt their galloping mule under his stomach. My uncles had probably shouted at their mules, while shouting at the priest. They would have had to untie him so that he could pronounce extreme unction. They probably untied him at gunpoint so that he could not escape—I would have.

The teakettle screamed, and Mahalia brought Isabel her hot water. Isabel removed a yellow tea bag from her purse, dropped it into her cup, and removed it almost immediately. When she lifted her cup to her lips, the water was pale, the same mustard-yellow of her shoes. Mahalia returned to the kitchen. I lay crossways over the chair, my feet sticking out over our coffee table. I leaned back over one chair arm until my head dangled upside down and I watched an inverted Mahalia rinse the last dishes. Behind her, the late winter sun crept through the window and stroked her red hair.

"I had a neighbor once, who just stopped cleaning one day," Isabel said, suddenly. "Nothing her husband did could make her lift a finger after that."

Isabel offered no more details. Her story ended right where one told by my mother would have started. I pulled myself back upright in the armchair and sat cross-legged, staring at her.

"What if she had to eat?" I asked. "Did she put food on a dirty plate?"

"She ate out of the can and then threw the can away," Isabel answered. "And if a chair got too filled up with men's hats or magazines or things, she'd sit on the floor. Her sister used to go over there just to clean sometimes, it bothered her so much." Isabel watched Mahalia scour the stove.

"I wouldn't use steel wool," Isabel told her. "It can scratch the enamel right off. Hasn't your mother told you that?" Isabel rose, opened the cabinet door under the sink and pulled out Comet. She stood next to Mahalia, sprinkled cleanser over the sponge, and rubbed at the stove top. "This is the easiest way," she said. She handed the sponge to Mahalia and remained beside her while Mahalia continued cleaning.

The telephone's orange light flashed again. This time, I reached it before Mahalia noticed. I raced behind her and tilted the receiver. The Graverobber's voice burst from the phone's speaker, startling Isabel: *"Marguerite! Marguerite! I know you're there!"* Isabel stepped back from the counter, looking around her. Mahalia quickly replaced the receiver.

Isabel studied the telephone.

"It's just the Graverobber," I told her. "He's always worked up about something and calling here."

Isabel frowned. "Someone who calls himself the Graverobber keeps telephoning you?"

I laughed—of course he did not know our name for him.

"You'll need something else for the inside of the oven," Isabel told Mahalia. Isabel reached behind the bottles of dish soap and Spic and Span, pulled out a fifth of gin, read the label, and returned it. She rooted around until she found oven cleaner, opened the oven, and peered inside. She reached into the back, and her long arm pulled out a bottle—a small, curved flask of whisky. Even to me, the oven seemed an odd place for my mother to have hidden liquor; she must have been tipsy when she thought of it. What if Mahalia had stuck some chicken in there one evening, without bothering to look? Isabel set the flask on the counter. A ray of sunlight passed through the trees behind our backyard and pooled in the whisky. The tree swayed; the light looked drunk.

"Baked whisky," Isabel said. One corner of her mouth bent up in a half-smile, as if acknowledging an inward joke, a joke she did not expect anyone other than herself to find funny. Faint wrinkles like tiny pitchforks appeared at the corners of her eyes.

Mahalia blushed. The telephone flashed again behind her. I lifted the receiver. *"I'm not giving up, Marguerite!"* the Graverobber menaced. Mahalia returned the receiver to its cradle and shot me a look of pure fury.

Isabel turned toward me and asked, "Did *you* put the whisky bottle in the oven?" I sensed that she somehow already knew the answer. Her question made me feel anxious and excited. When I shook my head, she said, "Because it could be dangerous to put alcohol in an oven. It could catch aflame. Where should this bottle go?"

I scurried to the sink. I pushed back the containers of dish detergent, and pulled out a tall bottle of vermouth and a fifth of gin and two half gallons of Wild Turkey, all half drunk. I had a sense that there was something trouble-seeking and mean-spirited about what I was doing. I could not have said whom my action was directed at—whether I was toasting or taunting my mother or Isabel or Mahalia or the whole wide unpredictable world.

"That bottle from the oven belongs with these," I said.

"Did someone have a party here?" Isabel asked.

Not understanding, I answered, "My birthday was weeks ago." I thought to ask, "Do you want a swallow?"

The phone's orange light winked on again. Before I could answer it, my sister unplugged the phone from the wall.

"I don't subscribe to liquor," Isabel answered. "I don't dance, drink, play cards, smoke, or make noise." She smiled the same half-smile she had earlier.

"It's everywhere here," I announced. "Every place you could dream up." My voice sounded strange and nervous, even to me. I stood, pushed myself up onto the counter on one knee, and opened the lid to the ceramic jar labelled FLOUR. I stuck my fist into the flour and rooted around. Mahalia gasped when I pulled out a half-pint of gin. It looked like a headless man covered with snow.

"She's hiding them from me," Mahalia said, to herself or to Isabel. Mahalia ran some water into a pot, sprinkled Comet onto it, and then unscrewed a bottle of liquid cleaner and lifted it over the pot.

"DON'T DO THAT!" Isabel cried shrilly. She grabbed the scouring pad from Mahalia.

Mahalia stepped back, bewildered.

"You can't mix ammonia with cleaners like Comet that have chlorine in them. The fumes can poison you. No one ever told you that?"

Mahalia shook her head, and a tear trickled down her nose.

"It makes the same kind of gas they used to kill people with in the World War," Isabel said. "Bon Ami is safer."

Mahalia left the dirty pot in the sink and threw her arms around Isabel, pushing her a little off balance so that Isabel stepped backward. My sister cried uncontrollably then, and Isabel patted her on the back, saying, "Now honey, now honey." I slid off the counter and lined up the bottles beside them as Mahalia wept. I put the small ones in the front, and the large ones behind. I remembered the telephone and plugged it back in.

When Mahalia's crying subsided, Isabel said, "I believe I saw your mother at the Stein Tavern."

"Oh, I despise her! I despise her!" Mahalia said.

I expected Isabel to answer, *No you don't,* but she just continued to pat Mahalia's back.

"Mama will stay at the bar for hours and come right home and drink all this," Mahalia said, gesturing at my array of bottles.

"Well, you can do something about *that,*" Isabel said. She let go of Mahalia and picked up one of the half gallons of Wild Turkey. Then Isabel opened the kitchen door, still carrying the bottle, and examined our backyard. The trees in the woods behind it tipped in the wind and sprang toward each other as if they were scuffling. Isabel stepped outside and peered into the tractor tire that had served as our flower bed in warm weather. Now the tire was filled with snow and gaped in our yard's center, a black-rimmed blind eye. Isabel upturned the whisky into the tire. The liquor left a stain on the crusted snow that looked like a wilted petunia or a puckered mouth.

Mahalia watched without moving. I felt a wild excitement; I unscrewed the caps on two of the gin bottles and carried them outside, holding them up jubilantly. I sniffed the mouths of the bottles: The gin smelled spicy, like my mother's breath; I loved the smell. I inhaled deeply, and then overturned the bottles into the tractor tire. The gin ate into the snow and left dark worm tunnels behind.

Together, Mahalia and Isabel emptied the rest of the bottles. I watched, jittery with a pleasant anxiety, until I couldn't stand still any longer. I bolted into the house, where I raced around like a dog unearthing a trove of fresh bones. I searched the hallway and fetched some rum bottles from the cedar box where we stored our winter scarves and mittens. Isabel and Mahalia emptied these too, silently, without talking. I brought them a sherry bottle from my mother's bedside table, a, flask of gin from the desk where she wrote the bills, and a bottle of vermouth from the back of the bathroom's linen closet.

Mahalia and Isabel poured the liquor out of all of these, and I carried the empty bottles inside and set them on the counter. The number was staggering. As Isabel and Mahalia returned inside, I stood back to admire the bottles: They looked like a church chorus of tall and slender and squat singers. The low late afternoon light snagged on them and folded like green and brown fabric on the counter. The tallest bottle caught the light in an odd way, so that trains of brightness spread out beside it, lacy and intricate.

"Maybe," Mahalia said, "when Mama sees them all at once, she might come to her senses."

"What's important," Isabel answered, "is to realize that you sometimes have to sweep the devil out with a broom, like dirt—it doesn't matter how often he comes back—just sweep him out." We were not accustomed to hearing people talk about the devil, but Mahalia did not react as if Isabel's odd language bothered her. My sister bent her head and looked at nothing at all; when the light fingered her hair, it turned wine-colored, like my mother's. I felt a rush of tenderness for my sister, and I turned away.

The telephone's orange light blinked; I lifted the receiver again. The Graverobber shouted, *"Marguerite, if I have to, I'll come over there!"*

Isabel took the telephone from me and said, "What do you mean calling yourself the Graverobber and upsetting this household? You are not to telephone here and bother the children anymore." She hung up before there was time for an answer.

Mahalia opened her mouth to say something, and then closed it—perhaps she intended to tell Isabel that the Graverobber was my mother's boss and that he had not known until that moment that anyone called him by anything other than his proper name. However, Mahalia must have feared that such facts would only make our household seem even more off-kilter. She turned her back to us and scrubbed at the pot in the sink.

A car rumbled in our driveway. I half expected the Graverobber to step out and rush up our walkway, angry and annoyed with Isabel. I ran to the front window and peered out. It was my mother; she sat in our Oldsmobile for a minute after the motor shut off. She rested her head on the steering wheel as if she were too tired to get out of the car. Just as I decided to go out to her, she lifted her head and opened the car door: I saw one of her legs touch the ground, lightly, as if she were testing the solidity of the pavement. Then the other leg followed, and she rose, closed the door, and walked slowly toward us across the front yard. I rushed back to the kitchen and stood before the bottles.

Mahalia strode by me and threw open the front door. My mother said, "It's nice to be home," kissed her cheek, and walked in. She sat down on the couch, pulled her feet onto the cushions, and laid her head back on the armrest. Only then did my mother see Isabel.

My mother propped herself up on her elbows and asked, "Who are you, the Lady with the Alligator Purse?"

Isabel perched across from her on the armchair.

"Mrs. Daigle," she said. "You must know who I am. I'm Isabel Flood, I do missions for Stein Evangelical Church." She paused and said uncomfortably, "I am aware that you are Catholic. I did not come here attempting to convert you. However, I will tell you that in my church work, I've had the misfortune of attending to the estates of people who have drunk themselves to death. I once sat by such a man while his wife called the hospital. But he was dead already—he had died sitting upright in the back seat of his car. His heart was ruined and his lungs had filled with fluid. He had drowned in himself. It was terrible to witness."

As Isabel talked, my mother sat up and looked behind her. My mother narrowed her eyes, focusing on the empty bottles crowding her kitchen counter: The light in them was dazzling. It filtered through a low tree and seemed to speak inside the bottles with a hundred tongues, dark green and pale blue, brown and blazing white. At first, my mother appeared puzzled, as if she could not make sense of that audience of bottles. Then she lifted one eyebrow and lay her head back on the couch arm.

"All things considered," my mother answered, slurring her words slightly, "it's especially nice of you, Miss Flood, to come in here and mingle with us degenerates." She pressed her finger tips against her temples. She kicked off her black high heels.

"I see I'm not reaching you, Mrs. Daigle," Isabel said. She picked up her puzzle from the coffee table and put it in her pocket. The fabric of her coat moved over her hand, and I heard the faint music of her puzzle's metal loops. Isabel waited for my mother to turn back around, but she did not. After a while, we all wondered whether my mother had fallen asleep or dropped into unconsciousness.

Isabel said, "Mahalia honey, remember our indoor picnic. Five weeks from today, the third Wednesday of February. I'd be thankful to see you there at five o'clock, an hour early. We could use a hand at setting up the tables. Can we count on you?"

"Okay," Mahalia said. "Yes."

Isabel gave Mahalia a quick hug, saying, "That's wonderful." She let go of Mahalia and looked at me, briefly adding, "You're always welcome too, Penny." She left, closing the door quietly behind her. I wondered why she had chosen to come over and invite us that day, if the picnic was five weeks away. I realized then that Isabel had not come about the picnic; she had appeared at our door for another purpose of which I was uncertain.

In the morning, the bottles were all gone when Mahalia and I came downstairs for breakfast. By then, my mother had also called in sick to work, and she lay asleep upstairs while we prepared breakfast and left for school. However, my mother either did not remember, or acted as if she did not remember, her encounter with Isabel. When we went grocery shopping a few days later, I spied Isabel at the end of our aisle. She wore a long coat that looked as straight and stiff as a corn husk. She was piling oatmeal boxes onto the top compartment of her cart, the one where small children customarily rode. I said, "Look, Mama, it's the Lady with the Alligator Purse!" My mother gave me a quizzical look, as if to ask, *What will you come up with next?*

Chapter Three

Quiet

J. X. once told me that when he was blind the quality of silence seemed different to him. Silence had texture: sandpapery grays and dark snarls like steel wool, whorls that tangled with each other and burnt jagged pieces that clawed one another at a white edge, and channels of black that ran swiftly to an invisible singing rim. Silence, when you concentrated on it, could lull you, or pierce your eardrums with a high pitch or drive you crazy by pulsing with vague repetitions as insistent as a leaky faucet. "No wonder the universe burst into being out of the void," he said. "It couldn't stand the quiet any longer."

Commencing with Isabel's visit, both my mother and Mahalia slipped into a battle of competing silences: My mother maintained her privacy, and Mahalia no longer opposed her openly. Isabel seemed to have left behind a kind of dampening over our house, a sense of resistance that made me feel as if I were breathing in dank cellar air. My mother and Mahalia never discussed the day we disposed of my mother's liquor. For me, their silence empowered Isabel's appearance at our home. She seemed to lurk on the edges of the mounting tension between my mother and sister, like one of those characters who skulk behind the fiendish masterminds of horror films—the silent Igors who witness everything and follow orders with a smoldering obedience that makes them more menacing than the Franken-stein monsters they help usher into being.

Instead of directly confronting my mother about her behavior, my sister made me the confidant of her disapproval. Two Wednesdays after Isabel's visit, my mother had one of her mornings when she stayed in bed while we got ready for school. Mahalia told me, haughtily, "She's hung over!" but I think my mother was simply trying to force herself to lie still, to hold the day in check so that she could not set in motion a wrong course of events.

Mahalia did not notice how my mother struggled with herself after the morning she got rid of all the liquor bottles we had emptied. When my mother came home after work, she sat restlessly at the dinner table, picking at her food, drinking only coffee or soda, and looking constantly at the clock. I think she had decided that she would try to make it until midnight every day, so that Mahalia would never have to see her drinking. My mother did not restock her large supply of liquor—she retained only a bottle of vermouth and a flask of gin under the sink—liquids that were so purely transparent, almost invisible, that they seemed to deny their own potency and very existence. Once I walked in on my mother in the bathroom and found her perched on the edge of the bathtub, emptying a flask of rum through the faucet's hot stream onto a hill of scented bubbles below. By then, however, Mahalia was so suspicious that she interpreted any mood, any transient loss of appetite, any giddiness, to my mother's drinking secretly, and so Mahalia missed my mother's efforts when she made them.

I came to see that Mahalia could not understand the vigorousness of the temptation liquor posed, and I was surprised there was anything I comprehended that she did not. To me, the allure of liquor and my mother's battle against it seemed almost familiar. I could easily picture myself lost in those turbulent tides (although, when I imagined that kind of struggle intensified, one which would have required me to break into two people, to fight against myself, I could not). I felt our lives as a hurtling forward, a motion I followed unquestioningly, heedlessly, beyond the bounds of my imagination, and I assumed that was what adulthood was—the place where you touched the bottom of the bottomless depths and tapped the ceiling of the dizzying heights.

The days when my mother lapsed, coming home late and walking unsteadily, built on one another inexorably, separating her from Mahalia and intensifying the differences between them until all their unspoken dissonance left me unremittingly on edge. When I entered our house I wanted to yell, to scare the quiet suspended between my mother and sister into something that could be heard and smelled and touched.

On the day of Isabel's indoor picnic, as we walked home from school, my sister tried to persuade me to attend with her. I refused. I did not want to go back to Stein Evangelical, and I sensed that appearing at the picnic without our mother would somehow be an indictment of her in the eyes of the other adults.

"I'm not cooking for you tonight!" Mahalia told me.

"I'm not hungry," I answered.

When we entered the house, we found our mother already in the kitchen, preparing an elaborate early dinner.

Mahalia whispered to me in the doorway, "Has she gone and gotten herself fired? Has she gotten fired? What's she doing home?"

My mother asked, "What's wrong, Mahalia? What are you hush-hushing about?"

"Mahalia wants to know why you're home so early," I said.

"That's *my life*," my mother answered, wiping her hands on an apron.

She set our supper on the table—smothered pork chops, Mahalia's favorite dish—and sat down across from us, eating nothing herself and holding a glass full of ice; whatever liquid had been in there was gone now. My mother still wore her work clothes, an ash-gray dress she saved for days when she went to court. There were lavender circles under her eyes also, and her hands shook slightly as she held her glass. She seemed sad and intent on reestablishing communication with Mahalia, but when she reached her hand toward my sister's arm, Mahalia drew it back. Mahalia did not mention the church picnic.

My mother looked sad or sorry, but Mahalia did not care; she stared at my mother's glass.

My mother asked, "Mahalia, back when you got in that trouble in October, what *had* Mr. Molinari done that caused you to write that note?"

"As if you care!" Mahalia answered, under her breath.

My mother waited a minute, and when no further reply followed, she said to my sister, "Your father named you after Mahalia Jackson, the gospel singer. I was dead set against it, but he filled out the birth certificate while I was lying dazed in the hospital. Oh, I was furious! People who strive on and on for goodness can be so blind to their own cutthroat selfishness. We had already agreed not to name you until we gazed at you and decided what kind of name fit you. But then, when I saw you, I found myself feeling tickled by your father's trickiness—he must have felt so daring, naming you on his own! Here he was, a man barely mean enough to survive the world, and his first look at you had inspired him to an act of pure, happy devilishness. And when I peered down into your little face, I thought: He's right, she does look like a Mahalia. He already knows his daughter. No other name in the world could have captured everything in that wide-eyed look you had."

Mahalia's reaction surprised me. She seemed annoyed, even angry. She said to me, not my mother, "My father named me after a gospel singer, and she never told me before?"

"Oh yes," my mother answered. "Your father loved gospel music. He sang it at all hours until I had to wear Kleenex in my ears for some peace. His favorite song was 'Were You There When They Crucified My Lord?'" My mother rose unsteadily and sang in demonstration:

> "Were you there when
> they laid Him in the tomb?
> Oh! Sometimes, sometimes!
> It causes me to tremble, tremble, tremble."

I thought she was funny. She sang in a solemn, false bass. Mahalia stood, pressed her hands to her ears, and yelled, "Shut up! Shut up!"

My mother kept singing. A fit of hilarity seized me. I started to laugh, choked on my dinner, and laughed some more, coughing while tears streamed down my face and my mother handed me a glass of water, still singing. Mahalia looked at me as if I had wounded her. I clamped my hands over my mouth, but the laughter sputtered through them.

Mahalia turned her back to us and shouted as she ran up the stairs, "I'm the only one in this family who's not all wrong!"

My mother picked up her glass, set it down, picked it up, walked to the sink, pulled the gin bottle from underneath, put it back without opening it, and restocked the glass with ice. She stared out the kitchen window until I thought she had forgotten where she was, and then she filled her glass with water from the tap and sat down.

She asked me, "Do you know what the difference is between you and your sister? If there was a bowl teetering on the edge of the table, Mahalia would reach over and grab it and move it to where it was safe, but you would just sit back, smiling, waiting for it to fall so that you could see what kind of noise it made when it broke."

I could not tell if she was praising or chastising me.

"Mahalia was so shy when she was little," my mother continued. "You wouldn't remember her like that—to you she probably seems big and in command. But when she was little, she wouldn't even say hello to any grown-up outside the family. She would have withstood the tortures of the damned before she answered a single question from a stranger. It was worse after your father died. A year after the funeral I once asked her what kind of animal she wished she could be, and I thought she would say a bird or a horse or a dolphin, but do you know what she answered? 'A turtle, because then I could close my shell if another animal tried to get me.' It made my heart hurt when she said that. She was so timid! She grew out of it when she was a little older than you, but she's still—cautious. She wants to know the ground is safe before she steps on it. I used to worry so much about her—when is the ground ever safe? And here I am now, upsetting everything—"

My mother rose, knocking over her glass: Water streamed across the table. "I've gone too far this time. I always go too far with her. How am I supposed to pull myself up short before I arrive at the place where Mahalia is? I have to talk with her."

She climbed the stairs, and I waited until I heard her murmuring above me. I walked as quietly up the steps as I could manage and sat down at the top.

My mother was telling Mahalia, "Then don't forgive me. I'd rather you didn't if that's how you feel."

Mahalia did not reply.

"Just listen if you won't answer me," my mother said. "Even if you stay angry, I really am sorry. I know it's hard for you to believe, but it's true."

"I don't believe it."

"I know. You're too young to understand."

"Understand what? I don't understand because there's nothing to understand!"

My mother fell silent—I could picture her, bowing her head slightly and biting her lip the way she did when she was worried.

"At least I'll be gone tonight, Mahalia," she said finally. "At least you won't have to be in the same house with me!" My sister said nothing. My mother exited our room and walked down the hall to her bedroom. "I'm just falling apart," she whispered to herself. "God, I'm falling apart!"

She closed her door. I listened to her rattling around inside her room— her closet door's hinges moaned, and there was a sound of shoes falling to the floor from the door's shoe rack. My mother asked, "What now?" and then a dresser drawer opened and shut. My mother emerged from her room wearing a seaweed-green dress I had never seen before. An iridescent blue scarf was woven loosely in her coppery hair, and shimmery earrings hung from her ears.

"Penny, what are you doing on the stairs, dancing?" she asked. "Did you clear the table? I have to go out tonight. I want you to do your homework and listen to your sister. Go to bed at eight-thirty, and don't give Mahalia any trouble. She's—she's feeling overtaxed." My mother kissed me and descended the stairs. Then she faced me and asked, "Do I look all harried like a bat out of hell, Penny, or do I look all right?"

"You look pretty," I said. "You look perfect."

She turned around once for my benefit, just as Mahalia opened our bedroom door.

"When is she coming home?" Mahalia asked me.

"The prodigal mother will be back by eleven-thirty," my mother answered.

She disappeared from the bottom of the stairs. She exclaimed, "What an awful coat!" The front door closed with a hush, as if offsetting Mahalia's repeated slammings of our doors.

Mahalia sat down on the stairs beside me and buried her face in her hands. "Where is she going?" she asked.

I wanted to make my sister happy—I scrambled to our bedroom, and looked out the window onto the street below. But my mother was gone already. The street was empty of cars in one direction. In the other direction, about three blocks away, were what I at first took to be the headlights of a slowly moving car, but as my perspective adjusted to gather in the barren trees fingering the twilight overhead, I saw clearly that the moving lights were too small to belong to a vehicle. Behind them, from around the corner of Main Street, other similar lights trickled. They moved gradually in the direction of our house, like molten lava. More lights followed, bobbing and flickering, and now I could make out dim ghoulish shapes carrying them.

"Mahalia!" I called. I ran past her down the stairs crying, "Something's outside!" I opened the front door and rushed into our yard. A moment later, I felt Mahalia behind me, holding my coat and lifting my arms to slip them into it.

Now lights streamed around the corner three blocks up our road, fifty or more bright winking circles that flowed into and away from each other in a glittering flood. Houses flickered on, and our neighbors materialized, silhouettes on their front porches, and stood as if transfixed by their closer vision of what approached us. The shapes that bore the winking lights grew more human. When they were a block away, I could distinguish a horde of dark coats and bright oval faces above them, illuminated by lanterns. A dim noise, barely discernible, preceded them—a humming noise, like the muffled furious hum of swarming bees.

"It's *them*," Mahalia said, stepping down from our porch onto the sidewalk. "The indoor picnic must be over."

I followed her for half a block, until the lit front border of the procession touched us. I saw now the clearly illumined faces of adult marchers. Mahalia called out to one of them, but he lifted his finger to his lips to silence her: It was Reverend Bender, hooded in a parka. He carried a lantern with a white-hot wick inside, and beside him two dim figures suspended between them a banner barely legible in the dusky air.

HOW MANY MORE WILL PERISH?

On either side of the writing were the painted curled shapes of infants trapped in containers shaped like halved hot peppers or punching bags. As Reverend Bender passed me, a deep, portentous vibration arose from the air beside him, and I realized with awe that the adults following Reverend Bender were humming—they were all humming together, and the humming grew stronger as they passed me, their lanterns held before them and lighting their faces.

I felt Mahalia's hand close around mine, and she pulled me into the vibrating current of light. I looked for Isabel Flood, but the lanterns half-blinded me so that when I stared at the ground I could barely distinguish my own feet. I felt propelled ahead as if by magic, as if I were moving without walking, and an increasing exhilaration filled me, a buzzing knowledge that Mahalia and I were now part of something enormous, larger than ourselves, larger than Mahalia's anger and my mother's tempest-in-a-teapot struggles with my sister and with liquor—we had entered the river that circled the world, what F. X. called the current of history, or what priests exhorting us in their dark robes called mankind, and I hummed into it all. My voice vibrated against my breastbone until I thought I would laugh out loud or burst.

The lights of new porches turned on as we passed. People emerged to watch us and stepped toward us like figures snagged by a current, and then passed behind us, dim shadowy floating forms, and we turned onto the street that led toward Stein Evangelical. Ahead of us, on the road, light flowed from the church, and a shadowy yellow bus sat beside it, its headlights channeling white into the darkness of the street beyond the church. Under the pinkish, inadequate light from a streetlamp, black words on the bus's side, **ARMY OF LAMBS**, were barely visible. As if the bus were a dam in front of our procession, the first marchers slowed, and a second wave of marchers lapped over them and commingled with the ones behind them until we stood in a sea of white-hot lights, half-blind in the cold.

Reverend Bender turned to a short man in a minister's collar and said, "Reverend Sloat, this has been exhilarating. We are enthralled that you chose to join us." Behind Reverend Sloat, a thin man with shadows pooling in his sunken cheeks held the banner, its loose end twisting white in the glowing air. My sister stood beside me, her face lifted, and illuminated by the myriad lamps, and then the humming ceased abruptly, a hand beside me turned a lantern key, and the lamps around me flickered out like the windows of houses on a dark shore.

———

The following afternoon when Mahalia and I returned from school, she set down her books on the kitchen table, retrieved my mother's gin bottle from under the sink, and set it on the table also. Mahalia moved like a person lit by fire on the inside, directed by a relentless unbending current of flame. She found a funnel in a kitchen drawer, removed a bottle of Tabasco sauce from the refrigerator, and poured it through the funnel, pounding the bottom. The red liquid dripped into the gin, turning it pink. I loved Tabasco sauce, the way a single drop of the red-pepper juice brought tears to your eyes and fire in your mouth, the fact that if you put it on a tarnished dark penny, the juice would leave it gleaming as if newly minted. When I was five, I had once eaten a quarter of a bottle of Tabasco sauce on a dare. I still remember the feeling of blood pounding in my ears, my heart racing, pepper-heat rising through my shoulders and neck and face. My mother had been so worried that she had rushed me to the hospital.

"What are you doing, Mahalia?" I asked.

"Saving Mama," my sister answered. "Teaching her a lesson." She returned the bottle to its place under the sink, behind the ammonia and Comet. I felt stunned by the deliberateness of Mahalia's anger. Her actions captivated me—I would never have been able to plan something harmful so coolly. Still, after my sister closed the cabinet below the sink and washed her hands, I reconsidered her strategy and thought my mother would never fall for such a trick; she would see the discolored liquor and throw it out.

"She's letting it happen," Mahalia told me. "Who does she think she is? I could just go to rack and ruin too, but I never have!"

After this, my sister finished her homework, and then bent her neck for an hour over the gold-dusted pages of a new Bible. When I leaned over her shoulder, I saw that some of the paragraphs were printed in red, as if the writer were afraid no one would read them if nothing set them apart from the small black print in the rest of the paragraphs. Mahalia closed the book and retired upstairs when we heard my mother's steps on the front porch.

As my mother began cooking supper, she took the gin bottle out from under the sink and set it on the counter. It remained there, unopened, as she blanched beans and turned on a burner under a skillet holding a coil of sausage. She poured rice into a pot, and sighed sadly, as if she were watching her own tears spill into the water.

The telephone rang, and my mother put it on "Speaker," as she liked to do when she cooked. I expected to hear the Graverobber's voice, peppery with exasperation or droning out some new assignment, but the words that boomed through the speaker were, "Help! I'm being held hostage by bullfrogs!"

My mother's face brightened, and she laughed. She set the rice box back on the counter beside the gin.

"What do bullfrogs eat, Marguerite? A chef I interviewed last year brought them over with a recipe for frogs' legs. He thinks I'm really going to eat them! I have to stop making friends with everyone I run into. Listen to this boy—" There was a silence, and then a deep croaking resounded through our kitchen. "The other eleven like him are singing themselves to death right now in my shower."

My mother laughed again and said, "Why don't you just let them go in some bayou, F. X.? Let them find their own food."

"Damn!" F. X. cried. "These devils pee on you to make you set them down. Imagine us doing that to everyone we dislike—*aah!*" There was a scuffling sound and F. X. came back onto the phone.

"Marguerite?" F. X. asked, as if my mother, and not he, had disappeared from hearing.

"F. X.?" my mother answered. "F. X., you have that tone in your voice. Are you in one of your blue moods? Is something wrong?" My mother stirred the rice, and then pulled down a glass from the cabinet over the sink, half-filled it with ice and tonic water, and poured in a small amount of pink gin.

"You bet, sister," F. X. answered. "I have a plague of frogs in my home. Hold on." We heard the sound of an object being dragged across the floor. F. X. returned to the phone and said, "They're all back in the shower. Can you hear them?" I imagined my uncle holding the receiver up to the bathroom, and I strained to hear the frogs' singing. "The real reason I'm calling you, Marguerite, is that your town, the godforsaken town of Stein, made the AP wire-service news today. Some antiabortion pecker from Ohio named Reverend Sloat is leading a pilgrimage from Cincinnati to Buffalo to Albany and stopping at a few out-of-the-way towns like Stein. The AP article says, 'Reverend Sloat descended on the small New York prison town of Stein, joined the Evangelical church there, and marched with his followers like a crusader.' It says his church took over some school board in Dayton, and now he plans to take over the country. Except New York City. He claims he won't go to New York City because it's 'lost to the Sodomites.' "

"I saw them," my mother answered. "A bunch of crazy people in a yellow bus parked here and herded down Main Street carrying hurricane lamps— no, *kerosene* lamps. Can you picture it? They were chanting in this huzzbuzzing way. Like horseflies! They sounded like a barn full of horseflies! The man I was with said, 'Well, here's the flies, so where's the manure?' The fire chief cited them for some kind of violation. It's the most dramatic thing that's happened in Stein in ten years. The only thing!"

F. X. snickered. "I hope your Reverend Sloat stays there on the edge of civilization, where he won't do too much harm. We surely don't need him down here. When the people of Louisiana don't want any more children, they just drown the ones they already have."

Our bedroom door slammed upstairs. My mother did not appear to notice.

"F. X.?" my mother asked. "Are you sure nothing is wrong?"

"Yes, Marguerite. I called to check on how *you* were."

"Things couldn't be better," my mother said. "*You* take care of *yourself.*" She turned off the speaker and asked, "How's your love life?" She talked to my uncle in an affectionate tone, inaudibly, for a few minutes before saying good-bye.

After she hung up, my mother sipped her gin absently and then stopped. She held her glass to the light streaming through the window—the light was mustard-colored and turned the gin to a pale rust inside the glass. Then she said, to no one in particular, "Well, okay." She summoned Mahalia for dinner. My sister said nothing when she saw my mother holding the pink gin.

At dinner, as my mother picked over her plate, she drank a second and third glass of gin and tonic without any discernible reaction, although the Tabasco sauce must have seared her mouth and the lining of her throat.

She asked, "How was school?"

"Penny got in trouble," Mahalia said. She looked at my mother as if measuring her. "She knocked out a sixth grader named Persis Boards."

"She hunkered right onto me," I explained. "First she hunkered down onto Laura Fiori, and then Lynn Cochran. When we were in the bathroom. Then Persis threw me to the floor and sat on my chest. She was mashing me."

"Penny knocked her out," Mahalia repeated.

"Persis pinned my hands down," I said. "So I fishhooked my foot under her chin, and brought her head down backward with my leg. It hit the tiles. She acted knocked out, then she came to, swirling her eyes around and moaning and saying, 'I was unconscious! I was unconscious!' If she was really knocked out, how could she have told she was? Sister Geraldine let her stay in the nurse's room all day." Sister Geraldine also had called me into her office, sat me down across from her, and asked, "Penny, how are things at home? How is your mother?"

I had felt giddy with trouble, and even at the very moment that I answered, I knew I was going too far. *"She's drunk as a skunk on the Fourth of July!"* I told Sister Geraldine.

Sister Geraldine pulled off her wimple. Her hair lay flat on her head for a few seconds, and then began rising in its natural disarray, like brush where a deer has slept. She rubbed her eyes and her temples.

"Does your mother have any relatives she's close to?" Sister Geraldine had asked.

Now, sitting across from my mother at the dinner table, I asked her, "What's Uncle F. X.'s last name?"

"F. X.?" my mother answered. "You know—Molineaux, just like my maiden name."

"That's what I thought," I said.

My mother did not ask why I wanted to know. Instead, she studied the glass in her hand.

"Mahalia—" she began, but did not continue. She stood abruptly and told us, "I'm sorry. I don't feel well." She climbed upstairs, still carrying her glass. I entered her room only a few minutes afterward, but she had passed out on her bed. I touched her, and jiggled her arm, but she lay there, lifeless.

When Mahalia and I got into bed two hours later, my sister murmured, "She didn't even notice." She switched off our light, turned on her side and escaped immediately into sleep—she never suffered from the insomnia that dominated my nights.

Nor did she ever show concern about my inability to sleep—she was oblivious to it, the way I sensed she tried to be about anything in me that was unusual. I felt a stab of fear that my sister must not care about me at all, if she was only willing to accept those parts of me that struck her as acceptable. I wasn't even sure I had such parts.

A skunk rustled below my window. It came every night to the garbage cans behind the house and unleashed its smell, usually at midnight, and again at two or three in the morning. I turned toward the window and breathed in the skunk's exciting, pungent stink. When I closed my eyes, I sank halfway to sleep until I dreamed I lay under a black water, listening to a rushing sound and waiting for something I could not name that I knew would come. I woke up frightened and was relieved to hear Mahalia tossing under her covers beside me. She was mumbling angrily in her sleep.

"Mahalia?" I asked.

She sighed and answered something in a groggy voice. I called her name again loudly, so that she would not teeter back into unconsciousness. I did not feel like being alone, and I wanted her company, even if she did not want mine.

"Mahalia?" I asked. "What the hell is abortion?"

I thought Mahalia would respond angrily, because I had cursed and jerked her awake, but instead she turned toward me under her covers and answered in the same earnest tone that colored so much of what she said in those days: "It's when a woman stops a baby from being born."

I had never considered that birth could be arrested in midstream. "How?" I asked her, glad to connect with her in any way if it kept her dog-paddling above the waters of sleep. "Does the man have to do something with his— sugar shaker?" I laughed and added, "Does he do what he does, and then do it backward?"

"It's not funny!" Mahalia answered emphatically. "They cut the baby up while it's inside you, or they poison it. It feels everything but it can't scream to make them stop."

Who would do that, and how? I wondered. My mother had told me that babies were protected within the womb, after I asked her why digestive juices didn't dissolve us all before birth. I imagined the womb as a bottle, a baby bobbing inside of it like a ship-in-a-bottle bobbing on the ocean. I asked Mahalia, "How do they get to the baby without poisoning you or cutting you up?"

"They go in through the bottom of your womb." Mahalia answered with such certainty that I knew she had asked the same question, or pored over a picture of a baby being murdered inside its bottle.

"Does the womb have a thing in it like a cork?" I asked. "Do they push things into it through the cork?"

"It's too horrible to talk about," Mahalia answered, as if she had glimpsed some blackness so pure that no two people who laid eyes on it could differ about how terrible it was; I longed to know what she knew. "Go back to bed, Penny." I heard Mahalia turn away from me and yawn.

I sat up under my covers and asked, "What did Mr. Molinari do that made you call him an asshole?"

Mahalia answered sleepily, "He only calls on the girls who flirt with him."

"Oh," I answered. *Was that all?* I thought. *So what?* I lay back down. "Mahalia?" I asked. "Can't the baby bite them or anything, when they attack it?"

"Babies that young don't have teeth," Mahalia answered. "I want to go to sleep, Penny."

I imagined being in a cave with poisonous red water whooshing in, its eddies sucking me under. When I finally drifted to sleep, I dreamed I was circling into a bottleneck, terrified. A black undertow sucked me down, and a dark warmth enveloped me with a crashing noise. A stream washed over me, cradling me and buoying me along, while black writing I could not read ribboned over a bright surface, and I knew that I was safe.

————

Mahalia took me to Isabel's house toward the end of March that year, on a Saturday when my mother said she was working for the Graverobber. I remember our walk vividly, because it occurred on a freezing morning that followed two weeks of unseasonably warm weather. Earthworms had dug in the hundreds from the top soil, and then been frozen solid in a late frost that reaffirmed the return of winter and left sheets of ice filled with their curled forms. The sidewalk that led to Isabel's looked as if it were made of a clear, fossilized substance from a primeval era predating even dinosaurs, like a chilly amber. The ice terminated in a salted cement landing in front of the house where Isabel lived as a first-floor renter, a narrow brick structure with small windows and a steep roof.

What I remember most vividly about my initial visit to Isabel Flood's was how orderly and spare her home was compared to our own. In what might have been her living room, for example, there were two folding chairs, a narrow rectangular table, and a single mustard-yellow armchair under a low-hanging lamp. There were no rugs on her floors, no pictures on the walls other than a single framed print of Breughel's *Massacre of the Innocents*, and an odd picture Isabel had painted herself. It showed a pink oval with a tail and two shadowy eyeholes, lying on a green background that undulated like grassy hills. At the bottom was the title, *The Seed*. Her kitchen was checkered linoleum, coal black and spotless white, her counters sponged and uncluttered by any of the appliances that crowded ours at home. One of Mahalia's mason jars containing boiled dirt and peat moss sat on Isabel's kitchen windowsill. The spores inside had not yet germinated. A label on the jar said: LOUISIANA RESURRECTION FERN.

At the end of a shotgun hallway was Isabel's bedroom, painted a pale blue, with a four-poster cherry-wood bed, a cherry-wood bedside table with a Bible, a clothing catalog, and a large glass lantern on it, and that was all. I had never seen a lantern like it before, except in the night procession. I leaned over it and breathed in its smell, which was oddly intoxicating to me. Isabel came up behind me and said, "Stay away from the kerosene lamp. It's dangerous." She lifted it onto the sill of a small square window, where I could not reach it.

While Isabel and Mahalia talked in the living room, I looked in the drawer of the bedside table. It was full of metal puzzles, piles of contorted loops and mangled half-letters. Under the bed were more puzzles: two large ones made of cast iron, and ten or more of interlocking wood pieces. A few dresses hung limply in the closet, and there were two pairs of slipperlike shoes on the closet floor. I tried the doorknob on a second door that looked as if it led to a separate room, but Isabel entered again and said, "This is my bedroom, Penny." She put her hand on mine—her fingers were thin, and her skin was dry and papery—but I could not turn the knob in any case; she kept the door locked.

"Why don't you join us in the front room?" Isabel asked. She wore a cotton dress, despite the weather, the same pale blue as her room, and cinched at the waist with a matching patent-leather belt. It reminded me of old dresses my mother kept packed in mothballs, which she liked to laugh at, referring to them scornfully as "those ridiculous outfits we wore when I was a girl."

I sat on one of the folding chairs. Isabel handed me a lemonade; it was too sour to drink. I asked her, "Where's your television?"

"We don't believe in television," Isabel answered. "Don't put your glass down on the bare table, Penny. Just hold it in your lap." She made me feel subdued and uncomfortable.

I leaned forward to peer around the table at Mahalia. Her lemonade was balanced in a ladylike way on the palm of one hand; I thought she looked silly. When I leaned back, I unsettled my own lemonade so that it splashed into my shoe.

"There's a sponge on the sink you can wipe it up with," Mahalia said.

I rolled my eyes at her. She got up to get the sponge. "Oh jeez," I said. "My shoe's going to stink tomorrow."

"We don't say that here," Isabel answered.

"Say what?" I asked. " 'Stink'?"

"We don't say the Lord's name in vain. We don't say 'God' or 'damn' or 'hell' or 'Jesus' or words that are just attempts to cloak those words, like 'jeez' and 'heck' and 'gee' and 'darn.' In that way, we fight against evil at every step, every moment of our lives. 'Jeez' is not even a true word, in any case, Penny."

"That's a lot of words," I answered. "It would probably be impossible to keep track of so many words." I imagined evil slipping through me, step by step, every moment of our lives, vital as blood, but denser, coagulating inside us like a black tar.

Isabel watched Mahalia mop up the lemonade and said, "That was thoughtful, Mahalia. Maybe Penny will clean up her own spills next time."

Isabel pulled a small pear-shaped piece of glass, clear as ice, from her pocket. She held it up by a slender metal chain. "This is a mustard seed,

Mahalia," she said. "It's special to me." I saw a small pale dot petrified at the center of the glass pendant. "Mustard seeds are a Christian symbol of innocence and purity, and I used to wear one like this when I was young."

She walked behind Mahalia and dropped the chain around her neck. When the clasp slipped, Isabel giggled girlishly—the only time I ever remember her giggling. After she had fastened it, Mahalia lifted the mustard seed and said, "It's pretty." My sister looked genuinely happy, at ease with herself and her surroundings. The thought came to me then that Isabel was just the mother Mahalia would have chosen if she had been allowed to cut one out of dough with a cookie cutter. I had an inkling in that moment of what it might have been like for Mahalia to live with a mother who was so different from her. When I looked at my mother, I felt the wildly stirring wind of which I knew I was part. When I considered Isabel, I saw a blankness, and felt that if I walked behind her quickly enough, I would find she was somehow not all there.

I peered at the painting on her wall called *The Seed*, wondering if it was also a mustard seed.

Isabel stood beside me and, lowering her voice, spoke slowly, as if picking carefully through words to avoid lighting on one that was sinful. "God sent that picture to me in a vision," she told me. "I didn't even realize what it was until I painted it. It was an unpainted child waiting to be portrayed."

"What do you mean, 'in a vision'?" I asked her. "Do you mean God firecrackered it down at you with His eyes?"

" 'Firecrackered' is not a word," Isabel answered. "You can't just make up words, Penny."

What did she mean, you couldn't make up words? Where had they come from if no one had made them up?

Isabel smiled one of her inward half-smiles and asked, "Do you know the story of Saint Hermine from school?"

When I answered, "No," Isabel told a religious tale that I have never been able to find as an adult, in any narratives of the lives of the saints. As she narrated, her voice thinned, and her manner of speaking was odd and formal, as if she had taught herself to speak or had learned to talk by reading the musty textbooks in the back of a school classroom. When I got to know Isabel better, I learned that she assumed this peculiar tone when she felt her religious mission needed elucidating or on those rare occasions when she disclosed personal facts about herself, usually for the same purpose—to explain or defend her mission.

"Saint Hermine was an ordinary girl, not particularly religious," Isabel said. "She had a vision one day while walking home on a dirt road. An angel stepped in front of her and refused to let her pass, and Saint Hermine, without being told, sensed what was expected of her and leapt onto the angel and wrestled with him. They wrestled all afternoon and all night, and during that period, the angel communicated through his touch and his fury the very way God's light felt. It was furry and smooth, like rabbit fur. And he carried the smell of heaven, which was like the smell of a candle the moment after it's blown out. Afterward, Hermine lived by herself, and what made her a saint was her refusal to speak, ever, of what she had learned in wrestling with the angel. She prized her relationship with God too much to do that. Despite what must have been an overwhelming temptation to impress others by saying, 'I've seen God, I know what heaven smells like, I understand now exactly what light is,' she resisted and remained holy through the purity of her experience, a memory she never muddied by retelling it."

When Isabel finished, I asked, "If that was true, then how did people know that Saint Hermine fought with the angel, or even that she was a saint? Did the angel wrestle someone else to the ground to tell them what he had done to Saint Hermine?"

Isabel acted as if she had not heard my question. She offered to walk us back to our house and asked my sister, "Are you going to be all right? Do you want me to accompany you?"

"That's okay," Mahalia answered. "I'll be okay."

I examined Isabel's painting more carefully: A baby with a vague face peered at me. It looked like a bank robber with a stocking pulled over his head, the nose and mouth mashed, the eyes partly obscured behind a tiny fence of red paint strokes. I tried to imagine myself as unborn, my mouth smothered against the womb, my arms and legs pinned tightly, my face so murderously desirous of freedom.

"Penny, we're going," Mahalia said.

I turned away from the painting—it was spooky. I followed Mahalia. She did not talk to me as we walked home; she seemed sunk in her thoughts. When we entered the house, our mother had not arrived yet.

"Maybe she's at the lake," I said. "Let's go look for her there. She likes to sit out there."

"No," Mahalia said. "Why should we make fools of ourselves by going after her?"

Mahalia cooked macaroni and cheese, made me do my homework, and then announced that it was time for us to go to sleep. I felt so restless after Mahalia turned out the light that I could have cursed her for falling asleep so easily. When I closed my eyes, I heard Isabel's voice: a litany of Don'ts that joined hands with itself and threatened to loop forever in its self-contained circle: Don't leave a ring of water on the floor with your lemonade glass; Don't say "heaven" (Why was *heaven* wrong?); Don't pick up coins off the ground and put them in your pockets, because they aren't yours and they'll cause holes to form in your pockets, and you'll forget to take them out before you put your clothes in the washing machine; Don't tilt backward on the chair arm because you could break the chair; Don't use Comet with ammonia; Don't touch my kerosene lamp. As I drifted on a circling edge of sleep, I found myself wondering whether Isabel was like other people, what adults would think of her. I missed my mother.

When I awoke, moonlight was streaming into the house. I heard a down-stairs door opening, and the lilt of my mother's voice followed by a man's grumble. My heart leapt when I heard her.

Mahalia sat up straight in her bed. She listened until the man's voice rose again, and then she turned on the light between our beds. "That's it," Mahalia said. "Now she's gone too far." Mahalia took a dress from our closet and pulled it over her pajamas. I thought she looked a little crazy, her pajama's lapel sticking up, her legs bare. I followed her out of our room.

"Mahalia!" I giggled.

"Shut up, Penny!" My sister's face under the hall's dim light looked fright-ened. I had thought she had climbed out of bed to express disapproval of our mother's arriving home with company so late at night. It hadn't occurred to me that we had anything to be frightened of. I followed my sister down the stairs.

The kitchen door that faced the woods was open. Outside, the bare trees bowed and wrestled and tossed snow over the yard into the small ring of light thrown from the back landing's single lamp. A man stood in the kitchen, backlit, tall and square-shouldered, a figure from the kind of movie my mother liked to call a chiller-thriller. He walked sideways, half-dragging and half-supporting the weight of the person beside him.

He leaned over the couch, and arranged my mother so that her head rested on the cushions there. He walked to the kitchen sink, got himself a drink of water, and returned to the couch. He bent over my mother and loosened her coat. He kissed her forehead.

"You can't stay here!" Mahalia stepped down from the stairway. "We'll call the police if you stay here!"

The man turned toward her, startled. "Your mother celebrated a little too hard at the party," he said, gesturing toward the couch where my mother snored quietly, her back to us all. "So I brought her home." The man wore a pair of blue jeans and a plaid hunting jacket. I had seen him around town, but I did not know where he worked.

He looked around him and said, "Are you here by yourselves?"

"Why do you want to know?" Mahalia asked.

"Well, that's a fair question," the man answered. "The front door was locked, so I came in the back. I didn't mean to scare you. We didn't mean to wake you up."

He extended his hand toward Mahalia, but she did not take it.

"I think you should leave," Mahalia said.

"Of course," he answered.

Mahalia and I followed him to the door. Curiosity pushed me forward, two hands at my back; I wanted to keep going after him, to find out more about him. Mahalia pulled me inside, and locked and chained the door.

————

All the next week, Mahalia refused to look at my mother, and when they had to pass one another in the hall or on the stairs, Mahalia turned away in a gesture of distaste. When my mother placed dinner on the table, Mahalia would take her plate and eat upstairs in her bedroom. If my mother asked her to clean the table, or sweep, or help with the dishes, Mahalia would do what she was told, but without verbally acknowledging my mother's requests. My sister wore her mustard-seed pendant every day and developed a habit of fingering it nervously while she maintained her prickly silences.

For the first few days of Mahalia's refusing to even look at her, my mother gave my sister a wide berth. Finally, however, on the fifth or sixth day, as Mahalia lifted her dish from the table, my mother grabbed her wrist and said, "It's not a good thing to fight people by sulking and slinking and smoldering around, Mahalia. I don't expect you to be brave all the time, but you should know that kind of fighting is cowardly. It allows you to march through the world like a general, convinced that you must be right because you make sure you don't hear the other side of things."

"There is no other side," Mahalia answered. I wondered then whether they could have resolved anything by mere talk. Mahalia's answers were so short and direct, how could my mother parry them with her circular apologies that joined head-to-tail with her ease of forgiveness?

Mahalia wrested her arm away, left her plate on the table, and walked upstairs. My mother cocked her head, waiting for the door to slam. Instead, Mahalia closed our bedroom door so quietly that its hinges made only a tired cry: This somehow seemed even more insulting than a slam. My mother sighed and returned to her dinner.

"Penny," my mother asked me, "do you have any idea why Mahalia has been watching me as if she's planning to poison me? Why is she so much madder than usual?"

"It's the man," I told her.

My mother dropped her hands in her lap and stared at me as if she did not know what I was talking about.

"Tell me more," she said.

"The man who brought you home last week."

"Oh," she said. She looked down at her plate and put her hand over her face. I was afraid she would cry.

"He acted nice," I told her. "He didn't do anything bad."

My mother nodded. "Of course not," she said. "David is a nice man. Possibly too nice for me."

My mother sent me to bed, but I knew I would not sleep; I tucked myself in, feeling as if most of my childhood consisted of lying awake at night, watching darkness swirl above my head. I took a flashlight from the table between my bed and Mahalia's. I held the bulb to my eyelid; F. X. had told me once that in the early stages of his blindness, looking though cataracts was like peering at a light held up to your eyelid when your eye is closed. When I tried this, I saw blood red surrounded by blackness.

I heard my mother on the stairs and switched off the light. Mahalia rustled beside me; she turned under her blankets so that her back was to the door. My mother sat down on Mahalia's bed.

"Are you awake, Penny?" my mother whispered.

I did not answer. I was afraid she would not talk to Mahalia unless I was asleep.

"I saw you move," my mother said. I held my breath, but then realized she was talking to my sister, not me. "Maybe you should feel glad to ease your burden a little, Mahalia. Maybe it will be better for you if I have some adult company."

My mother waited for a reply. She lingered for half a minute, and then stood up abruptly, as if she could not bear my sister's silence a moment longer. My mother brushed against my bed and slipped from the room. I heard her feet on the stairs and then water rushing in the kitchen sink below. There was a clanging of pots, the sound of the cabinet under the sink opening and closing, of dishes being rinsed. At one point, I thought I heard my mother sob.

I got out of bed and climbed downstairs.

"Mama?" I asked. She wiped her face on the dishrag. I approached her warily from behind—she wept noiselessly, with her back to me. She had never cried before in my presence. I must have watched her for a full minute, astonished, before I stepped forward and wrapped my arms around her.

"Oh Penny," she said. "Don't worry about me. I just feel like feeling sorry for myself."

I held her, my eyes closed, my face resting against her back.

"You have such a good heart, Penny," she told me.

Did I have a good heart?

"You act like a wild pirate, but you follow your heart," my mother told me. "Why can't that battle-ax teacher of yours see that? Why do adults think they can change children's fundamental qualities any more than we can change ourselves? Mrs. Fury's so peculiar. Do you know that blond wig of hers? It once belonged to Mrs. Fury's mother. Her mother wore it around town for a few months before passing it on to her. Isn't that strange and funny? It looked just as terrible on her mother, like a bleached rat crawling around on her head."

I laughed. I felt a relief I could not put a name to. I pictured Mrs. Fury, her face contorted with disappointment as she said something to me, and I knew I would never be able to wholly dispel this information from my thoughts when I looked at her.

My mother stooped down to my level and pushed my hair from my face. "Don't trouble yourself about me, Penny," she said. "Sometimes grown women go through little private hells they concoct for themselves. I'm going to take a walk to air out my head, and then I'll come up to bed."

I mounted the stairs, and as I climbed under my covers, I prepared again for a sleepless night. I listened for the front door to shut, and the sound of my mother locking it, and then I lay in the darkness wide awake while thoughts raced in a disconnected way through my head: I heard Mahalia say, "Because!" and saw Mrs. Fury, her mouth half open in reprimand, her blond wig sliding down over her forehead, all interrupted by the sound of a motor and dogs barking. I woke up abruptly, feeling as shocked as if I had been pushed into a ravine.

I heard voices outside on the street. I sat up and asked, "Mahalia?" but she did not answer. I peered outside. My mother stood under a streetlight, talking to a man who sat in a pickup truck parked below my window.

I pulled on my shoes and jacket and slipped downstairs. When I opened the back door, a winter wind chilled my face and woke me up. The night sky was a luminous dark gray: Stars appeared and dwindled like fish coming up for air. I held my hands out in front of me and walked toward the high tree on our neighbor's property until I felt a tangle of bushes and then rough bark. Our neighbor's dog was gone, and I pulled myself up high into the tree's branches, remembering my way. I closed my eyes to verify that it was true: I could climb blind. I did not open my eyes until I reached what I thought must be the last horizontal branch, near the top.

I felt a limitlessness up there: What if I were a sweep of night, my head always forty feet up, grazing heaven? And what if I were no more than the air I breathed, a darkness turned inside out? Up there, I felt suddenly that I knew what evil was, the evil that Isabel mentioned with such certainty: It was what pulled against everything, the energy that made the wind move, because otherwise everything would be a stock stillness, a waiting, a shout with a hand clapped over it. I felt myself slipping in the tree and sat up quickly, clenching the branch, dangerously awake, and the thought coursed through me: I'm not just going to fall asleep, I'm going to *fall dead.*

I heard the voices below again and saw my mother leaning into the front window of the pickup. The truck's motor idled, and white vapor billowed around it into the dark street.

My mother's voice was low and full of yearning, and the man's voice swooped under hers. The truck's motor shut off. The man emerged from inside, put his arm over her shoulders and laughed once. I heard my mother say, "Mahalia," with sadness in her voice. He pulled my mother's jacket collar up higher around her neck and leaned toward her to say something. It was a gesture full of such tenderness that I almost called out to them both, in order to hurtle myself into their moment of connection, but then I remembered that I was in the tree, that they would want to know why I was there, that they would pull apart and look up, craning back their necks until I climbed down.

They turned toward the house, and the man walked my mother to our door. She leaned into him. I imagined she looked both tired and relieved. They talked for a few moments longer. I climbed down slowly from my tree, feeling for the branches with my feet. My hands found grips with such sureness that I knew with absolute certainty I could never fall from that tree, in daylight or pitch blackness, asleep or otherwise. When I touched the earth, I stole to our front bushes, feeling the ground with my feet. I ducked down and peered into our front yard. My mother and the man faced each other, their foreheads touching. Then, instead of going inside, my mother hooked her elbow in the man's, and they turned and walked up the street in the other direction, until they disappeared in the darkness.

I felt pure longing watching them: I did not want to retreat into the house, to lie next to Mahalia while she slept through the night. I did not want to be shoulder-to-shoulder with my sister's indignant, disdainful dreams, in which she followed a slender trail only she could see toward a room filled with bright light where everyone sang and caterwauled out their claim to goodness. I wanted to forget everything cloaked in daylight, that harsh mustard-gold, to flee back toward some blackness in the wind, flitting like those summer insects so agile they eluded bats, jeering and veering through violet twilight. I wanted to plummet and soar after my mother into her secret life, to follow the scent of bad nights, of salt and blood skittering through my heart, to steady myself on a pinpoint of air or a howl of wind.

Men

any years after regaining his sight, F. X. claimed that he still had dreams in which everything was darkness and he felt his way along the edges of things, listening for echoes before and behind him to judge distance. After he earned his degree in anthropology at Tulane, these dreams often preceded an insight that allowed him to solve something that preoccupied him in his waking life—to decipher a Mayan glyph that had stumped him or to draw linguistic parallels between two words of seemingly unrelated languages. In his sightless dreams, jewels that were as black as the oblivion in which they were set appeared in his path. These were his favorite dreams, he said, because they led him "to understand that *Logos, the Word,* easily could have come precipitously out of the void, because it was there all along, a black diamond buried in black rock." Even now as an adult, I have dreams that suddenly contort and connect, as if through a black inherited vein, with F. X.'s description of his own dreams. I grope through relentless darkness and my hands abruptly touch movement, and the movement becomes F. X. talking with his nervous ebullience. His words stir around him and I know that I am on the brink of a rewarding discovery: The discovery will be F. X. himself, his face assembling across a dark surface.

Every child needs to have just one adult around who is like him or her, even if that adult is misguided or cruel or narrow-minded or off-kilter. Such an adult provides, if nothing else, a point of reference that allows us to get our bearings—without one, we have no way of judging whether we have stayed on course or departed from it or ever had a course at all; whether we are evil or saintly or neither; whether we are approaching land or being swept farther out to sea or whether we even want to return to shore. If F. X. had not been called by Sister Geraldine and I had been snatched up by Isabel Flood without his knowledge and influence and promise of return, I never would have weathered the months of my mother's drinking and her subsequent cure. Instead, I would have been knocked down and trampled in the holy war between good and evil, because in my childhood I never saw myself as good.

Of course, Mahalia had no such guiding kindred spirit in our family. I remember that I saw Mahalia's essential goodness as a burden to her—although many people say it is a terrible onus to be labeled bad as a child, I thought that the opposite must be worse: If you knew early that you had wickedness in you, you could learn to accept it, if not to wrestle against it. But if you believed that you were essentially good, then when you finally found the ocean of evil in yourself, surely it would come as a terrible shock.

In April, Mahalia began a pattern of rising and leaving the house at dawn so that my mother would have to confront my sister's empty bed in the mornings, just as my mother had forced us to face her late-night absences. On those mornings, Mahalia accompanied Isabel to church, or on visits she made to other members of Stein Evangelical.

On the third or fourth day that Mahalia failed to appear for breakfast, my mother asked me, "Penny, did your sister come home last night?"

I answered that she always came home early.

"She wasn't out gallivanting with a boy?"

"She doesn't have boyfriends," I said.

"So, where in heaven is she?"

"I think she's trying to make you mad by slinking out before you get up," I answered. I did not reveal what Mahalia had told me earlier that week. "Mama wants to make us witnesses to her sin," my sister had said. "She wants to make us part of what she's doing so that we forgive her, but I'm not going to let her."

"Why would Mahalia's rising early make me angry?" my mother asked, but she divined the answer before she finished her question, because she shook her head as if responding to an inner voice and said, "Oh, of course."

That evening after school, she called home and asked to speak to Mahalia. When I shouted for my sister, she refused to come to the phone.

"Mahalia?" my mother asked, thinking my sister had taken the receiver. My mother sounded exhausted. "I have to go see about a law-office job in Plattsburgh. Keep your fingers crossed for me. I spent an hour duddying myself up. I think they'll probably hire me. I'll just tell them they should get down on bended knee and thank God for sending them a woman who can type and do shorthand and spell better than they can." This was the first time I had heard my mother suggest that she had lost her job with the Graverobber. Until that moment, I had never seriously considered that she had. I wondered if she told Mahalia more than she told me.

"I hope you get the new job," I said.

"Penny?" my mother asked. "Is that you? Wasn't Mahalia on the phone just now?"

"No," I answered.

My mother replied, "I see. Can you tell Mahalia to fix the chicken I left in the refrigerator?"

Later in the evening, without my reminding her to, Mahalia took out the chicken and turned on the stove.

"I won't eat it," I told her.

"I already had dinner at Isabel's, but I don't mind cooking for you," Mahalia said.

"I just want cereal," I answered.

While I ate Cheerios, Mahalia pored over an old *Life* magazine from Isabel that contained pictures of embryos in different stages of development. When I was done eating, I leaned over Mahalia's shoulder and peered at the picture of the largest, nine-month-old fetus.

"It doesn't look real," I told her. "It looks like its fingers are made of wax." Mahalia ignored me and turned back a page to a smaller embryo. "That one looks like that doll, Talking Tina," I went on. "The one in *The Twilight Zone* who tells that little girl, 'My name is Talking Tina, and I love you!' and then later, it tells the girl's father, 'My name is Talking Tina, and I hate you!' And then later, when his wife finds him dead at the bottom of the stairs? Talking Tina lifts up her head and says, 'My name is Talking Tina, and you better be nice to me!'" I walked stiffly around the couch, blinking my eyes like the doll, and said, "My name is Talking Tina, Mahalia, and you better do exactly what I say!"

"It's almost time for bed. Wash your hair, Penny," Mahalia answered in a motherly tone that chafed me. I climbed upstairs and lay on my bed, scaring myself by thinking about Talking Tina—I found terrifying the idea of something that was not human rising up and acting with all the energy and spite of one of us. After I had seen the program, I had been so spooked that my mother had let me spend the night in her bed.

Around nine o'clock, our doorbell rang. I remember saying to myself in so many words: *When your mother falls apart, everybody thinks they can come pounding on your door*. Mahalia, I knew, would not answer. However, a minute later, the kitchen's back door squealed on its hinge and caught on the chain latch. I heard Mahalia's sharp cry and a man's baritone. I thought it must be the same man I had seen from my tree, who had appeared at our house two weeks before, and that surely Mahalia would get rid of him as quickly as she could. I pictured my sister standing at the door with the chain still attached, slowly inching the door closed as the man spoke frantically to her, asking her where my mother was. When I still heard the man talking a few minutes later, I grew curious and ventured downstairs.

"I don't think of our lives as repeating our parents' mistakes," the man was explaining to Mahalia. "I think of our lives as orbits. They go in circles. They zoom around and touch base with what they know and zoom on, always circling the things they love and fear most."

I recognized my uncle F. X. from his words before I saw him: Even in my earliest memories of F. X., he wears language like a house. Words build around him, dark supporting timbers and black slate. He is never quiet. His baritone expands the room; meaning and nonsense join, adding one annex of narrative to the next; his voice rises and rises again, keeping itself company with its architectural repetitions. In one of my first memories of F. X., he is sitting in our armchair holding his blind man's cane. His face is buried in his hands, his voice echoing hollowly as if he were speaking from a dark cavern, his eyes patched from new retinal surgery completed several years after his sight had been restored. My mother is telling him, "F. X., they have to hire you, you're so well-spoken and you have such *presence*." I remember understanding the meaning of that word without asking, for who else had such massiveness, such a tower of words, that wick of red hair that flamed from a block away, even when its bearer could not see it? *Presence* was a word my mother used often. It was what she liked to say when a man impressed her: a black-haired man cursing as he inspected a flat tire, his paw resting hugely on the car's hood; or a bearded man carrying four grocery bags at once and singing loudly, unself-consciously, as he stepped out of the store in front of her; or a one-armed man as tall as F. X., hollering to a friend while effortlessly hefting a bag of cement onto a truck. She described her own father with baffling satisfaction by saying, "My clearest memory of him is that he filled the doorway and his voice boomed through the house." She would express admiration for a man we met casually or passed on the street by saying, "he occupied the whole room," or "he sang like a bear," or "he was like Orson Wells—he walked in and filled the picture." Her sensual appreciation for such men was evident to me even as a child. Listening to her, I understood that a man's mere casual existence could be a gift, a delicious morsel a woman could drop into her mind like a chocolate into her purse.

Even so, as a small child I had once walked up behind F. X., about two years after the last follow-up surgery had been done on his retinas, and he had been so darkly fixed on himself, his arm over his eyes as he sat on the sofa with the lights off, that he had seemed less a presence than a vast absence. Looking at him was like leaning over a cliff and gazing into an abyss.

"Penny!" F. X. cried when he saw me, "You never grow! You're no bigger than a loaf of bread." He grabbed me by my shoulders and pulled me toward him: He smelled like whisky and cigar smoke and burnt matches. I vanished in his arms and reemerged: I was tempted to turn slightly to catch myself in the hall mirror, but I resisted. I had now broken what I thought must be a world record; I had avoided mirrors for 192 consecutive days. F. X. gave me a noisy, smacking kiss; his dark red mustache moved like a live animal, tickling me, and I laughed loudly.

"F. X. says he wants to visit us for a few weeks!" Mahalia proclaimed. She fingered her mustard seed, and I sensed the taut anxiousness in my sister's words, the pretense she was straining to sustain to make our uncle believe we were anything other than what we were. Her tone of voice made me feel an unpleasant spideriness, as if we were secretly, cruelly, trying to trick F. X. into entering what Mahalia must have seen as the dangerous web of our lives.

"So, where's your mama?" F. X. asked. "Out dancing on the hood of a policeman's car, at the head of a Shriner's parade?"

"She'll be so excited to see you," Mahalia answered.

"She lost her job," I said. "The Graverobber called and called and called until he had a conniption fit."

Mahalia flashed me her angriest look. I knew what I was doing. I was trying to unravel things before she could weave them together into something we were not.

"What a scene-stealer your mother is!" F. X. said. "I've lost my job too." He pulled me onto his lap.

Mahalia looked apprehensive; she said nothing. She sat in the armchair and doodled on a paper. Her eyes filled with tears, and I felt an impulse to apologize, to say something ridiculous to cheer her up.

F. X. studied her for a moment and told her, "There are never any main characters in our family—it's just a free-for-all with everybody wrestling with his own fates and flaws. Here I thought I'd be able to come here and scare up some drama around myself. I thought I'd have you all wringing your hands and thumping my back and saying, 'Poor you, out a job! You poor old thing!' Now I see I'll have to change my plans, and we'll throw a party instead. A job-changing celebration with lots of flashing lights and you girls kicking up your legs and singing "Carry Me Back to Ole Virginny.' "

My sister smiled faintly. F. X. continued, "Mahalia, I couldn't bear journalism anymore. It was all facts, facts, facts, parading after one another in the stark light of day. Reality was making me too gloomy. Believe me, Mahalia, not everyone has your wonderful olive-green eyes. You end up interviewing these old Baton Rouge politicians with eyes like catfish and triple chins who tell you, 'Bo', this wunner is such a co'd damn wunner it would even freeze a Yankee, and you quote me, Bo', put down that I said that.' "

Without taking her eyes off of the paper in front of her, Mahalia asked F. X., almost shyly, "What are you going to do now?"

"I've applied to graduate schools in anthropology. I want to specialize in archaeology or linguistics. And if that fails, I'm going to become a seeing eye man. I'm going to hire myself out to blind dogs."

Mahalia laughed and said, "Oh, F. X.!" I was relieved to see my sister at all happy, acting girlish instead of grown-up.

I told her, "Mama said she thinks she's getting a new job. In Plattsburgh."

"What kind of job?"

"I don't know," I answered. "Something with lawyers in it."

"What's that?" F. X. asked, pointing at the paper where Mahalia was doodling. "Arabic?"

"No, it's shorthand," Mahalia answered. I looked over Mahalia's shoulder. She had written: *I don't know, I don't know*.

"When I was blind," F. X. told Mahalia, "I thought there should be a Braille shorthand, but no one else I spoke to was interested in the idea. In the beginning, people thought Braille itself was a bad idea. Do you know Louis Braille's blind school in France outlawed Braille after he came up with it as a boy? The students had to write it secretly, passing notes to each other under their desks. That's why it endured. The Braille alphabet has the beauty of rebellion and the resilience of the underground. It's like a secret tongue. It's the kind of language Penny would have invented."

I grinned, thinking I would have liked to have been Louis Braille, but Mahalia said, "Penny *hates* languages. Her teacher is trying to teach her class a little French, but Penny resists every step of the way."

I could not tell if Mahalia was insulting me, or just speaking out of nervousness. "I despise French," I told F. X.

Mahalia fingered her pendant and said peevishly, "I liked Mrs. Fury!"

"Can't your mama help you, Penny?" F. X. asked. "She's the one who taught me French."

"Mama doesn't know French," Mahalia said.

"Of course she does," F. X. answered. "We grew up speaking Louisiana French. It was our parents' first language. Your mama read me all of Victor Hugo when my sight first became too bad for me to read. She made me practice the subjunctive over and over again. *She's* the real linguist in the family."

Mahalia fell silent. A blush started at her neck and crept into her face. F. X. looked at me with his eyebrows raised, as if to ask, *What did I say wrong?* His eyebrows were a dark red like his hair, two jagged wings flying over the hawk of his mustache.

"It's just like her not to tell us something like that!" Mahalia said. "Something as big as 'What language did I grow up speaking?' I once told Mama I didn't understand a French assignment, and she said, 'Oh, what use is French, anyway!' "

F. X. gazed at Mahalia, his head cocked, saying nothing. He closed his eyes, briefly, an odd mannerism that lingered from his days of blindness.

"Your mother wrote me that you're getting straight A's," he told Mahalia. "In French and everything else too."

"Would you like something to drink?" Mahalia answered, pulling herself back to her normal manner, responsible and adultish.

"Do you have any whisky?" F. X. answered.

"Mahalia dumped it out," I told him.

F. X. raised his eyebrows again. "Coca-Cola would be fine," he said.

"I'll get it," I answered him. Mahalia followed me into the kitchen. As I leaned into the refrigerator, she grabbed my elbow and said, "Don't tell him how bad things have been. You might as well tie a rock to your head and throw yourself into the Mississippi." I was surprised to hear Mahalia use one of my mother's favorite expressions. "Don't let him know that she's off with some man somewhere!"

"She's not," I answered.

"And don't let him know how desperate we are."

"We aren't desperate," I answered.

Mahalia whispered, "Well, if you don't know we are," she said, "then at least you won't let him know."

When we returned ceremoniously with his soda, F. X. asked, "So where *is* Marguerite, at nine-thirty on a Friday night?"

"Mahalia thinks she's out gallivanting with a man, but Mama called me and said she's looking for work in Plattsburgh," I answered. Mahalia glared at me.

"At nine-thirty?" F. X. asked.

Mahalia told him, "Anyway, a neighbor named Isabel Flood always checks on us when Mama goes out at night."

"Mahalia sneaks out to this church," I said, "where they talk in this crazy language. They jump and weasel their bodies around and holler like this: *murdo murdo murdo momy momy mom.*"

"Really?" F. X. asked. "They talk in tongues? I read a feature in the *Times-Picayune* in which a linguist claimed that when he recorded people talking in tongues, he found the grammatical structure and variations of a true language. He claimed it was not just gibberish invented on the spot by people trying to hog attention in church."

Mahalia's face was dark crimson with embarrassment. She would not even look at me.

F. X. stopped speaking and politely turned away from her. He leaned toward our piano, and then stood and tinkered with it. "Out of tune," he said. F. X. opened the piano bench and pulled out some dusty sheet music that had belonged to my father. Penciled notes rose and fell over a yellowed page of music paper; they looked like tacks pinning down the music. The song's title, "Waltz for Debbie," was written in neat cursive at the top.

"Bill Evans," F. X. said. "Your father must have written this out. He was crazy about Bill Evans. Only he would have tried to transcribe a jazz tune played by Bill Evans. Look at this, every single note." F. X. sat down on the bench and played a tune I did not recognize.

Mahalia bent over him to look at the music sheet: Nowadays she was curious about anything that had to do with our father. She kept his picture in her top dresser drawer. In it, he wore black robes from a graduation ceremony at Stein's blind school, and he was shaking the hand of an unknown student. His dark hair looked slicked down and his deep-set eyes were hidden under his eyebrows and his mouth was set in an ironic expression, as if he felt uncomfortable participating in public events. I had peered hard at the photograph in order to determine whether he would have put up with me: I couldn't tell.

"Look at this, a bowie knife among the music papers!" F. X. lifted a jackknife with a carved handle.

"Your father always carried that. He liked the woods and hunting. He was the kind of man who could have survived in the wilderness—unless he ran into a woman. He could have lived in the woods carrying nothing but a bowie knife and a compass, eating acorns and possums and catfish, and shunning humanity entirely. I think the reason he worked around blind people was that he enjoyed feeling invisible, away from the examining eyes of his own species."

F. X. handed me the knife, and I tried to open it, but it had rusted closed. I put it in my pocket anyway: I liked the idea of a father who could live wild in the woods.

F. X. told Mahalia, "I once wrote an article on how they make blind students learn music. Why do we all have to be Art Tatum and Ray Charles? Did they think those men had no talent? That blindness made them play like that? I had a roommate at blind school who hated all music. He said it irritated his ears. Why not make use of our other functioning senses? Why not train us as wine tasters, for example? The school director forced me to learn to play the organ badly—he kept giving me hymns to play. My roommate called it 'vampire music.' " F. X. tinkered on the piano a while longer and said, "Even Bill Evans sounds funereal on the organ."

"Did Daddy play the piano a lot?" Mahalia asked him. "I can't remember hearing him."

"He must have been overworked," F. X. answered. "He always worked too hard. He worked hard, keeping the forces of darkness at bay." F. X. laughed. "He played—he played mathematically. He could make Bill Evans sound like a marching song."

Mahalia studied F. X.'s profile, trying to divine whether F. X. was saying my father played the piano well or badly.

"So, have you eaten yet?" F. X. asked.

"I *told* Penny I'd cook her some chicken, but she didn't want any," Mahalia said.

"I'm starving to death," I answered.

"Then I'm taking you out," F. X. said. "I could eat a hundred elephants. Get your coats. It's cold as hell out there." F. X. did not notice, but Mahalia frowned when he said "hell." "Where do you all like to eat in town?"

"You have to go into Dannemora or Plattsburgh to dine out," Mahalia answered.

"There's the Stein Tavern," I said.

"That's a bar," Mahalia said.

"Do they serve any food?" F. X. asked, standing and pulling on his coat. "The roads were bad coming here. My car took off with a mind of its own when I turned off the highway into Stein. It went ice-skating down a hill into a mountain of snow that turned out to be your Main Street. It's better not to risk driving to the next town."

Mahalia seemed caught where she was, torn between refusing to enter a bar and accompanying F. X. out of a sense of propriety to a newly arrived guest.

"Are you worried Marguerite might come home while we're out?" F. X. asked her.

"The world doesn't revolve around *her*," Mahalia answered.

F. X. suppressed a smile; he watched my sister pull on her coat and hand me mine. When he stepped outside, cursing the cold, she followed him.

"Goddamn," F. X. said. "The climate here is vicious. Why did people ever settle in New York? Why would immigrants sail all the way across an ocean, and then not have the wherewithal to head south just a few hundred miles to Cuba or Mexico? It's almost May, for God's sake. How do people here survive?"

When we climbed into F. X.'s car, a rented Chrysler New Yorker, snow was swirling playfully through the air. "Hold onto your hair, girls," F. X. told us. "You know I haven't driven much in snow." F. X. had only started driving five or six years before. He had learned everything from scratch, right down to the colors in stoplights. (Franklin had no stoplights when he was a boy). F. X. loved driving in the way you only can when you've just mastered it. He drove like a teenager, revving the engine, and in the summer he would delight us by laying a patch on the road in front of our house. He liked big cars with expansive names: Galaxie 500s and Thunderbirds and Lincoln Continentals. I sat beside F. X. in the New Yorker's front seat, happy and exhilarated. Next to him, I had the sensation of being catapulted through black space toward a larger life, toward outrageous promise and upheaval and wicked joy.

Stein had no true restaurants. The Stein Tavern served hamburgers and cheeseburgers, coleslaw, and three-bean salad. The tavern was a medium-sized place rarely frequented by women or children after lunchtime. It had a counter and fourteen booths, and it was dark enough that even a sober person could not have judged whether it was clean or dirty. The counter, the booths, and the floor were all dark-stained pine or oak, and I still associate the color of the air there—a dark brown, the rich shade of loam—with men and the underbellies of their thoughts. The tavern was not a hub of social activity like the bars and restaurants so popular now in books and movies—it was not a common ground where the men of Stein met to embrace and reacquaint themselves with the details of each other's lives. It was simply a place where men went to eat and drink.

When we entered, the manager directed us to a solitary booth in an alcove at the back of the tavern, where I could not see the goings-on of the men at the bar without tilting sideways over the floor. The manager had a dark beard so dense that it looked like a mask of hair; it covered his upper cheeks and his eyes peered from deep sockets under his thick eyebrows.

He told F. X., "It gets too rough for kids here this late at night."

"Feed us fast then," F. X. answered, hanging our coats on the rack beside the booth. He ordered three Shirley Temples with our hamburgers.

Two men in the booth behind ours began an argument in Canadian French. There was a knocking against the back of my seat, and one of the men jumped up and yelled savagely a stream of words that sounded like, "*Mondyoumondyoudog!*" The man behind him pulled him back into his seat, saw Mahalia staring at them, and said, "Apologize to the pretty girl over there. She doesn't want to hear your racket." The man who had yelled was wearing an eye patch, and looking at him, I had the pleasant sensation that we were all riding on a pirate ship. He stared one-eyed at Mahalia, rocking unsteadily as if the floor were a roiling sea we were braving. The manager walked to his booth and spoke to him in a low tone, and the commotion evaporated as quickly as it had arisen.

Mahalia looked intensely uncomfortable: If there had been more light in the tavern, everyone would have seen her blush. She put her napkin in her lap, rearranged her silverware, and read the advertisements on her place mat.

"I know what that man just said in French," I told F. X. I stood up in my booth and called, "Get your mangy hands off my beer, or I'll smack your head off!"

"Penny, sit down!" Mahalia said. "She acts up all the time! That's why she's always in trouble in school."

F. X. laughed and said, "Don't worry about French, Penny. It's the language of debutantes."

"*No* one has ever heard of *anyone* taking French in third grade," I told him, scowling. "It's this crazy idea my teacher has about making us repeat things in French. How can you think in two languages anyway? Does it work the same way a whale works? The way a whale's eyes are too far apart on the sides of his head, so that he sees two different things at once and has to think two things at the same time, to keep track of them? Like, 'What's that up there on the left, a shark?' and 'Look at that fish there on my right?'—both at the same time?"

F. X. answered, "If you don't like French, Penny, invent your own language. All you have—"

He was interrupted by a bustle at the tavern entrance. Isabel Flood stood holding the door open just wide enough that an icy wind stalked through the bar. I felt opposite reactions to seeing her there: surprise at catching Isabel in a tavern, and a second more profound conviction that Isabel was somehow everywhere at once, witnessing everything, probing every nook and cranny of our lives. I thought Mahalia would jump up and wave to her, but instead my sister slid to the far side of the booth and pressed herself behind F. X. so that Isabel could not see her.

Isabel walked once around the tavern, peering into the booths as she passed them, as if taking a head count of the men there. She did not stop at ours. I thought I saw her gaze linger on me for a split second, but she acted as if she had not spied us. I leaned forward to watch her better, and Mahalia whispered, "Penny!"

Isabel examined the face of each man at the tables and counter carefully, and then she disappeared down the corridor leading to the bathrooms. She opened both bathroom doors—the women's and the men's—and looked inside. She came back up the hallway and passed the counter again. She exited the tavern without having said anything to anyone.

As she closed the door behind her, a woman outside yelled, "Are you telling me the bastard's not here!"

There was a nervous laugh at the back of the tavern and a contagious ripple of guffaws along the scattering of men in the middle of the bar.

The manager brought us our food. F. X. pushed his plate aside, stood, and pulled a small green reporter's notebook from inside the pocket of his coat where it hung on the rack. He sat down again, saying, "You see, Penny, any language you can make up will be more interesting than French." He wrote down a list of words and turned the notebook around to show me:

girl = *tika*
eat = *jom*
debutante = *tika-tika*
whale = *romodoofree*
at the same time = *romodoofreetik*
French = *oke*

The whale spoke French and ate
the debutante at the same time = *Romodoofree okmama romodoofreetik jomama tika-tika*

I took the notebook and puzzled over it.

"You keep it," F. X. said. "We'll write up a new language and then send it to the French prime minister and tell him we've found something he can use to replace his sorry tongue."

The tavern's door burst open again, and another woman stood there, her arms thrown wide in a dramatic posture. She was a large woman, with round calves and large hands and exuberant black hair, wearing a red coat and bulky shoes with heavy heels. Even I could tell that there was something not quite right about her. She carried her neck in an odd way, her chin raised defiantly and her head tilted slightly to the side. She made me feel homesick; for no reason at all, she reminded me of my mother.

"Where the hell are you?" she yelled. "You come out of here! I'll find you before you find us. I'll play your game!"

The manager stepped from behind the tavern counter, holding a white dish towel. He carried it like a flag of surrender, extended slightly in front of him, and asked the woman if he could assist her in any way.

The woman did not look at him; she surveyed the room. Just as Isabel Flood had, the woman followed a course along the circle of booths. She was less discreet than Isabel. She leaned far over the table of one booth to get a close look at a bearded man whose head rested beside his plate. She told a man at another table, "What's so fucking funny? Your own ugly smile?"

The manager stood planted, his lips pursed slightly, watching the woman's movement from one set of customers to the next.

Unlike Isabel, she peered into our booth. Our presence distracted her and seemed to make her forget what she had come for. For a moment, her eyes rested on me with an evaluating stare; she may have been surprised to see a child in the tavern at night. Mahalia stared at her plate. I wondered whether it was possible that Isabel really had not seen us.

When the woman arrived at the edge of the counter, the manager again asked if he could help her in any way.

Instead, she faced the center of the tavern and yelled, "All right, which one of you assholes is he staying with?"

Not one of the men in the tavern rose to speak with her or took her by the elbow and led her to a seat or even revealed more than mild curiosity as to what she was upset about. Two men turned around and went back to eating. She approached a man who appeared not to have noticed her at all. She leaned down and shouted, barely an inch from his ear, "They told me he's out! Explain to me how can they let a man like that out!"

Again the entrance door opened. This time Isabel Flood came in, leading a girl by the hand. She was small and elfish, dressed in cowboy boots and a baton twirler's skirt. She looked around her, gray-faced, and deadpan in the way of children who would prefer not to be noticed. She was around my age or younger with thick black hair that stood straight up, the kind my mother called "hurricane hair." I did not recognize her; I thought she must go to Stein's public school.

Isabel took the woman by the elbow and said, "This isn't the place. He must be at the Motor Inn. Katie's tired, Mrs. Balbeck. You need to get back to the car."

"*You* tell him when he comes in here," Mrs. Balbeck told the manager, "that he's not getting any money from us, and that if he even steps into our yard, I'll shoot him. Tell him that I'll be hiding in a bush with a gun."

Mrs. Balbeck followed Isabel reluctantly, saying, "Why do they want to protect him? Why does everyone protect him so that I have to be the one running around like a lunatic?" As she reached the door, she turned to us all and said, "That's what you think, isn't it, that I'm some female lunatic? Well, look at *you*!"

Isabel pushed her lightly on the small of her back, through the exit, leading the girl by her other hand. The girl turned to get a last glimpse of the tavern before she followed Isabel out; her expression did not change. The man at the table closest to me shook his head. Another man asked for a refill of beer. The voices of men, which at some point had dimmed to nothingness in the women's presence, now started up again to an accustomed, grumbling level. The manager poured a bag of peanuts into a dish.

F. X. tapped on the green notebook in front of me where he had jotted down words in a new language and he told me, "Now write, 'The big-haired woman mortified Mahalia.' "

I thought hard, examining F. X.'s translations and wrote: *Haarrota tika romotofied Mahalia.* I showed it to Mahalia and she half-smiled in a tight, unhappy way.

F. X. patted her hand and said, "Don't let your worries devil you, Mahalia. As you've just seen, with all the melodrama in the world, no one has time to notice us and our little problems." But F. X. did not know how afraid my sister had been that Isabel would see us, and so his words missed their mark and did not mollify her.

She pulled her hand away from him peevishly and showed him the same, tight, half-smile. "I'm done eating," she answered.

The manager placed a check on our table.

"I want blueberry pie," I said.

"We don't carry pie," the manager answered. He stood beside our table until F. X. handed him money. Mahalia was the first one out the door.

As we approached our driveway, Mahalia told F. X., "You should park the car in the garage."

"Your mama won't be using it?" F. X. asked. Mahalia shrugged her shoulders. "This New Yorker's too big for that garage," he told her. "It would make more sense to put the garage in the car." He stopped the New Yorker beside the curb.

"Your car might get snowed in," Mahalia answered.

"Then I'll dig it out," F. X. said, getting out of the car. "I'll dig it out with a spoon and a toothbrush, the way they excavate tombs to avoid scratching up some valuable artifact by mistake." But Mahalia was not listening. She stood, as if transfixed, on the sidewalk, staring at our doorway.

A man was there, knocking. It felt strange, watching him knock on our door while we remained on the outside with him. It was as if our house was not our own.

"Who's that?" F. X. asked. "The night mailman?"

"He must be at the wrong house," Mahalia answered.

F. X. approached the man from behind, and I ran ahead to see who he was. When he turned toward us, I said, "You're the man who brought Mama home the other night."

My sister looked at me, furious. The man stared at her as if trying to conjure her from the night when she had faced him half-dressed and angry in the darkness of our living room.

"Hi," I told him.

He nodded at me. "I wondered if Marguerite was here," he said to F. X. He looked tall to me, but he was not as large as F. X.

F. X. invited him in, but the man remained at the door.

F. X. appeared to draw himself in somehow until he seemed as cautious as the man. F. X. had once told me, "To be a good reporter, you have to be an Old Boy with the Old Boys, and count rosary beads with the old ladies and wolf around with the wolves."

"I'm F. X. Molineaux, Marguerite's brother," he said in a formal tone.

"Ah," the man answered, looking relieved. "David Slattery." He shook F. X.'s hand and stepped inside.

We followed him. Mahalia turned on the light, and we all looked around as if expecting the house's real inhabitant to greet us.

"Marguerite doesn't seem to be home yet," F. X. told David. I sat down next to F. X. on the couch. Mahalia withdrew to the kitchen and watched us from there.

David remained standing, glanced at Mahalia and me, and spoke tersely, as if measuring his words in front of us. "Marguerite was upset about this job thing in Plattsburgh," he told F. X. "She went up there to interview this evening, but they had already slated the job for someone who knew someone. I told her, 'Take the Civil Service Exam and come work for the state like me. You get good benefits: pension, vacation, sick days.'"

"Where do you work?" F. X. asked.

"Parole office," David answered.

"Then you must know Penny," F. X. said, patting my knee.

"Oh yeah," David answered, smiling at me. "Hoped to arrest her on a bench warrant tonight."

I grinned back. David sat down on the couch beside me. His hair and eyes were the same shade of silver-gray. He might have been ten years older than my mother; I could not tell, although I thought he looked as worn out as my mother. His mustache, cut on one side by a sickle-shaped scar, was silver also. He unzipped his jacket, a hunting parka the color of the fire newts I found at Stein Lake. Like F. X., David's size did not seem to diminish when he removed his coat: I thought the couch might break with both men sitting on it. I hoped it would.

"Do you want something to drink, like coffee?" Mahalia asked.

"Coffee?" David answered. "No."

"Have you known Marguerite long?" F. X. asked.

"We're engaged," David answered. "At least I thought we were."

"*Engaged!*" Mahalia cried.

"She hasn't told you?" David asked her. "We commemorated our one-year serious-dating anniversary two weeks ago by getting engaged."

"He's lying!" Mahalia said. "F. X., he's lying. He doesn't even know my mother." Mahalia looked stricken.

"Mahalia?" F. X. asked.

"We've known each other, through our work, off and on for about five years," he told F. X.

"It's just like her!" Mahalia said. "Everything has to dance in circles around her!" Tears trickled from Mahalia's eyes. She covered her face with her hands and ran up the stairs. She ran down again, and then back up like a crazy person. She came down again, wearing her coat, and rushed out the back door.

"I see she's like her mother," David said. "Emotional."

F. X. stood and asked, "Where's she going, Penny?"

"Just up the block," I said. "To the house of this baby-sitter who lives up the street."

"Well, let her go," F. X. answered, sitting down.

"It's the same lady who was at the bar tonight," I said. "The one with the little girl."

F. X. stood up again. "The big-haired lady?" he asked. "The one with piano legs?"

I considered his question for a minute: I'd never heard a person described as having piano legs. "No, the other one," I answered. "She's this religious lady named Isabel who churches around the neighborhood and baby-sits."

"All right then," F. X. said. He sat down again.

"Look," David told F. X., "just call me when Marguerite gets back." He stood, pulled out a card, and wrote his home telephone number on it. "I'm here because we had a fight, and she—" he glanced down at me "—I thought I should check up on her. But now that you're here—" David pulled on his parka. "I'm sorry I stirred things up with the older girl. I just assumed Marguerite would have told them about us."

"She holds her cards close," F. X. said.

"She sure does," David answered, grinning. He already seemed at ease with F. X. They talked briefly at the door. Their mustaches rose and fell as they spoke, like gray and red birds waving their wings at each other. I enjoyed having two large men filling up our living room, which usually had no men in it all. I liked the way they dragged in a snarl of excitement when they arrived and entered, and I hoped David would come back.

David looked down at me and said, "You two girls are all your mother talks about, you know."

He opened the door and a freezing wind whooshed into the living room. "Jesus!" F. X. said as David walked down the steps to his truck, "Give me hell any day over this cold."

"Stein is hell," David answered. Both men laughed wryly.

———

F. X. sat with me until around midnight, waiting for my mother. We played Parcheesi, first the regular way and then using all four sets of markers and pretending to be four people, each competing against three opponents. Then F. X. devised a new set of rules where the green and yellow markers progressed clockwise and the red and blue counterclockwise. "Clockwise men can only block counterclockwise men," he explained, "and primary colors can only take other primary colors, but not green, and green men can capture red men and trade places with them and reverse direction, and if you spin two fours in a row and have blue men, you can change places with any other person on the board if he's winning and you're not." By the third game,

F. X. proclaimed, "The board's too small! The board's too small! We need more boards!" The game became so full of reversals, of near losses suddenly converted into gains, of colors shifting into and out of alliances and rivalries, that I became lost in the tangle of our moves and played on my feet, circling the board instead of sitting down in front of it.

I felt jerked back into the world when F. X. grabbed me by my waist near the end of our third game and asked, "Penny, what kind of places does your mama like to go to around town?"

"She likes the tavern," I answered. "And she likes to drive down to the lake and sit in the car out there."

"It's too cold to drive around for pure pleasure," F. X. answered. "Let's go check back at the tavern." He did not appear as worried as he must have been, to bundle me in my jacket after midnight and load me into his Chrysler.

"I can't leave you by yourself," he said. "Do you want me to take you to that baby-sitter's while I look for your mother?"

"I don't want to go to Isabel's house," I told him. "She won't let me curse."

"Then sit up here with me," F. X. answered, patting the car seat.

We hadn't noticed, caught in the swirling turmoil of ourselves, that the weather outside had grown still, the temperature dropping so low that the air had frozen into a calm. Tomorrow, the softened snow would have a heavy crust, and by Monday we would be able to skate on our shoes across iced-over holes in the sidewalks and blacktop until Mrs. Fury wrested us out of the frictionless air, warning us against broken bones, against accidents, the peril of movement that cannot stop itself.

F. X. drove slowly down Main Street. The town's sole stoplight flashed ahead of us, a sudden, upturned bowl of green; a neon *Stein Drug* embroidered the darkness at the end of the road; the town's streetlights glowed dimly like multiple pink moons; a single lit headlight on a truck moved toward us, a tilted goblet of gold liquid, a nocturnal whisky. I imagined myself as a resident of a dark, future world, where humans wore glasses to accommodate night vision and convinced one another that the sun had always been invisible behind the layer of ash that had covered the continents since World War III. Anyone who spoke of the sun was carted away as a crazy person.

F. X. parked for the second time that night outside the Stein Tavern. "Lock the doors, Penny," he said. "Don't open them for anyone. Not even God. I won't be gone long enough for you to freeze." He dashed inside. Within a few minutes, I longed to follow him. I unlocked my door and prepared to step down into the snow, when he reappeared outside and opened his door, rubbing his hands together.

"She's not there," he said.

"We could try the lake," I told him.

"The roads are too icy to drive far at night," F. X. answered.

"It isn't very far," I said. "It's right outside of town."

"Okay, Penny," F. X. said. "If it's important to you, we'll look there."

When we turned down a back street, the snow glowed in a ghostly way, wrapped around street posts and garbage cans, and twisted into human shapes like men sleeping on the sidewalk. F. X. drove slowly along the road to the lake. A full moon's blind eye was rising over the black rim of the world ahead of us. We continued for about half a mile before F. X. said, "It seems pretty unlikely, Penny, that even Marguerite would want to careen around out here when it's so dark. Let's turn back home. Maybe she got snowed in somewhere and is trying to call us at this very minute."

"She doesn't call," I told him.

He did not answer me. He rested his arm lightly on my shoulders and took the wheel in both hands again almost immediately. The car inched toward the lake, its headlights stoking the snowdrifts as we approached them.

We both saw my mother's car at the same time. It was about fifty yards from shore on the ice. The car's interior light was on, so that it looked like a hot jewel resting there, melting the ice under it. Behind the shape of a woman in the front seat, I could see the black oval of my leering cut-out monster taped to the window.

"That's Mama," I told F. X..

F. X. stopped in the small park bordering the lake. Somewhere nearby, I knew, were swing sets with their cloth seats removed for the winter, their chains dangling in the darkness.

"Penny, don't you dare follow me," F. X. said. He turned the heat on high and left the motor idling. He opened the door, climbed out of the car, and then leaned back inside, saying, "You know better than to touch the ignition keys, right?" He seemed to deliberate for a minute, to weigh leaving me there with the motor running against taking me out to the dangerous place where my mother was, and then he closed the door. He opened it again, fished in the glove compartment, and found a flashlight. I thought he would take it with him, but instead he gave it to me and asked, "How frozen is that lake this time of year?"

"It doesn't unfreeze until the end of April," I said. "I've been on it lots of times."

"Because if I fell through, for example, you would know to walk the half-mile back into town to the baby-sitter's, right? And to call for help from there? You wouldn't be crackbrained enough to believe you could pull a three-ton uncle out of the water?"

"It's frozen," I told him. There was a shelf of rock that extended from the shore under the lake, so that during the summer, you could walk out almost a quarter mile before the water reached for the top of your head and tried to pull you under. I thought the lake could easily still be solid ice down to the rocky bottom, even out where my mother was. However, F. X. was not at all familiar with cold climates, and I thought he must have felt worried as he stepped onto the lake into the bluish-white path made by our headlights. He tested the ice with a branch as he must have tested for cracks and potholes in sidewalks when he had used a blind man's cane.

"If it will hold a car, maybe it will hold me," I heard him say.

I waited until he was about thirty yards out, and then I opened the New Yorker's door, left the flashlight on the seat, and followed after F. X.'s moonlit form in the muddy darkness ahead.

He stopped and said, "Goddamn it, Penny. I can feel you creeping up after me. Get back on the shore."

I wondered whether he had used powers of detection acquired in his years of blindness, or whether he just knew me well enough to guess, without evidence, that I would not obey him.

"Don't make me waste time walking back over the ice to carry you off, Penny." He stayed where he was, a denser blackness in the general darkness. I retreated, alarmed by the tightness in his voice. He waited until I walked to the lake's edge and climbed back into his car, before he continued on.

When he reached the halfway point to my mother's car, I could no longer see him. I climbed out of the New Yorker and examined the moon. I looked at my feet, indistinct shadows, and scanned the ground before them for the pale rim of ice where the frozen water started. I looked outward across the lake, to gauge the point at which my vision failed. Finally F. X. emerged in the dim circle of light around my mother's car, and I started toward them again.

F. X. knocked on the car's window. His knocks sounded as if they came right up against me, skating over the chill air. "Goddamn it, open the door!" he shouted. He continued to shout; half his words reached me and half were lost, his sentences torn in two by gusts of wind. I heard: "Out of your goddamn mind!. . .Get us both killed!. . .Mahalia. . .Penny. . .Goddamn cold!" The last thing I heard before the car door opened was "Freezing my ass out here!" He vanished inside.

There was the thinnest layer of snow on the ice as I approached its middle. It felt solid as cement. I walked steadily toward the car and circled around to the back of it. I crouched down and crept on all fours until I sat under my mother's window.

Her voice was too muffled for me to understand. It rose, and F. X. answered something, and then my mother's door opened. I froze, suddenly afraid that they would find me there.

"Leave me alone! I'm falling to pieces, F. X., and I don't even know why! That poor man has no idea what he's getting, what a mess I am! I'm not marrying anyone! I'm not going through all that, attaching myself to someone and then losing him! Not in this state! I'm not doing anything in this state! I'm terrified, F. X., every minute of every day. The feeling never goes away, except when I'm tipsy. I'm scared I'm going to turn into one of those mean drunks who are nasty to their own children. I'm scared to leave myself alone with Mahalia and Penny."

"Damn it, Marguerite, close the door!" F. X. said. "You don't even have the heat on!"

"I have this pit, right here," my mother said, "right in the center of my chest, right under my rib cage, that never goes away. And when I really think about it, what I think is that death is a great cruelty, something God will never be able to explain or justify."

I felt embarrassed to be there, listening; it made no difference that I only half-understood what she was talking about. The door remained ajar, while F. X. and my mother sat quietly, in their shared grief, a universe of darkness above them, the deadly cold suckling the ice under them.

"Well," F. X. said, finally. "Why didn't you tell me it was *death* that was bothering you."

My mother laughed, a lush, bitter sound. I felt so relieved to hear her laugh, and then F. X.'s snicker, that I laughed too.

"Penny!" my mother said, opening her door wider. "Oh, F. X., why didn't you tell me Penny was here? What's she doing here?" And then my mother was crying again.

F. X. flung open his door, walked around the car, and scooped me up. "Penny, I told you—" He opened my mother's door and said, "We have to go, Marguerite."

I thought he would set me in the Oldsmobile and drive us back, but instead he said, "I'm not taking this car over the ice, Marguerite. You have to get out." He pulled my mother toward him, and she stood, seeming to huddle into herself.

"Christ," F. X. said. "You're shaking, Marguerite." He wrapped one arm around my mother and said, "Penny, walk a little in front of me, toward the Chrysler. This is too much weight in one place on the ice." I went ahead, never turning to look at him or my mother. I felt irrationally that I could make them disappear if I did. I could hear F. X. rustling behind me, my mother quiet as the cold, and our walk seemed to take forever. When I touched the ground, F. X. said with relief, "Thank God! This is insane!"

He guided my mother to the New Yorker's back seat and pushed her in. "Sit in the front with me, Penny," he said. Beyond him, my mother's Oldsmobile still burned out on the ice: It looked like the dark center of a luminescent eye ogling the moon's wall eye.

As F. X. drove us home, I was afraid to speak to my mother. I looked once at where she lay, wrapped in both her coat and F. X.'s. Even through the two coats, I could see her trembling. How would they get her car off the lake? I wondered. Would they leave it there until the ice broke and the water swallowed it?

When we arrived at our house, F. X. led my mother inside as if she were a child and carried her up the stairs. He returned back downstairs and fished under the sink, saying to himself, "No Wild Turkey!" He found the gin bottle and poured himself a glass.

He turned to me and asked, "Penny, can you tell me the name of your baby-sitter again?"

"She's not *my* baby-sitter," I told him.

He bent down and said, "Honey, what's the name of the lady whose house Mahalia's at now, and where does she live?"

"Isabel Flood. She lives a block up the street."

F. X. took our phone book from its shelf in the kitchen and paged through it, and then he picked up the telephone and stepped out the back door into the cold night, without his coat. He closed the door on the phone cord. I wanted to know what he would say to Isabel, but when the door sprang half-open, jerked by the cord, I caught only the words, "Outpatient?" which made no sense to me, and then "Emergency? Which entrance?"

I slid away from the door as F. X. stepped back in. He hung up the phone and turned to me, saying, "Leave your coat on. I'm taking you to Miss Flood's."

"Why?" I asked him. "I don't want to go there."

"It's just until tomorrow," he answered. He led me by the hand outside and walked me up the street to Isabel's house. I hoped she would not answer her door because it was so late, but she seemed to respond instantly to F. X.'s knocking.

Isabel appeared before us fully dressed and asked F. X., "You're Mahalia's uncle?" Mahalia stood behind Isabel, ghostly in a nightgown that did not belong to her.

"I'm taking their mother to St. Mary's," F. X. told her. "Can you watch the girls until tomorrow?"

His words made no sense to me. Why did my mother need to go to a hospital? Hadn't F. X. already saved her?

"Of course I can," Isabel answered, placing her hand on my arm and guiding me inside. Her hand felt dry, like onion skin. Her narrow shoulders twisted above me as she reached for the door. I pulled away from her in time to see F. X. hurry back down the thin walkway of her front yard. His massive shape receded into the night's wooliness toward my mother, and the door shut, leaving me beside Isabel as she switched on her lamp, its single eye illuminating her armchair, her painting, her hallway and bedroom.

————

There is no real wall between dreams and waking, the blackness of true night and the blackness of the mind, because when we sleep our immediate surroundings seep into our thoughts like black water through a muddy membrane. Isabel slept in her armchair, propped upright beside her painting, after slipping a worn flannel nightgown over my head and directing me under her bedcovers, and I dreamed Stein Lake thawed and there rose to the surface crowds of unborn children with muted faces like the stocking masks of thieves. They were dead, frozen, and F. X. stood beside me and said, "This year the fish are different." I fell through the ice and froze below while calling for help, until my voice was cut by a knife of cold. I stayed there for an eternity of months, until I finally rose to the surface, a hand grabbed me, and a policeman said, "We caught her." Afterward I sat hunched, locked in a cell with waxy hexagonal walls, while up and down an outside hallway other identical cells stretched cradling half-formed children, colorless as wax, who breathed around me and moved featherlike antenna instead of talking. My cell door opened, and Mahalia stood beside Isabel and told me with a cheerfulness that horrified me, "Here's your mother! We have a new mother!"

I did not awaken until Isabel's voice plumbed my dreams and cranked me up. I struggled to open my eyes and found Isabel leaning over the bed saying, "Penny, are you with us? Or are you still asleep?"

Beside her lay a narrow cot Mahalia must have been using. My sister bent over it, tucking its covers tightly under the thin mattress. My clothes hung on a chair behind her; a flannel nightgown stretched past my toes. The events of the night before poured through me, and I sat there mutely, recollecting them all.

After Isabel made me dress, she served oatmeal for breakfast. I had never had oatmeal before, and I could not eat it—it did not taste like food. Isabel sat across from me at her small kitchen table, reading passages she had underlined in the Bible and looking up now and then to watch me not eat. She did not offer me something else as my mother would have. Nor did she ask me about my mother. At the end of breakfast, Isabel said, "I'm glad you can accompany Mahalia and me on my mission work today. Sometimes when our own lives are a challenge, dwelling on the hardships of others gives us a fresh perspective."

"What?" I asked.

Before Isabel could answer, someone rang her buzzer. Mahalia opened the door: I heard F. X.'s voice; they talked together on the front steps. I ran from the table to join them.

F. X. lifted me up. "Penny," he said. "I don't think you weigh ten pounds." He set me down on the steps and said, "I'm here to tell you that your mother's staying at Saint Mary's Hospital for a few days. Mr. Slattery and I are going to fix things up and bring her home next week. I'll be back for you this evening. Don't bite anyone while I'm gone."

"I want to go with you," I said.

Mahalia told me, in a grown-up tone, "F. X. needs to be free of us girls today for a few hours, so that he and that David man can go get Mama's car off the ice." Mahalia grimaced when she said this, whether at the idea of David or the spectacle of my mother's car sitting on Stein Lake, I couldn't tell.

I asked F. X., "Why is Mama at Saint Mary's? Did she get too knotted up with cold sitting in the car?"

"Mama's tired out," Mahalia answered. "She needs to rest and get her strength up."

My voice broke loose from me and seemed to shout with a will of its own, "Mahalia, you're not making any more sense than a dead dog!"

She stepped away from me, looking hurt.

I said to F. X., "Tell me why Mama's at the hospital! Is she sick because she's drunk all the time? Is that why?"

I heard a rattling noise in Isabel's kitchen, the sound of a timer going off and a pot lid being lifted.

F. X. answered, "That's partly why. I'm going to hang around and mess up your house for a while until I'm sure she's all right."

"Okay," I said.

"I talked to Miss Flood on the phone this morning, and I'm sure she'll take good care of you," F. X. said. "I'll be back around seven."

I clung tightly to F. X.'s hand and pressed my face into his leg. "Don't leave me with them," I said.

"Penny," Mahalia said. "You have to—"

"Stop trying to make my life a living hell!" I answered. I ran out the front door, before Mahalia or Isabel could stop me, and climbed into the New Yorker's front seat. Beside F. X., Mahalia stood peering at me, her face pale and sad. I leaned on the horn until F. X. joined me.

––––––––

The sky over the lake was a brilliant blue, and the ice sparkled under the sun. A lone man sat on a picnic bench in the park by the lake, smoking a cigarette—it was Luther Canon, the owner of the town supermarket, who had once called me "Captain" at the Stein Tavern.

David Slattery stood in a small parking lot by the shore with his hands in his coat pockets, waiting for us. He looked as if he hadn't slept; he was wearing the same clothes he had the night before.

When we stepped out of the New Yorker, F. X. asked David, "Which of us men is going to die? Do you want to drive Marguerite's car, so that I can scream for help when you fall through, or do you want to be the one who screams?"

"Why don't we just push the car off?" David suggested. "That way if the ice gives, we might have a chance to jump out of the way."

"All right," F. X. answered. "Penny can stand here on the shore and shout for help if the ice gives." He turned to me and said, "Penny, keep off the lake this time."

There was no one to shout to except Luther Canon, who I doubted would be much help, but I did not mind staying on the shore during daylight. I wrapped rocks in snowballs and threw them at trees while F. X. and David walked slowly onto the ice, testing it with sticks. It was so warm outside that I did not even need my mittens. I took off my hat and unzipped my jacket.

When the men reached the car, David opened the front door, leaned on the steering wheel and rocked the car. F. X. pushed from behind, and the two men managed to shift the car forward about three lengths before it got caught in a snowdrift. David climbed inside and the ignition made the coughing sound of a car that will not start. He climbed out and bent over the motor. F. X. asked him something. My uncle's voice skated over the ice so that he seemed to whisper right in my ear: "Dead."

"Shit on toast," David replied. He and F. X. walked back to shore.

"We must have left the interior light on last night," F. X. told me. "The car won't start."

David said, "Jumping it is out of the question. If we line up two cars next to each other, we're just asking to fall through."

The men discussed the car for a while in a businesslike way, as if they had retrieved many cars off many frozen lakes before: Listening to them, I longed to be in their men's world, casually braving catastrophes.

Eventually F. X. agreed to drive to the Esso station to buy a new car battery he and David could slide out to the Oldsmobile. After he left, David stood with me on the shore, studying my mother's car. He took my hand and said, "Don't throw any more of those rocks packed in snow. You might brain Luther Canon over there."

"How did you get that scar on your mustache?" I asked.

David answered, "A boy named Brian Nohilly gave me that when he tried to use my head as a hockey puck."

Luther Canon appeared at my side: I smelled him before I saw him, the odor of cigarettes and whisky, like F. X.'s smell but old and stale—the way F. X. might smell, it occurred to me, when he was old and stale. Mr. Canon's face was a grayish-yellow and his parka had a stripe of mud on it. He asked David, "How did the car end up on the lake?"

"Joyriding kids," David answered. I understood that he was guarding my mother's privacy.

Mr. Canon nodded. "I always wanted to do that," he said. "Just never had the nerve."

"A criminal who once came into the parole office where I work," David answered, "stole a whole tractor trailer in a robbery. He got rid of the evidence by driving the truck out onto Lake Placid. He hopped out just in time to get out of its way before it fell through the ice. This was around four in the morning, and no one saw it happen except for one little boy, who didn't tell anyone about it until two years later when the case went to trial. The man would have gotten away with it except that he bragged about it to his girlfriend, and when she left him, she dropped a dime on him."

"Body in there?" Mr. Canon asked.

David nodded, looking at me meaningfully, and answered, "You can imagine."

"Why would a man steal a tractor trailer?" Luther Canon asked. "Where in holy hell would he fence it?"

"He must not have thought much about details ahead of time," David answered.

"My God," Mr. Canon said. We all stared at my mother's car. "Too bad it's too far out for a winch. That's what people usually find best in a situation like this."

When F. X. arrived with the new battery an hour later, Mr. Canon offered the use of a toolbox he kept in his truck. He disappeared behind a cement building and came back carrying the box and a sheet of cardboard that he recommended David and F. X. use to slide the battery across the ice. He waited beside me and watched intently while they dragged the battery to the Oldsmobile. I felt a sense of sureness as I watched them; after this, I would always know how to get a car off a lake.

Once the new battery was in, F. X. pushed the Oldsmobile while David perched on the edge of the front seat, driving in reverse until the car's wheels were free. Afterward, David maneuvered the car slowly toward shore, keeping the door open so that he could jump out if the ice suddenly gave way. F. X. walked in front of him, testing for cracks. When the Oldsmobile was about fifty feet from us, F. X. crawled on the hood and rode the rest of the way, shouting and waving his arms.

"He's tempting the gods," Mr. Canon told me.

Chapter Five

Poker

$\mathcal{F}$. X. and David liked each other. Their presence in our house, and the easy camaraderie of these two men my mother had attracted into our lives, nettled Mahalia. The men sat together at our kitchen table or in our living room, drinking beer and playing cards and exchanging stories and laughing as loud as pirates. When she returned from her mission with Isabel, Mahalia kept her distance from them. My sister said hello stiffly to David, ran up the stairs, and stayed in our bedroom while he and F. X. banged around in the kitchen, making tacos from a prepackaged yellow box that contained tortillas, canned beans, and hot sauce.

David proved different from F. X. in one respect. David was more reserved around us—when he and F. X were talking about our mother, David would stop if he saw me, as if he were a wall between our child's world and the dazzling universe of adult women. When the men cooked in the kitchen, I sat on the stairs and stayed out of David's scope of vision, so that I could listen to him. I occasionally leaned forward to see how dinner was progressing: The counter was a mess and there were scraps of lettuce all over the floor. David and F. X. were entertaining one another with a long, ridiculous description of how they had retrieved the Oldsmobile off the ice.

"When you added your quarter ton to the car by climbing on the hood," David told F. X., "I had a mind to floor it in reverse, and watch you go spinning off!"

F. X. chuckled. I tilted forward: His red mustache hovered over his smile.

David's silver one rose with it in a devilish grin; I leaned back out of sight again.

"Even in the years of my youth when I played hockey like a demon all over that lake, I never walked on it in April," David said.

"Penny told me she thought the lake was safe."

"She did!" David said. "I hear Penny is a little hellion. Is it true?"

"Yes," F. X. answered.

"Marguerite worries a lot about those two. But Mahalia only seems shy and uncomfortable with how pretty she is, and Penny's just like one of those boys who should be run around a lot on the playing field until he peters out."

F. X. answered, "I'm sure your line of work will help you deal with Penny."

David laughed and proceeded to tell F. X. an avalanche of stories about Stein's parole office: How two days earlier, while David was at work, one of his fellow parole officers had tilted back his head and roared like a sick lion and beaten his own forehead against his own brick wall until two other officers restrained him. How one afternoon, two guards from the prison had drawn their guns on each other during an argument in the parole office's front hall, and shot an innocent bystander. How a drunk state policeman had once brought a burlap bag into the parole office, and when he opened it a raccoon had run out and raced twice around the office and through the door, stopping first to bite David's leg, so that he had to get rabies shots. David's stories relieved me. Our faults seemed like nothing, juxtaposed against the real despairs and lunacies of grown men.

And it was true that in the ensuing days David never acted as if he thought of me as hard to handle, and I never doubted that he liked me. On those occasions when I got too wild around him, he would pick me up like a bouncer, carry me to the living room, and thrust me into the armchair saying in a humorous tone, "Get a hold of yourself before I call the police!" or "That's enough, Penny. Do you want to get arrested and end up at Dannemora?" He did not do this with mocking disapproval, but instead with a kind of practical irony and swiftness that I thought he must have learned in his job.

David also liked to talk about the criminals he encountered at work, although I sensed that he held back when I was around; he never told me about the grisly murders and mayhem about which I suspected he held a store of information. However, his stories never involved Isabel's subtle kind of evil, the kind you strained to hear until you thought you would pass out. The lost souls David met revealed an evil that had density and exuberance, the kind that made the word "temptation" intelligible to me. David would tell me things such as: "I met a man at the parole office who hot-wired a Silverado and drove the stolen vehicle for a week before he discovered it belonged to his parole officer," or "Once a murderer who had just been transferred to Stein Correctional Facility escaped by knocking out the prison warden and hiding him in a storeroom. He told everyone the warden had been fired and claimed to be the new warden for five hours before he strolled out the front gates wearing a necktie."

Around Mahalia David acted with a delicacy that, at least during his first dinner at our house, failed to woo her.

"Your mother will be all right, Mahalia," he told her. "She's just stressed out and needs a break. If you want, you can come visit her in a few days, or even tomorrow evening."

"I won't be here," Mahalia answered, not even looking at him. She picked at her food, unrolling her taco and examining its contents. "I'm going on a church retreat with Isabel Flood for spring vacation."

"Don't you like our tacos?" F. X. asked her. "I put just about everything I could think of in them except communion wafers. They're not hot enough, are they? I ransacked the kitchen for Tabasco sauce, but I couldn't find any."

"Isabel Flood?" David asked. "You mean that one-woman police force who assigns herself to the delinquent families of Stein?"

I watched David's comment sink into Mahalia. It washed over her face like a rust-colored dye, beginning under her eyes and seeping outward to her neck and forehead and collarbones.

David stopped eating. He rubbed the scar on his mustache and turned away from Mahalia to look at nothing in particular. He set down his fork; one of his thumbnails was black. He said, softly, kindly, "You must be a breath of fresh air to Miss Flood, Mahalia. It must be nice for her to spend some time with a girl who has turned out right."

Mahalia ignored him. The silence that followed almost drowned us at the table. I stood up in my seat and leaned over my plate to reach a bowl of grated cheese near F. X.

"Penny," David said, "try asking for the cheese. Say, 'Uncle F. X., would you please pass me that plate?'"

I sat back down, dismayed, and F. X. handed me the cheese.

"Do you know that Mr. Slattery has a photographic memory, Mahalia?" F. X. asked. "He says that after he reads something, it's as if his head were a dark room with a lamplit desk in the middle, and he can turn the book's pages in his memory and review them. His ability allowed him to obtain a Regents scholarship at the state university, and aids him in his work. He remembers everyone's aliases and criminal records and faces after a single meeting. They call him 'the Record Room' at the parole office." I found this fascinating and looked at David with increased awe. F. X. added, "That's the polar opposite of the way I stored information when I was blind. Even now I remember what people are like and what they said by recalling the tones of their voices."

"I remember everything by the way it smells," I claimed.

Mahalia did not respond to me or F. X., but then, as if following an inner mandate not to be impolite, she asked David, "Where did you go to college?"

"Cortland," David answered. "A sorrowful dark hole. Are you thinking about college yourself?"

"Maybe," Mahalia said. "Maybe Bible college."

F. X. opened his eyes wide in mock horror and grinned at me.

David nodded and said, "My college roommate went to Union Theological Seminary. He said it was the best. Why don't you try for there?"

Mahalia looked at him uncertainly and said, "I've never heard of it."

"We can send away for their literature," David answered.

Mahalia showed no outward reaction to his suggestion, but after dinner, she lingered downstairs, on the edge of the men's conversation as they cleaned up the kitchen. It took them forever to do the dishes, and even at the end they forgot the pans on the stove. When they retired to the living room, F. X. said, "Parcheesi, anyone? Should we all play Parcheesi?"

"I will," David answered, looking at Mahalia, "but not with those crazy rules of yours that Penny was trying to explain to me before dinner." Mahalia was sitting in the armchair, turned away from us, reading a pamphlet. "Either we play straight or not at all."

"All right," Mahalia answered.

I did not join them—after playing with F. X., I was no longer attracted by the original game. I got myself a Coca-Cola from the kitchen, and when I returned to the living room, Mahalia was sitting across from David arranging her pieces. F. X. lay on the couch, reading a book on Mexican pyramids.

"If you think about it," F. X. said. "All the hieroglyphs carved into the sides of tombs are a kind of Braille. A language buried in darkness and raised in relief."

"You go first," David told Mahalia. "You got two and I spun eleven."

I hung over the back of Mahalia's chair. I thought I would jump out of my skin watching her move the pieces so stodgily around the board.

"How's your language going, Penny?" F. X. asked me.

I ran upstairs, retrieved the green reporter's notebook he had given me, and brought it back downstairs to show him. F. X. bent over it, reading. "Do you know the Kung peoples of the Kalahari make a sound we do not have in English?" F. X. demonstrated, making a loud *tock* noise with his tongue on the roof of his mouth. "Western peoples use an exclamation point to signal the sound when transcribing." He wrote !*Kung* and !*Komodofreetik.*

We wrote out a series of words and pronounced them, making clicking noises. F. X. introduced double exclamation points and question marks to signify other sounds, a snorting noise and a growl and an inward suck of breath. We wrote, ??*Pennatik* ??*X.ati!k* !!*Lunati!k!*

"You sound like a pair of wild woodchucks," David told us, looking up from the game.

Mahalia smiled and then caught herself, so that one side of her mouth hooked downward immediately.

"Where are you from?" Mahalia asked David.

"I grew up right here," he answered. "My father worked as a policeman in Dannemora."

"Have you ever been married before?" Mahalia asked.

"Yes, when I was a young man. My wife left me when I was twenty-eight."

"Why?"

"The marriage of my youth ended because I was hunting on Sundays and playing hockey on Tuesday and Thursday nights, and I came home and told my wife that some of the guys from work and I were going to start a baseball league and practice on Wednesdays and Saturdays. She kicked a hole in our kitchen wall, which was made of pasteboard, and she walked out and never came back."

After this, Mahalia concentrated on the board and did not ask any more questions.

F. X. added punctures to the paper, and I joined him, circling everything in imitation Braille. I threw in a few Roman numerals as well, a Mayan glyph from F. X.'s book, two jagged lightning bolts joined at the hips, and the symbol for infinity.

"Here you've gone and blocked me so close to the end," David told Mahalia. "I'm lost." My sister played as if she were not enjoying herself; but still, she moved her last pieces until the game was finished.

"You beat me by a mile," David told her. "Will you make it up to me by coming with us to the hospital on Wednesday to visit your mother? She wants to see you."

"No," Mahalia answered, standing up. "I'm leaving early tomorrow with Isabel."

———

The following morning, when she came to fetch Mahalia, Isabel did not seem comfortable around F. X. or David and lingered at the doorway until F. X. insisted that she come in. Isabel sat in a stilted way on the couch while Mahalia packed the last of her clothes upstairs. Isabel did not give F. X. or David any of her pamphlets during their meeting, or initiate any religious discussions. She nodded at David without asking his name.

F. X. introduced him and asked Isabel if she was from Stein.

"Is Mahalia almost ready?" Isabel answered. She pulled a puzzle from her pocket and tinkered with it: There were three narrow bars shaped like masts, with tiny crosspieces.

"What are those?" F. X. asked. "Captain Queeg's worry beads? Is that one of those puzzles? Watching you with it reminds me of those rosaries my great-aunts used to fidget with when I was a boy. Marguerite used to say you could tell how much sinning was going on in the family just by the speed of their fingers. Were you raised Catholic?"

"I'm not Catholic," Isabel answered flatly. "Once I saved baby-sitting money and made a trip to Rome. I visited the Vatican. I had expected a large church. Instead I saw gold and jewels and expensive paintings and marble. I learned that the Vatican was a monument to greed."

F. X. asked next, "Then you're not Mexican?" His face was deadpan; I could not tell if he was pulling Isabel's leg.

"No," Isabel answered. She ventured to add, "I read an article that said that if this country built a Great Wall like China's across our southern border, it would help keep out unlawful immigrants."

F. X. seemed caught off guard by this statement. He paused for a moment, his eyebrows raised, and then said, "But China had slaves to build the wall. Perhaps we could hire Mexicans to do it. Mexico's masons are among the best in the world. The United States could work out some mutually beneficial relationship with Mexico. They could reduce their national debt by building a Great Wall for us."

Isabel did not disagree or agree; she simply studied F. X. I could not tell whether she was trying to divine if he was teasing her the way he did us all, or whether she was considering his statement seriously, or simply had no interest in the topic. She looked mildly annoyed; she was not as patient with adults as she was with children.

"Would you like something to drink?" David asked Isabel. "Step into the kitchen with me, why don't you, F. X.?"

"A half glass of water," Isabel answered. "I'll be leaving shortly."

F. X. rose and followed David to the kitchen, and I tagged after them.

"Don't bait her like that," David whispered. "It's unfriendly."

"I can't help it," F. X. answered, also whispering. "She brings out the worst in me. It's as if she's the devil himself."

David smiled and shook his head. We returned to the living room. David gave Isabel her water and asked, "Where *are* you from?"

"I'm from southern Ohio," she answered. "I've lived in Stein for nine years." I saw her abruptly as the men must have—prim and restrained—but then that sense of her escaped me as she turned to F. X. and said in an even, commanding way, "I believe I spotted you earlier today, wearing black glasses and walking a blind man's dog down Main Street beside a real blind man. Mahalia told me that you were once blind, and that you often pretend that you still are."

F. X. answered, "Sometimes I close my eyes and walk, just to remember what it's like to be blind. I feel at home in the dark. Probably that dog would tell you the same thing. He'd say, 'I remember my days of liberty before I was melded with this man at my side, my days of woof and howl.'"

"That's the way a lot of people describe life before and after they're reborn," Isabel answered him.

"Before and after they're reborn?" David asked.

"I mean before and after a religious experience," Isabel said. "They recall their lives before they found God and after they saw the world in His light, and they feel as if they've been two different people, in two different lives."

F. X. asked, "Is that how it seems to you?"

Isabel answered, "I believe that until we awaken to see God as He is, we walk around in our lives not truly born yet, not understanding the nature of the world or why we are placed here." Isabel sipped her half-glass of water, and asked F. X., "Are you a practicing Catholic?"

"No," F. X. answered. "If I were a practicing anything, I'd believe in the Greek gods. The way they understood our petty jealousies and weaknesses! And their love of melodrama—parents eating their children and children murdering their parents and jealous wives turning rivals into cows and trees and snake-headed women! We had so much to learn from watching those gods." F. X. leaned forward and said to Isabel in a confidential tone, "Or, I would have a religion where we recognize that life on earth is in itself an eternity. Isn't that so? We sleep and rise up and sleep and dream until the months seem endless and the darkness repeats itself like a trick deck of cards. A single loss, or even one long lonely night is enormous as death—maybe vaster—and so life is at least as big as death. Or bigger. Death is merely the obsidian mirror in which we learn to glimpse and talk to ourselves. Our births spread out like suns to the rimless rim of time and the far stretches of the black unfenced universe where the gods run wild."

Isabel looked at F. X. blankly. She moved her hand in her pocket; the metal pieces of one of her puzzles jingled. She readjusted herself in her chair. She asked, "What does the 'F. X.' stand for?"

"Frederick Xylophone," he answered.

"It stands for Francis Xavier," Mahalia corrected him. She stood at the bottom of the stairs, a suitcase at her side like a dog brought to heel.

Isabel rose to leave, and I followed David as he showed her to the door. He waited for Mahalia to pass them, and once she was outside, he told Isabel, "It's generous of you to take Mahalia with you. When you return, I'd like to talk about hiring you to watch both children for a longer period."

Isabel gave him a steady, impenetrable look, and asked, finally, "Is there something wrong with the children's uncle?" Without waiting for an answer, she added, "If you need me to look after Mahalia and Penny, I'll consider it."

Mahalia accompanied Isabel up the street. F. X. came to the door and watched them go. "Penny," he told me, "if God thought the way churchy people do, He could never have created the world. He would have been too narrow-minded to think it up."

During the next few days, I barely had time to worry about my mother. While David worked, F. X. watched me, and accompanying him was like attaching myself to a whirlwind. Here are some of the things I remember F. X. doing in the first week he lived with us. He attended the funeral of a man he did not know. He engaged in a prolonged conversation in French with a Canadian woman who was eighty years old, and afterward drew up eight pages of notes on similarities between the Louisiana French my grandparents had spoken and her Canadian French. He accepted an invitation from a prison guard we met on the street, to come watch a pair of Percheron horses he owned pull a tractor out of a ditch. On Wednesday, the morning before I visited my mother at the hospital, F. X. drove me to an old mine shaft and asked me to wait outside while he walked into the shaft until he could turn around and see "no light at the end of the tunnel." Afterward we strolled to the nearby town of Swastika, which in those days was just an abandoned clump of buildings, and together we used seven rolls of film photographing snow while F. X. gave me detailed instructions on how to operate his camera—he loved photography the way he loved driving—it was a novelty to him, full of challenges and surprises. When he saw a wild turkey as we stood taking pictures by the road, F. X. crashed through the trees with me following, waving his coat in the air as if he believed he could lasso the bird to the ground. It flew away from us on thunderous wings while F. X. shouted to it, begging it to return, and I joined him, calling mournfully through the trees until we froze and returned to the car.

That afternoon, as F. X. led me along the sidewalk toward Saint Mary's Hospital, he spotted two men from the Stein School for the Blind walking Seeing Eye dogs.

F. X. came up behind one man and said, "Hey there, Raleigh."

The man stopped and told his dog, "Don't talk to him, Raleigh." The other man laughed. The man with the dog told his companion, "It's the reporter I told you about who's crossed the Styx into the seeing world. The one related to the Mr. Daigle who directed the institute before we starting teaching there. He's the fellow who was trying to teach Raleigh to walk with his eyes closed."

The three men engaged in a lengthy conversation that concluded with F. X. saying, "Why do they use Labrador retrievers for Seeing Eye dogs? Why not bloodhounds? After all, what dogs are about is smell, not sight. Why do we deny them the enviability of their noses? Why not admit that a dog with a great nose could lead us much more perfectly than any old dog who happens to be able to see? A blind dog could probably find his way around pretty well."

The men talked a little longer while I petted their dogs, who ignored me with a businesslike calm, and then the men exchanged phone numbers with F. X. As we continued toward the hospital, F. X. asked me, "Do you know the reason archaeologists couldn't decipher some of the Mayan glyphs was because they contained puns? Instead of etching a glyph into the side of a tomb that said, 'Sons of the gods,' for example, the Maya would carve the symbol for the *sun*, and leave it to posterity to puzzle out what '*Suns* of the gods' meant. Puns! A civilization that never used the wheel, but had puns!"

He added, "Except in toys."

"What?" I asked.

"Except in toys. They used the wheel in children's toys, in little carts that could be pulled by tiny toy animals. But in their real lives, their adult lives, they never used wheels, ever. It shows an endearing impractical fixation on children."

"What did they think about unborn babies?" I asked.

"Unborn babies?"

"What did they think about children who weren't born yet?"

"I don't know. In some ancient societies, children weren't even considered people until they were five years old. They didn't even name them until then."

We had reached the emergency entrance of Saint Mary's, and before F. X. could answer, a woman rushed in front of us, holding a bloody cloth clamped to her head. F. X. pulled me away, toward a set of elevators.

"Your mother might be a little tired when you see her," he told me.

When we entered my mother's room, David was already there sitting on the edge of the bed, his hand on my mother's arm. She looked brittle, like a tree with the sap sucked out of it. She pulled herself up as I approached her bed, and she said, "Oh Penny, I'm so sorry. I don't know what got into me."

Her apology made me feel uncomfortable. "That happens to me all the time," I said.

"Sit up here," my mother told me. She pulled down her covers on the side opposite David, and I stuck my feet under the sheets and leaned against her.

"I had a dream last night, Marguerite, about our own mama," F. X. said. "You and I were at a séance, and her spirit appeared in the room. She sat down at the table and pretended to be one of us, trying to call up a spirit. You looked at me and whispered, 'There's Mama, trying to fool us by pretending to be a ghost,' and I said, 'She's not pretending, Marguerite. She *is* a ghost,' and then Mama started laughing with that high, tittery chuckle of hers—"

"Oh, that chuckle," my mother said.

"And she turned to the man on her left and told him, 'This séance doesn't seem to be working. We don't seem to be able to get the dead to respond to us.' "

My mother laughed. "That's exactly what her ghost would have done at a séance," she told David. "She loved teasing people."

"I don't like dreams about ghosts," F. X. said. "They always give me a haunted feeling when I wake up."

"I've never heard you talk about your parents before," David told my mother.

My mother asked F. X., "Where's Mahalia?"

"She's with that scarecrow who takes her to those religious retreats," he answered.

"Isabel," I told my mother. "Isabel Flood who baby-sits. Who lives on the corner."

My mother nodded, uncertain about this news. "Isabel Flood who comes around with those pamphlets?" she asked. "What kind of religious retreat?"

"Something having to do with the prison," I answered. "They baby-sit prisoners' children who come up to Stein to visit them."

"My God!" my mother muttered frettingly. "What have I done? I've turned my daughter into a goddamn angel!" She clasped her hands together and let go of them and then folded her fingers in front of her as if to keep them still. I took one of her hands and held it.

"I thought you used Isabel Flood as a baby-sitter," David said.

"I never use baby-sitters," my mother answered. "I certainly wouldn't have thought of *her*. She's like a cake made of one ingredient."

David said, "Isabel Flood's all right, Marguerite. She seems to be responsible with the girls, and she's helped out a lot this week watching them."

"She could be an ax murderer for all I know."

"Well, Marguerite, it's true, you never can be too sure about anyone," David answered. "I heard at the office of a woman, five-feet-two and no more than a hundred pounds, with hair a different color each time you met her and eyes a flat nickel-gray, who was married to two different men who lived thirty-seven miles away from each other. She told one husband she was a day-shift nurse and the other that she was a night-shift nurse, but she really passed all day every day spending her husbands' money until she burned down both their houses on November 12, 1957. Her husbands met at her funeral because she set up each fire to seem as if she'd died in it. She supplied two local papers with her own obituaries, which listed her under two different names but gave the same cause of death and the same place and time for memorial services."

"Oh, for God's sake, David," my mother said, laughing. "It's just that Miss Flood is so churchy. I'd rather have Sister Geraldine checking in on Penny and Mahalia."

"Mahalia likes Miss Flood," David answered.

F. X. said, "I invited Sister Geraldine over for a poker game."

"You're invading my life," my mother told David feebly. "But all right, if Mahalia wants Miss Flood. Mahalia should get what makes her happy right now. God knows. I'm not going to succumb to competing with another woman for my daughter's affections." Although Isabel would test her later, my mother was not, by nature, prone to jealousy, and that day she must have questioned her own claim to Mahalia in any case.

David told my mother, "Isabel Flood seems to care genuinely for Mahalia too." He did not mention that he had asked Isabel about watching us both for a longer period. "Even after you get home on Sunday, Marguerite, you might enjoy a little baby-sitting help."

"Lord," my mother said. "I know what home will be like. I'll be stepping right back into a hurricane, with you two men carrying on in addition to

Penny. F. X. will be right in the middle of it all." She picked up F. X.'s hand, patted it, and said, "My favorite hurricane."

———————

That week, insomnia carried me from one night to the next like a cold wind blowing a black banner. The house lacked the noise of my mother's nocturnal stirrings, and I was not used to trying to sleep with Mahalia's empty bed beside me. The first night of her absence, I rifled her clothes drawer, put on one of her long nightgowns, and crawled under her covers. I lifted up the book beside her bed, a field guide to ferns, and read an underlined paragraph at the top of the page:

> Such is the life cycle of the true fern: The spore develops into a one-celled gametophyte that puts down a tiny rootlike hair to anchor it to the soil. Then by adding one cell to another, this one-celled being enlarges into a small heart-shaped green, membranous body.

I put down the book: It was dull and made me miss Mahalia.

By Wednesday night F. X. had moved from the living room couch into my mother's room, so that I would not feel alone on the top floor. Even so, I did not fall asleep until early morning. On Friday evening, a week after my mother entered the hospital, F. X. let me stay downstairs on the couch while he sat in the armchair, smoking a cigar, drinking whisky, and reading *Scientific American*.

"Do you know what makes fireflies shine?" he asked me. "*Luciferin*. The devil makes them shine." He drew a picture for me of a firefly with a horned halo and tucked it under my pillow. "I know what will help you sleep," he said. "Close your eyes, and I'll make you drop off by reading you *Scientific American*."

He read aloud to me in a droning voice from a page with a math puzzle on it, and I closed my eyes and pretended to fade until I appeared asleep. I did not want him to send me back upstairs.

When he reached the end of the page, he asked, "Penny?" I did not answer. He rose and clattered quietly in the kitchen, rinsing the dishes. I listened to the ring of silverware against the metal sink and half-dreamed Isabel was in the kitchen, washing the pots, and then rinsing her metal puzzles and hanging them up to dry on the dish rack.

The doorbell rang and startled me awake. I watched F. X. walk by me to answer it. I shut my eyes. He greeted David at the door. I felt David's foot-steps approach the couch.

"Is she sleeping?" David asked.

"She's having trouble falling asleep at night, so I let her curl up down here. She just dropped off a minute ago."

David got himself a beer from the refrigerator and told F. X., "I think we have to look around for some longer term facilities. I don't think Margue-rite's going to be ready by Sunday."

"I already checked out a place in Louisiana I once did a story on," F. X. said.

"Louisiana?" David asked.

"I thought she'd be more likely to agree to go if we sent her back to Louisiana for a while," F. X. said. "When I first mentioned the idea of treat-ment to her, Marguerite said, 'What do you mean? In a loony bin? I don't think I would like being locked up.'"

"Maybe Louisiana is a good idea," David said. "She'd be more likely to stay if it was harder to just walk home. And maybe the girls should have some time apart from Marguerite until she gets back on her feet."

The bell rang again. F. X. answered it and led Sister Geraldine into the living room.

"I'm glad you were able to respond so quickly to my call," Sister Geraldine told F. X. "It's been a rough year for Mrs. Daigle." She nodded at David and said, "I know Mr. Slattery. He was friends with my younger brother."

"I remember Gerry as plain as day," David told F. X. "She was an old teenager when I was little, and she had about ten brothers and she was always shouting at them to behave. 'Paul, stop stabbing Timmy! Aloysius, don't jump up off the roof! Thomas, don't point that gun in the kitchen!'"

"It cured the urge to have children right out of me," Sister Geraldine said, "and sent me fleeing to the church for safety. Where they made me a teacher."

F. X. laughed. I tried to imagine Sister Geraldine before she was a sister, but my knowledge did not stretch far enough to form an image.

I heard a general rustling of adults coming near. "Asleep?" Sister Geral-dine whispered.

"Dead to the world," David answered quietly.

F. X. said, "Whenever I pick her up to carry her to her bed, she moans, 'I want to stay here!' I'm afraid to touch her again now that she's sleeping. She hasn't slept straight through the night since I took Marguerite to the hospital."

"Poor little thing," Sister Geraldine answered. I felt hands pulling up my covers. "She doesn't look angelic when she sleeps."

"No, not at all," David said.

"Where's Mahalia?" Sister Geraldine asked.

"With a woman named Miss Flood," David said. "She's been watching the girls while we're at the hospital."

"Isabel Flood?" Sister Geraldine asked. "The one who pickets across the street from the public school?"

F. X. asked, "What does she picket about?"

"She objects to the high school curriculum."

"She does? Why?"

"Something having to do with abortion," Sister Geraldine said. "I'm not sure—I don't insert myself much in the affairs of the public school. Many people around here use Isabel Flood as a baby-sitter. She's thought to be responsible."

"Would you like a drink?" F. X. asked.

"Just a small one," Sister Geraldine answered. "Scotch or whisky."

"Another beer in a bottle for me," David said.

I heard the refrigerator door open, the clinking of ice, the rush of liquid into a glass.

"Are we really going to play poker?" David asked.

Sister Geraldine laughed and answered, "Of course." This was followed by the noise of chairs being pulled back around the table, a slapping of cards, and momentary silence.

"Penny ante," Sister Geraldine said. I opened my eyes slightly when I heard the word "Penny." Sister Geraldine was not wearing her wimple. She looked down her long nose and said, "F. X., you didn't ante." F. X. tossed a coin to the center of the table, while David grimaced at his cards. Their mustaches looked like two birds poised to swoop down on the money.

"Two cards for me," David said.

"None for me, and I bet a dime," Sister Geraldine said.

"None for me either, and I raise you three hundred dollars," F. X. answered.

"Quarter limit," David told him.

"Then I raise you twenty-four cents," F. X. said.

"I raise you another sixteen," David answered. He turned toward Sister Geraldine. "Sister Antonia Liquore, I hear, got a degree in mathematics."

"Yes, she left a few years ago to get a Ph.D. at Cornell. I raise you another ten."

"Mathematics?" F. X. asked. "What do you call her now? 'Doctor Sister Antonia Liquore' or 'Sister Doctor Antonia Liquore'?"

"As of graduation, she's Miss Antonia Liquore," Sister Geraldine answered.

"Well," said David. "I'm not surprised. All the boys on my block mourned when we lost her to the church."

"I think it was Brian Nohilly who scared her to us," Sister Geraldine said.

"Ah, Superintendent Nohilly!" David answered. "He'd ruin any girl."

"He was the worst behaved student in All Saints' history," Sister Geraldine pronounced.

"When he gave me this hockey scar, old Mr. Nohilly and the other team's coach had to pull him bodily off my unconscious bleeding head."

"He treated his wife and daughter the same miserable way," Sister Geraldine concurred.

"Meanest warden in the history of Stein Correctional Facility," David said. "Worst criminal in the whole place."

"A devil from hell," Sister Geraldine agreed.

"I call you and raise you another twenty-four cents," F. X. said. David and Sister Geraldine counted out piles of coins and pushed them to the center of the table.

"Three raise limit," David told him. "Show your cards."

I lifted my head slightly; it was a trial to hold still, even in sleep position. David turned in my direction, and I sank back quickly onto the couch. I waited without breathing until I knew he had not noticed me. I kept my eyes shut for so long that I wondered if I could see the backs of my eyelids, or the feel of darkness itself. I envisioned the words of the adults carrying information toward me like jewels presented in dark velvet ring boxes.

"F. X. had nothing at all!" Sister Geraldine proclaimed.

"Gerry wins," David said. "Three jacks! And she only raised us ten."

"And I kept you both in the game," Geraldine answered.

David's voice loomed over me. "I believe I saw Penny move," he said. He tucked in my covers. "We'd better keep it down."

His chair scraped the floor, and he said, "It's my deal, F. X."

"You're just what Penny needs," Sister Geraldine told him. "A parole officer."

F. X. said, "I'll take four cards."

"Where's your ace?" Sister Geraldine asked him. "Well—I'm surprised you have one. I'll bet a dime."

"I raise you twenty-four cents," F. X. said.

"You and Penny are two peas in a pod," Sister Geraldine told him.

"Penny, Marguerite, and I," F. X. answered, "all have the same bad blood. Chaotic blood."

"She's not bad at all, F. X., you know that," Sister Geraldine said. At first, I was uncertain whether Sister Geraldine meant my mother or me. "She's not mean to the other kids—she's not one of our bullies, like Persis Boards. And the other children don't shun Penny. She seems to be popular enough—they seem to enjoy her. I don't need any cards." I held my breath, waiting for more.

"I raise you eleven," David said. "Penny's not exactly sassy either. Not exactly. She's just—overly energetic. Extremely, extremely, energetic."

Sister Geraldine chuckled. "That's a nice way to put it," she answered. "I call you both. F. X. you've lost again. That's eighty more cents for Rome."

"Marguerite was completely haywire as a child," F. X. said. "But our mother claimed my sister settled down somewhere around the end of grade school. After that, she never acted up. Until now, anyway. When she was in grade school, she once locked a priest in a confessional."

"Hundreds of children have done that over the years," Sister Geraldine responded.

"Marguerite didn't like those French priests sinking their mitts in our brains. I've always wondered if confessionals went back to the days of the Inquisition—if the Inquisition was at heart motivated not simply by greed and a love of torture and anti-Semitism, but instead by a compulsion to pursue people into the innermost recesses of their lives and thoughts and fears."

"Hmmm," Sister Geraldine said, examining her cards. F. X., I perceived, was unable to rile Sister Geraldine the way he did Isabel. This interested me—I had assumed Isabel was unflappable, but now I readjusted my understanding: Isabel could be provoked in a way Sister Geraldine could not, but Isabel exercised some inner restraint to prevent herself from reacting. Sister Geraldine just did not care. F. X. also seemed to like Sister Geraldine more and to hold back more from baiting her: He hadn't once called the queen of spades "the Bony Sex-Starved Virgin," as he always did when he played cards with my mother.

David dealt a new hand, and the cards tipped through the darkness of my mind, while the adults proclaimed numbers to each other, and change clattered at the center of them. Their conversation moved in a circle with the betting, eddying around the table, and my thoughts followed it until I felt myself whirling and sinking into a drain of sleepiness. From a bottom darkness, I looked up and saw my mother, her body translucent green and weightless like a nightgown, sailing over me as if riding a current around the table where the adults were playing cards.

"Are you a ghost now, Marguerite?" F. X. asked.

I awoke, confused and frightened and realized I had been dreaming. F. X., David, and Sister Geraldine sat unperturbed around the table, examining their cards.

Sister Geraldine said, "You must have marked the cards, F. X." And then, "Penny's teacher thinks she should try taking Ritalin." A rush of consciousness swirled around me, and I found myself wide awake with my eyes closed.

David said, "Some of the juveniles I've seen were on Ritalin."

I heard a chair scoot back, and a moment later, hands pulled up my covers again. "Still asleep, you little murderer of men?" F. X.'s voice poised in the darkness over me. He scraped his chair forward again with a "Where was I? Oh yes, leading these lambs to slaughter."

"You've won again, F. X." Sister Geraldine said.

"Did the Ritalin work on those kids?" F. X. asked.

"Couldn't tell," David answered. "The parents said yeah, the kids said no. As usual."

"Children at All Saints have been on it before. With mixed results," Sister Geraldine said. "It helped one boy two years ago, but it gave Persis Boards bad headaches, and she had to discontinue it."

"Marguerite talked to Penny's pediatrician," F. X. said. I was surprised to learn this. "He said it has a lot of side effects, and that he wasn't sure Penny fit his description of the children who benefited from Ritalin. He recommended against it. He told Marguerite, 'Just put Penny's legs in two casts and keep her on a leash.' "

"That sounds like our Dr. Epstein," Sister Geraldine answered. "He's always recommending against Ritalin. Well, I'm not sure Penny fits the mold either. She's—unusual. Maybe it's worth a try. Maybe it's not. I don't like the idea of keeping children on drugs. Ritalin hasn't been around long enough for us to know everything about it. It might turn children into Protestants."

David laughed. I half opened my eyes: Sister Geraldine was staring intently at her cards. "I could just keep Penny in the office another three years," she said. "I could tie her to my desk. You're sure Marguerite calmed down after sixth grade?"

"Until now," David said.

"It's the first time she's ever been behind on tuition," Sister Geraldine said. She looked in my direction, and I closed my eyes imperceptibly slowly.

"So, let's play for tuition," F. X. said. "Doesn't anyone want more Scotch?"

Sister Geraldine laughed and told him, "I don't have the authority to do that. No more for me, thanks."

"None for me," David said. "Send me that bill, Gerry. And F. X. and I will read up on the Ritalin." He added teasingly, "Does All Saints still raise all its money through gambling the way it did when we went there? Chinese raffles and bingo games where the teachers act as bartenders and charge three dollars a drink and send the parents home tipsy with their children?"

"It's the Catholic way," F. X. answered. "I'll take care of the bill, David."

"Not *all* its money," Sister Geraldine answered. "Not even close. Why don't you both pay?"

David's chair moved, and his voice loomed over my head. "I saw an eye open just now.

I screwed both my eyes tight. The adults voices hovered over me a moment later, commingling like a flock of birds. I wondered if this was what people had sounded like to F. X. when he was blind—a confusion of disembodied words.

"I believe this girl is not asleep," Sister Geraldine said.

"There's only one way to know," F. X. said. A moment later, I felt fingers on my ribs, and I laughed out loud.

"Oh, you she-demon," F. X. proclaimed.

"It's our fault," David said. "We should have taken her upstairs before the game."

"Well, take her up now," Sister Geraldine told them.

F. X. lifted me in my blanket, slung me over his shoulder, and carried me to my bed. "Were you awake all this time?" he asked.

"I never sleep," I answered without opening my eyes.

"Then just go through the motions," F. X. said. He set me down on my bed and arranged the covers over me. "Keep your eyes closed until morning, and imagine you're sleeping. Imagine you're in a big bed the size of a ship and it's rushing off into the night and it won't stop until I check on you in the morning to see if your eyes are still closed." I heard the front door shut and Sister Geraldine and David talking outside in the yard. F. X. sat down on the foot of my bed, saying, "I'll stay here until you're unconscious." The bed tilted under his weight like a boat about to tip over. I clenched my eyes and rushed downward into darkness.

Mahalia came home on Sunday afternoon, about an hour before my mother was due to return from the hospital. My sister looked happier than I had seen her in weeks. She walked in the door, put down her suitcase, and said, "Hello, David. I had a wonderful time!"

"You have the glowing look of a girl in love," F. X. told her.

Mahalia blushed. "We did mission work the whole time," she answered. "We took some of the children to the prison to visit their fathers there."

"Good for you," David told her. "That's a kind thing to do." He was reading a book called *Forensic Medicine and the Criminal Mind*. He had been reading it and several other books all afternoon, and at one point had closed the book and said to F. X., "I don't know about this Ritalin." He had glanced at me and did not continue.

"Your mother's coming home in a little while," David told Mahalia. "I'm going to fetch her. I wanted to wait until you were here."

Mahalia sat on the couch, folded her hands in her lap, and said in an adultish voice, "I'm glad, David. I'm going to try to be understanding toward her."

F. X. rubbed at a dish and frowned, as though her tone, if not her words, troubled him.

"That's nice to hear," David said.

"Even though a lot of the men at the prison have done terrible things, it's still important to keep their families together," Mahalia said. "Some of the children's mothers don't like it, but Reverend Bender says it's important for them to keep up contact with their fathers."

"If the children really want to see their fathers in prison," David answered.

Mahalia nodded; she did not hear the question in David's statement.

David stood, dangled my mother's car keys, and told F. X., "I'll take Marguerite's Oldsmobile to the hospital, to prove to her that it didn't drown."

Mahalia waited for him to shut the front door behind him and said, "He's such a nice man."

"Mmm," F. X. answered, still frowning.

"What did Daddy ever see in Mama?" Mahalia asked abruptly.

F. X. lifted his eyebrows, took in a breath of air, and whistled it out. "I think your mother and father were attracted to each other because they couldn't see each other clearly, because they were so different from each other, neither one could even imagine the other. Because they were perfectly positioned in relation to one another—they stood in each other's blind spots."

Mahalia looked crestfallen. F. X. struck his forehead with his palm and said, "No, that's not what I should tell you. I should tell you that your father was a very good man, Mahalia. He was honest and hardworking and well-meaning. He was a very steady sort of guy."

"I remember how he used to let me ride on his shoulders when he swam in the lake."

"You do?" F. X. asked.

Mahalia answered, "I remember him perfectly. He used to let me sit in his lap and pretend to steer when he drove, and he used to take me kite flying with him, and I remember how he sang at church, and that he and Mama once danced to old forty-five records in the living room." Mahalia sat back and tugged at her dress, rearranging herself in her chair until she wore the holy expression she had when she first entered. "I think it would be a nice thing if Penny and I got some flowers for Mama," Mahalia said.

"All right," F. X. answered cautiously. He pulled ten dollars out of his pocket. "She likes those yellow roses with orange on the tips of the petals."

He sat down next to Mahalia and said, "Your mother taught me to tell the difference between roses when I first went blind. My mother grew roses in the backyard and Marguerite would lead me around and say, 'What color is this one? What color is this one?' She said that roses had so many smells, people should make different flavors of chewing gum out of them. And even now, I sometimes wonder, why not? Why not make rose Life Savers? You could offer them to a friend, saying, would you like a Baronne Henriette de Snoy? A Clotilde Soupert? Or a Viking Queen, a Complicata, or an L. D. Braithwaite?"

He closed Mahalia's hand around the ten dollars and told her, "You have no idea how bottomless Marguerite's generosity is. No idea."

"Of course I do, F. X.," Mahalia said, but the way F. X. looked at her, he did not seem to believe her.

I did not tell F. X. that Stein's florist never had roses. I followed Mahalia down the street, and she smiled sweetly at me in a way that made me feel nervous—she reminded me of the young woman who had talked in tongues the night I attended Stein Evangelical. My sister had a far-off look, and when she took my hand, I felt as if she were not really taking my hand, but instead that of some imagined younger sister who acted much better than I did.

The florist's was beyond Main Street, three blocks away. We passed Isabel's house and cut across a vacant lot. As we rounded the corner, a blue police light raced along the sidewalk in front of us like a scrap of sky blown by the wind.

Up the street, on the opposite curb, my mother sat with her head in her hands, talking to a policeman.

Mahalia stopped dead still. The far-off look left her face, and I was almost relieved to see her customary expression of suppressed outrage return.

"What's Mama doing?" she asked. "What did she do to make a policeman talk to her?"

My mother's Oldsmobile was pulled up against the curb at a crazy angle, her bumper touching the fender of the patrol car.

"Will you marry me, sir?" she was asking the police officer. "I'm a young widow. Will you help me raise these two lovely girls?"

The officer turned around and studied us, as if he were wondering if he could arrest us too. Instead, he asked Mahalia, "Is this your mother?" Mahalia nodded. My mother continued to talk: She gave the officer her account of how we were all displaced persons who had been dragged to where we all now stood. He sat, listening and nodding, his hand resting absently on his holster. He was missing part of his thumb, and I longed to ask him how he had lost it. He smiled at me once; he had crooked teeth. Finally he told Mahalia, "Stay here a minute with her." He crossed the street and walked fifty yards to the Esso station. I sat down beside my mother and wrapped my arm around the crook of her elbow. She looked sick: Her face was pale and her teeth were chattering.

"What are you doing here?" Mahalia asked her angrily.

"Mahalia!" I said. I turned toward her, to tell her our mother was sick, but the look on Mahalia's face stopped me—there was no tenderness or mercy in it.

"Mama, why do you have to make a scene out here?" Mahalia asked. "Now, everyone will know!" I looked away from my sister. I felt a sudden chill, overwhelming and spreading over the surface of my skin like an icy lake: Was it possible, I wondered, that Mahalia did not love us?

"Who's 'everyone'?" my mother asked. "God?"

The officer emerged from the Esso station carrying two cups of coffee. He recrossed the street, sat down beside my mother, handed her a cup, and listened patiently while she rambled on and Mahalia turned her back to them, her hands clutching her arms and her face red with anger. Then the officer set the second cup of coffee in my mother's hand, and tore up the ticket.

"She's drunk," Mahalia said.

The officer shook his head. "The Breathalyzer's negative. Does she—does your mother take some kind of medication for—some kind of medicine?"

Mahalia answered, "My mother already has a fiancé. She knows better than to propose to you."

"I feel sorry for the man who gets my daughter," my mother said. "Mahalia's too good for any of us."

Mahalia's face hardened. Her mouth lost its expressive curves, and her eyes narrowed, reflecting an internal adjustment. She turned on my mother not an expression of hurt or surprise, but one of pure disapproval.

My mother stood up unsteadily, spilling all of her coffee, and instead of walking in a straight line toward our car, she orbited us, returned to her original position, and looked around confused.

The policeman offered to drive my mother home, but Mahalia answered, "It's all right. She's a lot better if she walks."

My sister said this in such a cool, mature voice that the officer answered, "All right. If that's what you want." Perhaps he had guessed, as I had, that Mahalia could not bear the idea of a police car driving up to our house and unloading my mother there for all the neighbors to see. He watched frowning, as Mahalia took my mother's arm and half-tugged and half-led her toward the corner.

"Maybe you should try calling your future Daddy," he told her. Mahalia ignored him and kept walking. After he had driven away, she let go of my mother's arm.

As I followed her and my mother homeward, a woman I did not recognize approached us on the sidewalk with two girls around Mahalia's age. When my sister saw them, she took my mother's arm again, turned her around, and pulled her back in the direction we had come from. Mahalia walked quickly, almost dragging my mother.

I scampered after them, calling frantically, "Mahalia, stop, stop! Can't you see, Mama's falling to pieces!"

Mahalia answered. "Just shut up! Shut up! Go ahead of us and open the car door!"

She did not let go of my mother until I held the door wide for them. Mahalia pushed my mother inside onto the front seat. Mahalia tugged me around to the back seat, pulled me in beside her, locked the doors, and covered her face with her coat.

My mother turned on the engine without talking and grasped the steering wheel as if it were holding her up. She drove the car slowly toward home, wavering a little and crossing the dividing line, so that the woman with the two girls stopped on the sidewalk. They watched us with snickery ferrety faces.

I kneeled in my seat, leaned far out the window, and screamed to them at the top of my lungs: "WHAT'S SO FUCKING FUNNY? YOUR OWN UGLY SMILE?"

"Penny!" Mahalia cried. She yanked me back into the car.

F. X. ran across the yard as my mother parked in front of our house. He looked worried and asked, "Where's David? Didn't he fetch you?"

My mother answered, "I took the Oldsmobile while he was settling things with the hospital. I just couldn't stay any longer."

Mahalia sprang from the car and ran away from us toward Isabel's house.

"Let her go!" my mother said. "Let her go! Who can blame her?" She brushed past F. X., and he followed her inside and up the stairs. He turned around at the top and told me, "Stay *down* there." I sat on the couch, listening to my mother and F. X. argue until David knocked on the front door.

He let himself in before I could answer. "Your mother's here?" he asked. "Don't follow me, Penny," he said. "Stay *down* here."

I fled outside to my tree. The dog barked at me, and even after I had climbed to the tree's top, he continued to bark, as if he associated me with the noise in the house. From my perch, the house sounded as if it were speaking a strange language of roars and shouts and exclamations.

The noise died down, the dog settled into his hollow pit, and David came outside and called up at me, "Penny, come here. You'll break your neck." The dog barked at him, once, without standing up.

I obeyed. My arms and legs felt wobbly as I lowered myself, and when I stood in front of David, I felt more tired than I ever had in my life. I remember thinking, self-consciously, *So this is exhaustion*, certain that I had never experienced that state before.

"Penny," David said. "They gave your mother some kind of medicine at the hospital that didn't sit well with her, all right? It hit her the wrong way. It's making her act a little strange."

I could not tell if he was trying to protect me from a scarier truth. "What kind of medicine?" I demanded. "Like the kind Mrs. Fury wants me to take? Ritalin medicine?"

"No, something else. Penny, don't worry about that Ritalin for now." He sat down next to me on the back step and took my hand. He looked directly in my face and said, as if reading from a book typed onto me, "*Ritalin may depress appetite, slow growth or even retard it. The child may become weepy and lose his joy in life, and ebullience.*" I pressed my face into his shirt and cried.

"I know something's all wrong with me!" I said. "I'm just like Mama, completely messed up inside!"

"I like you just fine," David answered. "I can always tell exactly what you're thinking. There's nothing all snarled up inside about you." He put his arm on my shoulder. "And your mother cares about you girls, and she's never shown me anything but kindness. She's—she's just having some kind of breakdown. It could happen to anyone. She needs a rest, and she'll be fine again." I saw that he was lying to make me feel better—this was the kind of thing that happened to the Daigles, not to just anyone.

I leaned against him until the upstairs light in my mother's room turned off and the kitchen light turned on. F. X. stepped outside and sat beside us. He had lit a cigar, and its end bloomed and wilted in the air to my right.

"What's all the noise out here?" he asked. "Don't you know people are trying to sleep in there?"

David laughed. "Penny tells me she thinks she's all wrong inside."

"Oh Christ, Penny," F. X. said. "There's something all wrong with everybody. Don't you know that yet? We're all fools on a ship of fools."

"Where's Mahalia?" David asked.

"She stomped off to Isabel's," I answered. "She doesn't want to be around us." I thought of my sister, her face dropping its mask of kindness as we turned the corner and saw the policeman talking to my mother. And then I remembered Mahalia telling Isabel, "I despise her!" and Isabel failing to correct my sister—as if her words were true. I recalled Mahalia crying out even earlier, "I'll never forgive her!" and "I'm going to kill Mama!" and I realized that all along my sister had meant everything she had said.

"Mahalia hates us," I told David and F. X. "She hates all of us. She couldn't care less about any of us."

"She's just upset," F. X. said. "Don't be so hard on her." I let him lift me onto his lap and wrap his arms around me, but I knew my uncle was wrong.

———

Mahalia spoke with my mother only once before she left, on the day my sister faced my mother so defiantly as she sat upstairs in her bed, diminished and unraveled. David made arrangements with Isabel the following day: He told her that F. X. wished to join him a week after his departure with my mother; they all hoped to return in mid-August. Isabel rearranged her regular baby-sitting schedule and agreed to move in with us for the summer. After my mother and David left, in the few days that F. X. remained at our house, paying our rent and settling my mother's affairs, Mahalia radiated the joy of victory—as if she had drawn battle lines, won her silent war, and negotiated for my mother's disappearance. Watching my sister bustle around the house, scrubbing counters and dusting shelves and folding clothes to ready our home for Isabel's arrival, I understood more clearly Mahalia's vision of the world. She thought the world should behave the way she wanted it to, because she did what she was told and so had earned the right to certain rewards. For her, these rewards included the promise that all life would respond to her in an orderly way, and her acceptance by a larger community—some vague collection of grown-up girls that was unknown to me, or even adults generally.

I remember feeling appalled when I finally grasped my sister's view of things—I was on intimate terms with a wild universe that acted without regard to my desires but often fulfilled them nevertheless. I saw now that my sister gladly would have erased my world without a thought, like a scribble on a blackboard she did not recognize as writing, and I sensed that Mahalia hoped to accomplish this obliteration by replacing my mother with Isabel. I felt increasing dread at the prospect of Isabel's coming—she was the hand that would yank me into a slim world that had no niche for me. If I let my thoughts linger even for a moment near the emptiness left by my mother's departure, I felt a longing so desperate that it seemed to grab me by the shoulders and pin me in place. I wanted to toss myself after my mother into the dark chasm; her universe was also mine.

PART TWO

*I*SABEL

Chapter Six

Izzy's Girls

*T*hree days after my mother and David departed, a Western Union messenger arrived at the door with a telegram, which Mahalia opened:

> F. X. URGENT. MARGUERITE ESCAPED FROM SISTERS.
> WE ARE AT CYPRESS INN. COME AT ONCE.

My mother had bolted from the parking lot of The Place and refused to return despite pleas from David and two Sisters of Mercy who worked there. F. X. and David had anticipated something like this, which is why they had agreed that it would take at least the two of them to coax my mother to stay at The Place after she was free to check out voluntarily. David had hoped, however, that he at least would be able to get her in the front door by himself. Mahalia read David's telegram without expression and handed it to F. X. Afterward, he called Isabel and asked her to move into our house three days earlier than she had planned. As he reviewed odds and ends of my mother's life he would have to relinquish to Isabel, I saw that even F. X. was impressed by Isabel's efficient grasp of detail.

The day before he departed, carrying two extra suitcases for my mother, F. X. tacked the address of the Cypress Inn to our refrigerator and said, "They won't let your Mama make outside calls for a while, but she'll still write you all the time, and you can get hold of me here." However, when a letter from my mother fell through our mail slot a week later, Mahalia gave it to me, saying, "Take this. I don't have any use for it." I read the letter repeatedly:

My two sweet girls—

Here at The Place there are two old Ursuline sisters who told me that they made wine for years in a still in their bathtub. They said that now that they are no longer drinking, they are beginning to question their faith. F. X. tried to comfort them by telling them that most of us live without faith. F. X. entertains the sisters by playing the piano in the common room. He likes to play the songs backward because he says they sound diabolical that way. He used to do this at blind school.

He and David caught a hog-nosed snake yesterday and were keeping it in the hotel room, to bring back to you, Penny. They brought it here to show me, and it escaped out the window and crawled inside a drain pipe and out onto a wire leading from The Place to a telephone pole. I did not know snakes could balance on something so narrow.

David claims the entire population of Louisiana looks like it belongs in the parole office. He complains about the heat and drinks iced tea all day, and tells ice hockey stories. He told me it's too bad they don't let girls play hockey, because he claims Penny would be perfect for it. He says, "She would knock out their eyeballs."

Mahalia, let's all go ice-skating in the fall when I get back. Does your friend Isabel know how to skate?

After this first letter, no more came, and the absence of communication from my mother made me feel cut adrift and lost.

Mahalia blossomed. She loved following Isabel around, helping her set the house in a better order, resweeping and mopping and vacuuming the chaos from the corners and the shadowy places under our furniture. She helped Isabel settle into my mother's bedroom. Isabel brought her own sheets, which she said were made of 100 percent cotton, because she found synthetic fibers irritating. She also brought her own pillow, because she feared my mother's would be made of down. (It was.) Isabel used her own special unscented soap and shampoo and cleaned her bed sheets with a special detergent ordered through the mail. She never turned on the television that sat at the foot of my mother's bed, and which my mother sometimes watched late at night, laughing or exclaiming at the antics of comedians or monsters. Isabel went to bed earlier and was always up long before us; she claimed she enjoyed rising at dawn, and she set her alarm clock for five-thirty. Occasionally Isabel listened to morning radio evangelists. I would awake to hear their voices ringing tinnily behind her closed bedroom door, like the noises of a small animal trying to escape a metal cage. I wondered why television was sinful, but radio acceptable.

Mahalia ate what Isabel ate: oatmeal for breakfast, and meat without sauces, and vegetables that Isabel half-cooked in a metal pan with holes in it, which she had brought from her kitchen and called a "steamer." (It would be years before steamed vegetables came to seem wholly American.) Isabel believed that prepackaged foods and those containing artificial dyes were unhealthy, and she would not allow me to drink anything at meals except milk or water, or to eat barbecue potato chips or the blue Rocket popsicles sold by Stein's sole ice cream truck, or even canned soups because she said they contained monosodium glutamate. She would buy only white cheese, because yellow cheese contained chemical dyes, and she would not allow me to make sandwiches with Wonder bread. She herself ate very little even of what she allowed. She swallowed her small portions slowly, taking small bites. We never had desserts. After dinner, Isabel drank cupful after cupful of weak tea, reusing the tea bags until they were muddy-yellow and burst in the pale water, leaving flecks on the surface that made me think of tobacco spilling from the ends of the cigarette stubs that collected on Stein's sidewalks all summer.

Isabel divided most of her time between reading, corresponding with an evangelical organization in Ohio, and visiting homes during rounds of what she called her "missions." Her papers collected in four piles, which she laid out on top of our piano. She received literature from the National Conference of Catholic Bishops' Family Life Committee, which she kept in a folder labeled "Rome" and segregated from her other literature. She stacked together a Cincinnati newsletter called *Holocaust of the Unborn*, written by Reverend Sloat; issues of *The National Right to Life News*; and *Christianity Today* magazine. In a third pile were a clothing catalog and several small magazines and letters on natural medicine and nutrition, and in a fourth she kept issues of a weekly journal on puzzles. She read her literature daily and clipped pages that interested her with gold paper clips that were odd and old-fashioned looking, pointed at the tops instead of rounded. Other than her four stacks of papers, which built gradually and unobtrusively, she left no mark on our house. She never deposited her shoes on our porch, or a sock on the stairs, or her sweater on the back of a chair, or a ring of water on the coffee table.

The Jeep Isabel drove on her mission work belonged to Stein Evangelical

Church. It bore a bumper sticker that said, YOU BEEP, I CREEP, and another that demanded, RESPECT LIFE! The Sunday after F. X. left for The Place, Isabel asked me to dress in a jumper and accompany her and Mahalia on a late afternoon ride in the jeep. Isabel wore her mustard-colored dress and her slipper-shoes and a baseball cap with AMERICA BLESS GOD printed on the bill; her hair was twisted into a knot and tucked into it, and her ears stuck out a little, making her features look even sharper and foxier than usual. Mahalia sat in the front seat next to her and turned around several times to look at me; she was afraid I would misbehave. When I stuck my arm out the window to feel the wind, she shook her head, but I kept my arm where it was. With Isabel in the house, Mahalia talked very little to me, as if she had relinquished me to Isabel's care.

Isabel drove along the periphery of town toward Stein Lake. As we passed the lake, I tried to picture my mother's car at its center, but I could not hold the image—it was as if the lake were incapable of outlandish things with my mother gone and Isabel nearby. Isabel turned at the end of the lake onto a narrow country road that led north of Stein for a few miles, and then onto a steep mountain route banked by melting snowdrifts even in May.

If you take to the Adirondack roads or go hiking or climbing anywhere near Stein, when you look down, you see Stein Correctional Facility, a colossal grayish white weight that anchors the landscape and appears to be the reason all the wilderness is there. As Isabel's Jeep climbed to the top of a rise, I had a perfect view of the prison. Its concentric walls surrounded the central building like the circles of a whirlpool.

"They have to build the walls high and sturdy," I said. "To keep us Daigles out."

"What walls?" Isabel asked.

"The prison walls," I answered.

"I thought you meant the Walls of Jericho," Isabel said. She smiled at me in the rearview mirror—it was that half-smile of hers, vaguely slanted, and I smiled back having no idea what she meant. I liked the feel of the wind in my hair and the sensation of being up so high above everything. I thought of my mother at The Place, of how she would hate being confined, and I felt as if a hand had grabbed my heart to still it.

Isabel said, "It's far chillier up the mountain." She touched a panel near her elbow, and my window suddenly rolled up, surprising me. My cheek stuck to it and rose an inch before I pulled away.

"Who snucked up the window?" I asked.

"Not 'snuck,' " Isabel answered.

"What?" I asked.

"You can't use the word 'sneak' that way, Penny."

"Who *snaked* up the window?" I asked.

"*Rolled*," Isabel said. She crooked her arm around her seat so that her hand stopped in front of me, holding a hairbrush. "Comb out your hair a little." After I took the brush, Isabel said, "Not like that. Take your pigtail out of the rubber band first, then brush your hair, then you can pull it back again." Mahalia frowned at me.

Isabel shifted into a higher gear and the Jeep climbed for another forty minutes, until we came to an asphalt driveway that connected to the road miles from any other house. The driveway zig-zagged through the woods and stopped at the bottom of curving slate steps in a landscaped hillside of small frozen trees. Many of the trees were still in their burlap bags, as I had once seen trees at a Plattsburgh nursery. Small evergreens leaned against the house or on their sides, their short limbs bound like kidnapped children, their needles yellowing on the ends. The house itself was enormous, the house of rich people. I wondered how Isabel had found it, set so far back in the woods, how she had known there were people living there who would agree to let us in.

There was an International Harvester station wagon with one side collapsing in on itself from a collision that could not have been recent; the cracks in the paint had begun to rust. The left back door was twisted so badly that no one could have opened it. Isabel parked the Jeep beside the car and removed a large cardboard box from the back. Inside were packages of rice and beans, two hams, canned fruit and vegetables, and some baby clothes.

"Mahalia, can you get the second box?" Isabel asked. "And Penny, you take the sack."

I lifted a grocery bag: It contained powdered milk and four cartons of Quaker oatmeal. I felt sorry for the people in the house who were expected to eat it. Several of Isabel's pink pamphlets were tucked between two of the cartons. We followed Isabel as she mounted the steps and rang the doorbell. Mahalia set down her box on the doormat and leaned briefly over a muddy patch of ground beside the steps: A small clump of ferns poked from the ground. Ordinarily, Mahalia would have examined them thoroughly, and possibly cut off a piece of fern for herself if it was an unusual kind, but instead she straightened back up without saying anything.

The woman who answered cracked the door open only partway and said, "Oh, it's you. The Jehovah's Witness."

"I'm not a Jehovah's Witness," Isabel answered. "You'll remember I'm from Stein Evangelical. I just came to see how everything's going. I've brought some foodstuffs."

The woman peered down into my bag and said, "Come in." She looked beautiful in a way I associated with wealthy city people—tall, with dark brown hair that fell to her waist and gold bangles on her wrists and clothing that seemed sophisticated and exotic to me, a hot pink shirt printed with what looked like foreign writing. The shirt hung halfway to the floor, over matching pants. The woman wore pinkish-brown eye shadow and mascara—her eyes reminded me of scooped-out peach pits.

She led us into a front room larger than my house. Her floors were a polished rock I had never seen, light green flecked with white and pink. The walls rose to twice the height of our walls and were made of different colored stones, gray and pink and black. The sofa looked like three sofas joined together: It was long and made of white leather. Facing it was a leather armchair where a little girl around four years old lay curled up and asleep, her mouth open. There was no other furniture in the room.

"Sit down if you want to," the woman said. She sat on one end of the couch, and Isabel perched on the other end. The woman lit a cigarette.

"You shouldn't," Isabel said. "It's bad for the baby."

The woman arched her eyebrows, but put out the cigarette. "This," she said, making a vague gesture at the empty space in front of her, "is bad for the baby." I looked around the room but saw no baby.

"The church can find you a place nearer to town," Isabel said. "It would be better when your time came."

"If I leave here, he'll get someone to sell it, and he'll hide what he gets for it," the woman answered. "Then we'll really be a charity case. The last time we drove to town, when we came back, he'd sent a truck here that carried off every scrap in the house, lock, stock, and barrel, except these two ugly things." She pointed at the couch and armchair.

"I remember," Isabel said. "You mentioned that on my last visit. However, you could move in with your parents."

"I'm not bringing my children back into that madhouse," the woman answered. "That's why I hooked up with *him* in the first place—to get away from there."

"Your grandparents would be glad to take you too," Isabel said.

"My grandparents? You spoke to my grandparents? Do you do that to everyone, walk around prying into their lives like that?"

Mahalia interrupted the conversation. "I could unload the groceries and put them away," she volunteered.

The woman stared at us, as if just registering our presence and answered, "Well, okay."

"That's nice of you, Mahalia," Isabel said.

I followed Mahalia into the kitchen. The late afternoon light streamed through an enormous pair of glass doors from the top of the mountain, onto a small table standing in a large otherwise vacant area. The light seemed thin, watered down. My chest grew tight, as if there were not enough room for both air and light in a day spent with Isabel. I longed for my mother, for the thick richness of her conversation, her laughter that capsized onto itself. I missed the presence of the men too—the downstairs part of my house felt gutted without their too-loud voices, their smell of cigarettes and beer and whisky, the couches and armchairs tilting and sinking under their weight.

"They weren't even married," Mahalia whispered to me.

"Who wasn't?"

"The people who live here. He was arrested for something serious, and now he's going to jail." I was surprised my sister was taking me into this confidence. Before I could formulate an answer, Mahalia continued in a worried tone that struck me as off somehow—as if she expected me to feel concern for people I did not know at all. "Do you know who she is? She's the daughter of the prison warden! Of Superintendent Nohilly, who runs the whole correctional facility! Her name is Cicely Nohilly. She met the man who lives here and moved in with him and had a baby without being married. And then one day he just walked out and left her and her little girl and then the FBI came looking for him, and then she found out he was making all his money from drugs. And now she's going to have another baby! She's barely twenty-one. She had her first baby when she was only seventeen." Mahalia pulled Isabel's pink pamphlets out of the grocery bag and tucked one under a cutting board on the counter and a second one in the silverware drawer. She left several more face up on the counter. She looked under the sink, found some ammonia, and began scrubbing the kitchen cabinets.

I leaned back into the living room and stared at the woman. How could she only be twenty-one? She looked as old as Isabel to me.

"I have no goddamn idea what he expects me to do," the woman said.

I waited for Isabel to comment on her language, but Isabel merely said, "God will provide." I thought she must restrain herself from correcting adults she was trying to persuade of more important things related to her missions.

"I doubt that," the woman answered.

I leaned back into the kitchen and told Mahalia, "She doesn't look twenty-one."

"Life has worn her down," Mahalia answered knowledgeably. "And her makeup makes her look older." She opened the glass doors and rubbed at them with a dishrag. She stopped briefly to study something on the ground. "Wait just a minute, Penny," she told me, although I was not doing anything in particular. She opened several drawers in the counter until she found a steak knife and a plastic sandwich bag. She returned outside and quickly, almost furtively, cut a rectangle of mossy dirt from beside one of the glass doors.

"I've never seen one of these in Stein," she whispered. "I could just swear—I think this must be one of those Hart's Tongue Ferns they have in that book of Daddy's." She wrapped the plastic bag carefully around the soil. "Maybe it's growing here because we're up so high." Mahalia looked long-ingly toward the woods: She liked to walk around in woods to figure out how to recreate perfect controlled environments for her terrarium and gar-dens. Whenever she had the chance, she would get down on her knees and dig up humus to use in her fern beds.

"Maybe someone planted that fern you just pulled up," I said. "Maybe you're just stealing it."

As soon as I said this, I was sorry. I had felt glad to see Mahalia doing something unrelated to mission work, and I liked it when she talked about ferns. Mahalia put the bag in her pocket and returned to cleaning the glass, her back to me.

I walked around the living room, studying the stone wall and sneaking looks at the woman. I recognized some of the rocks from science class: rose quartz and granite and obsidian. There was a chimney whose opening came up to my forehead and I leaned down and looked up it. Its mouth was wide, the flue open. I stooped and tried to stand up inside it, but Isabel said, "Penny, that's not a good idea. Come out of there."

I ducked back down. I stepped forward to examine the little girl. She looked uncomfortable, wound up, the back of her head pressed against the chair's arm.

"Why's she all snailed up like that?" I asked.

"You should say 'curled,' " Isabel said.

I sat on the stone floor with my legs splayed in front of me. The floor was cool and pleasant, and I lay down sideways and pressed my cheek to it. The cold crept into my face until I thought: *I am the floor.* I laughed to myself.

"Is that child all right?" the woman asked Isabel, looking at me.

"Sit up, Penny," Isabel said. I sat up and saw a sooty print on the floor where my hair had been. The little girl had opened her eyes and was staring at me. Her thumb was in her mouth, which moved in a sucking motion. Her eyes were large and dark brown. She removed her thumb for a moment and coughed.

Isabel walked over to her. She placed her hand on the little girl's shoulder and said, "That sounds like a nasty cough. Does your throat hurt?"

"Keep your hands off my child," the woman told Isabel.

Isabel patted the girl's head and returned to the sofa. The woman rose and lifted her daughter onto her lap. "Sit here, Stormy," the woman said, clasping her arms protectively around the little girl.

"Her name's Stormy?" I asked.

"What of it?" her mother answered.

The girl took her thumb from her mouth. Isabel's hand moved in her pocket; I heard a muffled ringing, metal puzzling into metal.

"The church uses Dr. Cope in Dannemora," Isabel said. "His partner is a pediatrician. They'll see you and your daughter free of charge. I'll give his receptionist your name."

The woman did not react to this information. When I turned, I found her still facing me, both eyebrows arched. "You have soot on your head," she told me.

"Penny, stand over here," Isabel said.

She waited for me to move, and when I tried to sit on the sofa, she caught me by the shoulder and said, "Just stand."

Isabel handed the woman a pink pamphlet. I saw the heading, WE MUST CHOOSE SIDES! and the picture of the skull and crossbones in the bassinet.

"Huh," the woman said. "I've heard Reverend Bender at your church is into this kind of thing. I don't have any opinion about it." Her little girl peered at the picture, and the woman turned the leaflet over saying, "Don't look at that, Stormy."

"Penny!" Isabel cried. I looked down and saw a black handprint on the white sofa. Isabel examined it, walked hurriedly into the kitchen, and came back out carrying a dish towel and dish soap. She scrubbed at the soot mark, saying, either to me or the woman, "I like to think I don't take anything from any place where I alight." The woman gave Isabel a curious look as she wiped the area she had cleaned and stood back to examine it—there was not even a slight trace of my hand print on the white leather. "There," she said. She returned the soap and towel to the kitchen, reemerged a moment later, and sat back down on the sofa.

Isabel continued, "I know your family is of the Catholic faith, but why don't you come to one of our services? It will take your mind off things to hear about the issues Reverend Bender raises in his sermons."

"Take my mind off of things?" the woman answered. "That's what I'm supposed to do, isn't it? Just let my mind go all fuzzy? I'm not supposed to ask questions like, 'How am I supposed to take care of a baby in this mess?' I'm not supposed to think at all, am I? Well, I do. I think about the fact that some children have rotten families. Rotten parents, rotten childhoods, rotten lives. But you aren't allowed to consider that, are you?"

Isabel answered at length, in the same odd, antiquated tone she had used when she had talked about Saint Hermine. She told the woman, "I myself entered this world into bad circumstances, Miss Nohilly. I was an orphan. I was raised in a home for orphaned girls in southern Ohio. I never knew the love of a mother, and when I went to school, I never had any of the things other children had. We lived in a kind of poverty that had no name, because the people who ran the home would not even allow us to think of ourselves as poor. We were taught to feel lucky that we were cared for at all. But I did not believe then and do not believe now that we were lucky, or that I owe a debt to them. They fed us badly and some of the women who supervised us hit us, and they never looked for anything but bad in us. The home was eventually closed down for its ill treatment of the girls who lived there. And so I really can understand the kind of childhood you think I can't. Even so, I am thankful to have been born."

Stormy tugged on her mother's shirt. Her mother set her down on the couch. The little girl stared at me, her thumb back in her mouth like a stopper.

"That's the first time today you've addressed me by my name," Miss Nohilly answered.

Stormy climbed down from the couch, approached Isabel, and grabbed her hat by its visor.

"Do you want that?" Isabel asked, stooping in front of her. She removed her cap and placed it on the girl's head, so that AMERICA BLESS GOD faced backward. Stormy smiled and touched the cap.

"We're going now, Mahalia," Isabel called into the kitchen.

As Mahalia and I walked with Isabel to the Jeep, I turned and saw Miss Nohilly still watching us from the doorway. She lit a cigarette and closed the door behind her.

While we drove back down the mountain, I said to no one in particular, "I don't think she wanted us there."

"Of course not," Isabel answered. "The best way to discover evil is to turn toward the wind and see where you feel the most resistance."

"She took the food," Mahalia said. "She must have been glad that we helped her with the food."

"I go for the child," Isabel answered. "The adults can take care of themselves."

As we drove down the hill, I realized that I had felt intensely uncomfortable in Miss Nohilly's house, and this feeling barely ebbed as we approached Stein. Isabel and Mahalia sat next to each other without talking, as the land leveled off into barren horseradish fields, still muddy from melted snow.

"I feel completely strangulated," I said.

"What, Penny?" Isabel asked.

"Nothing," I said. I sensed that Isabel would not approve of the word "strangulated." But Mahalia had heard me—she frowned at me. I made a face at her.

As we arrived on the road into town, I saw Joel Renaud standing with a group of five boys from school: They were throwing rocks at cars. I leaned out my window and waved my arm wildly. Joel waved back, looking surprised to see me.

"Who are those children?" Isabel asked. She parked the Jeep on the road shoulder. "They should not be throwing rocks at cars." She stepped down from the Jeep and faced the boys, lifting her hand to shield her eyes from the setting sun as she peered at them. They shrieked and raced into the woods. Isabel waited and stared after them for a minute, and then she climbed back into the Jeep and traveled on.

Isabel passed our house and turned down the next cross street.

"Are we going on another mission?" I asked. I thought I would die if I had to stand by, waiting again, while Isabel carried out a new mission.

"No," Mahalia said. "We're stopping at a church member's house. At the Groots."

"Nicky Groot's?" I recalled my mother's description of him as a boy who would grow up to murder both his parents. I prayed for something interesting to happen.

Before we exited the Jeep, Isabel put a hat on her head, to replace the baseball cap she had given away. The hat was the one she had worn the night I saw her in front of the Esso station, and later when she had come to talk to David about caring for us. Even now I have never seen a second one quite like it. It came from another era—it was helmet-shaped and rimless, like a flapper's hat, and was grayish-violet, with a large knit like chain mail.

"Why do you wear hats all the time?" I asked Isabel.

"I cover my head to remind myself of my humility before God," she said.

I followed Isabel and Mahalia up the steep slope of a yard to a green stucco house that slumped on its foundations. One side of the house was higher up than the other. Basement windows grew out of the garage side of the hill, and on the uphill side the house narrowed at the foundation until there was barely enough room for the front door. A woman older than my mother answered. She was short and a little heavy, and wore a white pant-suit. Sallow skin with pockets of greenish eye shadow hung below her eyes; they made me think of hard-boiled eggs left out too long.

"Barb! Look who's here!" she cried. "It's Izzy!"

"Speaking of the devil!" a second woman called.

"We don't say 'devil' casually," Isabel instructed me. "Mrs. Wroblewski is a newer member of our church."

The woman at the door leaned down and took my hand. "I'm Myra Groot," she said. "Who might you be?"

"That's Penny, my little sister," Mahalia answered. She gave me a warning look.

We walked into the living room. It was tiny, crammed with armchairs and a couch, and tables covered with knickknacks and potted plants. African violets were everywhere: on the coffee table and the windowsill; sprawling over doilies set on the couchside tables; and spreading across the top of a television, like a miniature jungle. I wondered about the television—what had Isabel meant when she said, "We don't believe in television," if other members of her church watched it? There was a smell of something baking in the air. A dark hallway led from the living room, and I could hear muffled music—teenager's music—leaking from under a door midway down the hall.

A second woman rose from a flowered couch when we entered. I thought she must be the one who had called Isabel the devil. She was a large woman, my mother's age, with a reddish shag haircut that fell in feathery layers around her head. "Izzy, we're so glad you found time to pop in," she said.

"Penny, this is Mrs. Wroblewski," Mahalia told me. She leaned over and whispered to me, "Don't act up while you're here!"

"I just came by for a minute," Isabel said, sitting down. "I wanted to find out who's going to be taking Katie for the next few weekends."

"God knows I would have taken her myself," Mrs. Wroblewski answered. Neither Mahalia nor Isabel reacted to her saying "God." "But with the seven I've got already, the women's committee thought she'd be better off at Annie Strang's."

"Barb, you know not everyone thought that," Mrs. Groot said.

"That's true, Myra," Mrs. Wroblewski said. "It was mostly the Great Queen of the women's committee, Mrs. Esselborne."

"I'm sure Mrs. Esselborne tries her best," Isabel answered.

"If that's her best, I don't think much of her," Mrs. Wroblewski said. "I think she's a snoot."

"Well, as long as Annie doesn't mind taking Katie," Mrs. Groot answered.

She told me, "We'll have to get you and Katie together. I think she must be exactly your age." For a moment, I worried about being forced to play with a girl from Mahalia's church, but then Mrs. Groot said, "She's part of our church's Prison Visitor's Program." This detail made Katie sound alluring.

"My mother says we'll have a family reunion as soon as all our relatives get out of jail," I said. Mrs. Wroblewski laughed. I scooted close to her on the couch, and she draped her arm around me. The couch upholstery was covered with pictures of little birds—wrens and robins and sparrows. On a little table between the couch and the window was a jar of one of Mahalia's concoctions of dirt and peat moss and fern spore dust. I picked it up and tapped the glass: A small green tongue appeared in the dirt.

"Don't do that!" Mahalia told me. She took the jar from me and replaced it on the table.

"Mahalia brought that to me," Mrs. Groot said. "She's just a godsend. Here I was complaining about how little sunlight I have in my flower beds, and she knew just the thing—a fern garden."

Mrs. Wroblewski peered at it.

"It's a Marginal Woodfern," Mahalia said. "It's one of the true ferns. It will grow really easily."

"I always liked ferns," Mrs. Wroblewski said. "They remind me of the feathers on rich ladies' hats in old movies."

Isabel opened her brocade bag, removed a small spiral notebook from it, and wrote something down.

Mrs. Groot turned to her and said, "I would have liked a little girl staying here in my house. But you know with Nicky here, it's just not a possibility."

Isabel nodded, without explaining why she agreed.

"Izzy," Mrs. Groot said. "I meant to tell you that a girl Nicky knows said they're teaching that poem again this summer at Stein High School. The one by that lady, Guenivere Somebody? Guenevere Brooks? The one you were worried about last year?"

Isabel's head snapped up. "Gwendolyn Brooks? Her poem about abortion?"

"The one called 'the mother,'" Mrs. Groot answered. "I caught Nicky snickering over it with this girl."

Isabel looked perplexed. "I thought the school administrators had seen the light," she said. "I thought that drawing it to their attention would be enough." Isabel put down her notebook and stood up. "Let me talk to Nicky." She walked into the hallway and knocked on the door halfway down.

"Nicky!" she said. "Open up!" When there was no answer, Isabel pushed open the door herself. Eerie music crawled out of the room and scaled the air, and a black light threw violet marks like a twisted alphabet onto the hallway floor. Isabel stepped inside the room with a determined expression, closing the door behind her. The music and purple light pursued her inside. I felt impressed by her fearlessness—it was as if she had entered a tank full of monsters to wrestle with them.

Mrs. Groot stood up suddenly and ran into the kitchen. I heard her cry, "Just in time!" and the banging of a pan on top of the stove. I smelled cookies or cake, but she returned to us empty-handed and sat down again beside Mrs. Wroblewski.

Mrs. Wroblewski leaned over and half-whispered to Mrs. Groot, "Myra, I'm in a family way again. Every time I lie down, Mr. Wroblewski just crawls on top of me. It's gotten so I'm afraid to go to sleep."

"Oh Barb!" Mrs. Groot exclaimed.

"Can't keep his hands off me," Mrs. Wroblewski said. "I pray daily for the change of life." Mrs. Wroblewski rolled her eyes. I liked her; she added an element of ebullience to the cluster of girls and women that I hadn't felt all day.

Mrs. Groot laughed.

"Congratulations!" Mahalia said, laughing too; she did not even seem embarrassed.

"God knows what I'll do now for baby-sitters," Mrs. Wroblewski said. "Except for Izzy, I practically have to blackmail sitters to get them to watch seven kids."

"Barb—you took the Lord's name in vain," Mrs. Groot said teasingly. "For the second time in ten minutes."

"This time it wasn't in vain," Mrs. Wroblewski answered. "I meant it."

The door to Nicky's room opened, and Isabel emerged looking dismayed. The purple light clung to her clothing, then slipped back inside as she shut the door behind her.

"It's true," Isabel told Mrs. Groot. "Nicky showed me a handout he got from the girl who attends the high school." Nicky, everyone knew, attended the special school near Dannemora that was a step from juvenile prison. "I was afraid this could happen, but I prayed that it wouldn't."

"And after all the protesting you did," Mrs. Groot said sympathetically.

"I see now that it was wrong for me to try and tackle it all on my own," Isabel answered. "This is my just dessert for my own arrogance."

"You never act arrogant," Mahalia told her.

"She's absolutely right," Mrs. Wroblewski said. "You don't have a bone of conceited, arrogant pride in your body. You didn't deserve this at all. Why, you dedicated yourself to those protests at the school."

The phone rang, and Nicky's door opened. He emerged, looking taller than I remembered him. He was middle-school age, around thirteen or fourteen, with black hair and a faint mustache that looked like a crushed moth. He wore a small hoop earring and a tie-dyed sweatshirt with the sleeves ripped off. He padded by me on bare feet. A skull smoking a cigarette was tattooed on his arm: Smoke billowed around its top hat. He leered at Mahalia before he disappeared into the kitchen, but she did not appear to notice him.

A few seconds later, he returned to the room, looking disappointed and angry. "It's not for me, Mom," he said. "It's for you." Nicky leered at Mahalia again as he passed her, although her back was to him. She continued to chatter away with Mrs. Wroblewski as he walked backward down the hallway, watching us all. He placed his right hand on the muscle of his left arm, and bent his arm suddenly in a lewd gesture I had seen men make before, although I was uncertain what it meant.

"Who is it?" Mrs. Groot asked.

Nicky opened the door to his room without answering: The violet light pounced on him, and his door banged closed.

Mrs. Groot rose to answer the telephone and vanished into the kitchen. I heard an electric whirring as she talked.

Mrs. Wroblewski told Mahalia, "I really feel for Myra. She has the softest heart in the world. She just couldn't prevail against Mr. Groot. What woman can shield her children from a mean drunk? And now she has to live with what he left behind—that boy. She has to put up with him all by herself."

I looked at Isabel, to see whether she thought this was an inappropriate conversation for Mahalia to participate in and for me to overhear. But Isabel was preoccupied: She had taken out her notebook again and was scribbling something in it.

"What's a mean drunk?" I asked Mrs. Wroblewski. I recalled my mother using the same phrase when talking with F. X. out on the ice.

"Someone who uses liquor as an excuse to make everyone else's life a holy living hell," Mrs. Wroblewski answered.

I looked quickly at Isabel again, but she still was paying no attention to us.

"Excuse my French," Mrs. Wroblewski told Mahalia.

Mahalia chuckled mildly. I realized then that Isabel's clutch of women from her church made up the place where my sister felt valued and at ease, and forgot her awkward indignation.

Mrs. Groot reentered the living room and said, "It was Cicely Nohilly, Isabel. She wanted to know if you had really talked to her grandparents. I told her I was sure you would have." There was something white on Mrs. Groot's forehead—it looked like cake icing.

"I'm glad you told me about her," Isabel answered. "I've visited her three times now. She let me in the door today."

"As far as I'm concerned," Mrs. Wroblewski said, "the whole Nohilly family belongs in the zoo."

"Nicky used to do yard work for her," Mrs. Groot told Mrs. Wroblewski. "Cicely's husband, or whatever you call him, used to pick Nicky up here and take him to their mountain house on Saturdays. Then when I heard her husband or whatever he was had been picked up for drugs, I almost died. Nicky has a way of glomming onto the worst people."

As if he had heard her, Nicky burst from his room. He padded by us again, pulled on a pair of black leather boots with a grunt, and departed through the front door.

"Where's he off to?" Mrs. Wroblewski asked.

"I don't even want to know," Mrs. Groot answered. "I just don't ask anymore."

"Let me find out," Isabel told her. She opened the front door, stepped outside, and closed the door behind her.

"There's no one like Izzy," Mrs. Groot said. "She's a jewel."

"She's a saint," Mrs. Wroblewski agreed. "She's the only one who will watch seven children on a moment's notice without a squeak of complaint."

"She saved my life," Mahalia said.

She did? I wondered.

"Izzy appeared just in time," Mahalia told the two women, who listened to her with sympathetic faces. "I would have run away if she hadn't stepped in and rescued me from my crazy family."

Mahalia's words shocked me. I had never dreamed she had thought of running away.

"Just a minute!" Mrs. Groot said. "Hold that story right there." She hurried into the kitchen, where we heard her opening and closing drawers and cabinets. She reentered the living room carrying a plate of cupcakes.

"I know Izzy doesn't like children to have sweets," Mrs. Groot told me, "but this is her very own carrot cake recipe. It just has my icing on it. You go ahead and eat one, Penny, before Izzy comes back inside." Mrs. Wroblewski smiled wickedly at me and I lifted up a cupcake. The icing was so sweet it made my teeth hurt. I wolfed it down and took a second one.

Mahalia said, "Isabel seemed to materialize out of thin air, right when I couldn't take things for a second longer. I looked up, and there she was!"

"That's our Izzy," Mrs. Wroblewski said. "Isn't that just like her?"

"It was the same way with Nicky," Mrs. Groot said. "One day four years ago, I was sitting at home crying my eyes out after Mr. Groot had lit into Nicky and chased him out of the house, and the next minute there was Izzy ringing the doorbell. 'Mrs. Groot?' she said. 'I just want you to know that your son is safe with me. He tried to burgle my house, and now he's fine. I told him he could pass the night there.'"

"He broke into her house and she invited him to stay!" Mrs. Wroblewski cried. Mahalia and Mrs. Groot laughed together appreciatively. "Izzy isn't afraid of anything. She must have scared the hell out of him."

"When Mr. Groot died sitting upright in his own car," Mrs. Groot said, "it was Izzy who came over and held my hand while the police and ambulance people were swarming all over him."

I remembered Isabel standing in our living room, telling this story to my mother in different words. I thought to myself, *Well, Nicky didn't grow up to murder both his parents after all. One of them died before Nicky could kill him.*

"Izzy just sat there on the sofa and answered the policemen's questions for me, and chattered with me until the police left. She told me that a drunken priest once ran into her in a car and broke her arm."

"A priest!" Mrs. Wroblewski said.

"Yes, back in Ohio. She made the Church pay her a settlement. She thinks it's sinful for the Church to let priests drink. And even so, she didn't mention as she sat there with me that she had seen Mr. Groot weaving up and down our street in his car nearly every day. I thought that was nice and tactful of her. And then afterward," Mrs. Groot continued, "Reverend Bender himself came and invited me to attend Stein Evangelical. I thought it was really something, that the man-in-charge would take that kind of trouble, and I joined up right there."

"That's what I like about Stein Evangelical," Mrs. Wroblewski said. "When my father died, Father Flaherty couldn't even haul his bony ass over to the wake—he sent Sister Geraldine. I pulled my troops out of All Saints right then and there and put them in public school. 'The pope's just lost eight Catholics brought into this world to serve His Holy Highness,' I said."

Mahalia answered, "Isabel told me how you did that. She told me Mr. Wroblewski joined too."

"Oh yeah, him," Mrs. Wroblewski answered. "Before, he never attended Mass, and that made him Catholic, and now he never attends prayer meetings, and that makes him Protestant."

Mahalia chortled in a grown-up way.

The front door opened and Isabel came back inside. I could see Nicky standing in the twilight of the yard. An insect glimmered over him, and he reached out a shadowy arm and snatched it from the air. He lit a cigarette. None of the women in the room noticed.

"I think he'll come back in after a little while," Isabel said, sitting down on the couch between Mrs. Wroblewski and Mrs. Groot, her back to Nicky. He wandered off into the darkness.

"How many cupcakes did you eat, Penny?" Isabel asked.

I looked down at the plate; there were nine left. "Around three," I answered.

"That's too many for her," Isabel told Mrs. Groot. "Sugar fills her with nervous energy."

"Oh, you're right, Izzy," Mrs. Groot answered. "But you know how I am."

Isabel sat down and said, "While I stood out there talking to Nicky it came to me what I should do about the school. I should write up a petition and ask people to sign it."

"You know I'll sign anything you put together, Izzy," Mrs. Wroblewski said, "especially if it's commitment papers for Mr. Wroblewski."

In that odd tone of voice she used when she discussed religious matters, Isabel said, "I think what's special about our time, is that the devil has chosen to cloak himself in the disguise of institutions instead of particular people. I think that institutional sin is the greatest threat to children of this generation. We try so hard to protect them against sin, yet while we do our work, our very schools force dangerous ideas on them."

I saw that Isabel was losing the other women's attention—Mrs. Groot bent to scoop up some cupcake crumbs from the table, and Mrs. Wroblewski picked at a frayed place on her blouse. I concluded that Isabel did not merely fail to connect with my uncle F. X. and Cicely Nohilly; there were times when she failed to reach anyone.

"Can I go outside?" I asked.

"We're about to leave," Mahalia answered.

"Let her burn off a little of that energy before you go," Mrs. Wroblewski said.

Isabel nodded. She had pulled out her notebook again and was already writing something in it.

Mrs. Groot turned and watched with concern as I headed for the door.

"Leave the front door open," Isabel told me.

I searched for fireflies in Mrs. Groot's front yard, but it was too early in the summer for them to have started invading our neighborhood with their hordes of blinking lights. I followed a flicker I glimpsed at the edge of the yard. The early evening dark was mud-colored, with patches of deep blue. I pretended to be F. X. negotiating a shadow world with my eyes wide open—and what were they all, those women in Mrs. Groot's living room but shadows talking a shadowy kind of talk that meant nothing to me? I pictured Mahalia leaning forward to whisper something tittery and confidential about Miss Nohilly to Mrs. Wroblewski. I grimaced with distaste, then made my most hideous face in the dark, hitching up the left side of my mouth, screwing my left eye shut and baring my teeth. "Heh, heh, heh," I said aloud in a spooky voice.

The firefly ahead of me stayed lit for too long—I stopped and identified it for what it was—the end of a burning cigarette. It dimmed and brightened, illuminating Nicky Groot's chin. He stood on the edge of the yard, facing the woods as if waiting for something to come out from the trees and meet him.

"Talking to yourself?" he asked me.

"Maybe," I answered. The smell of his cigarette enveloped me.

"What's The Flood so worked up about Cicely Nohilly for?" he asked me. It took me a moment to realize that he was talking about Isabel. "Why's The Flood going after her like a cat in heat? Cicely can take care of herself."

"Hell if I know," I answered.

Nicky laughed, and his laughter made me feel liked and accepted by him. "Your sister's going to end up a dry old spider like The Flood if she doesn't watch it," he said.

"Why are they all so jumpy about you?" I asked him.

He guffawed and then fell into a coughing fit: He removed his cigarette and pranced in place, bending over and coughing, trying to catch his breath.

"Because I'm a boy!" he said, laughing again, straightening himself up. He sucked on his cigarette and said, "Ho ho ho," in a low, monstery monotone.

I liked the sound of it. I imitated him, jeering in my deepest voice, "Ho, ho, ho!"

"Nicky!" Mrs. Groot called. "Nicky!" I could hear an edge of anxiety in her words. Nicky puffed on his cigarette without answering.

Isabel stepped into the narrow rectangle of light in the front doorway. "Penny!" she called. "Come out of the woods and return here right now! We're going."

"Rescued from my clutches!" Nicky said.

"Penny! Penny!" Mahalia shouted, her voice charged with imitation anxiety.

"Penny! Penny!" Nicky copied her, whispering in a high girlish voice.

"Penny!" Mahalia repeated.

"She may be hiding," Mrs. Wroblewski said, and hearing her, I thought hiding would be a good idea. I backed a little into the woods and remained there, quiet as death.

"Penny Daigle!" Isabel called sharply. A flashlight snapped on in the darkness: Yellow light fell like a needle in the grass. My heart raced: I wondered if the sugar in the cupcakes was making it beat faster than usual.

Now the voices of the women all started in at once, tangling with each other and then swarming out over the yard like bugs. Nicky snickered, and I snickered just like him: We were two of a kind, two forest ghouls. Mahalia's voice traveled off to a far corner of the yard, and Mrs. Groot's and Mrs. Wroblewski's intersected one another near the road, saying, "She'd have more sense than to stray onto the street at night, wouldn't she?" and "I hope so!"

"Penny!" Isabel's voice leapt from the darkness only a few yards away. I heard Nicky's rustle, sensed him retreating off to my left into the woods. The beam from Isabel's flashlight wrapped my shoe in gauzy yellow.

Isabel's hand clutched my elbow. "Didn't you hear us, Penny?" she asked. "Did you just walk out of the trees or have you been standing here all along?"

"Izzy's found her!" Mrs. Groot called. Mrs. Wroblewski hooted.

Isabel pulled me across the lawn, her hand firmly on my arm, the flashlight in her other hand, unraveling the darkness in front of us until we arrived at the illuminated doorway where Mahalia waited.

"Where were you?" my sister asked sharply.

"Somewhere right there," I said, pointing vaguely into the darkness, knowing this answer would infuriate her.

"It's time to go home," Isabel said.

"I should have been home half an hour ago," Mrs. Wroblewski answered. "Mr. Wroblewski will be crawling the walls by now. He has a forty-minute limit with the kids before he starts coming loose at the seams. My oldest girl, Roberta, does most of the work anyway."

"Well, I'm glad you could visit at all," Mrs. Groot said wistfully. Behind her, a stack of uneaten cupcakes sat abandoned on the coffee table.

———

Mahalia avoided looking at me or speaking to me as we drove home in the car, but Isabel did not seem to notice my sister's smoldering silence. When Isabel parked the Jeep in front of our house, she said, "Mahalia, I'll need a few minutes tonight to do some typing. I would appreciate it if you would fold the clothes in the dryer."

Mahalia told her, "I'd be glad to," an answer she never would have given my mother, whose requests had seemed to weigh my sister down like boulders. For the first time, I wondered whether Mahalia had genuinely resented my mother heaping chores on her, or had simply disapproved of my mother's reason for doing so.

When we entered our house, Mahalia pulled her bag of Hart's Tongue Ferns from her pocket. She opened a kitchen cabinet and took out two plastic containers holding sterilized soil and peat moss, mixed small amounts of their contents together, and gently removed her fern from its bag and deposited it in a jar. She sprinkled water on the fern before sealing the jar, placed it on the windowsill over the sink, and then walked to the small laundry room behind our garage, careful not to address me or cross my path on the way. I followed her and lay on top of the pile of dry clothes she had heaped into the basket. She pulled as many as she could from around me until finally she said with exasperation, "Get off, Penny!"

"They're warm," I told her, nestling into the clothes.

"They haven't been warm for hours," Mahalia answered. She tipped the basket and dumped me out. She then lifted the laundry onto the dryer and folded our clothes there.

"Why is everyone so scared of Nicky?" I asked.

"Who's scared?" she answered. "Why did you pretend not to hear us when we called? Did you want to scare everyone? It was so embarrassing!"

She did not wait to hear my answer; she carried the basket through the garage into the living room. "*Pennatik romortofied Mahaliatik!*" I cried. Mahalia continued up the stairs when I followed her as far as the living room.

"Thank you, Mahalia," Isabel said formally. She had seated herself on the couch, a small gray typewriter in front of her on the coffee table. She still wore her helmet-hat, and she bent over a pale yellow paper, typing slowly and using one finger, her forehead wrinkled with concentration, her mouth opening and closing slightly as if chewing her words in slow motion.

Mahalia returned downstairs and, ignoring me, faced Isabel and said, "I'd be glad to fix us all dinner. Do you feel like ham and corn on the cob?"

"No, Mahalia," Isabel answered. "I don't want you waiting on me. I'll fix dinner when I'm done typing. I won't take more than a few minutes."

Isabel continued to strike one key at a time, painstakingly, so that I had a sudden vision of her as someone who would be lost in the man's world that my mother, pounding stacks of paper with her breezy typing, negotiated every day. Isabel rolled the paper up and down when she typed, checking each word as she printed it, apparently oblivious to the fact that my sister was pretending I was not in the room, and refusing to speak to me or even to look at me. My mother would have noticed the tension between Mahalia and me immediately. I was not exactly sure why Mahalia was so resentful of my conduct at the Groots'. It had nothing to do with her, and the fact that she thought it did struck me as off-kilter, as if she believed she was at the center of things—and her style of fighting was cowardly, as my mother had said, and falsely adultish. It was bad enough that adults generally seemed to lose the will to fight head on as we children knew how. When we were angry, we threw rotten fruit into moving cars; put dead animals in the confessionals before the wrinkled old women entered, counting their rosary beads like the fingerbones of babies; or we leapt on each other like ravenous animals, as I had done that time to Persis Boards—neither of us had believed we were strong enough to kill each other, but we would have liked to nonetheless, and we had aimed toward murder. Mahalia's sticky silence lacked our joy and hunger and liveliness and made me much angrier than Persis Boards ever had—poised between Mahalia and Isabel, I felt for the first time what the expression, "It makes my blood boil" meant, and I understood too how my mother must have felt all those months with Mahalia's silences tightening around her ankles like snares whenever she entered the house. The skin over my wrists felt tight, and heat spread up my arms and burst in my heart. I walked up to Mahalia and punched her as hard as I could in the ribs.

"Penny!" Mahalia cried.

"What is it?" Isabel asked. She turned around and saw Mahalia's mouth twisted with pain, and me standing beside her with the same leer on my face I had seen Nicky Groot flash at Mahalia that evening.

"She hit me!" Mahalia said. "She just walked up to me and hit me!"

"Penny?" Isabel asked, turning to me. "You're too old to hit people, and you're a girl, not a boy. This is what happens when you have too much sugar—you start spinning like a top gone out of control. Go up to your room and remain there."

As if I cared! I climbed halfway up the stairs and jeered, "I'm still here, Mahalia, and I'm not going away!"

"I don't know what's gotten into her!" Mahalia told Isabel as I entered our room. Was it possible that Mahalia really did not know? That her stingy, mean silence was something she maintained without thinking about it—that she was no more aware of me than a stump? I doubted it: I was impossible to ignore. At the same time, I had glimpsed the advantage of moving through that silence, that refusal to acknowledge anything. It was like a watery swamp that a monster could live in day after day, undiscovered. So that was how evil thrived, the evil Isabel was always pursuing and rooting out of words. It hid and grew, gargantuan and unmolested, in the murky everything they refused to talk about. I smirked like Nicky Groot again, throwing myself back on my covers and thinking, *Dry old spider!*

I half-closed my eyes and the dim air over me spun into a sticky net, gathering like cobwebs in the corners. A car's headlights tangled in the bedroom curtains and shut off below my window. The doorbell rang.

I heard Mrs. Groot's voice: "You go on in," she said. "Izzy won't bite you." I walked to the bottom of the stairs and leaned forward to see if Mrs. Groot had brought Nicky with her. I was disappointed—instead, Cicely Nohilly entered the living room, wearing different clothes than she had earlier—a dress and a button-down sweater. She looked more girlish: Her makeup was gone, and without it her eyebrows were plucked and colorless.

"I just wanted to thank you," Cicely said. She sat down on our couch, across from Isabel. "I wanted to thank you for calling my grandparents. I hadn't even thought to call them because my parents don't speak to them, and then my grandfather's been sick. I've hardly talked to them since I was little. I didn't even know they wanted to see Stormy. But I called my grandmother and she said, 'It's so lonely here. I'd love your company!' And she came and got me and my daughter."

Isabel smiled—a smile so genuine and effortless, it reminded me of the moment when she had given Mahalia the mustard-seed pendant. She reached over and patted Cicely's knee as if she were a child.

"I was rude to you," Cicely continued. "I'm sorry—I'm like that to everyone." She laughed. "Don't take offense."

"I'm just glad you've come to your senses," Isabel told her.

"Most people wouldn't have bothered," Cicely answered, adding with more energy, so that she sounded more like her earlier self, "most people would have left us up on that hill to rot. Christ, I didn't even know anyone knew we were there."

"That would not have happened," Isabel said, without correcting Cicely's language.

"My father knew we were there, sitting around in his big old prison, locking everyone up and bossing them around. But did he ever call me? Not once. He said, 'If you go off with that man, you're on your own!' And he meant it. No one's allowed even a little mistake around him. I'm lucky he didn't throw me into solitary after Stormy was born."

Isabel answered, "When you belong to a church, the church is your family. That's why we—"

Cicely interrupted, "That's just what I was going to say! It made me see for the first time how important it is to be part of a community, like a church." Isabel nodded. I thought of Nicky saying that Cicely Nohilly could take care of herself. I wondered what was true, his view of her, or the way she appeared here, shaping herself into the kind of person Isabel believed she could be. Cicely pressed on, "I was thinking maybe I could go to one of your services. At Stein Evangelical, I mean."

"That would be nice, Miss Nohilly."

"Call me Cicely."

"Isabel," Isabel answered.

"We call her Izzy," Mrs. Groot said. "And we call ourselves 'Izzy's Girls.' Now you're one of Izzy's Girls too." Mrs. Groot still stood just inside the door, clutching her handbag.

Isabel told her, "Sit down, Myra. I've typed up a petition about that literature they're making children read at the public school. While you're here, would you care to sign it?"

"Of course I will, Izzy," Mrs. Groot said. "I'd do anything for Izzy," she explained to Cicely. "She's the only woman in town who will baby-sit Nicky." She signed her name on Isabel's pale yellow paper without reading it.

"I'll put my name on it too," Cicely said. She read it quickly and remarked, "You put down your address here? Well, I guess I'll use my new one. Thanks to Izzy Flood." She handed the paper back to Isabel.

Mahalia said, "You should be proud of yourself, Isabel."

Isabel answered, "Oh, Mahalia," but she did look proud of herself.

I wondered what my mother would have thought of her and Mahalia and the other two women inhabiting our living room. I imagined I was my mother: I smiled her wry, bitter smile and heard myself think, in her very tone of voice, *There is no limit to human possibility.* I surveyed them all: Mrs. Groot wringing her hands for no reason; Cicely Nohilly smiling tightly, her lips pale in her unmade face; Mahalia resting a hand on the couch behind her as if to say that she owned the couch; and Isabel perched at the center of them all in her helmet-hat.

I recalled a phrase I had heard my mother use once to describe a beauty contestant on television: I said, in her very tone of voice, "Isabel looks like the cat that ate the canary."

The women stopped talking and turned toward me.

"Penny!" Mahalia said. "That was rude!"

"I'm sure she didn't mean anything," Mrs. Groot said.

"I don't think she's using that expression right," Cicely Nohilly said. "It's supposed to mean something else—it means you look guilty."

Isabel alone appeared unperturbed by my statement: She seemed to think suddenly of something else and bent forward to pick up her petition. She reread it, moving her lips slightly, unaware that the women around her had moved toward her, and now surrounded her protectively.

Chapter Seven

Daily Missions

School let out three weeks after my mother's departure, and when summer vacation started in June, Mahalia went to work at Stein Evangelical's Bible camp in the mornings and afternoons. According to Isabel, Reverend Bender had received money from an Ohio church to move into a larger, abandoned church on the edge of Stein that had once belonged to the Baptists, and this was the first year Stein Evangelical had held the camp. It included local children, as well as children who came to Stein to visit their fathers in prison. However, Isabel did not suggest enrolling me at the camp. She may have felt, with reason, that she could not entrust me to its inexperienced teenage counselors.

Isabel rarely let me out of her sight. On Sundays she stayed with me while she sent Mahalia to church services, and on Wednesday evenings, Isabel allowed herself to attend church only after putting me in bed early and assuring that Mahalia would keep an eye on me. Isabel always took me along on her weekday mission work. When she spoke to me, she was kind, correcting me doggedly with a fantastic patience. She did not talk about my mother. Nor did she ever discuss my mother's progress with my sister, but then, Mahalia never asked about it either. Mahalia chatted with Isabel about working at the church; they were both pleased with the new building, which contained an organ, although the church had no organist to play it. I remember hearing Isabel say one evening after dinner, "Mahalia, if I had a daughter, I'd want her to be exactly like you. I couldn't have had a better child if I'd ordered her from a catalog in the mail."

Isabel's handful of words filled my sister with light: She returned them with an expression of inordinate joy. Mahalia could have had no doubt that Isabel meant what she said. Isabel did not overflow with sentences in the way of people in our family, with their conversations in which every word contained a mouthful of words. Isabel's straightforward phrases held what she thought and nothing more, as if she believed she had nothing to hide— no shameful sweet secret or shocking joy or degrading precious covetousness.

As I spent more time with Isabel, I learned that her life was not usually dull, as I might have feared, especially on days when she executed her missions. Through her ministrations to the people of Stein, she introduced me to my own community in a way I had not seen it, and probably never would have otherwise. We entered homes where I sensed we were unwanted or desperately wanted. Once inside, Isabel acted as no other adult I knew would have—she was like a self-built person, made grain by grain, from thin air. The trait of Isabel's that impresses me most now, in retrospect, was her refusal to accommodate others in a manner that might have made her discourse with the world more relaxing; she was the carborundum against which all people she encountered were ground. She had no sense of irony, and because irony is the heart of humor, she had no obvious sense of humor either, although she often smiled her half-smile at some inward thought that amused her. She also appeared, for weeks on end, incapable of personal offense, or of being intimidated by the people she encountered.

We entered homes where there was no food; where toddlers were left unattended for hours; where twelve children occupied a single house trailer; where a father the color of pale liver sat at the kitchen table, with a glassy stare that reminded me of the young woman in church I had seen talk in tongues, and which I would recall and identify only years later as the wholly rapt expression of a heroin-user. Isabel often brought food, inquired about every child's health, and never reacted to violence or poverty or squalor with even a flicker of the kind of condescension or horror that would have added a burden of shame to the homes of the people she visited. In this way, she insinuated herself into peoples' lives, always half-invited by that variety of misfortune that leads people to call out fervently and indiscriminately to anyone.

Often her missions were fruitless: People greeted her with rudeness or indifference, or belligerence. One Monday in mid-June remains clear in my memory as particularly trying for her. That day, Isabel gave me a satchel to carry and said, "We're going on foot this morning." She told me to fill the satchel with a thermos of ice water, two apples, and some white cheese. I added several items of my own when she was not watching: some quarters I had found under the seat in the church Jeep; ten bittersweet chocolates I had purloined from a drawer in my mother's bedside table when Isabel was downstairs earlier that morning; a wallet my mother had given me, stitched on the side with lanyards and containing the picture of a child I had never met; a black stone from Stein Lake; the green reporter's notebook from F. X.; a paperback science-fiction novel by Ray Bradbury, from Sister Geraldine's collection; and my father's rusted bowie knife. As I threaded after Isabel through the needle-eye of her workday, the weight of the satchel comforted me. With my mother gone, the world had somehow thinned to its essentials: sky, clothes, rock, food, tree, road. The density of things seemed to have seeped out of life.

Isabel and I walked to the western side of town. On the edge of Stein, Isabel stopped at the brick building where my pediatrician, Dr. Epstein, had his office. She stood at the front desk until the receptionist looked up. "Has Miss Nohilly arrived yet?" Isabel asked.

The receptionist examined her calendar. On the wall of Dr. Epstein's office was a sign that said, THE VETERINARIAN, DR. EPSTEIN, IS IN, and under this was a picture of dogs playing poker: There was a bulldog that reminded me of Reverend Bender, and across from him, a boxer and a mean-looking little greyhound with his ribs sticking out. Leaning against the table were two girl dogs, a flirting poodle with a diamond collar and false eyelashes, and a fox-faced terrier looking off to the left as if the game did not hold her attention.

While I waited, I said a jingle out loud to myself that Joel had taught me: "*Hell-o* everybody, I am Harry Cemetery. If you're good you go to heaven, if you're bad you go to *hell-o* everybody, I am Harry—"

"Sit down and wait quietly," Isabel told me.

"Hello, Penny," the receptionist said. She told Isabel, "No, no one by the name of Nohilly has come in."

"Are you certain?" Isabel asked. "Our church made an appointment for her with Dr. Cope's office in Dannemora, but Miss Nohilly said she was bringing her daughter here instead this morning."

"No," the receptionist answered. "No one by that name is booked for today."

Dr. Epstein appeared from an adjoining hallway. He was a thin, tall man with a gray beard and hurricane hair. His white doctor's coat had a spiral of pink tie-dye in the middle: He had told me that his daughter tie-dyed all of his doctor's coats.

"Penny," he said. "Are you here because you have Yellow Fever? No? Are you in a coma?" He pretended to look in my ear. He tapped the top of my head. "No skull reflex at all. Come into my office, Penny, and we'll hook you up to a machine that will shock your heart into beating again. If you want a cast on your arm, we'll give you one of those too."

Isabel watched all this without smiling; from her expression, she might have taken Dr. Epstein's words literally. "Penny does not have an appointment today," she told him, but Dr. Epstein was already picking up a baby who had crawled out of an examination room and carrying him back down the hallway, saying, "Where has your mother gone to? Did she run off and leave you, or did you lock her in the medicine closet?"

Isabel frowned. She asked the receptionist to check the calendar for the next week, and when she found nothing, Isabel frowned again and said, "Thank you." She left a pink pamphlet and a yellow paper—a copy of her petition—on a table holding a pile of *Horizon* magazines, and we departed from the doctor's office.

I followed Isabel to the end of the road. We turned left onto a northbound highway. We walked for an hour or more. During this time Isabel was pensive and did not speak to me. She acted as if she thought nothing of walking several miles. At one point, a truck pulled up beside us and a man offered us a ride, but Isabel answered, "No, thank you. We're just getting some exercise." As the man drove away, I wondered if Isabel had chosen to walk in order to tire me out so that I would behave.

I was thirsty and hungry by the time we arrived at our destination, a gray house set by itself on the side of a lone gravel road that turned off the highway. Isabel stopped outside the house and told me to have a drink of water from the thermos and an apple.

"Don't ask for food when we're visiting," she directed me when I was finished.

She knocked on the door and said, "I wish to speak with Annie Strang." The woman who answered had thin white hair and wore a bathrobe with faded flowers on it. She held the door ajar while she measured Isabel from her bun to her yellow slipper-shoes, deciding whether to let her in.

"Isabel Flood from Stein Evangelical," she said.

"That's where I've seen you, at my daughter's church," the woman answered. "Don't you remember me? Annie asked me to sign your paper. I'm Annie's mother, Josephine Strang." She stepped back to let Isabel in. "Have you come to baby-sit Annie's children and that Katie girl?" Inside, a television played without sound and toys were scattered across the floor. A baby slept in a bassinet beside an armchair. A boy about three years old sat at a folding card table in the middle of the living room, eating a potpie.

A girl my size stood in the corner. She turned around to look at us with an elfish face. She was the same black-haired girl I had seen in the Stein Tavern with Isabel and the piano-legged woman the night F. X. took us there. Mrs. Strang told her, "I didn't say you could look away from the corner yet, Katie, did I?" Katie faced the walls again.

"Would you like a cola?" Mrs. Strang asked me. She walked into a small kitchenette and poured herself one.

"No, thank you," Isabel said. "And I'm not here to baby-sit. I won't be available for baby-sitting until late August."

Mrs. Strang looked disappointed.

"I had a meeting scheduled with Annie," Isabel said. She removed a metal puzzle from her purse and fiddled with it.

Mrs. Strang watched the puzzle for a few seconds and then looked away as if the sight of it irritated her. "Annie's gone and left the children with me for the day again," she said. "Even the one she agreed to take in for the church." Mrs. Strang pointed at Katie with her chin. "Annie's supposed to be watching her today, for that prison thing the church runs, and then she just up and leaves me with her. Here I am, fifty-eight years old and low energy. Every time Annie meets some potential husband, she dumps the kids on me."

The baby muttered in its bassinet. Isabel leaned forward and pulled up its blanket.

"I can count to twenty!" the boy at the table said suddenly. He cocked his head toward his grandmother, waiting for an answer.

"Don't interrupt, Charlie," Mrs. Strang said. "I could understand one," she told Isabel, pointing to Charlie. "Annie was too young, but at least my husband and I knew where the father was and persuaded him to marry her before he was killed."

"I can count to twenty!" Charlie said again.

"You must have a lot of brains," I told him. This is what my mother said to me when I showed her Sister Geraldine's twenty-by-twenty digit multiplication problems. Charlie leaned over his potpie, toying with a pea.

Mrs. Strang continued, "But to come home and say, 'Now here's another one!' and not even the same father." Mrs. Strang nodded at the crib. "Annie tells men she's a widow, but I don't see how you can still be a widow after you've taken back your maiden name and had a new child."

"DO I HAVE A LOT OF BRAINS?" Charlie asked in a stentorian voice.

"I'm speaking," his grandmother told him. "Don't inter—"

"HOW MANY BRAINS DO I HAVE? One, two, three, four, five, six, seven, eight, nine, ten, eleven, twelve, thirteen, fourteen, fifteen, seventeen, eighteen, nineteen, twenty!"

"You forgot sixteen," Katie said from her corner. "It's fifteen, *sixteen*, seventeen."

"Katie, I was speaking," Mrs. Strang said.

"NO, NO, NO!" Charlie shouted. "*Not* sixteen! I was talking about how many *brains* I have. Eleven, twelve, thirteen, fourteen, fifteen, *seventeen*—"

"Charlie," his grandmother said. "Didn't you hear Miss Flood and me talking? You'll have to join Katie in the corner if you can't eat quietly." Katie turned around to look at us again, and Mrs. Strang said, "I didn't tell you to move, Katie."

Charlie fixed a bright eye on Isabel: His eyes were a bottomless dark brown, his hair black, his nose small. He stood on his chair, held perfectly still for a split second like an otter in midsomersault above the water, and then dove under the table.

"Charlie, get in your chair," His grandmother commanded, but he did not respond. Mrs. Strang told Isabel, "I sometimes think there's something wrong with his hearing, but then I remember his mother was the same."

"I lost a pea," Charlie's muffled voice communicated from below. Charlie crawled back onto his seat, held up his pea jubilantly, and said, "Here it is! It's green." He put it on his plate, lifted his fork, and rolled it past a shred of crust.

Isabel said, "Charlie, don't eat things that have been on the floor." She picked up the pea from his foil bowl, and carried it to the sink in the kitchenette. Still standing, Isabel told Mrs. Strang, "Annie must have forgotten that I told her I would stop by today. I've brought some materials for her." Isabel placed a stack of yellow papers on the card table.

Charlie slid to the rug, and his grandmother said, "Charlie, off the floor! Now!" She waited for Charlie to climb back into his chair. "If you want to find Annie, Miss Flood, try the Motor Inn. She likes to go dancing there."

"Do pigeons pidge?" Charlie asked.

Isabel said, "Thank you, Mrs. Strang. Please give Annie the materials."

"DO PIGEONS PIDGE?" Charlie repeated. In her corner behind him, Katie giggled.

"That's too noisy, Charlie," Mrs. Strang said.

Isabel walked over to Katie, placed a hand on her shoulder, and asked, "Is there a reason you aren't at the church camp today?"

"I think the lady who's supposed to take me to camp forgot," Katie answered. Her voice was wispy and she ran out of air on the last word.

"I'll check into it," Isabel said. "You mind Mrs. Strang while you're here. Have you had lunch?" Katie nodded.

Mrs. Strang frowned. "Of course she has. She finished before Charlie even started, like she thought Charlie would steal it from her. And then Charlie just plays with his food and takes forever to eat."

As Isabel guided me out of the house, Katie turned to watch us forlornly. "Good-bye, Katie," Isabel said. "I'll see you in church."

Instead of returning to town, Isabel led me farther into the country. She stopped once to let me rest, after telling me to drink some more water and to eat some cheese.

"Don't swallow the candy you put in there," Isabel said. "Chocolate makes you lose control of yourself."

I pulled the Ray Bradbury paperback from my satchel and read while Isabel examined her yellow papers and underlined paragraphs in a new issue of *Holocaust of the Unborn*. I read for half an hour until I forgot where I was and that I was with Isabel. When I reached the middle of the second chapter, Isabel lifted the cover of my book: It was called *Something Wicked This Way Comes*. She shook her head, and before I understood what she was doing, she gently tugged the book from my hand.

"This book is too old for you, Penny," she said.

"It's only kind of hard for me," I answered. "I think I understand most of it."

"That's not what I meant," Isabel said. "I meant that the book is not suitable reading material for a child."

"Sister Geraldine loaned it to me," I answered.

Isabel frowned. She dropped my book into her purse. I wanted to know how the story continued—I felt as if I had jumped halfway off a cliff toward an exhilaratingly cold lake and been stopped in midair.

"But I'm not done!" I said.

"When you're under my care," Isabel told me, "you have to live by my rules."

She put her papers back in her purse with my book and continued down the road.

I followed her, singing under my breath, "*Hell-o* everybody, I am Harry Cemetery." She ignored me, and finally I stopped. It was too hard to hike and chant at the same time.

We passed a field where weeds wrestled with sunlight on pale patches of hard dirt. The field was surrounded by a barrier that made me think of the double walls of Stein Correctional Facility. The owner had strung a barbed-wire fence that sloped at a crazy angle from the ground. My mother had pointed out sloping deer fences to me before, explaining that deer could jump high but not wide—and she always added in the same breath that nothing could keep out a hungry deer. But I believed that this particular fence might work because it was surrounded by a second, upright fence made of every kind of wood imaginable—railroad ties snarled together with more barbed wire, and ordinary wooden posts tangled with cyclone fencing and iron rods, and even a rusted stop sign.

Isabel headed toward a house within the barricaded area, set back about forty yards from the road. The house was small, cabinlike, dark brown, and next to it was a small barn from which the smell of pigs emanated. The barn and the house had a barren neatness to them. There was a small yard, with a few stringy plants struggling upward out of hard-packed dirt. They were covered with small shield-shaped bugs I had never seen before, showily colored, with black and orange decorations.

At the other end of the yard was a flower bed, but someone had stuck white crosses into it instead of planting a garden. There were about twelve, as high as my knee. They reminded me of the small crosses children sometimes erected over the graves of their pets. Above them was a gray sign that announced: GRAVEYARD OF THE INNOCENTS. A chicken skittered away from us and fled around the corner of the house.

A girl Mahalia's age appeared on the front steps and called to Isabel. I recognized the girl as the one who had talked in tongues at Reverend Bender's Wednesday night prayer meeting. She had pale blue eyes and brittle-looking skin and wispy blond hair that made me think of the dry yellow grass that edged our sidewalk at the end of the summer.

"Lucy!" Isabel said. "You shouldn't be lifting buckets like that."

"I tell her that myself!" a man said, appearing in the doorway. He was the same height as David, but younger, with wavy brown hair and a beard. His beard had been cut a little unevenly, so that it was flat on the left side, but had two points on the right. He wore a plaid flannel shirt, as most of the men in town did, unless they were in uniform, on their way to prison work, and his clothes were unpressed and a little soiled, but no more or less than most men you saw in Stein. I remembered him now—he was the man who had grabbed the girl Lucy's elbow when she was talking in tongues.

"Penny, this is Lucy's father, Mr. Coker," Isabel said.

Mr. Coker handed Isabel a jar of horseradish, telling her, "Take this as a present." It had a hand-lettered label that read: COKER'S BITTER HERBS: NOT ORGANICALLY GROWN. "You know I couldn't get the horseradish to grow anymore without insecticide. The harlequin bugs lapped up the phosphate like it was candy." He invited us into the kitchen, where he poured us two glasses of milk. He stirred a yellow powder into them, which he called brewer's yeast, so that I was hesitant to touch mine. When I sipped it, I gagged—it tasted spoiled.

"You aren't used to goat's milk?" he asked.

Isabel said, "We'll be stopping for lunch here, Penny."

Lucy drank her milk and, during the rest of our snack, called her father "Pop" or "Mark" interchangeably, which unnerved me. No children I knew would have thought of speaking to their parents by their first names. Isabel sat at the kitchen table with us, reading a dog-eared copy of a thick tract Mr. Coker had given her called *Handbook on Abortion*, and paging through various other magazines and leaflets he kept on abortion, nutrition, and natural medicines. She pulled a plastic box of her gold paper clips from her brocade bag and clipped two pages of the handbook.

Mr. Coker busied himself in front of the stove, leaning into a cloud of steam and sprinkling spices over it. He wore an apron while he cooked, and his hair was tied back in a ponytail. He cut the ends off of a stack of kale, which I had seen before but never dreamed I would have to eat.

He told me, "We don't buy canned or frozen vegetables. They're full of chemicals." He went on to explain how canned mushrooms in grocery stores were cleaned by a leaching process that made them dangerous. He talked in an excited voice, as if the idea of frozen and canned vegetables profoundly bothered him. During the winter, I rarely had anything else.

"Democrat soup," he said, pointing at his cooking pot.

"Democrat soup," Lucy echoed, and I could tell that this must have been a private routine joke of theirs. I sensed that they probably had many such routines. Occasionally, Mr. Coker would pause in his cooking to ruffle Lucy's pale hair. Because I had no father, I felt an odd sense of foreignness, as if Lucy and her father took for granted something I had never been taught the word for.

"It's really venison stew," Mr. Coker told me. "Venison with homemade blood sausage and homegrown spices." I looked at Isabel in alarm, but she did not notice me. She was reading a pamphlet titled *Reverend Sloat's Handbook on School Board Takeovers* and clipping its pages with her gold paper clips.

"We shoot our own deer and raise our own pigs," Mr. Coker told me. "Commercial pigs have too high a rate of trichinosis." He stopped and grinned at me. I was not sure why. He asked, "Why do pigs like to root around in the ground?"

"I don't know," I answered.

"Because they have such tricky noses!"

"Get it, Penny?" Lucy asked. "Trichinosis—tricky noses!"

Mr. Coker laughed.

He pulled a bright red sausage from the refrigerator and sliced it into the stew. "Blood sausage," he told me. He asked Isabel, "Have you read about the beef blood yet? They brought it to a clinic and threw it on an abortion doctor." Isabel looked up at him but did not answer. "I have ten gallons of pig blood I'm freezing in case we ever need it for ammunition." He winked at Isabel.

While we ate, Mr. Coker hovered around the table anxiously, as if afraid he had forgotten something. I could not imagine eating a deer, and the disks of scarlet sausage that floated in the stew made me queasy. I wadded chunks of meat in my napkin when no one was looking and asked to be excused to use the bathroom.

I flushed the meat down the toilet. After I emerged from the bathroom, I peered into the rooms that adjoined the hall. The Cokers' house was smaller on the inside than it looked on the outside. It had a kitchen and living-room area with a woodstove in the middle and a hallway that led to back rooms. Mr. Coker's bedroom door had been left open, and I saw that his bedroom was literally a closet. There was a narrow bed in there that filled the entire space. Above it, on a thick wooden rod running the length of the area, his clothes hung. The longer garments, a bathrobe and three pairs of overalls, dangled down so that they were only an inch or two from the bed. He must have brushed against them when he slept. There was a mirror on the wall at the head of the bed, but it would have been nearly impossible to use, because it was partially covered by the overalls. The mirror caught me off guard—I had to glance down quickly to keep from seeing myself in it, and ruining my record of avoiding mirrors, which had now reached 240 days.

Entering Lucy's room was like walking through a magic door into another world. She had a canopy bed, which I had never seen, and a thick wall-to-wall rug that was a light gold. There was a collection of porcelain dolls with glass eyes that looked as real as those in taxidermized animals. I had seen such dolls in catalogs where you could order them on an installment plan. They cost as much as an engagement ring a girl in Stein might expect to get. Lucy's closet was open and inside were rows of black patent-leather shoes, as if a whole orphanage occupied the room—I kept a single pair for

All Saints, polishing them for holidays. Lucy's bedroom also contained a cabinet with a glass door and glass shelves holding small crystal figures that glittered like prisms and threw rainbows in ribbons along the floor. On the windowsill was a large mason jar containing a few small feathery ferns.

Lucy appeared in her doorway and said, "Hey, are you done eating?" She closed the door behind her. "Mahalia gave me those," Lucy said, picking the mason jar up off the sill and peering down into it. "She told me she'd help me make a fern bed for them when they grow bigger, only she hasn't come by again yet. I gave them all names. This one"—Lucy pointed to the side of the jar—"is Lady Lucy and this is Mr. Eisenhower and this is Bones." I laughed.

"Do you think that's weird, to name ferns?" Lucy asked. I shrugged my shoulders. "Do you think it's weird that your sister is so hung up on ferns, and is always talking about them and giving them to people and everything?"

Before I could think of an answer, Lucy continued. "Because I never can tell what people think is strange and what they don't. I was home-schooled until last year. You go to that Catholic school with Mahalia, don't you?"

"Yeah," I answered.

"I got to go to Stein High for one year," Lucy said, "and now I can't go anywhere!" She pointed at her stomach. I was not sure what she meant.

There was a knocking outside her room. It came not from the door, but from beside Lucy's closet, where a pipe protruded out of the wall, as large around as a coffee can. She removed a plastic coffee-can lid stretched over the pipe's end and fastened to it by a chain.

Lucy put her lips before the pipe's opening and called, "What?"

Mr. Coker's voice came back through the pipe: "You can give the scraps to the pigs."

"Okay," Lucy answered.

"What's that pipe?" I asked Lucy.

"It was sticking out of the wall when we first moved in," she answered. "So Mark chopped it off and we turned it into a sort of postbox, or we shout things through it." I bent down and looked through the pipe. It was about two feet long. At the other end was Mr. Coker's eye, large and green and startling.

"Gobble gobble," he said.

His eye disappeared, and behind him, I could see the whole kitchen clearly: the steam streaking like a genie from the pot, the table, and Lucy's father walking back to the counter and shaking a pan into a pail. "Those two are squawking away like barnyards birds in there," he said. I covered the end of the pipe with its lid.

"When I was little," Lucy said, "I was scared of the dark, and I used the pipe as a night light. I'd just take off the lid and the kitchen light would come through and I could stare at Mark doing things out there." She did not say this as if she felt called upon to explain the eccentricity of the eyehole. She spoke of it affectionately.

When we entered the kitchen, Lucy's father said, "You see, Penny, we use everything. You didn't have to flush away your food." He handed Lucy a bucket with leftovers in it.

"In a month or two she shouldn't even carry that much," Isabel said.

I followed Lucy outside to the pigpens.

"Where's your mother?" I asked.

"She ran off when I was little," Lucy said. "That's why I've gotten myself in trouble. No mother around to tell me what I need to know."

"What kind of trouble?" I asked.

Lucy guffawed. "Boy trouble!" She laughed. "You mean you didn't know? I'm going to have a baby." She lifted her skirt, revealing white streaks on her stomach: They looked like pale scars. I wondered what a boy had scraped her with to cause them. "Stretch marks," Lucy told me. "Your skin sort of gives out as the baby grows." I had never seen stretch marks before.

"Mark fought and fought to keep me from having to go to Stein High," Lucy said. "But he couldn't keep home-schooling me because he couldn't meet the state requirements for home-schooling parents. When the social services guy came here, Mark punched him in the face! He broke his nose! So they arrested Mark for assault and put him on probation and made him send me to school. And this is what I got for it!" Lucy pointed at her stomach. "And now I can never go back."

"Why not?" I asked.

Lucy said, "They won't let girls in the door when they look knocked up. And I can't even tell Mark who the father is. I'm afraid he'd violate his probation again. I told him I had too much punch to drink and can't remember who did it."

It hadn't occurred to me that you could be too drunk to know whether a particular man used his sugar shaker on you. It was news to me, too, that you could simply refuse to tell who a child's father was.

"It was Isabel who made Mark stop running on and on about it. She looked him dead in the eye, the way she does everybody, and said, 'If God thought it was important for us to know the parents of every child, he would have put our parents' names on all our foreheads.' Well, I'll tell you, they can all just keep guessing. Why should I let everyone know I was dumb enough to be tempted by someone who just turned out to be a big nobody?"

As we entered the barn, the smells from the pigpens made my eyes water. There were sacks of chemicals everywhere, printed with words that had the grandeur of an exotic language: chlorobenzilate, dimite, dovex, aramite, and tetradifon. There was a single fenced area in the middle of the barn. Inside was a darkness that moved like an ocean. When I leaned over the pen, I saw twenty or more pigs. They were brick-red and large. One of them approached the fence and glared at Lucy with small rust-colored eyes. His grunt sounded almost human, like a demand or a threat. His stink was overpowering; I wondered if the baby inside of Lucy could smell it.

After Lucy fed the pigs, Isabel allowed Mr. Coker to drive us back to the edge of Stein, where she asked him to deposit us beside the railroad crossing. Lucy stayed behind. Her father instructed her to lock the door when we left.

After we turned onto the road to Stein, he asked Isabel, "You still baby-sit that pretty girl who comes to the church?"

"That's Penny's sister," Isabel answered.

"You better keep an eye on her," Mr. Coker said.

Isabel frowned.

"I watched Lucy all these years at home, and then she begged me to go to 'real school,' and now look at her! I'd kill the boy if I could find him!" Mr. Coker handed Isabel an Ohio newspaper, which she put in her bag before we stepped out of his truck and watched him speed back to his farm.

———————

Most of Stein's black residents lived on a single road, Warden Avenue, which paralleled Amtrak's throughway. The backyards of houses on Warden Avenue were not merely on the other side of the tracks—they were right on them. A few times each day and night, trains roared behind the houses, segregating the neighborhood from Stein's downtown through earthshaking and deafening announcements of unrestrained, headlong danger. That afternoon, Isabel crossed the tracks for the first time that summer, looking for the address of a woman named Mrs. Turpin.

The appearance of the person who answered the door seemed to take Isabel off guard—whether it was because he was black or old or simply a man, I wasn't sure—I realized only at that moment that all of Isabel's missions had centered on girls or women my mother's age or younger, and all of them were white people. The only man we had ever visited was Mr. Coker, and that was because of Lucy.

The man at the door asked, "Yes?" tilting his head toward Isabel. He wore glasses and a gray prison guard's uniform, and his hair was cut so short that I could see two scars where he had injured his head. I had two scars on the side of my head also, where I had gotten stitches after trying to ride my bicycle on top of a cement wall. The man's face was reddish-brown and long, and his hand when he extended it to Isabel was also long and slender, with fingernails so delicately shaped that they reminded me of my mother's.

"I was looking for the house of a Mrs. Turpin," Isabel said. "Please excuse me." She did not take his hand.

"You've got the place," the man answered. "I'm Mr. Mackey, her tenant."

Isabel retreated to the bottom step. "We won't be bothering you further," she told Mr. Mackey. "I'll just leave some leaflets to share with you."

Mr. Mackey stepped down to where Isabel stood and took one of her pamphlets. He opened it and lifted one eyebrow. His eyeglasses were two lozenges joined by a slender gold filament. Standing beside him, I could see his eyes reflected on the back of the lenses, so that he seemed to have a second ghostly set of eyes that looked backward while his true eyes looked forward. He turned the leaflet over and read it to the end.

"Go ahead and come in," he said, placing his hand on the top of Isabel's back. She pulled away slightly as I slipped past her through the doorway.

"Penny," she said. "Come back outside. We should be going."

However, Mr. Mackey followed me, pulled a carton of milk from a tiny refrigerator, and told me, "If you promise to drink a whole glass of milk, you can have as many cookies as you want." He filled a miniature glass like the kind my mother sometimes used for whisky, and then he emptied a package of cookies into a bowl: They were circular with a hole in the middle and stripes of dark chocolate icing across the front. I sat down.

"Penny," Isabel called, entering the house.

Mr. Mackey removed his prison guard's jacket and closed the door. "So," he said to Isabel, "tell me about this 'infant genocide' you mention in your paper here."

Isabel remained standing. Mr. Mackey pulled out a chair for her. She set her purse on the table and removed her puzzle before seating herself.

"What is that?" Mr. Mackey asked. "One of those twisted loop things?"

"It is my mission to protect the rights of the unborn," Isabel began.

"You're one of those Moral Majority folks, aren't you?" Mr. Mackey asked.

"Moral who?" Isabel answered.

"One of those right-to-lifers."

"People call us that," Isabel answered.

"Can I see your toy there?" Mr. Mackey leaned forward, took the puzzle from Isabel's hand, and fiddled with it. "What about children born into poverty and all that?" he asked. "People must haggle with you about that all the time."

"We believe that conception is a miracle," Isabel answered. She continued slowly in her odd, formal tone: "It's the only miracle because without it, there would be no life at all. What's poverty compared to oblivion? What is woman's labor compared to that, and toil in the sweat of our brow, compared to that?"

"Presto!" Mr. Mackey said, holding up the puzzle's two parts. He handed them back to Isabel. She did not instruct him to reassemble the pieces. She put them in her purse.

Mr. Mackey squinted at Isabel and adjusted his glasses, as if trying to see something more of her that he might have missed. "Do you believe that people are resurrected after death, and then reborn? I mean, born again as themselves but in the trappings of a different person, almost as if they're reincarnated?"

Isabel seemed affronted by his question. "No, I don't believe that," she answered.

"Because I was thinking that if you're entitled to one life, why not two? If I had my life to live over again—" Mr. Mackey paused and leaned forward as if to gauge the effect of his words on Isabel, "I might come back as a murderer. After a whole life, it seems like you'd need a second one, there are so many scores to settle."

Isabel rose and said, "It's time for me to go." She took me by the shoulders, lifted me from my chair, and steered me to the door. After she opened it, she turned toward Mr. Mackey, who had not risen from his chair, and said, "You did not ask to be brought into this world, and yet God brought you."

"And I did not ask you to appear at my doorstep, and yet you did," Mr. Mackey answered. I heard him laughing even after the door shut behind us.

———

The last house that we visited that day was the home of someone who had already died. Isabel and I turned the corner together onto a residential block of white box houses and tiny lawns. The street was lined with cars, and in front of a large brick house was a long black car. People dressed in black stood at the door. Isabel crossed the threshold without knocking. A small group of people surrounded an elderly woman in a dark dress.

She approached Isabel and said, "Miss Flood, you'd be here to see my granddaughter Cicely—you won't know that Mr. Nohilly has just died. He passed on with our Cicely sitting right next to him on the couch. It was a stroke."

Behind her a casket lay on a draped platform. I had never seen a dead person before, and I wound around Isabel to have a look. A man with closed eyes lay inside it. His face was made up like a woman's, with lipstick and rouge. I reached forward to touch him, but Isabel called, "Penny, come stand by me."

"Cicely won't be making it," Mrs. Nohilly said. "She's staying with a friend in Albany." Mrs. Nohilly looked pointedly at Isabel as if trying to communicate something beyond that single fact.

"What do you mean?" Isabel asked.

Mrs. Nohilly's eyes filled with tears and she said, "She left for Albany this morning. My husband convinced her it would be all right to do it."

"To do what?" Isabel asked.

"Cicely's barely holding her own with the one little girl, but at least Stormy will be in kindergarten in a year. And Cicely can go back to night high school herself, to get her diploma. Cicely's just a child herself!"

"She's not a child," Isabel answered. "She's twenty-one."

"Mr. Nohilly said he wanted her to have more of a chance in life, and not to get bogged down so early on. The whole thing troubled Mr. Nohilly so much that he went to Sister Geraldine. She was there when our son, Brian, was in school, and Cicely's mother was fifteen and they had Cicely. Mr. Nohilly told Sister Geraldine he didn't think we ought to make Cicely go through it all again—she already has the little girl. And especially not with the father the way he is. Cicely told you he's just been picked up and sent back to jail on a parole violation? He's had that history of mental trouble, and Mr. Nohilly felt we were too old to help her as long as she's going to need."

"Are you telling me that Cicely has decided to have an abortion?" Isabel asked. Two people standing near the coffin looked our way.

Mrs. Nohilly lowered her voice and answered, "Mr. Nohilly said, 'I wanted Sister Geraldine to tell me it would be all right for my granddaughter to see the doctor in Albany. But I knew Sister Geraldine couldn't say that, and so did she. Even so, we both understood that if she didn't come straight out and say *not* to, she would somehow be letting me know it was all right.' I can't remember it all, Isabel, but I think that's how he said it to me. He made Cicely promise him afterward that she'd at least make an appointment and talk to the doctor. And then when he died, Cicely said, 'It was his last wish. It was the only thing he ever asked of me!' And she left first thing yesterday morning. Oh, don't be mad with her, Isabel. She threw the whole hog of herself into what you told her, but in the end she just couldn't do what you wanted."

"Is Cicely there right now?" Isabel asked. "Is it too late to find her?"

"To find her?" Mrs. Nohilly said. "What do you mean?"

"To find the doctor's office and stop her," Isabel answered.

"Oh dear—oh no, yes," Mrs. Nohilly said. "She's been recuperating at her friend's in Albany. She planned to come back today for the wake, but she's feeling poorly."

Isabel turned abruptly away from Mrs. Nohilly and walked through a group of people to the casket. I followed her. She leaned over Mr. Nohilly and glared at him as if she wanted to pull him from his coffin in order to fight with him. Her face was lit with that concentrated laser-light rage of people who are accustomed to holding their feelings in: I thought she looked frightening. Mr. Nohilly's failure to stir or flinch in the presence of Isabel's righteous fury impressed me more than anything with the finality of death. He slept on peacefully, the hint of a smile on his red lips.

"How could you?" Isabel whispered to him.

She grabbed my arm, tugging me away from the casket and around Mrs. Nohilly. "This is no place for us, Penny," Isabel said. She did not let go of my arm until we were outside. She crossed the lawn without using the walkway and strode away from the house so quickly that I had to run to keep up with her until we reached the corner. She stopped there and waited for me.

After we left the Nohillys', Isabel's face set in a silent grimace. She did not speak to me except to tell me to look both ways when I bolted into the street. She thereafter held my hand, her head lowered, her chin pointing inward toward her collarbone. I understood Isabel's anger. It was not difficult for me, as a child, to see how Isabel must have felt to have an accomplishment wrested from her. And I comprehended, in a dimmer way, that Isabel was outraged that a sin had occurred—that Cicely had stopped her own baby's birth by murdering it in its womb. Despite my recognition of these things, I found myself wondering if Isabel was also upset with Mr. Nohilly simply for dying—he had outwitted her through the somber sobriety of his own end. I tried to feel somber myself, to let the gravity of death sink deliciously into my bones, like the remembered scenes of a horror movie. As we approached the florist's a block from Main Street, I thought of my mother telling F. X., "I think death is a great cruelty." I tried to call up Mr. Nohilly's face, his peculiar look of contentment. I imagined his eye suddenly popping open to fix on Isabel as he said "Gobble, gobble!" like Mr. Coker— Isabel started and jumped back from the coffin.

"Gobble, gobble!" I said under my breath.

"What was that?" Isabel asked. "Are you talking to yourself, Penny? It's the effect of those chocolate cookies that man Mr. Mackey gave you. They made you jittery."

A woman ahead of us approached the florist's window and stopped briefly to examine the carnations in buckets outside on the sidewalk. She continued toward us, walking slowly and seemingly caught in a daydream. However, when she noticed Isabel, the woman halted abruptly and started up again, her expression altered. She looked as if she were recalling an argument.

When she came within five yards of us, she stopped directly in Isabel's path and demanded, "Why are you interfering with my husband's employment? He has a family to support!"

She was tall, tall as Isabel, with a heavy black braid down her back. Her skin was a golden brown and her hair was so wiry that the ends of her braid stayed twisted in place without a rubber band. She wore a billowing orange dress and an embroidered orange hat covered with round mirrors the size of dimes. I wondered if Isabel could see herself in the hat, multiplied into a dozen smaller Isabels.

Isabel looked baffled. She told the woman, "I don't know you."

"I'm Ms. Shipra Brewer," the woman said.

Isabel still did not appear to connect her to anyone she knew. "Where are you from?" she asked.

"Why are you asking where I'm from?" Ms. Brewer answered. "Where are you from? What are you doing in New York?"

Isabel did not answer. She stood stock-still, with the same expression of puzzlement.

"In New York of all places," Ms. Brewer continued. "You aren't from this town, are you? Why are you trying to tell us how to run our schools?"

"I'm from southern Ohio," Isabel answered. "You must be that teacher's wife. I didn't make the connection. He's not from India."

"I'm not from India either," the woman answered. "Or Ohio. I am from New York, and I know that you're the person who's circulating this petition to have my husband fired."

She opened her bag and rummaged inside it, looking through its several zipped compartments until she found a photocopied page. She held the paper before Isabel's face. At the top was a brief paragraph, and under it ten lines that held printed names and addresses beside nine signatures: Myra Groot, Cicely Nohilly, Isabel Flood, Mahalia Daigle, Annie Strang, Josephine Strang, Barb Wroblewski, Mark Coker, Lucy Coker.

Ms. Brewer turned the paper around and read to Isabel, in a scornful tone:

We the undersigned disapprove of the teaching methods of Mr. Martin Brewer of Stein High School. He has assigned books during the school year

and in summer school which contain material offensive to Christian values.
He has tested our children on their knowledge of blasphemous literature after
teaching them about such subjects as abortion and the lives of sodomites. We
demand that the School Board remove this literature from its classroom and
library, and that it ask for Mr. Brewer's resignation because he is undermining
the morals of our children.

"What kind of nonsense is this, Ms. Flood?" Ms. Brewer demanded. "What
do you mean, 'our children'? You don't have any children at the high school.
Why don't you go back to wherever you come from and protect people
there?" Her tone of voice reminded me of Mahalia: Ms. Brewer's outrage
made her majestic, and the mirrors on her hat flashed like a thousand furious
eyes.

"The unborn don't live in any particular place," Isabel answered. "It
doesn't matter where I do my work."

Ms. Brewer viewed Isabel with a baffled expression. It was as if the two
women spoke the same language but used its words so differently that one
might as well have talked in French while the other answered in !Kung. I
felt uneasy standing between them and made a clicking sound with my
mouth, trying to say !*Kung.*

Ms. Brewer peered down at me. "This child is fidgeting so much, she looks
like she needs to be released overnight into a field." She eyed Isabel and
said, "This is not *your* daughter."

"She's in my charge," Isabel answered.

"What kind of parent would let you—" Ms. Brewer began, but then she
glanced at me again and stopped in midsentence. She continued, "Do her
parents know you're dragging her around town while you go door-to-door
handing out your outrageous pamphlets? I see your literature talks about
abortions being wrong in cases of rape too. Do you parade this little girl
around and make her listen to you talk about rape? Are you teaching her
about abortion and rape before she even knows how babies are made?"

"I know how babies are made," I said.

"You do, do you?" Ms. Brewer asked. "And I suppose you know exactly
what you're supposed to say about abortion too, don't you?"

When I was eight, if Isabel had walked me into the mouth of hell, I would
have lacked the perspective to view her actions with a critical eye. Her
mission work seemed unusual to me, but most of the things adults did around
me seemed odd and unprecedented. If Isabel thought my favorite books were
unsuitable for me, Ms. Brewer thought talk on abortion was, and I concluded
from both women's reactions that what was forbidden was bound to be

interesting, and I was partly grateful to Isabel for allowing me to witness and hear about some of things that other adults would not. Her dedication to the rights of the unborn did not stir up any passions in me, but also did not seem unreasonable to me. It would be years before I heard the word *rape* uttered again in my presence, and no one had told me yet that women sometimes cried when they learned they were with child; that a woman who already had children might herald another as the extinction of herself; that she might view a child's birth as a permanent bond to a man who was cruel and destructive; that many women would consider Isabel a threat and an enemy and risk their lives or take them rather than witness what she deemed the miracle of conception; and so I accepted what Isabel proclaimed and basically believed her.

"I think it's mean to murder babies," I said to Ms. Brewer.

I felt Isabel's hand tighten on my shoulder. When I looked up, she wore the same enraged expression I had seen her turn on Mr. Nohilly. She said evenly, "I am not continuing this conversation. I don't let people insult my religious beliefs, or persuade me to stop doing what I know is right. I will not stop circulating our petition. I do not allow myself to watch institutional sin destroy our children."

Ms. Brewer put her hand on one hip, and the mirrors on her sleeve glittered. " 'Institutional sin'? What kind of crazy idea is that?"

Isabel continued, "I don't care if the institution is a public high school and its agent is a schoolteacher. Sin is everywhere. The only innocents are the children, and they need to be cared for and buttressed against sin."

"What could you possibly know about caring for children?" Ms. Brewer asked. "The only way you're going to have children is by an immaculate conception!"

This is when Isabel began to sing a hymn. She turned away from Ms. Brewer and sang steadily in a voice that was surprisingly high and clear:

"*Take my love, my Lord, I pour
At thy feet its treasured store.*"

Ms. Brewer told Isabel, "You are out of your damn mind."

Isabel continued to sing, slightly louder, so that I could not make out the rest of what Ms. Brewer said. I also could not hear the rest of Isabel's hymn, because Ms. Brewer continued talking. Finally, Ms. Brewer leaned down to me and said, "Honey, I'm sorry you've had to watch this." She put her copy of Isabel's petition in her purse, closed it, crossed the street, and hurried away.

Isabel sang until Ms. Brewer had turned the corner. Afterward, she sat down on the curb, doubled over slightly. I sat beside her. "Just wait a moment, Penny," she said. "Sometimes I get these panicky heartbeats." She put her narrow hand on her collarbone and patted her chest until whatever she was feeling subsided.

Chapter Eight

Letters

By the end of June, when I still had not heard from my mother, I concluded that her cure was so terrible that it left her no energy to write us. Once, I suspected that she called. I heard Isabel saying in a hushed tone into my mother's bedroom telephone, "No, not tonight, I don't think so," and then, "I'm sorry, but the girls are both asleep now." I missed my mother so badly that my longing for her felt like a fishbone lodged in my windpipe that choked me when I tried to breathe too deeply. A feeling that was new to me, pure anxiety, would ripple along the skin of my arms when I sat alone with Mahalia and Isabel during evenings at home.

On the difficult Monday when we visited the Nohillys, Isabel was so affected by her news of Cicely's abortion that we ended mission rounds early. Isabel took me home and lay in bed until suppertime. I rattled around the house "like a dried pea in a tin can," my mother would have said. When Mahalia returned from Stein Evangelical that evening, I heard Isabel tell her, "The most terrible thing has happened. It's Cicely Nohilly's baby. I allowed my pride to interfere with my vision and blind me. I should have known that Cicely could slip as easily into sin as she had into the church." Mahalia closed the door behind her, and her voice and Isabel's rose together in high excited murmurs and sank in low mournful ponderings. Mahalia emerged from the bedroom with a grim look that seemed to say, *I'm in control.*

She told me, "We have to do something to cheer up Isabel." Mahalia called several women from Stein Evangelical and arranged an outing at Stein Lake with Isabel for the following Saturday.

Isabel continued her missions during the rest of the week, but with an air of exhaustion that was unusual. On Friday, Isabel chose for the first time that summer to remain home for an entire weekday rather than embark on a daily mission. She stayed in her bedroom, studying the Bible, reading religious tracts and articles on nutrition, perusing mail-order catalogs, and listening to a Christian radio station. When I tried to leave the house, Isabel called me back in. She knew I would get into trouble if I played outdoors unsupervised. The brightness of the summer sky made the living room seem darker and cramped as a womb. The bass notes of religious hymns from Isabel's radio beat against the upstairs floorboards like a monotonous heart, and I felt bored and pent up and lonely. I looked out the kitchen window: My tree was there, wobbling in the wind, lively and bright green with summer, but Isabel had forbidden me to climb it; she thought climbing trees was dangerous.

I played a game I called Russian roulette, bouncing a tennis ball off the living-room wall and catching it in progressively more difficult ways, until Isabel called downstairs and directed me to stop and to clean my bedroom. As I stripped the bed (she made us wash even the mattress covers), I saw the mailman through the bedroom window, entering our walkway. I heard Isabel on the stairs, and a moment later when I looked out my window, she emerged from the house to take a catalog and an envelope from him before he put it in our mail slot. The envelope was red, and she tucked it into her brocade purse.

She closed the downstairs door, came up to my room, and said, "Penny, I'll be studying until dinnertime. Don't disturb me and don't leave the house until Mahalia comes home and can go outside with you." As soon as Isabel closed her bedroom door, I walked quietly downstairs, and guided by whim or intuition, looked inside her purse for the red envelope.

It was from Louisiana and opened easily with a single tug. The envelope contained two letters: one from my mother, addressed to Mahalia and me, and another written on a cocktail napkin and addressed to Isabel. I began the one for us first:

> My beautiful girls—
>   I miss you very much and hope you are not unhappy. Why are you always asleep or away when I call? David has found some anole lizards for you, Penny. We used to play with them when we were children. We held them up to our ears and made them bite our earlobes and dangle like earrings.

They change color like chameleons. David and F. X. also tore up some ferns from a swamp behind The Place and stuck them in jars of peat moss for you, Mahalia. F. X. swears they are something left from a time dinosaurs ruled Louisiana.

F. X. is all excited because Tulane has accepted him as an anthropology student. To celebrate, he explored part of the Appalachian Trail this last week and returned this morning wearing a red bandanna. He says the women hikers wear bandannas tied like pirates' scarves. Their dogs also wear bandannas, even the girl dogs. There's no doubting that hiking the Appalachian Trail is a life many dogs would kill for.

I understand camping to be the kind of thing you are supposed to convince people you enjoy, and I will try when we leave next week. I do not like lying on pine cones at night, or waking up cold and mosquito-bitten. I will miss my feather pillow.

I heard Isabel open her upstairs door, and I folded my mother's letter quickly and put it back in the envelope. The other letter, the one written on the cocktail napkin, was gone: It was not in the envelope, and I did not find it when I looked a little frantically on the floor around me and inside the purse. I stuffed the envelope back in Isabel's handbag. She did not catch me. I was sitting on the couch, three yards from her purse, when she came downstairs.

All afternoon, I waited for Isabel to mention my mother's letter to me. I reasoned that Isabel either would notice that the envelope had been opened already and would speak to me about pillaging her pocketbook, or in the alternative, that she would believe the envelope's flap had become unglued by itself, and would simply give me my mother's letter. Isabel did neither. When Mahalia came home, we all ate dinner together quietly, and then Isabel went to bed. As had happened on those occasions when she had not mentioned spying me at the Stein Tavern, and at Reverend Bender's Wednesday night prayer meeting, I was left to wonder whether she had simply decided not to acknowledge facts she must have in her possession.

———

The following day at lunch, while Isabel, Mahalia, and I ate cheese sandwiches and drank Isabel's sour lemonade, a current of letters rushed through the mail slot. Isabel picked them up, along with a paper she found protruding from under our doormat beneath the slot. I recognized the paper—it was the cocktail napkin, addressed to her, that I had lost the day before. Isabel studied the napkin at the kitchen table and said to herself, "Who would write such a thing?" She put down the napkin, frowned, and told me, "Penny, you know the rule. You have to eat five bites." She picked up the napkin again, reread it, and said, with a trace of satisfaction, "It must be that teacher who wrote this letter." She refolded it, and left it at her place, put the rest of the mail on the counter, and washed her plate. When she finished, she said, "You girls do your dishes. Mahalia, I'd like you to keep an eye on Penny while I stop by my house to retrieve some materials." Isabel put on her helmet-hat, lifted her stack of mail off the counter, and took it with her. Just before she stepped out the door, she turned and said, "Thank you, Mahalia, for arranging the outing at the lake."

I snatched the napkin from Isabel's place mat as soon as Mahalia rose to do the dishes. The letter scrawled on the napkin had no return address. It said:

Ms. Flood, Pro-Life Division
Stein Evangelical Church
Stein, New York

Dear Ms. Flood:

There is much talk out in your world about the rights of fetuses, yet rarely do any of you pause to ask how we fetuses really feel. I, for one, wish that you could assemble the resources of your medical community to assure that I will never have to leave the comfortable sofa of my being, this dark and temperate womb. Whether it be abortion or birth, neither is suitable to our needs, both are precipitate ends, both are terrifying deaths. We therefore request that members of the so-called "right-to-life" organizations stop speaking for us. Their alacrity to pose as mouthpieces for us, to project their anxieties onto the blank slates of our fledgling lives, recalls to mind that curious and objectionable title by Robert Penn Warren, "Who Speaks for the Negro?" No one may speak for us, and those who do, do so at their peril, for what ghost is more potent than the ghost of What Might Have Been, of Who Might Have Been? Silence out there! Silence! We must sleep!

Sincerely,
F. E. (Fetus Elegante)

I recognized the handwriting as F. X.'s. I did not grasp the meaning of most of his letter, but I remember understanding its tone well enough to guess that F. X. hoped to ruffle Isabel.

Mahalia washed her plate and Isabel's, and then told me, "I'm not doing your dishes, Penny. You can wash your own plate yourself when you're done." I did not answer her. She continued, "Don't act bad when we go to the lake, Penny. A girl your age named Katie is going to be there, so try to act nice." Mahalia wore a yellow shirtwaist dress, and her mustard-seed pendant. Her hair was pulled back over her ears in a ponytail, the wiry strands that usually escaped pinned down with barrettes; at least she had not begun to wear a hat. She no longer seemed related to me; a tempest no longer blew through both our lives and bound us together like sailors braving crashing waves. At night, Mahalia read children's religious books in order to prepare for classes she taught at camp, or she read the Bible, whispering the verses aloud. When I looked at her, I felt an emptiness swell inside me. The night before, I had dreamed that I leaned over to touch her in her bed, and she had no depth—she lay on it like a shadow and seeped into the sheets like water into sand.

As the Jeep headed to Stein Lake's picnic grounds for the outing Mahalia had planned, Isabel told her, "This is so thoughtful of you, Mahalia. I've been so focused on myself all week, that I've failed to prize the people around me."

Mahalia sat in the back seat between two coolers filled with corn-on-the-cob and barbecued chicken she had made not from our mother's perfect recipe, but from one of Isabel's nutrition magazines. I sat beside Isabel in the front seat. Light glinted off the sun shade's mirror above me—I pushed it up hastily, to avoid catching my reflection.

I said, "My mother once swam naked in the lake with one of the other secretaries. It was so dark they couldn't see the beach."

"Penny," Mahalia began.

Isabel interrupted, saying, "That would be a dangerous thing to attempt, Penny. If you can't see the shore, you could drown." She took my hand and held it the rest of the way as she drove, as if she were concerned that she could not let me out of her grasp even as I sat in the Jeep next to her.

We stopped at a small yellow house with a collapsed porch and paint peeling in large sheets onto the ground around it; it made me think of a woman whose slip is showing.

"They must be piss-poor," I whispered to myself.

"What did you say?" Mahalia asked, but I ignored her. A girl who looked about Mahalia's age stood at a front window, jiggling a baby. Mrs. Wroblewski emerged from the front door, wearing black maternity pants with a small hole in the knee, and carrying an enormous orange cooler. She sat down beside Mahalia, holding the cooler in her lap. "I made enough punch for an army," she told Mahalia. "And not a one of my children would come. Maybe I should have had sixteen instead of eight, and then at least one would have liked to go to church!"

Mahalia laughed, but Isabel answered, "Sometimes you just have to make them attend, Barb."

"I'm glad to get away from them!" Mrs. Wroblewski answered.

"Who's staying with the children?" Isabel asked.

"My oldest girl, Roberta, can pretty much watch them single-handedly now," Mrs. Wroblewski said. "She hates it. I figure, good! Let her get a little taste of it now, and maybe she'll postpone boyfriends for a while."

Mahalia laughed again, a little uncertainly, looking at Isabel, but Isabel was concentrating on the road and did not answer. She turned toward the lake. Evening was collecting in stagnant pools on the edges of the woods bordering the water. The lake looked still and well-behaved.

Mrs. Groot and Nicky were already at the shore when we arrived. Lucy Coker sat at a picnic table wearing a faded sundress, and her father appeared behind her from a clump of woods, carrying a stack of kindling. Mr. Coker had braided his beard and secured the end with a rubber band; I had never seen a man do this to his beard before.

As we disembarked from the Jeep, Mrs. Groot called, "Here's Izzy, the girl of the day!" Isabel waved as she got out of the car.

"Where's Annie Strang?" Mahalia asked.

Mrs. Groot answered, "Annie's still on her way with Katie." Mrs. Groot had tied a red scarf around her neck that reminded me of a turkey wattle. She wore a red pantsuit and heeled red sandals that made it difficult for her to walk in the sandy soil around the picnic table. She told me, "You and Katie should have a good time together."

Lucy and Mahalia unloaded the bags of food. Mr. Coker had dug a pit and filled it with coals from a paper sack. "Everyone knows by now that this charcoal is not healthy," he said to no one in particular, his back to us all. Off of his own property, he seemed uncomfortable and did not approach Isabel or the other women. He continued to talk, half to himself, as he bent over the coals. "It's a shame," he said, "to ruin good corn and chicken and sausage this way." On the picnic table behind him were a stack of his red blood sausage and one of his jars of horseradish labeled COKER'S BITTER HERBS: **NOT** ORGANICALLY GROWN.

"Don't worry, Mark," Isabel said. "We've wrapped everything carefully in aluminum foil to protect it."

"One day they'll tell us that aluminum is as dangerous as lead," he answered.

Mrs. Groot hovered behind him, watching. "Why don't you come to our women's group meetings, Mark?" she asked him. "We need a male voice to guide us sometimes."

"Now, what would I do there?" Mr. Coker asked. "With all you women gabbing away around me? I just come to things like this outside the church to chaperone Lucy."

"Lucy," Isabel asked. "How's your poem for the pregnant teens' motherhood booklet going?"

"I'm kind of stumped on it," Lucy said. "I'm having trouble thinking up rhymes."

"She'll get it done on time," Mr. Coker said.

As Lucy and Mahalia unpacked the food onto picnic tables, Nicky wandered down the beach without saying hello to me first. I waited with the women for Katie to come and loitered beside Mr. Coker as he pushed corncobs wrapped in foil between rocks laid in a circle around the coals.

Isabel kneeled to help him, but Mrs. Groot stopped her, saying, "No Izzy, you just sit. You're the Lady of Honor." Isabel perched at the table and perused a pamphlet. Mrs. Wroblewski and Mrs. Groot shook out a large green tablecloth and laid out dishes and silverware.

"I'm so glad that little girl Katie will have a playmate," Mrs. Wroblewski said. "She hasn't made it out to the church get-togethers too much this summer."

"Sometimes Annie's a little disorganized," Mrs. Groot said. "But she promised to bring Katie this time. She couldn't believe it about Cicely Nohilly!"

"What's to believe?" Mrs. Wroblewski answered. She rummaged through a bag and asked, "Where's the dessert, Myra?"

Isabel replied, "I called Myra and asked her not to bring dessert, because of Penny."

"What's Nicky doing?" Mrs. Groot asked.

We all turned around—it was plain enough what he was doing. He was standing in the water with his shoes on, halfway down the beach, smoking a cigarette.

"Penny," Isabel said, "run and fetch Nicky. Tell him we need to know what he wants for supper."

I skittered down the beach, thinking, *No dessert!* I turned once and saw that neither Isabel nor Mrs. Groot had taken their eyes off of me, as if they intended to come after me immediately if anything went wrong. I wasn't sure whom they were watching—me or Nicky. When I arrived where Nicky stood, he turned away from me, into the wind, cupping his hand around a match; he was lighting a new cigarette. He wore blue jeans and a blue jean shirt and a black windbreaker, and his hair was pulled back in a miniature ponytail. The bottoms of his jeans were soaked, and his shoes were filled with water.

"Why are you standing in the water with your shoes on?" I asked him.

"Because I feel like it," he answered.

"They all want you to come back and tell them what you want to eat." I walked into the water next to him, smirked, and said, "They want to know do you want Mr. Coker's *blood sausage?*"

I thought Nicky would smirk with me, but instead he answered, "Mark's a cool guy. He showed me this." Nicky pulled a crumpled paper from his windbreaker pocket. "Do you know what this is? It's a Justifiable Homicide Pact." I looked at the paper: It was a typed page with a place for two signatures at the bottom. He crumpled it back into his pocket. "It says in some cases, it's all right to kill people because they're killing *you.* Know what I mean? Like, if people kill babies, you can kill them to stop them. This man named Mr. Petty gave the pact to Mark, and he signed it, and now I'm going to sign too." I was flattered that Nicky was speaking to me as an equal.

"I think that's cool," I said. Nicky nodded, as if my opinion mattered to him. "I think you should be able to kill people who are trying to kill you," I told him. I did not want to upset our momentary friendship by asking what you had to do if you signed a justifiable homicide pact.

We heard the women's voices rise behind us in a flurry of laughter. I turned to look at them across the rim of the lake: They seemed unrelated to me, like a distant, disturbing recollection. I thought abruptly of my mother, and how far away she was. A frightening image came into my mind, of her standing far away, on the opposite side of a hazy gray river, gazing at me as if she could not remember my name. I felt a stab of anxiety and turned back toward Nicky.

Nicky snickered. "Mark says those women from The Flood's church are like a pack of cackling barnyard chickens."

"I heard him say that too." I did not tell Nicky that Mr. Coker had directed a similar statement at me and his own daughter. I was uncertain how to carry on a conversation with a teenager. I added, "I think they sound like bony sex-starved virgins."

Nicky guffawed, and then doubled over laughing. He straightened up and said, "I can't believe you're Mahalia's little sister."

I laughed too; I liked him, because he liked me. "Sometimes, I can't believe she's my big sister," I said honestly.

He laughed again. "She's such a stuck-up priss," he said. "I once whistled at her when she was walking along the road with Isabel, and she didn't even turned around. She pretended like I wasn't even alive."

I thought that no one except Nicky Groot would whistle at a girl who had Isabel at her side. It occurred to me for the first time that this was part of the reason my sister had attached herself to Isabel. I found myself defending Mahalia, in spite of everything. "She's sort of shy," I told Nicky.

"Naw," he answered. "She just thinks she's better than everybody else." He turned his back to me, and I drew up alongside him, the lake lapping my shoes: He pulled a glass flask from his windbreaker pocket, unscrewed it, and took a sip from it.

"Vodka," he said, putting the cap back on. "The thing about vodka is, if you mix it into juice or soda or punch or something, it doesn't have any taste and so it's hard to smell on your breath. Dump it into a can of Coke and you can drink it all day and no one will know. I can't take these women's church things without it."

"How come they're all so het up about you?" I asked him. "No one will tell me."

"Oh, different stuff," he said. "I steal things. I hit this teacher. I set a fire in Mr. Canon's parking lot. Big deal. I didn't burn anything except a pile of garbage." He handed the flask to me and said, "Do you want to taste it?"

I unscrewed the cap; I did not want to turn down Nicky's gesture of friendship. I sipped the vodka: It burned my throat going down and left a bad feeling in my mouth, like bitter medicine.

"Penny!" Mahalia cried, right behind me. I stuck the flask under my sweater. "What are you doing with your feet in the water!"

She had come down the beach with Mrs. Groot, and when I turned around, I noticed that Mahalia was trying as hard as possible not to look at Nicky—that his very presence bothered her. The expression on her face irked me. It was the same one she wore when she was trying to ignore me, and I felt sorry for Nicky. I backed toward him, but he was already walking away from us, down the beach. I saw him as Mahalia must have, as a dangerous boy, and then as I believed he was: as someone who had talked to me as if I were a regular person, who did not try to make me feel small because I was younger than him.

"Nicky! Nicky!" Mrs. Groot called, walking after him. "Supper is almost ready to serve!" I felt the vodka flask pressed between my upper arm and rib cage. I wondered how I would get the flask back to Nicky.

"You shouldn't talk with Nicky that long," Mahalia said. "Why did you copy him by standing in the water? Why couldn't you just have done what Isabel told you, and asked him what he wanted for supper and come back?" There was an edge of something in her voice—worry or discomfort or anger.

"He's a lot nicer than you are," I answered, but she acted as if she did not catch my words. I followed her back toward the picnic tables. Mr. Coker had arranged a stack of logs in a campfire pit and was bending over a small flame, fanning it. I screwed the cap on the flask underneath my sweater. I took the flask from under my arm, slipped it inside my skirt pocket and buttoned my sweater over it. I was disappointed to see that Katie had not arrived yet—I worried that she might not come at all.

"Now Penny's cold," Mahalia said with exasperation. "Look at her buttoning her sweater!"

"Take your shoes and socks off," Isabel told me, "and let them dry next to the fire. I brought some dry socks in case something like this happened." She pulled a pair of my knee socks from her brocade bag, and I pulled them on.

Behind Mahalia, Mrs. Groot was trudging toward us up the beach, without Nicky. Nicky was at the far edge of the lake, strolling slowly away from us all.

"Look at the sun over the lake!" Lucy cried. Everyone turned politely toward the sun: It had dipped into the trees over Nicky's shoulder, turning them dark yellow. Tree shadows fell like broomsticks across the water.

"This is the most romantic time of day," Lucy said.

Mrs. Wroblewski teased her, "That's the kind of thinking that got you into the state you're in." But Lucy didn't laugh: She turned away, looking upset. Mrs. Wroblewski stopped setting out paper cups. Her eyes on Lucy, she pronounced, "I only wish I could say that's what got *me* into the state *I'm* in." Then Lucy laughed, and Mrs. Wroblewski turned back to the table.

"Where's that girl, Katie?" I asked.

"Penny," Isabel told me. "Annie Strang's flaw is that she's not always punctual or dependable." I heard a familiar jingling—it was Isabel tinkering with one of her puzzles.

"Maybe she'll still show up," Mrs. Wroblewski told me. She opened a pack of paper cups and filled them with bright red punch from the cooler.

Mrs. Groot arrived, saying, "Nicky will be coming back on his own steam."

Mr. Coker told her, "I'll go get him, Myra, if you keep an eye on the chicken and sausage." He set off down the darkening shore. I thought he looked relieved to escape the women gathered around me. He walked quickly and did not wait for Mrs. Groot to answer him.

"Barb, none for Penny," Isabel said, as Mrs. Wroblewski began filling an eighth cup with punch. "Penny, I packed milk for you."

I must have looked disappointed, because Mrs. Groot asked, "She can't have Hawaiian Punch?"

"The dye in those punches makes Penny antsy," Isabel said.

"It makes her punchy!" Mahalia cried. She and Isabel laughed together, infuriatingly.

"I don't want milk!" I said.

"Then just drink water," Isabel answered. "But I thank you for bringing the punch, Barb. And I'd be glad if you poured me some." It did not occur to me that Isabel might simply wish to be gracious to Mrs. Wroblewski, despite Isabel's own compunctions about drinking punch herself. I felt that Isabel was flaunting her right as an adult to do whatever she wanted.

"What good is a barbecue where there's no kids and no dessert and no punch?" I asked.

"Come sit down here by me," Isabel answered. She removed her helmet hat; her hair slipped down, so that I could see only her foxy pointed nose. She tugged me beside her onto a slab of rock near the campfire. I wondered if she could smell the vodka on my breath, despite Nicky's pronouncement that this was not possible. However, Isabel did not lean too close to me, and I reminded myself that Isabel had not ever kissed me on my mouth, or even hugged me. I felt the flask of liquor in my pocket. I took off my sweater, and hiding the flask under it, moved the bottle to my lap.

"Everything's ready!" Lucy called. "It'll burn if we wait any longer."

I could not make out Nicky's or Mr. Coker's shape on the shore. The fire flickered on the ground beside us. I stared at it until I was able to imagine it as a piece of hell that had broken through the earth.

"We'll stick some food aside for the boys," Mrs. Wroblewski said.

Everyone sat down on the ground around the fire. All the women asked for chicken, and turned down Lucy's offers of blood sausage. Mrs. Wroblewski waved the sausage away, saying, "Lucy, I have to tell you that stuff makes me want to scream when I look at it."

"I'll have sausage," Isabel told her.

"Which one do you want?" Lucy asked.

Isabel balanced her cup on the rock between her hip and me, and she turned toward Lucy, leaning over the plate of red sausages and examining them in the firelight. In the darkness behind her, I pulled the vodka flask from under my sweater and unscrewed the cap.

"I'll have the small one there," Isabel said.

I poured half of the remaining vodka into Isabel's cup of punch.

"My only regret is that Cicely Nohilly can't be with us here tonight," Isabel said.

"We don't need her, Izzy," Mrs. Wroblewski answered.

"No, but her child needed us," Isabel answered. "And I take responsibility for the fact that my pride prevented me from protecting him." She took a sip from her punch. I waited for her to sputter when she drank the vodka, but she betrayed no reaction at all. I could not tell if Isabel was refusing to register outwardly a fact which she was privy to, or whether she simply had so little experience with liquor that she could not recognize it when she tasted it. Or could what Nicky said be true—that mixed with punch, vodka was oddly undetectable to adults?

"What's all this about your pride, Isabel?" Mrs. Wroblewski asked. The twilight had blackened into night, and the fire made her feathery hair look shiny and dark, like the hackles of a rooster.

Isabel answered, "I allow my pride in my dedication to God to let me believe I am infallible sometimes, and at every step God proves me wrong."

"I think it's too much, the way you keep dwelling on your pride, Izzy," Mrs. Groot said. "You're the only one who sees yourself that way."

Isabel took another sip of her punch and said, in her peculiar, formal tone, "That's because I know myself, Myra. It has to do with how I found God. You know I was raised in a Catholic home for girls. The priests and nuns there were very harsh with us, and one of the ways they used to punish us was by making us feel that if we were in their bad graces, we would be cut off from God. The priests acted as if they held the key to God's kingdom. One of them even told us that the children of unwed mothers could never go to heaven." Isabel stopped speaking, as if this subject upset her so much that she could not talk easily about it. She sipped her punch again and continued, "One morning when I was about ten years old, I woke up and thought, 'Why, I don't need priests to talk to God. I don't need their permission to rejoice in God's creations. I can speak directly to Him.' After that, I refused to go to Mass—I saw how wrong the Holy Church was to try to hold a child at a distance from God, by forcing her to communicate through priests. I was amazed no one else had ever thought of such a thing." Isabel took another swallow from her cup, smiled her half-smile, and exclaimed, "And then when I was twelve, I found out someone else *had* thought of it—and his name was Martin Luther!" The women smiled with her, a little uncertainly, as if, like me, they were not quite sure who Martin Luther was.

"You can imagine how foolish I felt, thinking I had invented a new religion on my own! My pride had allowed me to pull out of the clutches of the Catholic church, but it had also prevented me from knowing there was such a thing as Protestantism. Imagine!" Isabel's formal tone seemed to lose its grip on her words, so that she finished speaking in an ordinary voice. "That's why my pride has been so hard for me to wrestle with. Because although it's my flaw, it's also the thing that led me out of darkness toward God. I have trouble knowing when it's a bad thing, and when it's a good thing. I can't tell you how I used to feel when I lay in bed at night, believing that the only church I knew had the power to separate us from God. I was afraid I would die in my sleep, and then end up in the flames of eternity. It was the injustice of it all! It was bad enough that they withheld meals to punish us and denied us privacy when we bathed and hit us with their switches and paddles and shoe-soles. But the fact that a child could be allowed to fall into hell and kidnapped from God so easily—" Isabel took a large gulp of her drink, and then she began coughing—I thought surely she would realize now that the punch had something else in it. Instead she stood up, thumping her chest and saying, "Excuse me!"

Lucy patted her on the back, and Mrs. Wroblewski said, "Get her some more punch!" She ran to the table, filled Isabel's cup at the cooler again, and handed the cup to Isabel, who waved it away. Mrs. Wroblewski put it on a rock near the fire and said, "Just take shallow, short breaths, Izzy." I poured the rest of Nicky's flask into Isabel's punch.

Isabel sat back down and said, "What a commotion!" She breathed deeply and took a deep swallow of her punch. "I feel much better now. Thank you, girls."

"I could tell stories about nuns that would make your skin crawl," Mrs. Wroblewski said. "There was a nun at All Saints who used to punish boys by making them take their arms out of their shirtsleeves, and then tying the sleeves behind their backs so that they had to go all day without the use of their hands. And before her, there was Sister Jane who—"

Isabel interrupted her, to my dismay, saying, "I'm older now, Barb. I've learned that it's not productive to harp on those things. I try instead to see my own flaws clearly and to keep abreast of them. It was a proud thing for me to believe I could rope in Cicely Nohilly with three visits! I don't know what I could have been thinking!"

"If you ask my opinion," Mrs. Wroblewski said, "all the Nohillys should have been drowned at birth. Cicely's mother married a living nightmare. Do you remember Cicely's mother, Myra? She went to All Saints and worked at the drugstore after school? Her name was Carol and she looked like a wet mouse? No one could believe it when Brian Nohilly's parents made him marry her. That boy was born with a heart missing. That fellow David your mother's going around with," Mrs. Wroblewski said to Mahalia, who looked down into her lap as if she did not want to be reminded of our mother at all, "once took out Brian Nohilly's lights for tying Antonia Liquore to a telephone pole in seventh grade after making her take off everything but her slip and kneesocks. A few days later, Brian tried to kill David in a hockey game. It took two men to pull Brian off of him, and both Father Flaherty and Father Lafayette went and hid in the bleachers. The entire Catholic church was terrified of Brian Nohilly by then. God knows how he even noticed Cicely's mother. He must have stepped on her by mistake one day. I never heard her say a word during all my years at All Saints. That girl Essie Starkey used to sit on her during every lunch period, in the school bathroom—"

"There's a girl named Persis Boards who does that to people in my class now," I said.

"Nothing ever changes," Mrs. Wroblewski answered.

Isabel took another swallow from her cup; when she set it back down, I saw that it was nearly empty.

"What Cicely Nohilly does is not your fault," Mahalia told Isabel. "And I still don't know why you're always blaming your pride for everything." Mahalia told the other women, "I've never seen Isabel being snooty. And anyway, she has a right to be proud of herself. She never acts angry or falls apart like a lot of people. She has—she has inner strength." I doubted my sister's judgment—I had seen Isabel fastening that look of rage on Mr. Nohilly's corpse. I knew, at least, that she could get angry.

"We all have flaws," Isabel said. "Annie Strang's is that she lacks punctuality and maturity—no one would ever think to call her 'Miss Strang,' would they? It's always 'Annie.' And Penny's flaw is that she has to learn restraint." She put her hand on my leg, half patting it, half holding it down. "Not that that's not such a terrible fault as faults go, Penny. And Myra's flaw is that she cares more about appearing to be kind than standing up to people to do what's right." I saw Mrs. Groot's face crumple in the firelight across from me. She looked hurt, and then a little furious, and then hurt again. "And Lucy's is that she dissembles and does not keep the command-ment to honor her father by being forthright with him. If she had not been inclined to dissembling, she would not have fallen into a situation where she got pregnant." Lucy did not answer; she bent her head so that I could not see her face. "And yours, Barb, is that you make jokes about things that aren't funny as a way of excusing your irreverence, and this is an insult to God."

"Well, I plead guilty to that!" Mrs. Wroblewski said and laughed, but she stopped, suddenly dampened, when no one laughed with her. I realized then that Isabel never smiled at Mrs. Wroblewski's jokes.

"What's Mahalia's?" I asked. "What's her flaw?"

"Mahalia," Isabel said. "Mahalia's still in the making. To be honest, I never have found any flaws in her yet."

If I had been a little older, I might have recognized this as a pronounce-ment of love—as the kind of unconditional acceptance of someone that accompanies love, but instead I simply thought that it was unfair.

"And my flaw is pride," Isabel said. "And oh, I work and work away at it, and sometimes I think I just get farther and farther from overcoming it."

"At least you don't have to wear your fault sticking out to here like I do," Lucy said. There was a dead silence, and Mrs. Wroblewski laughed. Lucy joined her, and Mrs. Groot followed with a relieved, high titter. Mahalia looked at Isabel and chuckled, and Isabel laughed once, loudly, a big belting guffaw. I was shocked—I had never heard Isabel laugh outright before, or even chuckle or snicker. I had heard her giggle once, and had seen one corner of her mouth drawn up in a half-smile, but that was all.

"You sound like a flock of night crows!" Mr. Coker pronounced, appearing suddenly out of the darkness. The women cackled a little longer, as if they were laughing at him.

"Myra, I talked to Nicky for a while," Mr. Coker said, "and he just wanted to walk home by himself, so I let him go."

"Oh dear," Myra answered. "He'll be hungry."

"We'll wrap the boy something and send it home with you," Mrs. Wrob-lewski said.

"No you won't," Mark said. "I'm so hungry I'm going to eat everything." However, when Lucy handed him the plate of sausages, he seemed dismayed that so many were left.

"No one here likes my sausage?" Mr. Coker asked.

"Isabel had one," Lucy told him. "And she ate some horseradish too."

"Well, God bless Isabel," he answered.

"I don't feel well," Isabel said suddenly.

"What's wrong?" Mahalia asked.

Isabel stood up and said, "I feel—headachy and woozy."

The women fell into a jumble of clucks and exclamations around Isabel.

"We need to get this lady home," Mrs. Wroblewski pronounced.

"You just go right ahead and take her," Myra said. "We'll clean up." I heard her mutter, out of Mr. Coker's hearing, "I wonder if it was the sausage. She's the only one who ate it."

"Come on, Izzy," Mrs. Wroblewski said. "I'll take you home in the church Jeep, and then drive myself home and return the Jeep to you in the morning."

"Lucy," Isabel said. "If you start to feel bad, you should see a doctor right away. These sudden things are sometimes food poisoning, and that wouldn't be good for you in your condition."

"I feel fine," Lucy answered.

"I'll keep an eye on her," Mr. Coker said.

"I hope we haven't gone and poisoned Izzy when we meant to give her a good time!" Mrs. Groot cried, leading Isabel to the Jeep. She settled Isabel into the front seat, and Mahalia and I climbed into the back while Mrs. Wroblewski turned on the ignition.

"You've just had a long week, Izzy," Mrs. Wroblewski ventured as she took the road home, but Isabel did not answer. She had fallen dead asleep. When we reached the house, Mrs. Wroblewski had to shout her name three times before Isabel woke up. Mrs. Wroblewski carried in Isabel's brocade bag and walked her up the stairs. She left Isabel's purse on the armchair. Seeing it, I suddenly remembered my mother's letters: I opened Isabel's brocade bag and went through it quickly. It contained a comb, a plastic box of her gold paper clips, some pamphlets, and a coin purse—the red envelope that had held my mother's letter was gone.

Mrs. Wroblewski came back downstairs and said, "You girls call if Isabel needs anything."

After she left, Isabel lay in bed for two hours with a wet rag on her head. When Mahalia brought her a cup of pale tea, Isabel told her, "I no longer think it's food poisoning. It must be a flu. I have the beginnings of a bad headache, although I'm not running a fever. Mahalia, I don't want you to miss church in the morning out of worry for me. Call Mrs. Wroblewski and ask her to use the church Jeep to take you with her in the morning. Please get Penny into bed."

I felt a little sorry for Isabel. Even then, it did not occur to me that she was not sick—I did not connect her symptoms with my mother's hangovers.

After Mahalia and I put on our nightgowns and got into bed, she told me, "Don't you dare give Isabel a hard time when she's sick. I'm coming straight home after church tomorrow!" The tone in her voice was threatening and scornful. (I realized at that moment that Isabel was never scornful.) When I turned over all the events of the day, I felt worn out by Mahalia's constant admonishments—I saw that we had not just grown apart; Mahalia had moved imperceptibly toward a state in which, when she was not ignoring me, she constantly strove to keep me in line in a way she never would have with my mother home. In fact, Mahalia would have resented my mother if she had asked her to take such a heavy hand in correcting me. I could not puzzle out what it was that had made Mahalia change toward me, but I saw by its timing alone that it had to do with Isabel's presence.

I asked Mahalia, partly to goad her, "Why doesn't Mama call us?"

"She called right after F. X. left," Mahalia answered. "But I told her I didn't want to speak to her."

I asked angrily, "Why didn't you get me?"

"She wasn't even supposed to be using the telephone," Mahalia answered. "She said it was against the rules."

"Has she written us any letters?"

"No," Mahalia said. "She hasn't bothered." And then, perhaps out of concern for me, Mahalia added, "Maybe it's hard for Mama to find paper where she is." The idea was so ridiculous that it irritated me. While Mahalia drifted off to sleep, I lay in bed, staring at the luminescent dust motes that were always there, swirling like a whirlpool in the air above me. After half an hour, I heard Isabel's steps outside in the hall. The bathroom door shut, and the bathwater turned on. The pipes vibrated and made a mournful sound: *ooooh*. I closed my eyes and asked Mahalia, "Are you awake?" She did not answer. I pressed my face into my pillow until I saw sunbursts of color behind my eyelids that dissipated at the corners in a blackness that seemed friendless and ungiving. I realized that Isabel was never going to deliver my mother's letter to us. I wondered if there had been others she had hidden.

I slipped out of bed and walked down the hall, past the bathroom. I heard Isabel splashing inside. I thought of how my mother would sometimes let me skip taking a bath for a week "just to enjoy the feeling of being dirty," she would say. "Only children really know how to enjoy being grimy." I slipped into Isabel's bedroom—my mother's bedroom. I opened the top drawer of my mother's bedside table, but found nothing there—Isabel had emptied the drawer, so that my mother's supply of chocolates was gone. The water in the bathroom turned off, and I stopped dead still, listening like a burglar: The bathtub was quiet. I opened the bedside table's other drawers, but none of them revealed that bright red flash of envelope, or any other envelopes like them. Isabel's puzzles filled the bottom drawer.

I looked on the shelf of my mother's closet, but the red envelope was not there either: I found only my mother's feather pillow, stripped of its cover, pushed into the back of the closet like a hidden murdered man. I tried the top drawer of her wardrobe, and there, behind a nest of scarves, were my mother's chocolates! They were high mounds full of dark liquid. I put three in my mouth and a handful in my pocket. My mother had once made fun of those chocolates, saying they looked like women's breasts, something that would never occur to Isabel, sploshing away in her bathtub with the bathroom door locked. My mother was not afraid to bathe with the door open, to walk around the house naked, revealing the red hair between her legs, her friendly bottom, the dark stripe that raced downward from her navel.

On top of my mother's dresser were her familiar bobby pins, and her lipsticks: coral, bloodred, rose-red—and eye shadows in every shade of brown and green, like chameleon dust. There were several compacts containing blush. My mother had once let me try on her blush—it felt as if I had a light coat of pink fur. In the middle of her dresser top was a brass stand of six cylinders joined at the hip, each holding a perfume. I had smelled them all before, and I reopened them now: There was the one that almost made you faint, like a lilac pushed up to your nose; the one beside it was the mere memory of a smell, a plum sniffed a year ago; next were a scent that was heady and dizzying, like Wild Turkey; vanilla mixed with wet leaves; skunk; and rose water. Every scent reminded me of her. It was almost as if she were in the room, as though, if I only turned around quickly enough, I would find her there.

Inside my mother's second dresser drawer were more scarves—green and blue, and every shade in between: sea green, pea green, snap bean green, parakeet blue, peacock blue, the blue of iridescence, of oil on water; and browns—cinnamon brown and black-brown like dark tea, and chocolate and coffee. (No red envelope underneath.) There was a green oriental scarf with a pressed wrinkled pattern that looked like lipsticked mouths. In a separate, inner drawer was my mother's hefty jewelry box, containing a pirate's booty of jumbled jewelry: her single real jewel, her engagement ring with a pawnshop tag on it from a time she had hocked it. All around her ring were enamel bracelets, plastic necklaces thrown from Mardi Gras floats, gaudy pins shaped like fruit or flowers or animals with pin sabers, all made of glass more glittery than diamonds—oh the joyous power of being my mother! I loved the idea of imitation diamonds, rubies, sapphires—a trick played on the rich—I thought our reds were redder, our greens greener, our blues as sparkly as the ocean. (But I would not wear jewels; I would carry a sword.) Under these was a flat drawer containing a sheaf of letters.

I recalled again what I had come into her room for—her letters. And here was a thick stack, all the letters she must have written that Isabel had hidden. I pulled them out—they were too old, a pile of typed carbon copies with my father's name at the bottom of each—letters my father must have sent to my mother. I felt disappointment and began to put them back, but stopped when I saw one which was not a carbon. It was written in blue ballpoint, and it fell away easily from the others—it had been clipped with several of Isabel's gold paper clips. I was mildly shocked to learn that Isabel must have looked in my mother's jewelry box at least once—I could not imagine her admiring jewels.

The date on the letter was Christmas, 1965, four years before I was born, and it began, *Dear Francis Xavier*. It took me a moment to identify F. X. with this name, because no one I knew had ever called F. X. by anything but his initials:

I welcomed your phone call, Francis Xavier, as I did not have any notion where to look for Marguerite until she called me, and was considerably worried. I had never been to the Stein Motor Inn, and when I went to retrieve her I was shocked that she would have subjected herself to circumstances that were so inherently dangerous.

It grieves me to tell you that your sister felt unable to rejoice in her pregnancy in part because her girlhood had been burdened by caring for a sibling with a handicap. I had no idea that she felt she could not mother a child who might have suffered the effects of exposure to German measles. As you know, I find the idea of truncating the lives of children because they might be handicapped repugnant, although my church is not opposed to such procedures. How could I, director of an institute for the blind, feel otherwise?

I believe our daughter Mahalia would have benefited from the company of a younger sibling, whether or not the sibling proved impaired. Even at her young age, Mahalia is a girl who possesses an unnerving timidity and insistence on predictability, qualities which I have always wrestled against within myself. The presence of a sibling might have made her less rigid in this respect.

I was not offended that you told me I was being hard-hearted and judgmental, any more than I thought you would be offended by my suggestion

*that you see a psychiatrist to determine if your bouts of mania could be organic
in origin and regulated with doses of some kind of medicine.*

    *It is difficult for me to accept the decision of my wife, but I remain dedi-
cated to our marriage, in consonance with my marriage vows. Marguerite
has never been a simple person to—*

My father's letter ended abruptly here. Under his fine, neat blue print
were the words, written furiously in my mother's script: *Joseph, you are a
damn fool if you really intend to mail this to my brother.*

Attached to the letter with one of Isabel's gold paper clips was a carbon copy
of a second, short note written by my father, also addressed to *Francis Xavier:*

    *I regret to inform you that Marguerite miscarried our child on December
27, this year of 1965. It was a boy. The baby apparently suffered from the
effects of Marguerite's exposure to German measles, and his premature end
was an act of God's wisdom and charity in these matters.*

With Fondest Regards,
Joseph Daigle

Although I saw that Isabel had been interested enough in the private details
of these letters to clip them with her paper clips, I do not think that I came
close to guessing that my father had been writing F. X. about an abortion
in his first letter, or that the second letter about my mother's miscarriage
might have been an effort to cover up an abortion. I already knew that my
mother had once lost a child in pregnancy. I also knew that German measles
damaged babies carried by pregnant women, because Mahalia and I had both
been vaccinated against German measles for this reason. However, I was
surprised to learn that my mother had lost her baby because she was exposed
to German measles, although I was not surprised that my mother had kept
this, like so many other things, secret from us.

    I heard a creak in the bathroom, and the sound of Isabel's body rising
from the water and stepping onto the cold tiles. I forced the sheaf of letters
back into the drawer, closed the jewelry box, rammed the drawer shut, and
headed for the hallway, but not in time. Isabel emerged from the bathroom
in her terry-cloth bathrobe, my mother's favorite towel wrapped in a turban
around her hair. "Penny, go to bed," she said. "Don't come into my room
to look for your mother's chocolates. They keep you up at night and they
aren't in the bedside table anymore." She waited in the hallway until I
climbed back into bed.

The following morning, I rose early, before Isabel and Mahalia awoke. I wrote my mother a letter, furtively, on an index card which I sealed immediately in an envelope. On it I printed the address F. X. had left on our refrigerator, although I fretted both that the letter might not reach my mother before she left for the Trail, and that I might be addressing it wrong in any case—I had never sent anyone a letter on my own before. I wrote on the envelope's back, *All you Sisters, please get this to my mother if she is on the Trail.* The letter said, simply:

> Dear Mama,
>
> Why can't I hike with you? I don't see why I have to stay with Isabel anymore. She steals your letters and pries around your dresser and messes with your things. I walk around every living minute in strangulation and cannot take this anymore.

I hurried down the street immediately, to mail the letter—I was not about to leave it around the house where Isabel could find it.

When Isabel and Mahalia arose that morning, Isabel was still feeling poorly and stayed in bed while Mahalia attended church. When Mahalia returned, I acted sullen and untalkative around her. She asked me what was wrong, but I smirked at her and did not answer: I saw that my silence irked her, although until then she had pretended she was unaware that her silences affected me. I huddled over my secrets, polishing them like rocks from Stein Lake. I had never had a real secret before, and now I was full of them: Isabel stole my letters, Isabel snooped in my mother's things, my mother still kept our father's letters. I understood for the first time how secrets were born— they came to be because you had no one with whom to share your fears or discoveries. I had never felt so lonely in my life.

Chapter Nine

Katie

*I*solation and belonging are not absolute, provable states of being. They arise completely out of the nothingness within you; you measure their dimensions against your own firm or shaky sense of who you are. This is one way I can explain the draw Stein Evangelical had on Mahalia. She believed that we were somehow cut off from the whole, outcasts who did not even know we were cut off. Before my mother left for the summer, I could not have understood Mahalia's feelings. If anything, I believed that our home was the center of things, the eye of the storm that made up our lives. However, two months after my mother's departure, I often had moments when I experienced an inversion of perspective and suddenly found myself on the craggy edge of everything, looking in.

Most of June and the first days of July, I followed Isabel like a shadow, from one house to another until I began to feel as if I had never had a different life, but had always resided in Isabel's world: a world inhabited by adults who barely acknowledged my presence and children who did not play with me. By the end of each day of mission work, I felt tenuous and unconnected to things, like a piece of flotsam dissolving upon the ocean.

The week of July 4 (Isabel did not take us to see fireworks), Mahalia told me that I was expected to attend a Sunday evening potluck and service at the church. I did not want to visit Stein Evangelical with Mahalia and Isabel. I longed to go to the lake, to ride an inner tube down the stream that crashed into the lake's mouth, to join the other children shrieking as if their necks had been cut when they submerged suddenly into white water.

"If you act the way you do at school," Mahalia told me, "they won't invite you back to the church." I was sitting on the back steps when she said this; I had hoped to sneak to our neighbor's yard and climb my tree. Mahalia passed me, carrying a small sack of peat moss and her jar of Hart's Tongue Ferns. She pulled out a trowel and dug in the fern bed nearest to the steps. The Ostrich Ferns that lined the house's back wall reached the top step now. When I squinted, I could make them look like the wild hairdo of a crazy woman.

"What if I don't want to go to the potluck?" I asked Mahalia.

Mahalia tucked the ferns from her jar into the dirt. They were tiny and pale, and curled into themselves, making me think of the *Life* magazine pictures of fetuses.

"Penny," Mahalia said in a patronizing tone. "Isabel told Reverend Bender she was inviting you."

"Why did she do that?" I asked.

"Because you don't have any friends," Mahalia answered.

In the days before the church's potluck supper, Isabel seemed fretful in a way that was unusual to her. She stayed up later at night, reading tracts written by Reverend Sloat, and a book called *The History of the World Foretold* that Mr. Coker had given her. I never guessed that Isabel might have found it a taxing burden to have me around every second of her day. I assumed something was bothering her that was of no concern to me.

"Reverend Sloat is coming from his church in Ohio to talk to the congregation," Mahalia told me. "Isabel is doing all the arrangements."

On the morning of the potluck supper, Isabel took us with her to the grocery store to buy fruit and cheese. As Isabel and Mahalia hovered over the cheeses, trying to find ones that did not contain yellow food dyes, I said, "Why can't I stay home instead of going to the potluck? I don't want to go."

"Penny," Isabel answered, "you'll come, and if I leave you to your own devices, I trust you to act right. Sometimes I have business of my own to attend to. This time, Katie will be there. Mrs. Esselborne is in charge of her now."

After Isabel paid for the food, as we exited the store, we ran right into Cicely Nohilly. She was leaning against a cement pillar, talking to Mr.

Canon and smiling. She looked nothing like she had on either occasion I had seen her earlier. She had frosted her hair, and she wore blue jeans and a midriff blouse and a leather hat. She had drawn her eyebrows back on, and did not look so young anymore.

Isabel walked by her without saying hello, and we followed. I might have dismissed Cicely at that moment as someone unlikeable, someone who had betrayed Isabel's kindness, but then Mahalia said, "Look at her, just standing there having a good time after what she did! She should be crying her eyes out." Mahalia's condemnatory tone angered me, and as we reached the jeep, I looked back at Cicely again: She laughed loudly at something Mr. Canon had said, and I realized how long it had been since I had laughed like that myself. I felt as if I were suddenly coming up for air, out of a silent gloominess into a world where I could be like Cicely, happy, joking around with someone I enjoyed.

Mr. Canon walked back into the store, and as Cicely turned to leave, she spotted me staring at her. She saw Mahalia and Isabel beside me, loading the bags into the Jeep. Cicely crossed the parking lot toward us.

"Miss Flood," she said. "I want you to stop pestering my grandmother. Don't you have any mercy? Her husband has just died."

Isabel finished loading her last grocery bag and without looking up, said, "I spoke with your grandmother in order to understand more clearly why you had changed your mind so suddenly, and decided to kill your baby."

"How dare you judge me," Cicely Nohilly answered. "You, of all people!"

"My judgment doesn't matter," Isabel answered wearily. She closed the Jeep's backdoor. "It's God's judgment that matters."

"And you have a direct line to God, is that it?" Cicely asked. "Your judgment just happens to be the same as God's?"

"Miss Nohilly," Isabel said, still without turning around. "You approached me in this parking lot. I did not approach you."

"No," Cicely said, "You just had your little dwarf give me the evil eye."

Isabel pushed her empty cart past Cicely without answering and walked it to the front of the store.

Cicely followed her, saying, "What did you expect? You knew how desperate I was when you found me. How can you expect a desperate person to be honest? All those people you visit—don't they act the same way? They accept what you have to offer because they don't have any choice! And then you drag your pack of gossipy women into our lives and try to suck us into your church."

Isabel did not answer. She tilted her head down like someone braving a strong wind, and walked on, her helmet-hat balancing precariously over her barrettes. She mounted the Jeep, and Mahalia and I climbed in behind her.

Isabel drove back to the house without discussing what had happened. When we pulled into the driveway, Mahalia said, "Cicely Nohilly's poisonous, Isabel, she's poisonous!"

"She didn't seem poisonous to me," I said. "She just seemed upset."

Mahalia glared at me and said, "Penny, how can you—"

Isabel held up her hand and told Mahalia, "I've already given what happened with Cicely a great deal of thought, and I accept that her antics are part of my cross to bear."

Isabel then asked Mahalia to put away the groceries. "I have to gather together some papers at my house," she said. "And Penny, I will return immediately. Mind Mahalia while I'm gone." She headed quickly up the block, her face set in a grimace as if the events at the grocery store had troubled her after all.

Mahalia simmered as she put away the groceries, keeping her back to me. When she finished, Mahalia told me, "You can't wear those sneakers to church. Put on your good shoes."

"I don't know where my school shoes are," I answered.

"I'll find them," Mahalia said, and headed upstairs to get them. She wore thin-soled slipper-shoes like Isabel's. They slapped the steps as she climbed them. Her hair was pulled back in a coil pinned to her head, the way Isabel liked to wear hers. Mahalia never wore lipstick or jewelry like other girls her age.

I passed my dish once under the faucet without soaping it, stuck it in the dish rack, and stepped outside into the backyard. The tractor tire was full of sunken mud. I leaned down to see if I could smell gin and whisky in the soil. I imagined I detected a sweet fermented scent like old cantaloupe.

The doorbell rang, and I returned inside to answer it. A boy stood on our front porch. He had curly black hair, and olive skin like my mother's. He was almost as tall as David, but he was dressed like a teenager. He wore a T-shirt that said, "Stein High Sucks the Wazoo!" His chin and cheeks were darker than the rest of his face, as if he were already old enough to shave, and needed to shave again soon.

"I'm answering the advertisement the church put in the paper for an organist," he said.

I let him in and called Mahalia.

The boy seated himself at our piano and asked, "What's this? Bill Evans? Who transcribed sheet music for Bill Evans?"

"What do you want?" Mahalia demanded.

"My God!" the boy said when he saw her. She frowned. He repeated his reason for arriving. "What's that you're reading?" he asked Mahalia. "A Bible? Oh, well." He turned back to the piano and looked through the music there.

The boy read from my father's penciled notes, and played them more fluidly and quickly than F. X. had. "*Un*believable," he said when he finished. "*Un*believable." He asked Mahalia, "Is this yours? Do you like Bill Evans?"

In that peculiar way I associated with Isabel, Mahalia ignored his question by answering him with her own: "Why are you here? Did Penny invite you?"

The boy pulled a newspaper clipping out of his back pocket and showed it to us. It gave Isabel's name and our telephone number, and said, **Organist needed for Wednesday Night Prayer Meetings and Sunday Services.**

"You have to know how to play church music," Mahalia told him.

He played "Bringing in the Sheaves," but stopped halfway in the middle, and said, "I can play 'Wednesday Night Prayer Meeting' " and shifted suddenly into a crazy escalation of notes—the music sounded like a train going up a spiral staircase. I did not notice Isabel standing in our front doorway until the boy had reached the tune's end.

"Mahalia?" Isabel asked. "Did you invite this boy here? What is this boy doing in the house?"

Mahalia flushed. She looked hurt and then annoyed. "No," she answered. She peered over Isabel's shoulder into our hallway mirror and composed herself. "He's responding to the ad for the organist."

"I play for the Presbyterian church when their regular organist is out," the boy said. "And I accompany the high school's choir and the band. I did it all last year and I'm doing it now for summer school."

"You're young," Isabel told him.

"I'm going to Eastman next year," he answered. "I can handle whatever you want me to." He turned back to the keys and began playing "Silent Night."

"I wouldn't know how to judge your skills," Isabel interrupted. "Reverend Bender's choir conductor is the one who's handling the hiring. I'm just gathering names."

"Oh," the boy said. "Well, I'm Ben Fisher." He continued to play. He had long black eyelashes, and under them, his eyes were dark brown, like tea where the leaves have soaked for hours, stealing the soul of the water. His hands were wide and square, and black hairs covered his forearms. I saw Mahalia bend forward slightly, as if she were looking at them.

"We've already hired someone," Isabel said.

The boy stopped playing. He pulled the rolltop cover down over the piano keys and looked straight ahead, his back to Isabel. He raised his chin slightly, as if the piles of Isabel's papers had caught his attention, or as if he were trying to control himself. Then he turned toward Isabel, studying her. He crossed his arms and said, "You didn't tell me that before I gave you my name."

Isabel answered, "I'm sorry, but you'll have to go now."

She showed him to the door. I followed her, asking, "Who did the church find to play the organ?" Isabel did not respond.

The boy brushed past her and crossed the street. When he reached the other side, he turned and called, "Mahalia, you sure are beautiful! *Unbe*lievably, *un*believably beautiful! Let me know when she lets you out of her jail!"

———

On the way to church potluck that evening, Isabel drove her Jeep to Mrs. Groot's house to pick her up. Mahalia jumped out of the front seat and ran to the door. She rang the bell, and then pulled a piece of paper off the door that had been tacked there. She read the paper, bent over and lifted a plate from the front steps, and returned to the Jeep.

"Mrs. Groot's not here," she said. "She left this note."

I read it over Isabel's shoulder:

Dear Izzy,

Nicky has been arrested. I won't be able to make the potluck after all. I left the frosted brownies on the steps. Please get in touch with me tomorrow morning.

Myra

Isabel restarted the Jeep, telling me, "Penny, I don't want you eating those brownies. There will be less sugary desserts without chocolate in them at the potluck." She circled the downtown area, and then asked Mahalia in an even tone, "Do you think you might have invited that boy named Ben Fisher to the house?"

The back of Mahalia's neck darkened to a violet-red. "How could you think—of course not," she answered. "I can't believe you would ask me that!"

Isabel turned onto Stein's largest street, the one that had once housed all of the upper echelon prison officials in the initial days of Stein Correctional

Facility's construction. Now the town's few store owners, doctors, and lawyers lived here. The houses were large and white, with wraparound porches.

Mahalia asked, "Who will be playing the organ at the church?"

"I'm not in charge of that," Isabel answered.

They were both quiet after this, and I sensed tension between them for the first time since Mahalia had introduced me to Isabel.

Isabel parked the Jeep in front of an enormous house with a mailbox labeled **ESSELBORNE** that depicted men on horseback chasing a fox. Isabel told Mahalia, "I need to speak with Mrs. Esselborne. She'll be joining us with Reverend Sloat at the church a little later. She needs to retype some of our leaflets onto mimeograph forms." My sister did not answer. She remained with me in the car while Isabel rang the bell. A blond woman appeared at the door, and Isabel handed her a stack of papers. Mrs. Esselborne pushed a girl my age toward Isabel—Katie, the same elfish girl who had been at Mrs. Strang's house when I was accompanying Isabel on her missions. Katie wore the cowboy boots she had the night I had seen her at the Stein Tavern, and her baton twirler's skirt. Her hair had been cut short like a boy's.

Isabel said something to Katie and returned to the Jeep.

"We're just waiting a minute while Katie changes her clothes," Isabel said.

Katie emerged a few minutes later in a jumper, similar to the one Isabel had insisted I wear that afternoon, and tennis shoes. Mrs. Esselborne waved to Katie. Katie did not wave back.

"Well, we'll let the shoes go," Isabel told Mahalia, smiling at her in shared complicity. Mahalia did not notice. She had pulled down the sunshade and was staring at her reflection in the small rectangle of mirror there. She tucked a stray hair into the braid she had bobby-pinned in a circle around her head.

"This is Penny," Isabel told Katie. "Put on your seat belt." Katie slid into the seat beside me and stared out the window: There was nothing there but a vacant lot that fled from Mrs. Esselborne's yard to a ragged horseradish field.

Mahalia pushed the shade to its usual position and drew herself up in her seat as if pulling herself together for Katie's sake. As the Jeep left Mrs. Esselborne's neighborhood, Mahalia turned around and told me, "Katie sings in the church choir."

"What did your father do to end up in prison?" I asked Katie.

"*Penny!*" Mahalia said. She scowled, turning her face into a mask of adulthood.

Katie examined me: She had tilted brown eyes. "I don't know what he did," she answered. "No one will tell me."

I ignored Mahalia. I had an enduring curiosity regarding the prison, and hoped that Katie might be able to tell me something about it. There were three kinds of people who lived in and around Stein, other than the handful of residents who worked in the town's few businesses and schools, or had some loose and usually unpromising connection to the land: those who worked at the prison, those who were in prison, and the people, mostly transient, who came to visit men at the prison. Some members of this last group tried to live in Stein, but usually they left after a while, because there really was no permanent niche for them; there was considerable hostility in Stein toward friends and relatives of prisoners. I knew from my mother that families or associates of prison inmates at correctional facilities in Stein and Dannemora sometimes spent a night or a week at the Stein Motor Inn. My mother did not allow us to walk on the road that ran by the Motor Inn and eastward from Stein's prison to Clinton Correctional Facility in Dannemora. This road was called Dannemora Road in Stein, and Stein Road by people in Dannemora. I had never strayed onto the road before, mostly because it was too far from our home and the lake, which were on the other side of town.

The new Stein Evangelical Church was on Dannemora Road, and as we left the town's outskirts, we passed Stein Correctional Facility. Just looking at it gave me a trapped feeling: Guards, rifles in hand, looked down from the watchtowers over their snarls of razor wire.

"There's the public high school," I told Katie, pointing at the prison walls.

She looked at me with a perplexed expression, her forehead wrinkled above her tilted eyes, and finally smiled.

I did what I always did when my mother drove us by the correctional facility. I imagined I was a prisoner there. Sometimes I let myself be falsely accused. Other times I imagined I had been rightly convicted of a serious crime, an armed robbery or murder, and that in prison I befriended a priest or pastor who dazzled me by revealing to me the mystery of remorse. On the day I rode by the prison with Katie, I imagined that I was a burglar who knew how to break out of jails as well as he knew how to break into homes. As soon as I had the image in my head, I was free, slipping through the watery darkness outside the walls.

Isabel sped past the Stein Motor Inn: It was a low building with trucks parked outside of it, and neon signs that flashed the names *Coors*, *Molson*, and *Budweiser*. Two men scuffled in its doorway, and a little beyond them, in the parking lot, a man lay asleep on the hood of a car. Four or five miles down the road, Isabel turned onto a gravel driveway and pulled up in front of a white wooden church. It had a steeple, unlike the old church, and the lettering over its door still read: FIRST BAPTIST. Before the steps was a sign with the name STEIN EVANGELICAL on it, and under this, spelled out in moveable white letters on a black background was the question:

WHY DO THOSE WHO CRY OUT
AGAINST CAPITAL PUNISHMENT
FOR CONVICTED CRIMINALS
SUPPORT FIRST DEGREE MURDER
OF THE INNOCENT UNBORN?

When we stepped down from the church's Jeep, Reverend Bender greeted Isabel and said, "This is the big day. Hello Katie. It's good to see you again." He smiled at me with his bulldog grin, and reached down and lifted my hand. His fingers were as rough as the pads on dogs' feet.

"And who's this?" he asked Katie.

"She's Penny. *I'm* Katie," she answered.

"All of you come look at our new organ," Reverend Bender said, without acknowledging his mistake. "The organ's a gift to the church. It's still in the annex until we find someone to play it."

"Our uncle F. X. plays the organ," I said.

"Maybe he would perform for us some time," Reverend Bender answered.

"He can play backward," I said, but no one commented on this. We all followed Reverend Bender through a large church with pews divided by a red carpet, down a hall with office and bathroom doors, and into an adjoining small building where food was laid out on tables to the left and right of the organ.

Mrs. Wroblewski approached Isabel, saying, "I guess you've heard about Nicky Groot by now."

"Mahalia!" Lucy called. She was so enormous that at first I did not recognize her: She looked like a fat lady. She had dyed her hair as well, a bright red color. Mr. Coker rose when he saw Isabel: He wore the same work clothes he always did. His boots were muddy, and his beard had grown more ragged. He had not braided it.

Mrs. Wroblewski asked, "Mark, why don't you come socialize with us girls?"

Mr. Coker told her, "When I was fifteen, I realized that there was no person out there I liked talking to as much as my dog, and that's the way I've conducted myself since." Mrs. Wroblewski laughed loudly.

"Lucy," Isabel said. "What did you dye your hair with? Some commercial hair dyes are dangerous for pregnancy."

Lucy's face fell. "It was just some kind of henna," she answered.

"I told her not to do it," Mr. Coker said. "But she dyed it one day when I was gone."

"I'm sure there's nothing to worry about," Mrs. Wroblewski said. "I dye my hair every time I get the news, just to keep from feeling low about myself, and not one of my children has been born a redhead yet!"

"Are any of your children here?" Isabel asked.

"No, it's just me," Mrs. Wroblewski answered. She told Lucy, who still looked upset, "Thank God for the church. It's seems now like it's the only time I can get away. It's the only thing I can really use on Mr. Wroblewski to induce him to stay with the kids. 'You can work me like a slave most of the week,' I tell him. 'But you have to respect my religion and my time with God.' It actually works. Next time, maybe I'll say it on a Wednesday before prayer meeting and go have my nails manicured instead."

She got Lucy giggling, and as Mrs. Wroblewski continued to talk, Katie and I approached the dessert table. I picked up a Dixie cup of Kool-Aid and reached for one of Mrs. Groot's brownie's, but Isabel appeared from behind me, took the Dixie cup from my hand, and said, "Not now, Penny. That's for the picnic supper. And water's fine. I don't want you drinking Kool-Aid." Katie and I walked around, longingly examining the food. There was fried chicken and corn on the cob, hot dogs and hamburgers and mashed potatoes, potato chips, and pickles. On the edge of one table was a platter of dark red sausage, and in front of it was a jar labeled COKER'S BITTER HERBS: **NOT** ORGANICALLY GROWN.

"My mother will expect me to sing," Katie told me.

"Where's your mother?" I asked.

"In Schroon Lake," she answered. "We belong to the same church there."

"I saw you once at the Stein Tavern with her. That time your mother came in and looked around. Remember? When she was yelling at all the men there?"

"She thought they'd paroled Roger, but they hadn't. I remember you too. I wondered why that man would take you to a bar like that."

"Who's Roger?" I asked Katie.

"My father. Is your father in prison too?"

"My father's dead," I told her.

"Then why are you here?"

"Because my mother's away. Isabel's looking after us, so she brought me here. My sister likes to come."

"Why?"

I shrugged my shoulders.

"The choir's practicing," Mahalia told Katie, interrupting us. Mahalia led Katie away from me into the church's front room.

Isabel followed Reverend Bender toward an older man I did not recognize, a balding man a head shorter than Isabel, with child-sized hands that made me think of a possum's paws. He wore a minister's collar and carried a backpack, which he removed. Inside were posters featuring embryos with the title *2001: A Space Odyssey* under them. On each poster, a black X had been drawn over the words "*A Space Odyssey*" and, printed underneath in block capitals, was the sentence: THE MILLENNIUM WILL UNLEASH THE WRATH OF THE UNBORN.

"Isabel," Father Bender said, "this time, Reverend Sloat's come without his yellow bus—he's giving himself completely to Stein Evangelical this evening."

She extended her hand. "I'm Isabel Flood. We're grateful that you're here."

Reverend Sloat grinned; he had jagged, pointy possum teeth. He took Isabel's hands in his and said, "Belle Flood? It's a pleasure."

"Isabel," she answered.

"Miss Flood brings in a lot of members," Reverend Bender told Reverend Sloat.

Isabel turned to me and said, "Penny, I have to trust you to wait for me." She accompanied Reverend Bender and Reverend Sloat down the hallway into an office.

I helped myself to two brownies from the refreshment table. I found a large canister of coffee and poured myself some. I had never had a whole cup of coffee before. I added three teaspoons of sugar and some milk, and gulped down my cup quickly and refilled it: My mother sometimes let me sip her coffee at breakfast, and the taste reminded me of her, lush and bitter, although the church's coffee was weaker than hers. I poured myself another cup, and then a fourth.

A tall woman with custard-colored hair came up behind me saying, "What is this girl drinking?" although no one else was standing near either of us. "Is that coffee? Get this young lady some Kool-Aid." She wore a navy blue dress with a pattern of large gold chains running across it. A gold heart-shaped pin held in place a scarf with the same pattern. "You must be Penny Daigle. You can call me Mrs. Esselborne. I'm president of the women's group. We all certainly hope that you'll be joining us at services like Mahalia." I recognized her now as the woman who owned the big house where Katie was staying. Mrs. Esselborne removed the empty coffee cup from my hand

and said, "You probably didn't know there was Kool-Aid, did you? Look right over there." She guided me to the other end of the table and poured me a cup. As I raised the Kool-Aid to my lips, I could already feel the coffee working in me. I was surprised by its energy; my heart lurched three times in a row, as if it were trying to get ahead of itself. I finished the Kool-Aid before Isabel returned.

A pale, cadaverous man entered the room briefly. I thought I might have seen him with Reverend Sloat's followers the night of the church's march the winter before, but I was not certain. He wore a gray jumpsuit embossed with a yellow script that read *Hank Petty—Former Member of the Legion of the Unborn*. He said something to Mr. Coker that made him smile, but Mr. Petty did not smile back. Thin arms poked from the sleeves of his jumpsuit, and lavender shadows pooled in the depressions under his cheekbones. When he looked at me, his expression was flat; he did not even seem to register that I was there. I thought with satisfaction as he looked away, that he was so small and frail I could have tossed him through the air or wrestled him to the ground.

"Mr. Petty!" Reverend Bender called, stepping out of his hallway office. Mr. Petty vanished inside. He moved swiftly, making me think of an animal darting through water. Mrs. Esselborne waved to Reverend Bender and approached him, saying, "I'd like you to read one of these papers Miss Flood asked me to mimeograph—I have some compunctions about it." He took the paper, and they both stepped into his office.

Isabel emerged from the office briefly afterward and sat beside Mahalia and me, looking preoccupied.

Mahalia did not speak to either of us during dinner, and Katie ate with the choir. Isabel would not let me eat any hot dogs or dessert. I felt jittery from the coffee; my heart did a polka in my chest, and I jiggled my plate as I ate. When the hour for church services came, Isabel said, "Penny, if you don't think you can sit still during the sermon, find yourself a seat in the back pew, so that you can leave without causing a disturbance. You can wait on the church's front steps if you need to."

At the end of our meal, Isabel turned toward my sister and said, "I'm sorry I doubted you, Mahalia. It's entirely my fault. I allowed myself to get too caught up in my work, and it made me snappish and impatient."

"That's all right," Mahalia told her.

Isabel patted Mahalia's leg. Mahalia smiled—she looked relieved to be back on good terms with Isabel. When services started, Mahalia nestled into a pew beside her.

I seated myself far in the back, fidgeting until the man next to me said,

"Do you think you could stop that?" I sat on my hands and listened to the choir sing without accompaniment.

Reverend Bender led Reverend Sloat to a platform at the front of the church and told the congregation, "We all know what Reverend Sloat's people are stirring up in Buffalo right now, and we're honored that he's made a special visit to help us stir things up in our tiny corner of the world." The congregation laughed, and Reverend Sloat placed himself before a large podium that still said "First Baptist" on it. He grinned, showing his jagged possum teeth, and led the congregation in a chorus of "My Country, 'Tis of Thee."

Once the choir was seated, Reverend Sloat began, "Birth is nothing special. It's just a change of scenery." The congregation laughed again, and he continued: "But birth seems to be causing quite a foofaraw among the Pro-death people. Why? Because a me-first attitude has robbed America of the family values that are its brick and mortar. The twentieth century is the Me-First Century. How have we arrived at such selfishness? The selfishness that makes a person say, 'I'm glad I'm alive, but right now, I don't have time for you to be born. God's creation of you is an inconvenience to me.' How have we come to this?"

I left before he could answer himself. I slipped out the back doors and lay down on the church's steps, looking up at the purple-black sky. I liked black when it was just tasting color: the red black of cast iron, the night drinking the last violets of evening sky, the green-black of brackish water cuddling skunk cabbage. And I liked the pure, absolute blackness these could turn into. Mrs. Fury had once asked the class what our favorite colors were. I knew what she wanted us to answer: red, yellow, green—the pure colors— or maybe sky blue or, if we were frivolous and not very smart, pink. "Pitch black," I had answered, and her eyes had slid over me to the next student; she judged that I was trying to milk the moment for whatever badness it offered. But this was not true. I relished the sound of the words *pitch black*— they made me think of something pitching forward off a cliff, or of music that climbed too high, of creosote and smoke rising into your cupped hands, because Sister Geraldine had told me that pitch was an old form of tar that caught fire, tar so black everything else looked light in comparison.

I threw gravel at the silhouette of a pine tree until the stones seemed to erase it and the tree vanished entirely in the invading darkness. When blackness filled in the last section of sky overhead, I rolled down the steps sideways until I hit the gravel path below. I ran once around the church, in the darkness. When I reached the front of the building again, I did a flip in the air and landed on my feet on the black earth.

Katie sat on the church's front steps, holding two flashlights. She asked me, "Why did you come out here?"

"It drives me crazy to have to sit still and listen," I answered.

"I told Isabel I didn't want to sing any more songs, and she sent me out to find you," Katie said. "She said we can sit here together if we want. She said we should each have a flashlight." Katie handed me one. "What did you just do by the sign? Did you do a frontward flip in the air?"

"Yeah," I said. I took one of the flashlights, and its beam burrowed into the darkness. I turned it toward the church's sign, and read: SUPPORT FIRST DEGREE MURDER.

"Oh no!" I whined, clutching my heart. "Murder! Murder! Someone's murdering me!" I fell to the ground. Katie watched me, tilting her elfish face, and said nothing.

I walked over to a front church window. The adults were rising from their pews to sing. Mahalia and Isabel stood up together. I circled the church, looking in all the windows, one by one. I heard Katie following me. I peered inside the back room that held the organ. The room was empty, and the refreshment tables had been cleared.

I tried the window to see if we could get inside to play the organ. The one at All Saints had a button you could press that made drum noises.

"What are you doing?" Katie asked, drawing up beside me.

"Breaking in to try out the organ," I told her.

"Why? Reverend Bender said I can play on it whenever I practice singing. He'll let us go in there while the grown-ups are meeting in study groups."

"Naw," I said. "It's okay." I did not want to talk with a minister.

"This is what I'm learning now," Katie told me. She stood still and sang in a serious voice, like a grown woman:

> "Around the throne of God in heaven
> Thousands of children stand:
> Children whose sins are all forgiven,
> A holy happy band."

I thought that she was strange, to sing out loud that way, without any adult forcing her to. She made me feel nervous and excited.

"My mother sings in the choir at home," Katie said.

"Does you father sing at the prison?" I asked.

"I don't know." She peered inside the building, so that her face lit up like a mask of light. "I thought they would tell me more about him at the church's prison camp, but nobody does. My mother only sends me to prison camp because the church tells her to. All they do is drop me off at Stein Correctional and Roger and me play checkers, and then I leave and they say, 'Did you pray for him?' "

I felt disappointed. I had hoped she would know more about the prison, that she might be badly behaved and reckless like me, because her father was a criminal.

"And when I get home," Katie continued, "Mrs. Esselborne makes me take a bath and looks through my hair with rubber gloves on. She's afraid I'll get lice at the prison. She took me to the beauty parlor to have my hair cut shorter."

I reached up and tickled the nape of Katie's neck and said, in a tiny voice, "I'm a louse, and I'm going to bite you, Mrs. Esselborne!"

Katie lifted her eyebrows, so that her elfish ears moved. She sucked her mouth into a pucker of amusement.

I made my voice smaller and said, "Mrs. Esselborne! I'm breaking into your house with my louse friends! We're going to sit on your sofa and kiss your neck and drink all your whisky!"

Now Katie laughed, and I found her laughter infectious. I laughed boisterously.

Reverend Bender opened the door that led into the room where the organ was. Katie and I stopped laughing and drew back into the darkness as Reverend Bender opened a second outer door and stepped outside, accompanied by the guest minister. In the church behind them, the choir sang loudly: *I was blind, but now I see.*

"You did fine in there, you old gasbag," Reverend Bender said.

Reverend Sloat laughed. "When I get back here later in the summer, let's talk about school board elections. That's the best place to start. You can bootstrap yourself up from there. Lord, this is good," he said, sipping from one of the Dixie cups. "My father used to make something like this in Kentucky, straining fermented apricots and wood alcohol through Wonderbread. Mr. Petty gave it to me. You talked to Mr. Petty? He's the one who first told me about you. Before he came to Ohio, he lived in Dannemora."

"He doesn't say much," Reverend Bender answered.

"He's indispensable," Reverend Sloat said. "A great strategist." Reverend Sloat lifted a thermos and poured a clear liquid into his cup. "If nothing else, this certainly makes it easier for *me* to listen to myself talk."

Reverend Bender chuckled. Standing in the half-lit doorway, he grinned his bulldog grin; Reverend Sloat smiled back with his jagged possum teeth.

"Have a taste?" Reverend Sloat asked.

"No," Reverend Bender answered. "I can't have my congregation smelling that on my breath."

"Who's the girl following around that lady with all the pamphlets?" Reverend Sloat asked.

"Mahalia Daigle?" Reverend Bender answered.

"Pretty name, pretty girl," Reverend Sloat said. "Hair like wildfire."

I wandered away from the building so that the men wouldn't catch us if they came outside again. I heard Katie's footsteps behind me. When we were about fifty yards from the church, Katie asked, "Do you know how to sing any songs?"

I answered in a loud, rasping voice:

"Just open the door
and crap on the floor
sang Barnacle Bill
the Sailor!"

"I've never heard that," Katie answered matter-of-factly.

I snapped on my flashlight and shone it upward under my chin. I knew from practice that I would look devilish lit that way. "Heh, heh, heh," I said in my monster voice. Katie did not respond.

I ran off, past a ledge of darkness where the flashlight suddenly seemed more brilliant. Katie followed me. I felt a desperation to make her laugh again, to make her do something wrong, to draw her away from the church with a pull stronger than the church's antics had on Mahalia. Far ahead, my flashlight illuminated a road shoulder, and I staggered toward it pretending to be drunk. The flashlight's beam danced crazily on the ground in front of me as I sang:

"Just open some liquor,
I'll show you my pecker!
sang Barnacle Bill
the Sailor!

It's twelve inches long
and never goes wrong
sang Barnacle Bill
the Sailor!"

I fell to the ground, clutching my stomach the way I had once seen a man do outside the Stein Tavern, and calling as he had, "Oh baby, baby, give me a drink, I have to have a drink!" Only then did it dawn on Katie that I was being funny. She giggled a little. This was all the incitement I needed. I sang incoherent words in a drunken tone, staggering, my hands clenched in two fists. I called out, "Give me some pussy! I have to have some pussy!"

Katie gasped, "Pussy!" and giggled again. She followed me as I staggered. She pointed her flashlight in my face. When I pretended to fall again, my shadow twisted under me like a wrestler, and then stretched out level along the ground, reaching for the edge of the road.

"Oh my darling shadow," I said, "come back to me! Kiss me, oh kiss me!"

Now Katie laughed out loud: Her laugh sounded like a whinny. I directed my flashlight at her, and she copied me, falling to the ground and kissing her shadow.

"Oh my darling!" she said, kneeling and pretending to clutch her heart. "My darling, don't run away!"

We were in stitches then. We dragged ourselves up, hands over our hearts, and chased our shadows to the road, shining our lights behind one another to make our shadows longer and calling, "Come back! Come back! Don't ever leave me!" As we hit Dannemora Road, we were wild with laughter. We were pure craziness, what no walls could lock up, hysterical with joy.

A car came around the bend toward us. "Let's switch off our flashlights," I said, and we did. The car slowed down as it neared us; its headlights lit us up like angels before it raced on.

"*Morny morn!*" I yelled, running after it. "I'm talking in tongues! *Morning morn!*"

I stopped and waited for Katie to catch up with me. She drew beside me panting and said, "Listen, listen! I can do that even better. They sound like this: *Bozel murkik Beezlebub! Porfinny murk murkin Lucifork!*"

I snorted and repeated, "*Lucifork!*" and then a stream of my own words, "*Lucifork jomama tika-tika! Tika-tika romodofreeka Luciforkmama!*" Katie laughed, and we talked in tongues until we reached a bend in Dannemora Road. As we walked on, we kept our flashlights off. I imagined I was an escaped prisoner quietly wending my way through the night, savoring my personal freedom. I did a flip, once in the air, through the dark over the dark ground. No one saw me do it, not even Katie. I did it for myself, for the sheer perilous pleasure of it.

Around the bend, we saw a Volkswagen van on the road shoulder. Its interior was dark and its motor off. We shone our flashlights up and down

Dannemora Road, but no one was around. We peered inside. The van's middle seats were littered with papers. The door was locked, but the triangular side window was ajar.

"I can open the door if you let me stand on you," I told Katie. She got down on all fours, and when I stepped onto her back, she laughed so hard that we both fell over. She crawled beside the window a second time, and I stood on her again. She said, "Whoosh, wait a minute," and braced herself, giggling, against the van. I stuck my arm through the side window, up to the elbow, twisted my wrist around, and pulled up the lock. I opened the door. We shone our flashlights inside again. There was nothing of interest: a briefcase with an unopened bottle of rum tucked under it, a tennis racket, a pair of men's oxblood leather shoes, a suit on a hanger, two dirty white shirts thrown to the floor, a torn and trampled *New York Times*, a pile of white paper stapled to thicker blue papers like the ones my mother typed for the Graverobber, and a cigarette lighter, which I pocketed.

I sat in the front and turned the steering wheel, pretending to drive. "Let's head to Albany," I said. Katie sat down beside me, her hands braced on her knees, her flashlight in her lap. She was so excited that when she spoke her voice came out hoarsely.

"Let's go to Schroon Lake!" she said.

"Let's go to New Orleans!" I answered.

We switched our flashlights off and pretended to drive a little longer. Then I turned mine on and said, "I'm going to look in the back." I pushed between the front seats and leaned over the middle. I shone my flashlight downward and slid on my belly into the rear seat. Katie crawled over the middle seat and I straightened up beside her.

"We could stay here until whoever owns the car comes back, and then scare them," I said. We turned off our flashlights again. I imagined jumping forward, grabbing someone by the shoulders, shouting in his ear. I sat quietly until the coffee in my veins pummeled my heart. I stood up and felt for the switch on my flashlight.

We heard men's voices. They were coming from the woods beside the van. I peered out the window and saw the sudden flash of a match under a cigarette. There was a single, shouting laugh, and then three men emerged from the black woods, carrying flashlights. Two of them walked away from us; their lights bobbed in the darkness like drunk animals. The third man approached the van by himself. He wore a suit and tie, and carried a paper bag.

"Duck down!" I said. We slid to the floor, and I pushed my eye to the crack between the middle seat and the side of the car. The front door opened, the car's interior light flickered on, and a man leaned over the briefcase, snapped it open, dropped the bag inside, and locked the briefcase. His suit was gray, and he loosened his tie, which was red. He had brown hair and a mustache, and looked a little younger and shorter than David.

I turned to Katie with my finger to my lips. She stared at me in alarm for the split second before the car door closed and the interior light turned off. The ignition whirred and the motor rumbled under us. The car pulled onto the road and made a U-turn in the direction of Dannemora. I felt a rush of feelings, each hanging on for dear life to the next—excitement and exhilaration and fear and sneakiness and meanness and dangerousness. I don't know what Katie felt as we crouched there on the backseat floor, because I could no longer see her face, and she didn't make a noise. I whispered her name very quietly over the grumble of the motor, but she did not answer.

The van increased speed and raced along a river of darkness until we came to the lights that shone from the towers and walls of Clinton Correctional Facility in Dannemora. We continued into the town of Dannemora and out again, and past a mossy green sign bearing a white luminous arrow and the words PLATTSBURGH—9 MILES. I felt Katie reach out and grab my hand. Her fingers were warm and damp, and made me feel so jittery that I almost cried out. After fifteen or twenty minutes, the houses outside Plattsburgh began to rush by on the sides of the road. They looked like fat ghostly women running out of a dark lake. I thought vaguely that we would announce ourselves when we entered Plattsburgh, but the van slowed at a sign: ALBANY—161 MILES.

When we hit the highway, I heard the snap of the briefcase lock, and a rustle in the front seat like a paper bag opening. The van skimmed along the black highway, and there were no more landmarks or road signs. I felt a fidgety chaos start up inside me, from having to sit so still. I jiggled my knee, dropped Katie's hand and picked it up, and dropped it again. I heard a burst of air, smelled sulfur, watched the driver light a cigarette, and then breathed in air tainted with smoke that did not smell like cigarettes—it was sweeter, horsey. I peeked over the seat to get a better view of him, and then ducked back down.

I heard Katie crying beside me: small, whispered sobs she was trying to keep quiet, and then a louder cry.

I looked over the back seat to see if the man had heard her. He turned halfway around, his face illuminated slightly by the cigarette, but he did not seem to be able to make out what he saw in the darkness behind him. He slowed, switched on the interior light, and looked in the rearview mirror.

"What the fuck?" he said. He turned around again, saw us both, and cried out, loudly, "Jesus fucking Christ, Jesus fucking Christ!" He pulled the van over with a jerk, as if he were avoiding oncoming traffic that had gone out of control.

He turned around all the way. "What are you doing in here?" he asked. Katie looked at him, frozen, her dark eyes opened wide. "How old are you? Eight or ten? Jesus fucking Christ! I can't believe this! I can't believe it!"

The look Katie fastened on me asked one question: Why had I gotten her into this situation? It was not a look of blame or reproach, but fearful concern.

The man's expression matched hers. He seemed worried, even frightened. "How did you get in here?" he asked. "Are you running away?"

Now Katie was crying in a gasping way, sucking in her breath and almost choking on it.

"Where did you get in?" the man demanded, but Katie was unable to answer him.

I said, "Dannemora Road."

"What?"

"Dannemora Road," I repeated.

"Jesus fucking Christ!" the man said again. "Where the hell is that? Is it near the prison?"

Neither of us answered him. He opened the glove compartment and fished through a stack of papers, saying, "Christ, Christ, Christ, I don't even have a road map! Two little girls in my car! Fucking Christ!"

A car's headlights approached us from pitch blackness. The car seemed to lift in midair and direct itself toward us though the black sky, without any highway to guide it. The man stared ahead as if mesmerized, and then switched off the van's interior light and turned on the ignition. He rolled down his window and tossed his cigarette into the dark air: It scattered like fireworks. He pulled onto the road about a half minute after the other car passed us.

"All right," he said. "Here's what I'm going to do. I'm going to drop you off at the next town we come to, do you understand?" He paused to reflect for a moment. "I'll let you off near the first Holiday Inn or McDonald's or whatever that we come to, and you go in there and ask to use the phone and call your parents and tell them to come get you."

We sat tensely until we came to an exit, and a sign that said TOWN OF FLORENCE. There was no McDonald's or any hotel. The man let us off on a road shoulder about a quarter mile from where we saw a streetlamp.

First, he opened his door, got out, and looked down the road. Afterward, he leaned his head back into the car and told us, "Walk toward that street-light until you find a pay phone somewhere." It was cool outside, but sweat ran down his face like tears. He placed a dime in my hand, and I looked down at it, uncomprehending. He pulled his head back, opened the middle door, and then, in one motion, seemed to be standing me up on the back seat and jerking me off it, onto the ground outside the car. Then he pulled Katie out, stood her next to me, and climbed back into the van. The van made a U-turn and sped away into the darkness.

Katie stopped crying and walked beside me, without saying anything. We had forgotten our flashlights in the van. When we reached the streetlight, we saw that we were not in a town at all, but instead by a gas station located at a V-shaped intersection. We walked around the station and peered into pure blackness beyond the darkened windows. A pickup truck was parked in the front of the station, but when we knocked on the doors and windows, no one answered. There was no pay phone outside.

"I have to go to the bathroom," Katie said. She sounded panicky.

"I'll wait here," I told her.

I sat down on the front steps of the gas station. I took out the cigarette lighter I had pocketed and tried to make it catch flame, but it was empty. I threw it onto the road. It occurred to me that the gas station must have a telephone inside, and that if we broke in, we could use the phone there. I thought of possible things I might say to Mrs. Esselborne and sat waiting to tell Katie my plans when she came back.

Too long a time seemed to elapse without her returning. Two trucks passed on the road without seeing me, and then a camper, and a car. I stood up and called out, but Katie did not answer.

I walked around the back of the gas station. I called again, but still she did not answer. I called until I was hoarse. I walked into the woods across the road from the station and called out for her there. The wind jerked the trees and they made a sound like the rush of crashing waves. I walked back to the station and pressed my face against the front window; I could not see a thing. I felt myself break open and a sense of terror flooded the hollow space left behind. Something I had never felt before as a child, simple despair, took me over.

I stood for a long time on the edge of the road, with my hands shoved into my jumper pockets. In every direction, the night looked the same, an undifferentiated darkness. I stayed perfectly still. I had never stood so quietly for so long in my whole life: It might have been forty minutes, or hours. Finally, I walked back to the gas station and crawled into the cab of the pickup truck parked in front of it. I closed my eyes and lay down. I thought of Isabel saying, "I have to be able to trust you," and then I heard Mahalia telling Isabel, "I can't believe you would ask me that!" and Isabel answering, "I get these panicky heart beats." Sinking into the pale of night, I saw Isabel in my mind's eye, treading an edge of a yellow sky sidelong, like a solitary crab, and understanding how alone I felt in her company, I felt sorry for her.

———

Later I would learn that it was long after midnight when a police car found me at the gas station. The patrol car drove by me, and then slowed, and backed up. I had left open the front door of the pickup truck. An officer's flashlight passed over the truck, and a finger of yellow nudged me awake.

"How did you get here?" the officer asked.

I struggled upright and saw his uniform. I wondered if I was being arrested for sleeping in a truck that was not mine.

"A man drove me from Stein," I answered, "and let me out right here."

The policeman pulled me from the truck and said, "Get in the car and we'll take you back to the Florence police station. You can call your parents from there."

"I can't," I told him. "I'm here with my friend, Katie. She got lost. I'm waiting for her."

"We found your friend two hours ago," the officer said. "Her mother's come to get her. She wouldn't tell us how you two ended up here."

The officer opened the police car's back door, steered me into the seat, and sat me down behind a metal grate that separated me from him. I had seen such grates in police shows on television and knew that they functioned to cage in criminals.

When we arrived at the station, the officer asked for my telephone number and sat me at a large desk in an empty room. There I unwillingly ended the contest I had enjoyed for 259 days. I saw myself reflected in the police station's mirror, which covered the entire wall; it might have been the mirrored side of a window meant for viewing lineups. In it I looked exactly the same as I remembered myself, an ordinary girl with deep-set dark eyes and a crooked brown pigtail and burnt olive skin. There were no obvious changes in my features or the color of my hair. I walked over to the mirror until I stood too close to focus. I stepped back and allowed my eyes to unfocus. I duplicated into a double image of myself, and my four eyes had the same glassy, distant expression that Lucy Coker had had when she talked in tongues at the church. So that was how they did it, I remember thinking— that was how you made yourself look as if you were under God's spell, in a saintly trance—you let your eyes wander.

"Penny, what are you doing?" Katie's elfish face appeared behind me, and I turned around.

"Did you get arrested?" I asked her.

She wrinkled her forehead. "I didn't tell them about Mrs. Esselborne!" she said. "I gave them my own telephone number, and my mother came all the way here to get me."

"Where did you go?" I asked her.

She shrugged. "I just turned the wrong way and got lost, and after that I decided to walk to Schroon Lake."

"Katie!" a woman called.

I followed Katie into the next room. A large woman with piano legs and complicated waves of black hair stood at a counter talking to the officers who had brought me in. She looked different than she had the night I had seen her at the Stein Tavern, more relaxed and good-humored, although I could still picture her clearly the other way: worried and furious and threatening. She told Katie, "Well, you imp. It's home for you. I never should have let those church women talk me into these visits." Katie wrapped her arms around her mother and buried her face in her dress. A wave of homesickness overpowered me.

Katie's mother stooped in front of me and said, "I'm sorry if Katie got you in trouble. I guess she didn't want to stay in Stein anymore. Will you be all right here until they come get you?"

I nodded. "It was mostly my idea," I said.

As Katie's mother led her out of the station, Katie waved to me and grinned.

The officer who had found me gave me 7UP and showed me back to the desk. "We can't get a hold of anyone at your house," he said. "But we'll keep trying."

After he left, a different officer brought a handcuffed man into the adjoining room—he kicked over a chair and shouted, "I never took the money! I never said I wanted his money! He's a goddamn liar!" He strayed and stumbled through the doorway, near the desk where I sat, and looked at me in a confused way. I remember thinking, incongruously, *Just say, "You're rich. Give me your money. I want it."* The police officer jerked him away and down a hall.

I leaned over the desk and filled the front pages of a pad with twenty-digit multiplication problems, and wrote over and over, *"I will not act recalcitrant during lunch period."* A hard unnamable feeling lodged in the middle of my chest, and when the officer returned to tell me that no one answered the phone at my house, I gave him Sister Geraldine's name, not Isabel's or Stein Evangelical's.

The officer turned my paper toward him, read it, raised his eyebrows without commenting on it, and returned it to me.

"Are you arresting me?" I asked him.

He laughed and answered, "Not this time." He had a chipped tooth, and wispy blond hair that caught the light behind him; he walked like a swaggering angel into the adjoining room and spoke to some officers there. I heard another burst of laughter. Afterward, he brought me a sweet roll, and asked me one question after another. As I answered him, I watched his face grow graver and quieter. I sat stiller than I had ever sat, the triumphant, intoxicating jitteriness that almost always accompanied me suspended as he questioned me. Why would we crawl into the van voluntarily? What happened when the man was alone with us? What had we done after the man let us out of the van? Had we walked toward the town or away from it? At one point, the officer asked, looking at no one in particular, "Why would a man let two children off on a dark road in the middle of night in the middle of nowhere?"

I recalled the man's expression when he first discovered us, and I answered soberly, "He was afraid of us?"

Sister Geraldine arrived about an hour later. I had dozed in my chair, and perched there on the edge of sleep, unable to fall. I opened my eyes and found Sister Geraldine standing in front of me, saying, "How do you like jail life, Penny?" She wore her full habit and wimple. She helped me to my feet and led me outside to the station wagon that belonged to the school. She buckled me into a center seat belt, so that we touched ribs when she turned on the ignition. She took off her wimple. Her hair looked like smoke.

As she backed out of the police station's parking lot, Sister Geraldine asked, "So, how did all this happen, Penny? I'd like to know."

I answered, "I don't have any friends."

Sister Geraldine put her hand on my knee and drove quietly down a dark road. "Maybe Miss Flood needs a break," she said. "I'm going to try to call your uncle in the morning. Our summer school begins in two weeks, and you should come. You need to spend more time playing with other children during the day." *Is that the only problem?* I wondered. I felt as if a snarled cord had been cut inside me, and a springing sensation. Sister Geraldine turned back onto the road north, and the night flowed ahead of us, wide and endless. Trees and mailboxes and cars drank our headlights and sped by on the rim of a world that held me at its center. The hum of the motor lulled me, and for the first time I could remember, I struggled futilely against sleep and gave into it helplessly.

Chapter Ten

Poetry

*T*he night I ran off to Florence, a man named Thomas Buskin broke into an abortion clinic in China, Ohio, and threw gasoline in the eyes of a young receptionist, before setting the clinic's waiting room on fire. His actions were among the first violent crimes against clinics in those days; the previous February, a man had burned down the administrative offices of Planned Parenthood in St. Paul, Minnesota. The Ohio receptionist was temporarily blinded, and F. X. followed her story assiduously—the event would mark the beginning of F. X.'s excursions into investigating right-to-lifers. In late summer, he would actually call the receptionist and speak to her, and she would tell him that even though she was regaining her sight, she felt that part of her would be trapped forever in her week of blindness, that she had been indelibly marked and altered by those seven days. F. X. would then tell her that he had always felt out of sync with his own identity, because after years of adapting to the idea of being blind, he had suddenly been "forced to shed his skin and reenter the world aboveground and socialize with its inhabitants, who no longer seemed related to me in any way, and who did not understand that I was just as blind as I had ever been. I never became a seeing man—I simply became a blind man who could see. A black chaos whirling through people's lives."

Isabel did not learn about the clinic firebombing from the radio, or read about it in the morning paper, because she was too upset and worried about my disappearance. She spent the night searching Stein with Mrs. Esselborne.

They walked along the border of woods behind the church, imagining that they glimpsed Katie and me and calling into the darkness. While Reverend Bender notified the local police, Isabel and Mrs. Esselborne drove up and down Dannemora Road with the Jeep's brights on, scanning the road shoulders for any sign of us. They traveled down Main Street and through the grid of streets around it, slowing whenever they saw a girl child, to peer in her face and identify her. They even ventured to the park by Stein Lake and walked along the periphery of the water, shouting our names. Sister Geraldine was unable to contact them until after she returned from Florence.

That night, Sister Geraldine led me into All Saints Convent, a building that to me seemed imbued with the soft murmurings and night shufflings of women who were mysterious and set apart from children by their incomprehensible communal devotion to God. I felt the appalling and sobering piety of the convent's atmosphere as if it were palpable as fur. The hush of its dim hallways, and the stillness of the spare room where I was put to bed, I did not interpret as the quiet of early morning, but as the holy secrecy of the Catholic sisterhood. As I drifted to sleep, I envisioned the wicks of a hundred vigil candles illuminating the small hands of robed women, their whispering voices tossing in the shadowed air.

Isabel woke me up in the afternoon. She stood at the foot of my bed and said, "Penny? Don't sleep any longer or you won't be able to fall asleep tonight." Sister Geraldine was not there; I realized she must be at the school. Isabel waited as I slipped out of my sheets in my rumpled clothes and put on my shoes. She led me through a corridor, without pausing to speak to whomever had let her in, or turning back to make sure I was following. She walked quickly, as if exiting a place she considered perilous to herself and unattractive.

After we climbed into the Jeep, Isabel said, "I've learned that you've asked Sister Geraldine to call your uncle." She drove me home without questioning me about what had happened the night before; I understood that she would deal with my transgression by covertly stamping it as unmentionable and relegating it to a silent corner of her universe. I felt intensely uncomfortable beside her. Isabel had never shown anger toward me before, but I could sense both annoyance and wrath in her now. The fact that she did not reproach me with words made her dissatisfaction with me all the more intolerable.

When we arrived home, Isabel fed me a cheese sandwich and celery, and sat in the living room working one of her puzzles while I ate. Once she looked up and said curtly, "Your uncle has left on his hiking expedition and Sister Geraldine has not been able to connect with him yet." I heard Mahalia in the shower upstairs. The water remained on throughout my lunch, as if she were avoiding greeting me. When I finished eating, Isabel told me, "Wash your dish." While I rinsed it, and still had my back to her, she said, "I need to go to my house to complete some papers. You'll have to come with me, Penny. I don't feel I can leave you alone."

"Mahalia's upstairs," I told her.

My slight defiance found no purchase in our conversation. Isabel waited to hear the shower turn off, and then she spoke to Mahalia through the bathroom door. Isabel descended the stairs, picked up her brocade bag, dropped her puzzle inside, and told me stiffly, "I won't force you to accompany me."

After she left, Mahalia came downstairs, a towel wrapped around her head like a turban. When she saw me lying on the couch, she said, "Everyone was looking for you! They searched for hours! Isabel and Mrs. Esselborne drove all over town. They called the police, and the police were looking for you too. Isabel was mortified. How could you do something so dangerous? How could you?"

Was Isabel mortified? I had not known I had the power to unsettle her. My sister glared at me, looking righteous and indignant, her green eyes narrowed, wisps of her hair escaping like small flames from the edges of her towel-turban. I understood then that in the tug-of-war between good and bad, Isabel had lost hold of and relinquished me. Somehow, I had won, and a tremendous sense of relief overwhelmed me.

I wanted my sister to vanish and leave me to myself, so that I could feel unattached for just a little longer, freed of supervision and the hovering, circling presence of authority.

"Penny—" she began.

But I did not want to hear any more from her. I interrupted her—I asked, hoping to push her away, "Don't you ever miss Mama?"

"Of course," Mahalia answered. "I miss the way she used to be."

"I miss her any way at all," I answered. My sister turned to head upstairs. I had derailed her from whatever she had intended to say. I watched her climb, and as her slim feet touched the middle step, I suddenly did not want her to go.

"Mahalia?" I asked.

She stopped. "What, Penny?"

"What will happen to Isabel when you turn into a grown-up?"

"What do you mean?" my sister answered.

"I don't think Isabel likes people after they grow up," I said. "She only likes them before that."

Mahalia made a noise halfway between a guffaw and a cry of exasperation. She returned to the bottom of the stairs and said, "You don't understand anything about Isabel, do you? Isabel has kept you at her side every day, day after day, morning, noon, and night. Who else would do that for you? Don't you see how much she cares about you? She was worried sick last night."

I felt a flicker of remorse that I had made Isabel worry. However, Mahalia's next words were: "Last night Isabel was so upset! She told me that a child in her charge had never even been injured before. She told me that you were the most exhausting person she's ever been around, and she saw that she had failed with you completely!"

This hurt my feelings. I pressed my hands against my eyelids, holding tears back. I saw blossoms of blackness and a red glow that darkened to the color of iron. "Mama loves me when she can't see me," I told my sister. "Isabel only likes me as long as she's watching me."

"That doesn't make any sense, Penny," Mahalia answered. "I wish Isabel would stay with us longer. She was supposed to be here until August at least. If F. X. comes back now, she'll have to move out early. Why did you make things so hard for her?"

For the only time that summer, I experienced a terrible doubt that Mahalia did not want Isabel to like me as much as her—that Mahalia's disapproval of me was calculated, that she liked pointing out my faults to insure that she would have Isabel all to herself. And then I wondered: Did Mahalia think my mother loved me more, because we were more alike?

Mahalia interrupted my thoughts by saying, "Don't give Isabel any trouble when she gets back!"

All that day, after Isabel returned, Mahalia doted on her. My sister washed Isabel's dish before Isabel could get to it, and brought her hot water for her tea before Isabel had drawn out a tea bag. My conduct, if it had helped to free me, seemed to propel Mahalia more fiercely to Isabel's side.

"You're spoiling me, Mahalia," Isabel said, when my sister made dinner that night: baked whitefish with steamed rice and vegetables. Hugging Isabel from behind, Mahalia wrapped her arms around Isabel's narrow shoulders. Isabel took Mahalia's hand for a moment, looking grateful, and then quickly leaned forward to retrieve the tea bag from her cup.

———

For the next few days, Sister Geraldine kept me at All Saints until late afternoon. The school's summer session had not started, and she let me sit reading science-fiction novels at the secretary's desk outside the principal's office and released me periodically to run around the playground outside the office window. When Sister Geraldine brought me home in the evenings, Isabel would greet her in a formal way. At dinner, Isabel read her pamphlets and nutrition magazines or catalogs, and discussed church business with Mahalia, and never asked me about my day.

On Friday, F. X. called Sister Geraldine from a hiking lodge off the Appalachian Trail. My mother was worried because she had been unable to speak to my sister or me before leaving The Place, and she had dispatched F. X. to the pale of civilization to contact us. When Sister Geraldine related to him my journey to Florence, the words she chose induced him to head back to Stein the next day.

F. X. arrived at our house a few hours after midnight on Sunday. All that night, nightmares had ransacked my sleep: I dreamed repeatedly that I was lost in a neighborhood with a hundred houses identical to mine. When I tried their doors, they opened into buried rooms or fields of beaten ground. In the last dream, the ground inside one house began to tilt. I lost my footing and clutched desperately at small weeds to keep from slipping: I saw that I was going to fall not merely out of my neighborhood, but off the earth itself.

When I awoke, F. X. was sitting on the foot of my bed. It sloped under his weight, and the room smelled like cigar smoke.

"Penny?" he whispered. "Are you awake? I heard you moaning up here."

I sat up, trying to free myself from my dreams. I saw the beacon of a lit cigar: Around it smoke broke into wafts of ghosts scuttling off, *Boooo!*

I cried, "F. X.!" and threw myself onto him.

"I intended to stay with your mother and David at least two more weeks on the Trail," he said, "but by the time Sister Geraldine spoke to me, your mother and David were acting like unwed honeymooners and I felt like a chaperone. I was glad to escape, so I took the red-eye."

"I almost died while you were gone," I said.

"I heard about your escapade," he answered, but I hadn't meant that I had almost died when I ran off with Katie—I had been thinking of the whole summer leading up to that night. When I considered explaining what I meant, it made no sense, and I let it go. I clung like a shipwrecked man to F. X.'s bulk and fell asleep.

In the morning, I awoke to the sound of my uncle's voice downstairs. Isabel already had begun to evacuate the house. Her clothes, her bathroom articles, and all of her papers fit into a single cardboard suitcase that leaned against the wall by the piano. She stood at the door, ready to leave, while F. X. carried in a canvas backpack from his newly rented Galaxie 500. By the time I came downstairs, he was unloading his pack onto the living-room couch.

"Penny!" he told me. "I brought you something." From the top of his pack he lifted a small wood-and-wire cage with two wedge-headed brown lizards inside. He took one of the lizards out. It opened its mouth wide and made a silent squawk. He held it to his earlobe and it clamped on. "Lizard earrings," he said, batting his eyes. Isabel regarded him silently. I heard noises in the upstairs bathroom and realized that Mahalia must be up already, and that Isabel was waiting for her.

"Mama wrote me about those!" I told F. X. I turned away from Isabel, realizing I had betrayed the fact that I had seen my mother's vanished letter, but if Isabel had registered my slip, she did not show it.

Mahalia came down the stairs a few minutes later, fully dressed, her hair pulled back, and wearing her slipper-shoes. Isabel picked up her suitcase and said in a peculiar, stilted way, "It's nice of you to walk me home, Mahalia."

F. X. did not seem to notice that Mahalia's eyes were red, as if she had been crying in the bathroom. F. X. handed me a lizard and told me, "You know they change color like chameleons? I have this theory that their colors shift when you hum to them or make noise around them. I was experimenting on the airplane." I held the lizard to my earlobe and felt it grab hold like a tiny hand.

"Mahalia, you have to see these ferns David and I have been carrying around for you." He lifted a small Tupperware container from his pack, pulled off the lid, and held the container in front of my sister: Tiny wine-colored fiddleheads spiraled outward from a single brown knot.

"They're Royal Ferns!" Mahalia cried.

"David found them in this swamp," F. X. said. "The big ones were about a hundred feet high. They looked primordial, like brontosaurus food."

"They grow to six feet," Mahalia told him. "Oh, these will be hard to keep in a garden," she announced happily. "They like a lot of water."

"If it's easier for you, Mr. Molineaux," Isabel said, "I can continue to take Mahalia to Stein Evangelical in the mornings, as long as she's teaching at the Bible camp."

F. X. turned toward Isabel and thanked her.

"I can take Mahalia to church services as well," Isabel continued.

I said, thinking it would irk my sister, "The church doesn't have anyone to play their organ. You could play it for them, F. X."

"That's not necessary," Isabel answered.

"Isabel," Mahalia said. "F. X. could play for choir practice." I was surprised Mahalia would want F. X. at the church. Perhaps she felt that her life might end at any minute, and she hoped to draw him closer to her world before he could pull her from it.

"That's an interesting idea," F. X. said. The other lizard still clung to his ear, and I leaned forward, pried it off, and put it on my bare one. "I'd be glad to."

"He could help the choir on Tuesday," Mahalia told Isabel, "and afterward, he could attend the women's meeting with us. Mrs. Groot is always complaining that we need to have more of a male presence at the meetings."

Isabel capitulated to Mahalia, saying, "Well, possibly just this once." Isabel may have feared, a little, that now that F. X. had returned, she could lose Mahalia just as she had lost hold of me. She added, "And I'm sure Penny would be happy to attend with her uncle." Isabel put down her bag and walked over to me. She did not touch me, but she bent down and said, "You have been a test for me, Penny. I realize now how much I'll miss your company. I'm glad you'll be coming to the church. We can all go as one family."

Isabel lifted her suitcase. She told F. X., "Several letters arrived from the children's mother. I was not sure whether I should deliver them to the children, because they contained material that did not seem appropriate for them, and so I discarded them. I am sure when Mrs. Daigle returns that she can communicate to the children any essential news that was in the letters."

F. X. received this information with one eyebrow raised. "I see," he answered.

Mahalia reached for Isabel's suitcase; my sister wanted to carry it for her. Isabel relinquished it, and she and Mahalia walked together up the block. My sister spent the rest of the day with Isabel.

When F. X. picked me up from All Saints on Tuesday afternoon, Sister Geraldine gave me a novel for the weekend. It was *A Wrinkle in Time*. She told F. X., "Isabel Flood came to the convent yesterday evening to tell me that she didn't think Penny should be reading the science-fiction books she borrows from the office."

"She did?" F. X. asked.

"I just want to reassure you that any books Penny gets from All Saints have been scanned thoroughly for anything that might not be right for a youngster."

"Well, of course," F. X. answered.

"Anyhow," Sister Geraldine said, "I told Miss Flood that the Catholic church has considerable expertise in the area of censorship and not to worry. She didn't laugh. She doesn't seem to have a sense of humor."

F. X. laughed.

What Sister Geraldine did not say, until several months later in a casual conversation with David, was that Isabel had written to the Family Life Division of the Conference of Catholic Bishops to inform them that Sister Geraldine had condoned Cicely Nohilly's abortion. When Sister Geraldine related this story to David, she said, "The Catholic Conference wrote me a letter of inquiry, and I replied that Isabel Flood had collected her story second- or thirdhand, and pried into a privileged and subtle conversation with a man who had since crossed into the next world. I was in the middle of a fund drive for All Saints in any case, and the politics of family planning and Isabel Flood were the last thing on my mind because she hadn't done anything criminal yet."

The evening after he spoke with Sister Geraldine, F. X. wrote the second in the series of letters he would continue to deliver to Isabel that summer:

Dear Ms. Flood:

> *The Fetal Committee has met. Our community wishes to hold a referendum on the question of our "right to life," as it is now called. Some of us lean toward the uncharted experience of birth, some toward death, with its promise of reawakening in a larger womb. Whatever else is said, death is quicker, and therefore less painful. However, we lack sufficient empirical data. Please supply us with more information so that we can make an informed decision. In the interim, we continue to request that you refrain from speaking for us.*

> *Sincerely yours,*
> *The Fetal Committee*

F. X. chuckled and guffawed as he composed this letter; he stood as he wrote, until he sat down to sign it. I looked over his shoulder.

"Isabel didn't know your other letter was from you," I told him.

"Which other letter?" F. X. asked.

"The one you wrote on that napkin and stuck in with Mama's letter. It fell onto the floor, and Isabel picked it up later and thought that teacher had sent it."

"What teacher?"

"A teacher from Stein High School who she doesn't like," I said. "But I knew it was your letter because I saw it when I took Mama's letter from Isabel's purse. I took it because Isabel stole all of Mama's letters, just like she told you!"

F. X. answered, "Penny, Isabel probably thought she was doing the right thing by keeping those letters from you. In fact it was wrong, but she thought it was right. She's a strange fish."

Was she a strange fish? This was the first time any adult had admitted such a possibility—I felt a rush of relief, an inward swirling of my parts, a reassembling of myself into something closer to what I had been before my mother left, and suddenly the whole summer with Isabel telescoped into a dry, hard ball, and seemed far behind me.

"Mahalia doesn't know Isabel's strange," I said.

"Being strange is not necessarily bad," F. X. answered. "Sometimes it's a person's only redeeming quality. Besides, Mahalia sent me a letter saying that Isabel was kind and patient with you all summer."

"Mahalia wrote you and Mama?" I asked.

"She wrote me, anyway," F. X. answered. "I don't think she wrote your mother. Is what Mahalia says about Isabel true?"

It was true: She was always kind and patient with me. She was a far cry from Mrs. Fury. "Yeah," I answered.

"Well, *that's* good," F. X. said. Even so, when Isabel came to our door in the morning to drive us to Stein Evangelical, F. X. had the letter from the Fetal Committee in his pocket, in an envelope addressed to Isabel, and when we arrived at Stein Evangelical, F. X. put the envelope in the container marked "Suggestion Box" at the front of the church.

F. X. played the organ vigorously all morning as the choir sang. Isabel and Mahalia busied themselves collating leaflets in Reverend Bender's office while I sat beside F. X. on the organ bench to see whether, as he claimed, "A deaf man could learn the organ because the vibrations are so vivid. Sit next to me and close your eyes while I play, and put your fingers in your ears, and you can feel the darkness twist and slither."

I had brought the anoles in a plastic bag in my jumper pocket, and I peered in at them to see how they reacted to the music. They looked mesmerized; they had closed their eyes and turned browner as the music progressed, as if they thought of hymns as being the color of silty lake mud. At several junctures, the choir conductor asked F. X. to play more softly. When practice was over, she told F. X. with evident relief, "I'm sorry you won't be playing for us regularly."

After the chorus dissipated, we ate bag lunches prepared by Isabel, and then the women's committee president, Mrs. Esselborne, arrived. She pushed a podium before several rows of folding chairs set up in the front of the church annex, assumed the podium, and readjusted the heart-shaped gold pin that held her scarf in place. Her blond hair lay knotted on top of her head. Although she wore a different dress than she had on the evening I ran off with Katie, the fabric had an identical pattern, gold chains linking across a blue background.

Mrs. Esselborne said, "Well! Where did Penny come from? Did you just drop from the sky?" Her mouth turned up in a fretful smile, and I felt uneasy. As she looked down to page through a stack of papers, her brow furrowed. She could not have been happy to see me.

The attending women's committee was barely larger than the clutch of church women I had met already through Isabel. There were no other young girls present, and the only teenagers were my sister and Lucy Coker, who burst into the room shouting, "Penny! Mahalia told me you were coming." Before I could answer, Isabel emerged in the hallway outside the back doors, and Lucy ran to her calling, "I have an important message for you!" Mrs. Esselborne kept her eyes on Isabel and Lucy and frowned slightly.

Mrs. Groot entered the room with a cake on a plate, a dark devil's food with icing that was almost black, and I longed for a piece. I wondered whether the cake would be served before or after whatever kind of meeting the grown-up women were going to have.

"You can put the cake on the card table, Mrs. Groot," Mrs. Esselborne said.

Mrs. Groot set her plate on a low wooden table and settled herself in a folding chair beside her cake. "Oh, Penny," she told me. "I'm so glad you're back with us. You gave Isabel such a scare. I told her not to worry—Nicky used to disappear like that as a boy." Mrs. Groot wore a dark brown pantsuit, the same color as the cake. The yellow pockets under her eyes seemed heavier. She leaned forward and said hello to a woman named Mrs. Hatter who had seated herself in a back row.

Mrs. Hatter did not look up; she read from a maroon Bible with a large bookmark, her lips moving slightly. She was older than the other women, with pale gray hair and a wrinkled neck, but she wore a red dress and red sandals, as if she were young.

I sat down in the row of chairs between her and Mrs. Groot, within a yard of the cake.

"Ever since Mr. Groot died," Mrs. Groot told Mrs. Hatter, "snatches of the Bible have been floating up at me from nowhere, when I'm just walking up the street or in the middle of a conversation with someone. Does that ever happen to you? 'Blessed are the meek' and 'Nearer my God than thee' and 'Blessed art thou among women.' All in an unconnected way where I can't make sense of them. It makes me feel unsettled."

Mrs. Hatter closed her Bible over her thumb and said, "That would be God trying to reach you."

"I don't know," Mrs. Groot said vaguely.

I stood and leaned over the table. I found a knife and lifted it to cut myself a piece of Mrs. Groot's cake. Isabel loomed beside me and laid her hand on my arm. "Not now, Penny," she said. She took the knife from my hand and guided me to a chair several yards from the cake. I felt my anole lizards wiggle in my pocket as I sat down.

"Izzy!" Mrs. Groot said. "Nicky's back home. I'm so relieved they didn't decide to try him as an adult! I can't thank you enough for speaking up for him at the police station."

"I'm glad for Nicky that things worked out," Isabel answered.

"I don't know what moved him to steal that car," Mrs. Groot said. "It's so nice of Mark Coker to offer to take Nicky under his wing and let him help him farm. Of course, Mark would never leave him alone with Lucy."

Mahalia appeared at the back doors and signaled frantically to Isabel. Mrs. Esselborne watched Isabel as she disappeared with Mahalia into the hallway.

Mrs. Groot turned back to Mrs. Hatter and asked, "Are you new here? I used to attend the Lutheran church when I was young, but the minister died and they replaced him with Reverend Fowler, and I could never understand him through his accent. He was from the city. 'Hawk, the angel of God,' was the first thing I ever heard him say, and it took me days before I realized what he meant. So I just stopped going to church until Izzy invited me here."

Mrs. Hatter answered, "The church I attended for years in Dannemora burned down."

Isabel returned to the meeting room and announced, "Mrs. Esselborne, Penny Daigle will be sitting beside me and carefully watched. Mahalia has brought her uncle, Mr. Molineaux, with her today as well. He played the organ for the choir this morning."

Mrs. Esselborne frowned, but at Isabel instead of me. I was not sure why. I was not sensitive to territorial struggles among women. However, as the meeting progressed, I would notice that Mrs. Esselborne was quick to disagree with Isabel at almost every opportunity, and that Isabel steadfastly resisted her.

"It will be nice to have a man's guiding voice," Mrs. Groot told Mrs. Esselborne. "Mr. Molineaux will make things more balanced." Mrs. Groot groped under the table, where she found bags containing cups, napkins, and plastic forks, which she arranged in front of her cake.

I fidgeted on my chair, wishing I had brought my science-fiction book. I read the back of a hymnal in front of me, and then a scrap of paper resting on the seat beside me. It was a set of notes in an adult's script:

Men
Still no male members! Mahalia's uncle by invitation.

Catholics
Barb Wroblewski—7 children! married, however to Protestant.
Mahalia Daigle (teen) and Penny Daigle (pre-teen).

Protestants
Esselborne—CHAIRWOMAN. Married but no children.
Annie Strang—tardiness problem. 2 children & unmarried.
Lucy—our pregnant teen!
Mrs. Hatter—from Pentecostal.
Mrs. Groot—Widowed. 1 child.

Isabel picked up the paper and inserted it in a loose-leaf notebook she held. She sat down right beside me.

A discordant tune arose at the back of the room. F. X. was fiddling with his left hand on the low keys of the organ. "That's the kind of music that's better than it sounds," he said, smiling at Mrs. Groot. "Boulez." Mrs. Groot smiled back uncertainly. Now F. X. played something else, even odder, stopped after a few bars, and said, "That's 'Amazing Grace' played backward." I left my chair and reseated myself beside him, peering at the anoles in my pocket. As the organ hummed next to them, the lizards looked as if they were blushing green: Color came into their cheeks and flowed backward to their tails.

"Excuse me, Mr. Molineaux," Mrs. Esselborne called. "Is it necessary for you to practice now? We need to start our meeting."

Mrs. Groot turned to Isabel and said, "Let him sit here with us." She tugged at her devil's food pantsuit, patted the seat beside her, and smiled at F. X.

F. X. stayed where he was on the organ bench. "Thank you, Mrs. Groot, but I like sitting near the back." He whispered to me, "That way I can bolt if I have to." I snuggled happily against him, and he slung his arm over my shoulders.

"Penny, stay here with me," Isabel said, taking my hand and leading me back to the chair beside hers. She clearly assumed that F. X. could not keep me in line during the meeting.

Mahalia emerged from the hallway with Mrs. Wroblewski and said in an exasperated voice, "F. X.! I thought you were going to come to the office before the meeting. I didn't even get the chance to tell you what it's about."

"Mahalia," said Mrs. Esselborne. "We're glad to have your uncle here. In the future, please let me know when you want to bring visitors, so that we can give them the welcome they deserve."

Mahalia nodded and colored slightly. She clasped her mustard-seed pendant and sat down on the other side of Isabel.

"Barb Wroblewski and Lucy, please don't do that here," Mrs. Esselborne said. "Please find a chair."

Mrs. Wroblewski and Lucy stood next to one another, comparing their stomachs. Mrs. Wroblewski rolled her eyes in Mrs. Esselborne's direction. Mrs. Esselborne was not looking, and Lucy giggled. Both Lucy and Mrs. Wroblewski were wearing smocks and red headbands: Lucy's hair was still reddish-orange, and Mrs. Wroblewski had a new shag haircut and a feathery halo of short bangs. Lucy pulled her smock up, exposing her stomach. It looked artificial, as if someone had stuck an oversized cantaloupe under her skin. Lucy's smock was new and pressed, but Mrs. Wroblewski's was a washed-out gray, oyster colored, with faded ruffles, and her ankles were so swollen that she appeared to have no ankles at all. Her shoulders hunched forward, as if they were being drawn into the pocket of herself. I touched my own stomach; it was flat, with two brackets of muscle. I decided I would never bear children.

A fly attempted to land on Mrs. Groot's devil's food cake. She shooed it away.

Mahalia called to Mrs. Wroblewski and Lucy, "Sit next to me!" She waved at some seats on her right, and they nestled in beside her. Mrs. Esselborne scowled again.

Mahalia put her arm around Lucy and laughed when she could not reach very far. They readjusted themselves in their seats, and there was such a flurry of whispers and muffled laughter that I almost did not recognize my sister: Lucy said something to her and Mahalia cracked up just as I would have if Joel Renaud had whispered *fuck a duck* into my ear during one of Mrs. Fury's French lessons.

"We have two special visitors today," Isabel said, standing up.

"Let's wait to call the meeting to order," Mrs. Esselborne told her.

Isabel continued, turning around in her seat to face the other women, "You all see that Penny Daigle is with us today. This is her first time at a Stein Evangelical women's committee meeting." Lucy flashed me a smile, and Mrs. Groot and Mrs. Wroblewski clapped. I saw that this bothered Mrs. Esselborne. "And her uncle, Mr. Molineaux, has come by special invitation."

Mrs. Esselborne said, looking directly at me as if she were avoiding responding to Isabel, "As long as it's all right with your uncle, you're certainly welcome, Penny."

Isabel sat down.

"Where is Annie Strang?" Mrs. Esselborne asked.

Another fly attempted to land on Mrs. Groot's cake. She stood and covered it with a napkin.

Lucy cried, "Wait a minute! I have to use the bathroom!" She rushed into the aisle. Mrs. Wroblewski followed her saying, "Don't you worry! I'm right here with you!" Mahalia followed them. She whispered something to Lucy, and Lucy burst out laughing.

"Oh hush, you terrible girls," Mrs. Wroblewski told them.

"Where is Annie Strang?" Mrs. Esselborne repeated.

Mrs. Hatter looked up from her Bible, to watch Lucy, Mrs. Wroblewski, and Mahalia. Lucy leaned her forehead against the wall beside the back door, and Mrs. Wroblewski took her by the arm saying, "Just a few more steps to the bathroom, honey." While Mahalia grabbed her other arm, F. X. stood to open the door and let them through. F. X. reseated himself and tinkered absently on the organ.

"Mr. Molineaux," Mrs. Esselborne said.

I leaned toward F. X. and whispered, "Is the cake for us?"

He stopped playing and whispered back, "It's the reward we get for lasting through the whole meeting."

"Oh," I answered. I checked my lizards, pulling them part way out of my pocket. Mrs. Hatter stared at them and turned away, looking ruffled.

"Mrs. Hatter," Mrs. Esselborne said in the same tone Mrs. Fury had used to draw out students who never raised their hands. "Is there anything you'd like to say to the group about today's agenda while we're waiting for Lucy?"

"No," Mrs. Hatter said.

"Would you like to share what you're reading?" Isabel asked Mrs. Hatter.

"Let's try and keep to the agenda," Mrs. Esselborne said.

"Well," Mrs. Hatter answered, with a puzzled expression. She gazed down at her Bible and said, *"And he shall turn the heart of the fathers to the children, and the heart of the children to the fathers, lest I come and smite the earth with a curse—"*

"Thank you, Mrs. Hatter," Mrs. Esselborne said. "But we like to start with the first order of business. As usual, it's finances."

"We're so sorry!" Mrs. Wroblewski cried, reentering with Lucy and Mahalia. Lucy had her arms hooked around Mrs. Wroblewski's arm and Mahalia's waist.

"Hey-ho!" Lucy called. "I'm okay now."

"Morning sickness, and so late in her pregnancy!" Mahalia whispered to Mrs. Groot, who smiled knowingly. Mrs. Groot's dark brown sleeve slipped forward, revealing a smear of devil's food icing on her forearm.

"The meeting is called to order," Mrs. Esselborne said. "And the question on the floor is"—she waited for Lucy, Mahalia, and Mrs. Wroblewski to sit down—"whether anyone knows if Annie Strang, our treasurer, is coming. She was in charge of bringing our financial records."

"Annie asked me to tell you—" Mrs. Wroblewski answered. "She asked me to say that she'd be held up because both of her kids have been sick with chicken pox since Monday. Annie had to locate a baby-sitter, because her mother claimed she felt sick as well. Annie said she'd try to be here in half an hour."

"We're moving on to the second order of business," Mrs. Esselborne said. "Poems for the *Motherhood Booklet for Pregnant Teens*."

"I wrote a poem," Lucy announced.

"That's wonderful, Lucy!" Isabel told her. "Let's hear it."

"Wait just a moment," Mrs. Esselborne directed. "Did you bring extras? So that people have your poem in front of them when you read?"

"Isabel made copies for me," Lucy said.

Mrs. Esselborne watched silently as Mahalia handed a pile of copies to the row of women behind her. There was a rustling as each committee member leaned over to take a paper, or to hand the pile to the woman behind her. In her confusion, Lucy passed two copies to F. X., who returned one. "I'm sorry," she told him shyly. When Isabel stood and leaned forward to assure that everyone had Lucy's poem, I scooted down the row of chairs and situated myself beside the cake table.

"I need a copy," Mrs. Esselborne said. She stepped forward and got her own. "Now, let's all settle down so that Lucy can read." Everyone faced Lucy expectantly.

The table holding the cake suddenly tipped dangerously. I looked down and realized that I had stood up and was leaning on it. Mrs. Esselborne stepped forward and grabbed the table. Isabel pulled me away and stopped the cake with her free hand from sliding off the table edge.

"Sit on the other side of me, Penny," she said. She and Mrs. Esselborne did not look at one another. They each returned to their respective places.

"Let's have complete quiet," Mrs. Esselborne said.

Before Lucy could read, however, Isabel turned to her and said, "Share the poem with us now, honey."

Resting the paper on her stomach, Lucy read:

> "I hope that you will
> fight the people who kill
> the babe in the womb.
> There is plenty of room
> in our great big life
> although I am no wife
> although I am not wed
> although I am not married
> you will not be buried
> when all had been said.
> With our conscious to lead us
> you will come out and greet us
> my feetus, my feetus."

All of the women clapped.

"You did a good job, Lucy," Isabel said.

"We're all proud of you, Lucy," Mrs. Esselborne followed swiftly. "I know Mrs. Hatter is proud. Mrs. Hatter?" she asked. "Do you have any commentary on Lucy's poem?" But Mrs. Hatter was reading her Bible; Lucy's poem was tucked in its back pages.

"Hmmm?" Mrs. Hatter answered, looking up.

"I wasn't sure how to spell *conscious*," Lucy said.

"It should be *conscience*. C-o-n-s-c-i-e-n-c-e," Mrs. Esselborne answered.

"But this is not a spelling test, is it, Mrs. Hatter?" Mrs. Wroblewski asked mutinously.

Mrs. Hatter frowned obligingly.

Behind her, Mrs. Esselborne looked furious. She returned to reading Lucy's poem, smoothing the page in front of her. I found myself siding with Isabel against Mrs. Esselborne. Isabel was bent over her loose-leaf notebook, where she wrote several sentences on a blank page. Her dime-store barrettes pulled her hair back tightly over her ears, and there was a look of tenderness on her foxy face, as if Lucy's poem had moved her.

"I wasn't sure about *feetus* either," Lucy said. "I wanted to say *embryo*, but nothing rhymed with it."

"It's just precious the way it is," Mrs. Groot told her.

"*Try to remembry-oh,*" F. X. said. He had spoken for the first time since the meeting had been called to order. All of the women, except for Isabel and Mrs. Hatter, turned toward him. He continued:

"*Try to remembry-oh*
The days of Septembry-oh
When you were an embryo."

"Mr. Molineaux," Mrs. Esselborne said. "Everyone will get a turn. Who else brought a poem?"

No hand went up. Isabel continued to write in her notebook, and Mrs. Hatter turned to a new section of her Bible.

Mrs. Groot stood and moved her cake slightly toward the center of the table. She waved her hand in the air as if she had risen in order to brush away another fly, but I saw that she was distressed by the disarray created when the cake had slid toward me. She quickly rearranged the plates, forks, and napkins in front of the cake and sat down again before Mrs. Esselborne had time to comment.

Isabel closed her notebook, stood, and announced, "I have a poem I'd like to share."

"Did you write it yourself?" Mrs. Esselborne challenged her.

"No," Isabel answered, looking around at us all. "It's a poem by a woman named Gwendolyn Brooks that's being handed out to summer school tenth graders by a Stein High English teacher. He also used this material during the regular school year last spring. I believe it's important for us all to read the poem, and know what children are being taught in our public institutions."

"Maybe you can place that on the agenda for next time," Mrs. Esselborne said. "People were asked to write their own contributions for the *Motherhood Booklet*."

"It's essential that we attend to this now, before the regular school year begins again," Isabel said, turning her back to Mrs. Esselborne, and facing us. Isabel half-smiled with satisfaction, as if she had befriended us all for this moment alone.

"You should take a look at that poem," Mrs. Wroblewski told Mrs. Esselborne. "It really is a shocker."

Mrs. Esselborne's face registered the fact that Mrs. Wroblewski and Isabel already had discussed the poem with one another. Mrs. Esselborne said, "Let's follow procedure and place the poem on the agenda before we read it."

"I wouldn't mind reading it now," Mrs. Groot answered.

"I'd like to see it too," Lucy said, "because I've been in high school, so this concerns me a lot."

"And I'm still in high school," Mahalia said.

"But you don't go to Stein High, honey," Mrs. Esselborne told her. "You go to the Catholic school."

"She's old enough to know what counts," Lucy said knowingly.

"Can I see it?" I asked.

"Let's simmer down," Mrs. Esselborne said.

But Isabel was already handing around the Gwendolyn Brooks poem. Even Mrs. Hatter took one, although she tucked it, like Lucy's, in the back pages of her Bible. When Isabel handed me my copy, she grasped my shoulder and half-smiled; she was not angry at me anymore.

"Is there any other business?" Mrs. Esselborne asked.

"Annie!" Lucy cried as, just at that moment, Annie Strang bustled in. She was a thin, giraffelike blond woman with a large nose and a pock-marked face. She looked as if she had been in a fistfight on her way to the church. A label protruded from the back of her dress, and her collar stood out strangely under her chin; she had buttoned wrong. A large space between her second and third buttons revealed the lace of a violet brassiere.

"Don't stop things for me!" Annie Strang cried, seating herself. "Charlie and the baby are down with chicken pox, and I had to hunt for a sitter after my mother suddenly discovered she's feeling too exhausted to help out. I couldn't ask the girl that usually comes, because after the last time she baby-sat, the bathroom smelled as though someone had gotten sick, and I found an empty six-pack in the bathroom cabinet, and, of course, Izzy was *here*. So I called Mrs. Skelter—"

"We use her, in a pinch," Mrs. Wroblewski said. "There's not many who are willing to watch over seven. Except Izzy, of course." She smiled at Isabel.

"Mrs. Skelter flatly refused to watch my Nicky four years ago," Mrs. Groot said.

"And," Annie Strang continued, "Mrs. Skelter said she could come for two hours, but she had to run an errand first—"

"Our meeting has already commenced," Mrs. Esselborne interrupted. "Do you have our financial records?"

"I just didn't get to them," Annie Strang answered. "I hoped we could save them for next time."

"You don't have the records?" Mrs. Esselborne asked.

Annie Strang looked down at her shirt and rebuttoned it. A large section of violet brassiere flashed and then disappeared. "It's not my fault," she said. "Tell my kids not to get sick! You don't know what it's like to have kids. You have all the free time in the world!"

There was an uncomfortable silence, although I was uncertain why: Mrs. Groot exchanged looks with Isabel, and Lucy and Mahalia whispered to each other. Mrs. Wroblewski turned halfway in her chair and rolled her eyes at Annie Strang, who grinned back. F. X. raised his eyebrows. Only Mrs. Hatter seemed unconcerned about whatever had stirred up the other women in the room. She turned the page of her Bible and read on.

"Why don't we vote on whether we're going to share the poem I've brought?" Isabel asked.

"Isabel—" Mrs. Esselborne began.

"What's wrong with voting?" Mrs. Groot asked. She smoothed the front of her devil's food pantsuit and smiled at F. X.

"Annie," Mrs. Wroblewski said, "Isabel's brought a poem that's being taught at the high school." She handed her a copy from Isabel's pile. "We need your opinion on it as much as anyone else's. Let's see a show of hands. Who wants to read the poem?"

Before Mrs. Esselborne could say anything, everyone's hand except Mrs. Hatter's went up. Even F. X. and I raised ours. He was reading his copy of the poem with a swallowed-looking smile. When Mrs. Esselborne asked for a show of hands against, Mrs. Hatter did not raise hers then either.

"Mrs. Hatter?" Mrs. Esselborne pressed. "How do you vote?"

Mrs. Hatter answered, "I was remembering that Job cursed the day wherein he was born. '*Let it look for light but have none; neither let it see the dawning of the day: Because it shut not up the doors of my mother's womb, nor hid sorrow from mine eyes.*' "

"But how do you vote, Mrs. Hatter?"

"Don't make her vote," Mrs. Wroblewski said. "At this point, we already have a vast majority, so it won't make any difference anyway."

The lizards in my pocket had grown too quiet. I pulled out their plastic bag and laid it on my paper. They were still breathing and had turned a dark brown. I bit a small airhole in the bag and stuck it back in my pocket.

Isabel said, "This is by a poetess named Gwendolyn Brooks and it's called 'the mother.' " She read aloud slowly and in a mildly dramatic voice, as if she thought poetry should be read in a particular way:

"*Abortions will not let you forget.*
You remember the children you got that you did not get,

> *The damp small pulps with a little or with no hair,*
> *The singers and workers that never handled the air."*

"Wait," Mrs. Esselborne said. "This is not appropriate. We have a child in the room." She asked, "How old are you Penny?"

Lucy answered in a challenging tone, "Penny is twelve."

I was not twelve, of course; I was about to turn nine. It was amazing to me that a girl Lucy's age could look at me and imagine she could put me forward as even a day older than I was, but no one questioned her. Mrs. Wroblewski winked at me. Mrs. Esselborne scrutinized me and said, "I think it would be easier if people read the poem to themselves. Why don't we do that?"

As the adults around me read silently on, I scanned the next few lines:

> *You will never neglect or beat*
> *Them, or silence or buy with a sweet.*
> *You will never wind up the sucking-thumb*
> *Or scuttle off ghosts that come.*
> *You will never leave them, controlling your luscious sigh,*
> *Return for a snack of them, with gobbling mother-eye.*

I thought of Mr. Coker saying, "Gobble, gobble!" as he stared through the pipe into Lucy's room.

Mrs. Esselborne snatched the poem from my hands.

"That's exactly Isabel's point," Annie Strang said. "Who would want their little daughters reading this?" She touched her collar, realized it was tucked into her shirt, and turned it back right-side out. "If I had known there were people who thought about this kind of thing when I was a girl, God knows what more trouble I would have gotten into."

Mrs. Esselborne returned to the podium, with my copy of the poem. Annie Strang leaned toward Isabel and whispered, "I see what's going on here. And I want you to know I'm on your side."

Mrs. Groot stood and bent over her cake. I thought the meeting was over and got up also. However, Mrs. Groot merely spread a new napkin over her cake to protect it and returned to her chair.

"Just bear with us, Penny," F. X. whispered. I sat back down.

Isabel announced, "This poem is about a mother who has killed her own children."

"You know what I don't like about this poem?" Mrs. Wroblewski asked.

"I'll tell you what I don't like about this poem. It's all told from the point of view of the mother—how she feels about it all. No one asks how the baby feels."

"It tells you the mother feels bad," Mahalia answered.

"She feels terrible," Lucy agreed.

"They're right," Mrs. Groot said. "You-know-what's don't let you forget."

"We could print that up for lapel buttons," Annie Strang said. "*Abortions will not let you forget.* We have enough in our budget for buttons."

"Let's not use that word in front of Penny," Mrs. Esselborne cautioned. "In fact, this whole discussion should be tabled for another time."

"You see?" Annie Strang said. "Do you see how you yourself feel about a girl being exposed to this?"

"The person who is speaking the poem appears to have had several you-know-whats," Mrs. Groot said.

"Do you think that's what it means?" Lucy asked F. X.

Before he could answer, Mrs. Esselborne proclaimed, "Lucy is a teenage mother, and even she can't understand it."

"Exactly," Annie Strang answered. "And yet they're giving this to girls younger than her at the high school."

"Which is why it's necessary for us to begin picketing the high school as a group," Isabel said. "During the last year, I picketed there myself. I hoped that this literature would not be given to the students in the future, but afterward I learned that it has been assigned to the summer students, and that the school plans to use it again next year. My individual efforts to stop them were not enough. This problem needs to be tackled by a larger community."

"I think it's time to serve the cake," Mrs. Esselborne announced.

Mrs. Groot set down her poem, leaned toward Isabel, and whispered, "We can meet at my house privately later, Izzy—don't you worry." Isabel patted Mrs. Groot's leg.

I stood up again, to get a piece of cake. Mrs. Groot picked up the knife as I reached for it—she wanted to be the one who cut the slices. She handed out pieces to Mahalia, who passed them around to the committee members, stopping first to give one to Mrs. Hatter. Mrs. Esselborne collected the papers on her podium and departed out the back exit without cake.

Smiling her half-smile, Isabel rose, stepped toward Mrs. Hatter, and murmured something to her. Mrs. Hatter looked up, a little surprised, and took a yellow paper Isabel held before her. Mrs. Hatter examined the paper with a puzzled look, but accepted a pencil from Isabel, squinted, and then signed her name on a line to which Isabel pointed. When Mrs. Hatter had finished, she smoothed the pages of her Bible and closed it over her bookmark.

Around me the women rose and talked all at once. I saw that Mr. Coker was right; they did sound like barnyard birds squawking. Isabel stood slightly apart from them, watching us. She bent her head a little, and her half-smile reappeared. For the second time that morning, I had the odd feeling that although Isabel loved us all, strongly or faintly, every word she had ever spoken to us before that day had been directed toward her triumph at the meeting.

Mrs. Groot handed me a piece of cake, but Isabel touched my arm and told F. X., "Penny shouldn't have chocolate, Mr. Molineaux. If she eats even the smallest amount, it will keep her up all night."

F. X. answered, "Is that so?"

I looked at him crestfallen.

When Isabel stepped away from us to speak with Mahalia, F. X. asked Mrs. Groot to cut him an enormous piece. He told her, "I've been eyeing your delicious cake the whole meeting. I could hardly think of anything else." Mrs. Groot smiled broadly and gave him a napkin and a gigantic slice, almost a fourth of the cake. Plate in hand, F. X. walked into the hallway, and I trailed after him. He wrapped the cake in his napkin and told me, "We'll devour this in the secrecy of our home."

Behind him in the hallway, Reverend Bender sat in his office with his door open. Mrs. Esselborne stood before his desk, her back to me. She said, "Reverend Bender, what I'm trying to tell you is, I think she's dangerous."

"Oh, you women just had a little squabble, that's all," he answered.

Mrs. Esselborne turned around and saw F. X. and me. She closed the door.

As Isabel drove us home in the Jeep, I worried that F. X. would forget the cake, that he would lean too far forward and squash it, or that it would melt and stick to the napkin he had wrapped it in. But after Isabel dropped us off, he pulled the cake from under the napkin and handed it to me intact, saying, "Voilà! A chocolate cake is born!" He poured me a glass of milk and offered a forkful of cake to my lizards, who were green again. I watched, wondering if they would turn brown when they ate devil's food, but they simply stared at it. I devoured the first half of the cake slice standing up, and then had to stop—it was too rich, even for me. That night I could not sleep at all: My mind fidgeted, and when I closed my eyes, I saw Isabel calling to me down a tunnel, "How do you vote?" Words from her poem repeated themselves nonsensically: *gobbling mother-eye, gobbling mother-eye, gobbling mother-eye*, and Isabel's eye winked at me from the end of the pipe in Lucy

Coker's room. A whirlpool opened in blackness, the lid of a gyring eye, and spun me crazily until I sat up abruptly and gave up trying to sleep.

I pulled on some shorts and a dirty T-shirt and walked downstairs to eat the rest of the cake. I poured myself a glass of milk and carried the cake outside to enjoy it on the back steps. Mahalia's Ostrich Ferns tickled my legs as I sat down. I was deliciously aware, as only a child can be, that it was almost dawn. I had been up and outside at dawn only a handful of times in my life. The sky was a soft purple-gray and seemed to belong to me alone. Clouds swiveled above the horizon, and a few stars still teetered over our street. Below them, a globe of light burned in the window of Isabel's living room: She was up already, but she was back in her own home, banished and vanished by whatever tides left the rest of us breathing after the darkness receded.

PART THREE

MAHALIA

Chapter Eleven

Marguerite Returns

*M*y mother and David arrived home on July 31 and announced that they were married. A hiking Unitarian minister had performed the ceremony in a rowboat on a mountain lake, and when my mother and David stood to kiss each other, the boat tipped over, and David had to save the minister from drowning. It turned out that he could not swim, and that his agreement to preside over the wedding had been an even greater act of bravery than David and my mother's. David had wrapped his left arm around the minister's neck, in what David described as "an illegal choke hold," and pulled the minister to shore while he kicked and struggled with terror. After his feet touched ground, the minister had regained his composure and reported that he hoped "never to participate in a full immersion wedding again."

David and my mother returned from the Appalachian Trail with the lean, rangy look of people who have been hiking for long periods, with their clumsiness in adjusting to civilized places. My mother greeted us at the front door wearing one of David's shirts, her dark red hair tied back with a broken bootlace. She sprawled on the living-room floor, set down her backpack, and removed its contents: dirty tin plates; fermenting oranges; her muddy socks intertwined with a pair of David's pants; a mildewed washcloth; and several rumpled blue jay feathers, which she handed to me. David carried the damp and twisted parts of a tent into the hallway and laid them out on the floor, counting them and lining up a series of metal poles that we tripped over as we walked into the living room. A stubble of silver whiskers covered his chin and extended above his mustache.

I sat on my mother's lap while she told F. X. the story of the drowning minister. "What an extreme cure," my mother concluded. "Marriage."

Mahalia was appalled. When my mother explained that David would move into our house until they could find an affordable larger one, Mahalia said, "He's even crazier than everyone else here!"

Before my mother could respond, my sister escaped out the front door. I followed David when he tried to talk to her. "Mahalia!" he called. "Your mother's been through a lot. She's accomplished a lot. Stay and welcome her home."

Mahalia turned around, but continued to walk backward, toward Isabel's. "You," she told David, "don't even have a good reason for marrying Mama!"

"Mahalia, stand still!" David answered. She stopped, but turned forward halfway to signal that she intended to pause for as brief a time as possible. David told her, "This is not as sudden as it seems. Your mother and I dated on and off for years before we started going out seriously a year ago."

But this information only infuriated Mahalia more. She answered in a tone of voice that was at first even and instructive like Isabel's, but then rose progressively until it was too scornful and furious to be anyone's but her own: "Everything in your lives is so crazy! I don't want to live like that. I don't want to live in the middle of your—everything in that house just moves and moves and moves around and I'll never have any peace and quiet!" She turned her back to us and fled down the sidewalk.

I thought of Isabel's rooms—how still they were, and how our house had felt with her in it, drowned in calm. When I considered that Mahalia might be as chafed by the tumult in our home as I had been by Isabel's restraints, I felt bad for my sister—I could afford to, now that she would no longer have such authority over me.

I trotted after her, but David pulled me back saying, "We knew Mahalia would have trouble with this, but we didn't think if we waited it would be any better. Mahalia's just going to have to work it all through by herself." He sounded a little disappointed nonetheless.

———

The evening of my mother's arrival, we ate our welcome-home supper without Mahalia. I sat next to my mother, basking in her, my ankle entwined around hers. I felt joyful for the first time that summer. F. X. had prepared tacos, and he overcrowded the table with dishes of odd toppings, singing:

"They had an itch
to get themselves hitched."

On Mahalia's place mat he set a bowl holding whole okra, two plates of stacked bacon and sliced hot dogs, and an opened can of jumbo black olives. He sprinkled them all over his ground hamburger and cheese, red beans and tomatoes and avocado, lettuce and hot sauce, and sat down.

"Just let Mahalia cool off," David told my mother. "I'll walk up there myself tomorrow morning and talk to Miss Flood."

"Miss Flood," my mother answered, "seems to want to steal my daughter."

"I'm sure she doesn't," David said.

My mother rolled her eyes and told him without venom, "What men don't know about women would fill a set of encyclopedias. Lon Chaney wants to whisk my daughter away, just like the Phantom of the Opera."

An hour later, Mahalia called and informed David that she would be spending the night at Isabel's. My mother told him, "Let it go for now. I'll come up with a battle plan in the morning."

After she walked up the stairs to put me to bed, my mother sat beside me, leaning against my pillow, and told me about her summer. I was glad to have her all to myself, without Mahalia's constraining influence.

"There was a man who had been hiking back and forth along the Trail for two years, can you imagine?" my mother asked me. "He looked like Rip van Winkle. He had this long jaggedy beard and a two-foot ponytail. He said he thought we would destroy ourselves in a nuclear war by the year 2000, and that he wanted to be completely self-sufficient and learn to find and grow food for himself in the woods, so that he would know how to survive when all the food in grocery stores was contaminated." Her description of the man made me think of Mr. Coker. "He said he had been eating fish and plants he found in the woods, although he was very happy when David gave him a root beer. His name was Philip. He was the witness at our wedding. When the minister fell in the water, Philip kept shouting, 'Save yourselves! Save yourselves!' "

I laughed. I knew the world would never end, now that my mother was sitting beside me.

"Penny, it will take some getting used to, having a man around the house. If all the changes start bothering you, just tell me, all right?" Before my mother tucked me in, she waited for me to shine my flashlight on my lizards, to see if they soaked in the darkness of night. They did not—they were bright green. I shut the flashlight off, wondering why they had such a narrow range of color, brown and green; it was like the opposite of being color blind. My mother kissed me good night. I lay back, listening to David and F. X. and my mother laughing uproariously downstairs. I felt a secure joy, wrapped in the arms of noise and bustle. I was glad to have David with us. I dismissed my mother's concern about my adapting to him as one of those odd apprehensions about children to which grown-ups fell prey.

I heard F. X. say, "I like sleeping on the couch," and then my mother and David climbing the stairs. The hallway light turned off, and I got out of bed and peered down to the first floor: F. X. was sitting on the couch under a blanket, reading.

"Penny," he said, "I can smell you at the top of the stairs." I scoffed and returned to my room.

After my mother and David went to bed, I listened to their muffled titters and whispers, to see if I could detect the precise moment at which they fell asleep. However, after dinner, F. X. had told my mother that Isabel believed chocolate kept me awake, and my mother had not laughed and served me the chocolate ice cream in the freezer. Instead she had told me to "try an experiment and save dessert for breakfast." Now, without chocolate, my mind did not race for hours until it collapsed exhausted. I failed to stay awake longer than David and my mother.

During the next few days, Mahalia returned home only briefly, while we were not there, to leave us the note saying that she had packed a bag and taken it back to Isabel's. (I noticed Mahalia also had taken the mason jar into which she had transplanted her Royal Ferns.) My mother did not talk with me about this; nor did she talk to me about her own general condition. Once she grabbed my hand and said, "Penny, I'm sorry for everything. Anything you can think of that I should be sorry for, I am." But I did not want her to apologize to me; I wanted to know how she was. No one pronounced her cured, or wavering in her cure, or half-cured. She seemed happier. She took long hikes in the mornings, up through some trails in the Adirondacks nearest Stein, and sometimes at night, before the dishes were even done, she would get up suddenly and say, "I need a walk," and race out the door, as if she were fleeing some memory of herself. She drank copious amounts of root beer, something she had never kept in our refrigerator before, and David would not allow F. X. to bring liquor in the house. "Who can resist temptation?" David asked him, as if thinking of the trials and failures of paroled prisoners. He and F. X. stored beer in an ice-filled cooler hidden in the garage and talked together there in the evenings while my mother was off on her walks.

Five days after she and David arrived and Mahalia departed, my mother lingered at home in the morning and made one of her giant breakfasts. She served eggs and ham, grits and biscuits, melon and oranges, and Virgin Marys with Tabasco sauce. When we were all seated at the table, she announced that she would pay a visit to Isabel, and lay down what she called "ground rules for my older daughter's abduction."

David laughed and said, "Go ahead and try, but the basic problem is that Mahalia thinks she's better than the rest of us." I could not tell by his tone whether he felt hurt by Mahalia's rejection of him.

"Mahalia *is* better than the rest of us," my mother answered.

"Then she's dangerous," F. X. said, patting my hand.

After breakfast, my mother knocked on Isabel's door and requested to speak to Mahalia. My mother set forth what she called for Mahalia's benefit, "guidelines for camping away from home." These were, simply, that Mahalia had to spend time with me each week, and that she had to eat dinner at our house on Fridays.

"I told her to bring Isabel with her for the dinners," my mother announced when she returned home. "We'll just invite Miss Flood right into the chaos." Although I did not understand my mother's motives then, her strategy strikes me as startlingly perceptive now. My mother must have believed that Isabel needed a family, and rather than take Mahalia from her, my mother had the largeness of heart and tactical intelligence to hand Isabel more than she asked for, by offering to include her in our entire extended family.

After confronting Mahalia with her ground rules, my mother drove to a trail twenty miles from Stein and hiked for seven hours. When she returned, she told us that she had gotten "lost in the wilderness," because she had strayed from the path by following a ring-necked pheasant down a hill. "Those birds have never looked real to me," she told us. "They look like something out of those Chinese fairy tales I used to read to Mahalia, where a boy catches a peacocky kind of bird, and the bird says, 'Don't kill me, and I'll give you three wishes.' By the time I hiked to the bottom of the hill, I thought, I'll ask him for a bath and a warm dinner and to point me the way home. Then a prison van whizzed by me on a road I hadn't seen and I knew I was headed back in the right direction."

———

After a week, F. X. became uncomfortable in the house. He said that he felt like a "fifth wheel from the fourth estate," and announced in a mildly disgruntled voice that he was moving into the Stein Motor Inn until the end of August, when he intended to return to Louisiana to find an apartment closer to Tulane. My mother implored him not to move out, but he claimed that it was impossible for him to concentrate when he studied in our living room. He told her, "The Stein Motor Inn holds a community that would enrapture any anthropologist. There, teachers from the blind school drink with the families of prisoners and prison guards alike, and adulterers toast criminals who run drugs to contacts from the correctional facility." He pronounced the Stein Motor Inn "an ethnographic dissertation in the making," and took notes on his midnight conversations there, but demurred when my mother told him to plan to write his own dissertation on the Motor Inn so that he could return to us regularly. "No," he told her. "I'm not doing ethnography. I fled journalism to escape logging the repetitious truths of humanity. And ethnography is really just extended journalism. Instead of interviewing three people and figuring things out in a day, you interview a hundred people and realize you can't figure out the same thing in a year. I'm going to stick to the archeological side of anthropology." He had decided on his next profession with certitude and gusto and wrote a twelve-page letter to an anthropologist named Tatiana Proskuriokov, because, he claimed, she had discovered that "Mayan glyphs do not proclaim the greatness of the gods, but instead, the silliness of man." He announced to us that he wanted to photograph and decipher glyphs in Mayan tombs. "I don't want to preserve what people did," he said. "I want to know what people *say* they did." He reconsidered this statement and added, "I want to know what they say they did and then decided to bury in a dark place."

My mother was afraid F. X. would get lonely at the Motor Inn, but she need not have worried; he kept himself busy. He visited Mahalia at Stein Evangelical summer camp, where Mrs. Esselborne asked him politely but firmly to stop playing the organ for Mahalia's group of six-year-olds. He did rubbings of old gravestones in Stein's Catholic cemetery, trying to ascertain which kind of paper and charcoal would be best for obtaining impressions of Mayan glyphs. He engaged two teachers from the blind school in a seven-hour poker game at the Motor Inn, using Braille playing cards. According to a complex cheating scheme devised by F. X., each player marked all of the cards first according to his own system, so that in order to win, players had to distinguish their own marking systems from their opponents', and from the Braille as well. (F. X. played blindfolded and threw in random marks on every card, but lost, because his marks were so elaborate that the other men recognized them immediately.) After reading a letter to the editor in the *Stein Record*, F. X. introduced himself to the newspaper's staff, which consisted of three part-time employees, only one of whom did any local reporting—the editor himself, Mr. Harkless, an elderly man with two different-colored eyes, who also taught clarinet in the afternoons.

The letter to the editor that impelled F. X. to meet Mr. Harkless was from my own pediatrician. It read:

> *It has come to my attention that one of our finest teachers at Stein High School is being harassed by religious extremists because he chose to assign a poem by the established poetess, Gwendolyn Brooks, which touches on the subject of abortion. As an experienced pediatrician I can attest that the patients most in need of exposure to this subject are teenage boys and girls. I am also appalled that anyone among us would call for the First Amendment to be swept aside in order to satisfy the vengeful fantasies of zealots.*
>
> *Sincerely,*
> *Donald Epstein, M.D.*

Mr. Harkless did not reply to the letter or refer to it in his weekly column. He told F. X., "I may have run the letter, but I'm not touching that one with a ten-foot pole." F. X. told my mother and David, "Now *there's* a man who should be studying the dead instead of the living," but he still accepted Mr. Harkless's invitation to go fishing. F. X. spent the afternoon inducing Mr. Harkless to fish with his eyes closed. F. X. told me, "We tried to see if blind people would make better fisherman because they can concentrate more subtly on the feel of the line." F. X. caught three small sunfish that Mr. Harkless persuaded him to throw back in. Mr. Harkless hooked one medium-sized bass, which he kindly gave to F. X., and which F. X. asked my mother to cook.

The following evening fell on the first Friday Mahalia and Isabel were invited to dinner. My mother stuffed F. X.'s bass with crabmeat, apricots, bread crumbs, and various spices, and set it on a side dish for F. X. The dinner she prepared for Mahalia's coming was far more elaborate. My mother made a gumbo with thirty-seven ingredients; gumbo was Mahalia's favorite dish. At least seven of those ingredients were hot peppers of one kind or another, which my mother had purchased dried or bottled in Louisiana and asked the sisters at The Place to mail to our house.

F. X., who had arrived early for the occasion, stuck his nose over the pot and said, "It's hot as hell in there! The okra is trying to crawl out of the water like boiling lobsters." We all loved gumbo like that—in the old days, before my mother and Mahalia had occupied enemy camps, they used to like to lay out hot peppers on paper towels and nibble their ends, proclaiming in a barely believable way that they were ignoring the hotness of the peppers and concentrating instead on the subtleties of their different tastes. As F. X.

lifted me to sniff the gumbo, I had a sudden flash of memory from my earliest childhood, in which Mahalia touched the end of a dark green pepper with her tongue and exclaimed, "This one tastes like a fried poodle!"

I sat down on the back steps, crazy with hunger, waiting for Mahalia and Isabel to show up so that we could eat.

F. X. stepped outside to join me and said, "Come look at the film I just got back in the mail." He led me to the Galaxie 500 and pulled from its trunk a cardboard box containing dozens of packages of newly developed photographs he had taken during his summer in Stein and Louisiana, and on the Appalachian Trail. There were at least ten rolls of my mother and David, several hundred pictures of ferns, and fifty or sixty photographs shot at such odd angles or from so far away or so close that I had difficulty identifying their subjects. F. X. spread out the photographs he was most pleased with on the hood of the Galaxie 500, for me to puzzle over.

They revealed a vision of the world extravagantly different from most people's. There was a picture that was almost entirely black, with a tiny mouth of light near the middle, and a figure balanced inside it like a dark star: It was me, peering at F. X. looking for light at the end of the tunnel. There was a close-up of black spots repeating themselves with unvarying regularity on a dark green background. I mistook them at first for polka dots on a green dress, but F. X. revealed they were spores on the back of a fern frond. In a third picture, a series of black car tires under bright fenders spun out of focus into a murky corner that rippled like swamp water—when I stood back, I saw a fern's tendrils curling darkly in on themselves.

F. X. gave me a stack of pictures to keep. One was a portrait of a Seeing Eye dog, half-obscured by a billow of smoke, wearing dark glasses, and being led by a hand holding a leash and a pack of Raleigh cigarettes. There was a picture of red snakes coiled inside a mason jar labeled CAUTION: PUFF ADDERS—they were Mahalia's Royal ferns. There was a posed snapshot of my mother in a red dress: She stood before a large photograph of a debauched-looking General Grant at a Civil War tourist exhibit, holding a white tract emblazoned with bright red letters saying TEN GOOD STRATE-GIES FOR AVOIDING ALCOHOL. My favorite pictures were a photograph of a statue of St. Francis, both hands outstretched and holding two red bras-sieres; one of David standing in a swamp, submerged past his chin, with two yard-long red ferns coiling outward under his nose like an enormous han-dlebar mustache; and a timed self-portrait of F. X. sneaking up behind a statue of Robert E. Lee with a heavy stick, my uncle's arm cocked as if he meant to brain the monument, while a blurry woman ran from a building in the background, waving her arms at him.

"I hope you're ready—You Know Who is coming," F. X. said. I looked up from the pictures and spied Isabel and Mahalia crossing Isabel's yard.

F. X. put his boxes away, and I carried my pictures to my room. As I returned downstairs, I heard my mother say, "You can't just lock Mahalia up like a parole violator, David. And I've already decided what I'm going to say to Princess Isabel. I'm going to say, 'Thank you for taking such good care of my children while I was gone. I don't think anyone else would have been as patient with Penny.' "

The doorbell rang. F. X. answered it, and Isabel entered, looking stilted and ill at ease. Mahalia followed her, without greeting any of us.

My mother said, "You came just in the nick of time. Dinner will be ready in five minutes." Isabel immediately seated herself and placed her napkin in her lap. Because of this, my mother had no opportunity to ease her into a conversation before serving supper.

My mother could not have guessed at Isabel's eating habits. No one had told her how carefully Isabel filtered the food that reached her from the outer world, or that Isabel rarely permitted herself to eat a meal she had not prepared with her owns hands and preexamined with her own eyes. It might have occurred to my mother that a woman from southern Ohio would not be accustomed to spicy food, but it is also possible that my mother was concentrating so hard on trying to please Mahalia that she forgot to take Isabel into account.

David pulled F. X. aside at the bottom of the stairs and said, "Don't start any of your talk about the Greek gods and the Great Wall of China."

"I'll be on my best behavior," F. X. answered.

F. X. must have tried, at least in the beginning, because after we all seated ourselves, he commenced the meal in complete silence, a state so unnatural to him that in itself it created tension at the table.

"Is the gumbo all right?" my mother asked him.

F. X. nodded.

David finished his glass of water and rose to get another one, which he drank, standing up, beside the sink. He propped open the kitchen door to let a breeze into the house from the backyard. He filled a pitcher with ice water and set it on the table.

Isabel took one bite of her meal and asked, "Could someone tell me what this stew contains?"

"I never reveal my recipes," my mother answered, smiling at David. "The secret to good cooking is secrecy itself."

Isabel put down her spoon. A frown wrestled with her mouth and then retreated.

"This might be okay," Mahalia said, passing Isabel a plate of cornbread. My mother looked up sharply when Mahalia said *might*.

Isabel took a piece of cornbread and ate it without butter.

"Mahalia," my mother asked. "Is something wrong with your dinner?"

David refilled Isabel's glass.

"No," my sister answered. She swallowed a bite of gumbo, and then set down her spoon beside Isabel's.

No one talked—it was so quiet, you could hear bugs jitterbugging in the yard outside. Mahalia picked up a piece of cornbread, while Isabel chewed on hers and the other adults clanked their silverware against their teeth and gulped down water. F. X. rose, bent over the stove, and asked David, "Will you have some more?"

David's neck was red, and rivulets of sweat trickled from his hair. After I got to know him better, I would learn that David always reacted this way to hot peppers. They made his hands shake, and his heart beat faster, and caused sweat to pour from him like a lake from a burst dam.

"Sure," David answered.

I reached for some cornbread and overturned my glass. Everyone was relieved. David and F. X. jumped up to catch it, and while they and my mother mopped at the floor, and Isabel bent over to wipe up the water around my place mat, Mahalia upturned Isabel's bowl into F. X.'s and gave me a pleading look. I was happy, I was conspiring, I smiled at my sister for the first time in months.

"David's sweating to death!" I said, when the adults reseated themselves.

Everyone looked at David. He mopped his face with his napkin and said, "I'm not complaining."

Isabel peered at her empty bowl, looking mildly surprised, but said nothing.

F. X. asked, "Mahalia, do you know that on the Appalachian Trail, David ran into an ex-parolee named Mr. Buckley who used to like to explore Buffalo's sewer pipes and storm drains? Just like the Phantom of the Opera?"

David drank a full glass of water, and then offered, "He was the first burglar I encountered during my early days at the parole office. He had broken into his next-door neighbor's apartment by digging a tunnel under his floors that came up in his neighbor's closet. It took the man thirty days to dig it. Well, of course they caught him! A tunnel only leads in two directions. I was amazed that someone could be so determined and hardworking and stupid at the same time. And here he was standing in front of your mother and me, employed as a forest ranger on the Trail. He was explaining to a pack of Catholic brothers from Italy how beavers build dams.

I pretended not to recognize him. I wondered, 'Does he like beavers because they build underwater tunnels? Could it be that all along it wasn't stealing that tempted him, but just a love of underground routes?' "

"There is no limit to human possibility," my mother said. "Maybe the Catholic brothers should show him the catacombs in Italy those old monks used to keep."

F. X. included Isabel in the conversation. He said expansively, "I understand that the Archbishop of your stomping ground, Joseph Bernadin of Ohio, has been threatening Catholics with damnation if they enter Planned Parenthood clinics. Do you think that your Evangelical church has fallen under the spell of Rome?"

My sister burst into tears.

"Mahalia—" David said.

"Don't do it! Just don't do it!" Mahalia cried.

F. X. looked stricken with remorse.

"F. X. didn't mean any harm," my mother told Mahalia. "He was just being himself."

Mahalia stood, wiping her tears on her napkin—I knew how awful it must have been for her to lose her composure like that, in front of us all, in a way Isabel never would have. My next thought was that I was glad my mother was back to deflect some of Mahalia's righteous indignation away from me.

Isabel rose and said, "Thank you, Mrs. Daigle. Or is it Mrs. Slattery?"

"Daigle," my mother said. "That's the name my daughters have grown up with, so it feels like mine too. After all, who am I but their mother?"

"Mrs. Daigle," Isabel answered. "It was very kind of you to cook dinner for us."

"You're not leaving," my mother said.

"Is dinner over?" I asked. "Can I have dessert?"

My mother did not appear to hear me. She was watching Mahalia. My sister opened the front door and waited on the porch for Isabel.

"Penny should avoid all sugary foods late in the evening," Isabel told my mother.

My mother turned back to Isabel and answered, "I don't believe in that."

"Believe in what?" Isabel asked.

"I don't think it's a good idea to have too many rules about food. It can cause children problems when they grow up. They can become the kind of person who thinks he has to control every little scrap of food that enters his mouth. Or they can become the opposite—eating everything in sight, just to prove a point. Look at me, the one food I ever longed for and was denied as a child was chocolate, because we couldn't afford it. Now I eat chocolate every opportunity I get." Although my mother had made me wait to eat chocolate ice cream on the night of her arrival, she concluded, "I can't imagine a project more futile than trying to keep children from eating chocolate!"

"But—" Isabel answered.

Mahalia stepped back into the living room and told my mother, "You don't even realize how much she did for Penny! While you were off drinking and gallivanting around with men, Isabel was the one who figured out that Penny gets all hyperactive when she eats certain things. Isabel's the one who got Penny to behave when you never could."

"Mahalia—" Isabel said.

"They don't even value you," Mahalia told her.

"But I wasn't looking for anyone's approval," Isabel answered. "That's not why I do what I do."

"She's right, Mahalia," my mother said. "Isabel has her reasons." My mother may not have intended it, but this last phrase was spoken in an ambiguous, slightly insulting way.

"What are you insinuating?" Mahalia asked her.

"I didn't mean anything," my mother answered.

"I'll wait for you outside, Mahalia," Isabel said. "This is a private conversation between you and your mother." Isabel stepped behind Mahalia onto the porch and closed the front door.

"Look what you've done!" Mahalia shouted at my mother. "You can't stand the fact that I'm fitting in. I'm making a life for myself outside this house. I'm normal and you're all deranged! You and your boyfriend from the parole office and F. X., who races around like a crazy person, and your father who left you, and your mother who drove herself into a lake!"

Even I was surprised by the meanness of Mahalia's words. I was afraid to look at my mother and F. X.

Mahalia put her hand on the doorknob, but my mother told her, "You are not stomping out and making one of your grand exits, Little Miss. It's high time you stopped judging everyone around you and finding yourself superior. The one kind of child I will not turn loose on this world is someone who looks down on everyone."

Mahalia pulled on the doorknob, but my mother blocked her.

"Mahalia, everyone's a little deranged, even you. Even your precious Isabel who can't act like an ordinary woman and has to roam around the neighborhood snatching people's children!" My mother's voice rose on her last sentence, so that I was afraid Isabel might hear her through the door.

"Get out of my way!" Mahalia cried.

There were a few sharp raps on the door. My mother and Mahalia both took a step back. Isabel opened the door and leaned in halfway.

"Mrs. Daigle—" she began.

Mahalia wrenched the door open and pushed past my mother. My mother almost lost her balance—she took a sidestep to keep from falling.

"Isabel, let's go!" Mahalia called from the sidewalk.

"Mrs. Daigle," Isabel said. "I had no idea that you and I were at such cross-purposes with regard to Penny. I thought you were aware of what strides she made this summer. I am genuinely sorry about the incident in which she ended up in Florence with the other girl. It resulted from a lapse of oversight on my part. She was making progress until that day."

"Isabel!" my sister called again.

"Mrs. Daigle, you must know," Isabel continued, "that you don't have to worry about Mahalia. I'm not sure what's troubling her today. I've never seen her lose control of herself like this. I'll talk to her. You know she's not a girl who's inclined to engage in destructive behavior."

"No, of course not—" my mother said.

Isabel closed the door quietly behind her. I thought she must have been afraid to let things go any further, before something could be said that would cause an irreparable rift between her and my mother. I perceived only then that Isabel did not see herself as having that luxury, because my mother had the power to forbid another adult from letting my sister board with her. Isabel must have divined the opposite as well—that if my mother forced Mahalia to return to her, her hold on my sister would be meaningless and illusory, and that once home, Mahalia would have the ability to make our lives a living hell if she chose.

———

Two weeks after my mother returned, she obtained a temporary position as a records clerk at the parole office. She walked to work after walking me to summer school in the mornings, and she made a point of stopping at Isabel's each day along the way to say hello to Mahalia. Their conversations were painfully brief.

"Good morning," my mother would say when Mahalia came to the door. "Do you like those long dresses now? They must be hot in this weather. They were a fashion when I was a young woman, but I always thought they were a shame for girls like you who have nice legs."

"Good morning," Mahalia would answer.

I spent most of my days in Sister Geraldine's office, not because my summer-school teachers sent me there, but because Sister Geraldine pre-empted them by deciding to release me only for gym and recess, and for a single hour of English class each day. The English teacher—a reedy middle-aged woman named Mrs. Sizemore who once pulled up her shirt to show us her cesarean scar and was not invited back the following summer—did not seem to notice my antics in class. She talked to herself while she talked to us, saying things such as, "Try to write a story or an essay on something other than 'What I Did This Summer' or—what was it I thought was a good idea? Now, Mrs. Sizemore, what was it? You don't remember? Well, if I don't, why should you? Just try to be original! Write a scary story if you can, or an essay about your parents, or instructions for building a model airplane."

I read science-fiction books during her class, or composed paragraphs in a nonsensical language no one would ever decipher:

> Murdo morny morny morn Lucifork?
> Pennytik luciforkmama oke. Luciforkmama
> mamamama Mahaliatik Isabeltik! Pooka pooka
> porfinny mohodofreetik murdo hoke!

Once I felt moved to write a story in English about a murderer, which Mrs. Sizemore pronounced "Wonderful and insightful, and I'm going to send a copy right now to *Jack and Jill*." She may have forgotten to mail it to that magazine, or those in charge at the children's publication may have found my story inappropriate, because I never learned of their reply.

In the afternoons, Sister Geraldine directed me outside to act as a water boy for the middle school's field hockey team, a practice she would continue until I graduated from elementary school. F. X. picked me up in the afternoons, except on Tuesdays, when Mahalia, following my mother's ground rules, came with Isabel to get me. Isabel maintained extreme caution around me, and would never let me out of her sight when we were together.

On a Wednesday in mid-August, F. X. arrived at All Saints driving his Galaxie 500 and announced that we were going on a photography expedition at the abandoned mine near Swastika. He wanted to experiment with techniques for taking pictures in "lightness places," so that he could prepare for the subtleties of photographing Mayan tombs. However, we never reached the mine that day because as we turned south off Main Street and passed the public high school, we saw a group of adults walking and holding signs, and Mahalia was with them. I had never encountered grown-ups picketing before, and I could not understand why they were marching in a closed circle, seemingly going nowhere. Isabel stood to the side with a clipboard, handing out pink pamphlets.

"Look," F. X. said, "it's Captain Ahab and the fetus."

F. X. parked his Galaxie 500 in the lot behind the high school. As I followed him toward Mahalia, I saw that my sister and the other women with her—Annie Strang, Mrs. Groot, Mrs. Wroblewski, and Lucy—were carrying cardboard signs with pictures of *Life* magazine's nine-month-old embryo on them. The signs proclaimed ABORTIONS WILL NOT LET YOU FORGET. The women wore lapel buttons printed with the same words. Mahalia frowned with annoyance when she saw us. She turned her back to us in order to peruse a stack of literature on a card table in the middle of the picket circle.

Nicky Groot leaned against a tree twenty feet away from the women. He did not carry a sign. His hair was pulled back in a short ponytail, and he wore blue jeans and a leather vest without a shirt underneath. He drank Coca-Cola and stared off into the distance, to the right of the school, at nothing at all. I wondered if he had vodka in his Coca-Cola can.

"Izzy, I'm taking Lucy home," Barb Wroblewski was saying. "Our feet are giving out." She and Lucy put down their signs. Both of them were enormous now—I had never been so close to pregnant women and had no idea how far they expanded before they burst open.

"Next time, we should bring folding chairs," Mrs. Groot said. "I don't see why Lucy and Barb can't just sit and hold their signs instead of marching."

"That would be fine," Isabel answered. She saw F. X., but continued talking as if she had not noticed him. "Lucy and Barb, you can sit in front of the literature table from now on."

"Izzy, I have to get going too," Annie Strang said. "It's almost two-thirty, and I promised the baby-sitter I'd get back by two o'clock." She alone among the women had dressed up: She wore a brown mini-dress that accentuated her giraffe legs, and gold espadrilles. She hunted for a compact and lipstick, in her purse, blotted her large nose, and then drew underneath her eyes two dots of lipstick, which she rubbed vigorously over her cheekbones with a piece of Kleenex.

"It brings out the color better than blush," she told me.

F. X. leaned over the literature table and leafed through the pamphlets and books there.

"In the future," Isabel said, "you should plan to stay longer, Annie. We need people here for the three o'clock bell as well as the two o'clock."

But Annie Strang did not respond. She was already leaning her sign against Lucy's and Mrs. Wroblewski's, and saying to Mrs. Groot, "I hope you can handle taking all of these things home."

"It's not a problem," Mrs. Groot answered. "I'm glad to do anything to help Izzy."

Mahalia still held her sign. She watched Annie Strang hurry away and asked Mrs. Groot peevishly, "She never helps very much, does she?" Behind Mahalia, Nicky grinned as if he found her ridiculous.

"Oh, Annie does what she can," Mrs. Groot said. "I think she just feels a little scattered sometimes. It's a shame though, that Mrs. Hatter couldn't join us. She seemed like a nice lady. Mrs. Esselborne told me that Mrs. Hatter has been church-shopping in Plattsburgh."

A bell rang inside the school. Students began drifting out as Annie Strang drove away behind Lucy and Mrs. Wroblewski. Most of the students ignored Isabel when they sauntered by. One boy leaned over her literature and leafed through a booklet on the table titled *Life or Death*.

"Gross!" he said. He carried a music book, and I recognized him as the boy, Ben Fisher, who had come to play our piano in response to Stein Evangelical's ad for an organist. Several other boys carrying black musical instrument cases gathered around him. They guffawed at *Life or Death*, and one of them said, "Jesus! Yuck! What is that, a photo of a baby in a hospital garbage can?"

I walked over to see what they were peering at, but F. X. pulled me back, saying, "Penny, that's too grisly even for you. Stay over here." F. X. closed the book before I could view the photograph.

Mahalia watched the boys drift away. She did not take her eyes off of them until they disappeared around the corner. Then, she set down her sign and rearranged the leaflets the boys had riffled on the table.

I wandered over to Nicky and waited for him to say hello to me. He was watching the high school students walk by.

"What a bunch of jerks," he told me. "Look at them."

"Which ones?" I asked.

"All of them," he said, making a sweeping gesture with his hand that took in the whole school. He shook his head, to show he thought they were hopeless. "They don't know anything," he said. I nodded in agreement and stood beside him, watching the high school students with a superior expression. This gave me an odd feeling of being excluded myself, as if I were an outlaw standing with his cohort, surveying the warm houses of a village that did not want us.

A man who looked like a teacher came up the slope of the hill and stopped in front of the literature table. He had a short black beard and wire-rimmed spectacles, and carried a book called *Rose, Where Did You Get That Red?* He wore a white shirt, blue jeans, and an electric-green necktie. "What the hell is this?" he asked.

Nicky set down his Coca-Cola by the tree and stepped toward the table to examine the literature that was causing such a stir. Mahalia moved to the other end of the table, away from Nicky.

I followed him, but F. X. said, "Whoa, Penny," grabbing the top of my jumper. He pulled me away again. "That stuff really might give you nightmares."

"When grown-ups say something will give me nightmares, it never does," I told him.

Nicky closed the book as if it did not interest him and returned to his Coca-Cola can.

The young bearded man told Isabel: "You must be the one-woman circus who's been circulating those petitions around Stein. Let me introduce myself. I'm Mr. Brewer. Meet the devil, Ms. Flood."

F. X. grinned.

"We don't use that word in such a casual way," Isabel answered.

"What word?" Mr. Brewer stood with his hand still extended, but Isabel did not take it.

Isabel answered, "It's important to recognize the devil when he asserts his special character in every situation, and so we don't use the word recklessly."

"The Word?" Mr. Brewer asked, uncomprehending. He adjusted his gold-rimmed spectacles. "Do you mean you don't preach *The Word* recklessly?"

"No, Mr. Brewer," Isabel answered irritably. Mr. Brewer looked at her with the same bafflement his wife had exchanged with Isabel weeks before. "I was speaking of the devil. We don't use the word *devil* in a reckless way."

Mr. Brewer laughed. "Oh! The *devil*—" he answered. He picked up a flier, examined Isabel's yellow petition without evident interest, and then opened *Life or Death* and said, "Jesus! Where do you get this stuff!" Isabel frowned.

Mr. Brewer closed the book, turned back to Isabel, and said, "Let me tell you what I think is reckless, Ms. Flood. It's reckless for you to set up your little table here. It's reckless and a waste of time and destructive. Many of the children who go to summer school are here because they can't read. I'm trying to interest them in books by whatever means I can." As he spoke, Mahalia moved alongside Isabel and laid her hand on the crook of Isabel's elbow. Mr. Brewer glanced at her and continued, "The Gwendolyn Brooks poem that's keeping you awake at night, Ms. Flood, reaches these children because it touches on some relevant issues. It's not even straightforwardly pro-abortion—it's ambiguous and provocative, it makes you think. But that's just what you're afraid of—*ambiguity*—isn't it? That poem also happens to be the only thing many of our students have ever read by a black writer. Not that you need the works of black writers at Stein Evangelical, which as I understand, has no black members."

F. X. interjected in a conversational tone: "In southern Louisiana, where I grew up, the Catholic church had black members, but it was segregated, so that they had to stand in the back rows where there were no pews. I have always believed that the most racist institutions in this country are real estate and the Catholic church."

Mr. Brewer asked him, "Who are you?"

"An innocent bystander," F. X. answered.

Mahalia glared wrathfully at F. X.: If she had been an angel, she would have wrestled him to the ground. "*He* doesn't belong with us," she told Mr. Brewer.

"Who does?" Nicky sneered. "Who would want to?"

Mahalia ignored Nicky.

"Look, Ms. Flood," Mr. Brewer said. "You can preach whatever you want at your church, and you can circulate your little petitions, and no one objected when you used to come out here and parade yourself around with your sign across the street. But you can't set up this table on school property."

Isabel answered, "It is not this institution's right to rob children of their innocence."

"They are not innocents!" Mr. Brewer replied, angrily. He asked Mahalia, "What are *you* doing here? You don't go to our school, do you?"

Mahalia answered, "No, I go to All Saints."

"Oh, All Saints!" Mr. Brewer answered sarcastically. "I understand you have a real *library* at All Saints. Stein High School doesn't. Our new library is in a trailer." He pointed behind Mahalia to a long aluminum house trailer beside the school. Mahalia turned around to look, and Mr. Brewer said to Isabel, "You're here with students from the private Catholic school to tell me to take books out of a public school library? A library that's a goddamn trailer, and you want me to take books out of it?"

F. X. asked, "Is that what this is about, Mahalia? Are you asking that books be removed from the shelves of the high school?"

Isabel answered for my sister: "Mr. Molineaux," she said, "this is my battle. I will handle it myself."

"A school is a great place for you to stage a battle!" Mr. Brewer told Isabel. "Why don't you set up your own little Inquisitorial Tribunal right here, Ms. Torquemada? Why don't you print up a little list of all the books you think the children *shouldn't* read and pass it out to them as they walk into the building? I think you could reach most of the students here with a list like that. I think most of them would agree not to read any book you told them not to."

"I'm not Catholic," Isabel answered. "I'm from Stein Evangelical."

"Oh dear," Mrs. Groot said. Her words seem to come out of the blue: I had forgotten her. I turned in the direction in which she was looking: Nicky was jogging away from us toward the road. Isabel and Mr. Brewer continued to talk, and Mrs. Groot said to me, "I think something upset Nicky." When Nicky reached the end of the school driveway, he stopped to light a cigarette, and then disappeared around a row of bushes lining the street.

Almost immediately afterward, another boy ran down the school driveway toward us. He was one of the boys who had scoffed at the literature on the table. I wondered what he had come to ask: Had he been persuaded by Isabel's literature and decided to join us? Instead, he passed behind Isabel, grabbed Mahalia's elbow, raised her arm, and stuffed a note into her hand. She looked at her hand in bewilderment, and then turned toward him, but he was already running back up the driveway toward the road. Nicky was still there, watching intently. He threw his cigarette on the grass, and ground it under his heel.

Isabel missed all this. She continued to talk to Mr. Brewer. "I did not choose your school as a battleground, Mr. Brewer," she said. "You did. You knew very well when you assigned this poem that you would cause a stir. That's why you did it. You knew that church people would be bound to protest your decision."

I crooked my neck around Mahalia's arm as she read the note. *Mahalia from Ben*, it said:

Mahalia, Mahalia, Mahalia
I've got to nail ya.
Don't look so uptight
You're such a dazzling sight
I dream of you all night.
I promise I won't bite.

Mahalia turned pink and crumpled up the note.

"—and we're not going away," Isabel concluded.

"Do you think what she says is true?" F. X. asked Mr. Brewer. "Did you anticipate that Isabel's church would object to your teaching materials?"

Mr. Brewer adjusted his gold-rimmed spectacles again. "I could not have imagined a person like Ms. Flood before she showed up here," he answered.

"Why are *you* here?" Mahalia asked F. X. Her face was livid now; everyone looked at her, a little surprised. "You don't have any business here, F. X.! Did you come to bother us? You just push and push and push people until you get them on the brink! Why don't you leave me alone? Why doesn't everyone just leave me alone?"

F. X. answered evenly, "I happened to see you here when we were passing by, and I stopped out of curiosity."

"Mahalia," Isabel said. "Your uncle's presence should not serve as a hindrance to us."

F. X. took my hand and said, "Let's go find something else to gawk at, Penny." He guided me to the Galaxie 500. After we closed the car doors, he told me, "My God, your big sister has certainly chosen a strange way to act *normal*." He cackled to himself.

As the Galaxie 500 exited the school grounds, we passed Nicky Groot. He sat on a low wall, only twenty yards or so from the school's entrance, smoking another cigarette.

F. X. seemed to forget Isabel and her battle immediately, and on the ride home, he talked instead about photography and an idea he had for a further experiment in photographing lightless places. When we arrived at the house, he took a collection of old wine goblets from a kitchen cabinet, pink with crystal facets, saying, "I tried this yesterday at the Motor Inn with old champagne glasses." F. X. half-filled the goblets with water, took two flashlights from under the sink, and then turned off all the downstairs lights and pulled the shades.

He handed me a flashlight and pointed it downward into the goblets. They cast intricate shadows on the floor that looked like jellyfish. As F. X. lowered the flashlight, they contracted their bodies, and as he lifted it, their bodies thinned and expanded, and spun out lines of light that wrapped like tentacles around one another.

"Look," F. X. told me. "Pure light reflected across darkness takes on the same forms as simple organic life. What if the most primitive life at the beginning of time, jellyfish and sponges and worms, just imitated patterns of light?"

He retrieved his camera bag, pulled out his camera, a metal cable, and a beanbag, and said, half to himself, "We'll open the aperture way up, use an extension cable, and set the camera on a beanbag as a makeshift tripod. Then we'll use as slow a shutter speed as possible, and maybe we'll capture scraps of the Holy Ghost—who knows?" Thereafter, we spent an hour on the kitchen floor, shining light through goblets and then half-filled root-beer bottles, and a jelly jar, and an old glass doorknob. Around us, luminous forms scuttled under the cabinets and skimmed across the floor and whirled upward to the ceiling, until I forgot who and where and what I was, and felt like God Himself, marveling at the creations I spun out of mere light, out of solitary and twinned and multiplying flashes of visibility in an ocean of darkness.

After we had each taken several rolls of photographs, F. X. finally said, "Damn! This is the last picture!" He was lying upside down on the kitchen floor, eye level with a champagne glass.

"Can I go outside?" I asked.

"All right, Penny," F. X. answered. "But don't wander away."

The sunlight hurt my eyes when I stepped outside: It took me a moment to adjust to the ordinary world. If Mahalia had been home, I might have run off, just to trespass beyond the sphere of her influence. But I did not want to escape F. X.; I liked having him nearby. I did two front flips over the back walkway and headed for my tree. It looked lonely from all those weeks without me. Its yellowing leaves trembled in the late summer wind. Our neighbor's dog stared at me forlornly from inside his house; he looked too lonely to bark. I grabbed a low branch and swung upward—and then caught myself, because high in the uppermost limbs was a person. It was a boy—he wore black high tops and blue jeans, and had the long legs of a teenager. I could not see his face. His body was turned toward our house, and smoke drifted down from him through the branches.

I climbed up to investigate. I wasn't sure whether I should move stealthily, in order to startle him, or whether I should announce my presence by singing loudly. When I reached the halfway point on the tree, I lost my grip and decided to yell. "Damnation!" I shouted. "I'm going to die if I'm not careful."

"What the hell?" the boy asked. He craned his neck downward: It was Nicky Groot.

I pulled myself up beside him.

"What are you doing here?" he asked.

"This is my tree," I answered. "I've been up here a hundred times."

"Oh," he said. He turned away from me, looking disgruntled or embarrassed. He drew hard on his cigarette, and then tossed it to the ground below. We watched its glowing embers swirl though the trees: The wind looked like it was on fire.

Nicky watched the ground after the cigarette hit, although it was not interesting—the downward fall had put it out. He kept his back toward me, twisting his body just slightly away from our house. I realized that before I spied him, he must have been facing our top windows. Directly in front of me was the upstairs bedroom where Mahalia and I slept.

"Were you trying to watch us?" I asked.

"Why would I want to watch you?" Nicky answered. He lifted his head and twisted his body a little more, to create the impression that he was simply staring toward the woods.

I offered, "Do you want to come inside our house?"

"Why would I want to go in there?" he answered.

I shrugged my shoulders.

"Is your sister home?"

"No," I said. "She's still at the high school. But she stays at Isabel's house nowadays, anyway."

"She does?" Nicky asked. "She lives with The Flood?"

"Yeah, she's mad at us, so she won't live with us."

Nicky lit another cigarette, and I sat quietly beside him while he smoked for a while, until he asked, "So Mahalia's not home right now or anything?"

I shook my head. I sensed that he desired something. I offered again: "You want to come inside? You want some root beer?"

"If you want," Nicky answered. "I'll go inside, if you want."

"Okay," I said. I swung myself off my branch, and I heard him snapping twigs as he followed me down.

I acted as if I were luring a stray animal into our house; I did not turn around as I crossed our yard, and I walked slowly, so that Nicky did not feel that he had to hurry in behind me. I heard F. X. rattling around in the garage, and I veered away from it, to the path that led along the side yard to our back door. I heard Nicky's tennis shoes on the steps behind me as I entered.

"So this is it," he said, looking around.

"What do you want to drink?" I asked him.

"What's on the second floor?" he answered.

"That's where we sleep," I said, following him up the stairs. He entered my mother's room, glanced once at her dresser, where David's shirts lay in disarray, and then Nicky backed out of her doorway. Nicky turned and pushed open the door to the room I shared with Mahalia and stepped inside. The covers on my bed spilled to the floor, but Mahalia's bed was neatly made. On top of her bedspread was a stack of church literature, a folded peach sweater, and a children's Bible she had used at Stein Evangelical's camp. The ferns in the terrarium pressed against the glass top as if trying to escape; she had not been home to trim them.

Nicky picked up the peach sweater. He shook it out and dangled it in front of him. "This belongs to your sister?" he asked. "It looks like an old lady sweater." He made it dance in front of him, and I laughed.

A downstairs door slammed. F. X.'s feet pounded up the stairs. "Penny?" he called. "Are you up here?"

He stopped at the bedroom threshold when he saw Nicky.

"Who—?" he asked, but Nicky pushed by him before F. X. could finish. Nicky took the stairs in three steps, still carrying Mahalia's sweater, and then I heard him race toward the front door and outside.

"Who was that?" F. X. asked. "Is he the boy who was at the school with Isabel?"

"He's just someone from Mahalia's church," I answered.

"Well," F. X. answered. "That's good. It's good Mahalia knows at least one boy. Nothing but a boy is going to pull her away from her passionate dedication to bloodcurdling religious literature."

I moved over to the window and peered out: Nicky was loping up the street away from town, as if he had been spotted committing a crime. My sister's sweater caught the wind and fluttered beside him like a struggling abducted child. He jumped over a flower bed, turned the corner, and was gone.

Chapter Twelve

An Abortion Remembered

"If we order Mahalia not to go to those pickets, we might push her into making a martyr of herself," my mother told F. X. and David over breakfast, the day after I visited Stein High School. F. X. had described Isabel's encounter with Mr. Brewer, and David had advised my mother to warn Mahalia not to attend Isabel's pickets anymore. My mother continued, "Mahalia and Isabel and those other church women are not going to do anyone any damage marching around in circles with a few signs. Of course, they might make themselves dizzy." My mother smiled and pounded the bottom of the Tabasco sauce bottle above her eggs. "Have you ever seen that Evangelical minister those women follow around? He wears a diamond stickpin and has an underbite—he has the look of an alligator that just swallowed your mother." She laughed and added, "I think it's smarter to let Mahalia grow out from under Miss Flood on her own. It can't be much fun to follow Princess Isabel of the Stiff Neck around, and that's my advantage. I know what happens to growing girls."

David disagreed and announced that he would talk to both Mahalia and Isabel about the picketing when they came to dinner that week. However, on Friday morning, Isabel called and said she could not accept my mother's invitation for supper "because of a foreseeable emergency with Mrs. Groot's son." My sister appeared alone for dinner, looking, my mother whispered to David, "as uncomfortable as a social worker visiting our house to inspect it in the middle of a meal." Mahalia wore a long skirt and her slipper-shoes, and had twisted back her hair in a braid so tight that it seemed to tug at the corners of her eyes. She walked upstairs first to check on her terrarium ferns. She watered and trimmed them and then returned downstairs. She sat at the table and picked gingerly at my mother's barbecued chicken, as though it was too exotic for her.

F. X. said, "Penny, I'm going to outeat you." He put half the chicken on his plate. I reached over his arm and took his biggest pieces and arranged them on my plate. He growled at me, and I growled back at him.

"Mahalia, I hope that whatever happened with Mrs. Groot's son is resolved," my mother said with half-suppressed amusement, as if she believed Isabel might have fabricated an excuse for not joining us.

"Nicky was arrested for shoplifting false eyelashes and batteries," Mahalia answered. "He's been skipping summer classes at the school for juvenile delinquents. Isabel always helps Mrs. Groot with Nicky. Isabel is always there for people in distress."

"Does that include you?" my mother asked. "Are you a person in distress?"

Mahalia looked at her coldly.

"Because if that's how you feel, you should tell me."

David cut in, trying to avert an argument. "Nicky Groot?" He asked. "The boy who set a fire in the parking lot of Canon's grocery?" He told my mother and F. X., "There's a boy who might as well have been born in jail. He's been in and out of the juvenile court for years. Once about five years ago, I was having a beer at the Stein Tavern, and old Nicholas Groot, Nicky's father, came in with him. Mr. Groot was tight, even though he looked like he had just left work—he was still in his prison guard's uniform. He ordered two Scotches for himself, and when the manager brought them, Mr. Groot pushed one of the Scotches in Nicky's direction. Nicky shook his head and looked at the floor. He started to slide sideways out of his booth as if he wanted to make a quick escape, but his father grabbed his arm. Mr. Groot tilted his head back in this weird leering kind of way." David lifted his chin and looked at us oddly, his eyes slitted over a snarl. The effect was unsettling. "Then Mr. Groot pushed the Scotch closer to Nicky and said, smiling meanly, 'I'm sure your mother wouldn't approve.' Nicky picked up the glass and drank it down, all at once, leering back at his father. The manager asked them to leave. I've never felt so sorry for a kid in my life."

"Nicky Groot's a pervert," Mahalia told David.

After trying vainly to engage my sister in small talk, David decided to bring up the picket at the school.

"Mahalia," he began, "I hear you've been accompanying Miss Flood to Stein High to stage protests there. You and I both went to Catholic school.

If we go down to Stein High and tell them how to run things, they'll say the pope wishes he could take over American education."

"And they'd be right," F. X. interjected.

"F. X.," David said. "Just let it go for a minute. Mahalia, people don't want you wandering over from All Saints to tell them what to teach their children."

"I'm not Catholic," Mahalia answered. "I'm a member of Stein Evangelical. My father was Protestant." She looked away from David when she spoke, as if she did not particularly care if he heard her or not. "My father was a Protestant, and I doubt he would have forbidden me to do what's right."

"Your father was a Baptist," my mother said. "He was a Baptist and his Baptist church here was not against abortion. I happen to know personally because—"

Mahalia pushed her seat back abruptly and said, "Stop talking! Just stop talking! Do you think I want to hear what you have to say!" She turned away from us, knocking over her chair.

This time, Mahalia exited the house out the back door. I followed my sister into the yard, but she did not see me. She stepped on one of her own fern beds, and then cut straight into the woods, hurrying through the trees to God-knows-where. Her anger was electrifying; it seemed to charge the air behind her.

I heard my mother say in the kitchen, "This is my fault," and I returned inside. "It's my fault for not being sensitive enough to anticipate how Mahalia feels about things."

David answered, sounding mildly exasperated, "Marguerite, she's acting just like you."

"My Lord, David," my mother said. "Are men really that blind to the differences between females? Mahalia is not behaving like me. I've acted a lot of ways, but never *that* way. I've never acted principled. I never had a time of leisure as a young woman when I could feel idealistic. Let her have her day. Let her save the world."

"I don't know," David answered. He looked annoyed; his frustration with my sister was increasing by the day. Perhaps he was wondering why his fifteen years as a parole officer were not giving him a handle on a teenage girl. "I once supervised a boy over at probation," he said, "whose own minister got him involved in a scheme of selling the same church cemetery plot over and over to dozens of people. They collected thousands of dollars. His parents used to send the boy to the church because he had a history of arrests, and they claimed that he stopped getting in trouble once the minister took him under his wing. The parents only became suspicious when he bought a new car."

"David!" my mother said. "Mahalia doesn't have a history of getting her-self in trouble. She's fundamentally good in a way that none of us are. She just sees everything in black and white. It must be hard to face the world that way—you've got to fit yourself and everyone else into neat little boxes. I have to be patient, with her. After all, I've played my part this year. Mahalia never caused anyone any worry in her life before now. I have to wait for her to find her way, and I have to trust her."

"Well, I don't," David answered. "I think Mahalia and Miss Flood are wandering outside the pale. When people live by their own rules, they always get in trouble."

"If Isabel steps too far beyond the pale, she'll lose Mahalia," my mother said. "At least that's what I'm counting on. I know my daughter, David. I know her in a way Miss Flood never will."

"Why not just sit back," F. X. asked David, "and see where Mahalia leads herself? I'm sure she'll end up just fine. Mahalia knows how to watch out for Mahalia."

"Has she been this hot-tempered all summer?" David asked me.

"Mahalia was never fighty when you were gone," I said. "She just smol-dered around and bossed me to death all the time." I had a passing sense that Isabel's beliefs invited the kind of fury of feeling Mahalia added to them. But I let this perception flitter away. Isabel had not badgered everyone with angry criticism the way Mahalia did—it was Mahalia I felt exasperated with now, not Isabel.

"I've always wanted to join some off-the-wall political crusade like Isabel's," F. X. told David and my mother. "To pretend to be a fervent follower, and rise through the ranks like a sheep in wolf's clothing, until I held some high-ranking position. And then, in some pivotal moment when I was representing the group, in some keynote speech that had a critical effect on their group's fu-ture, I would suddenly lose it and act completely discombobulated. I would stand up and say something like, *Do you know what's behind all these abortion-ists? The Arab-Jewish conspiracy! This conspiracy is everywhere. It's trying to in-vade the fallopian tubes of our society. It's stealing everyone's sperm!*"

"I can just picture you," David said.

"F. X. would be wonderful at doing something like that," my mother agreed.

"Is Isabel's picketing off-the-wall?" I asked.

"Well, Penny," David answered. "Some people might see her cause as being a little extreme. They might see her picketing as a little nutty."

I was surprised to hear this. Why hadn't anyone told me this before? Did Mahalia know that adults thought Isabel's cause was nutty?

"But you don't have to judge Isabel that way," David added. "Just judge her according to how she treated you. If she was nice to you, you have the right to like her."

"That's why I like you, David," my mother said. "You're so levelheaded." She leaned over the table and kissed him.

David stood to meet her and answered, "I'll be levelheaded for you all night."

I cried, "F. X. said *sperm* out loud, right at the supper table!"

David sat back down. He said to F. X., "Miss Flood and her women's pickets may seem a little laughable to us now, but what if they aren't so innocent at all? You know what that guy Buskin did in Ohio. Who knows, maybe in the next twenty years some of these right-to-lifers will become the first serious terrorists our country deals with. Maybe twenty years from now, their children and followers will be sitting across from me at my desk in the parole office."

"Maybe," F. X. said, "their children will emerge from the womb armed to the teeth, carrying little automatic rifles."

"Oh, F. X.," my mother said. "Just picturing that gives me the willies."

After dinner F. X. sat in our armchair and composed a new letter to Isabel. He read it aloud to my mother:

Dear Ms. Flood,

An embryo has returned from the netherworld to tell the Fetal Committee that it is a lonely place full of bright lights, and warning us away from it. He stirred up quite a commotion before he was exposed as a charlatan and impostor. Even at such an early stage, we are not without complication and wickedness. Sin enters through the umbilical cord.

I have become despondent with this existence and hope that the Birthworld is less isolated than this one. Here, life is tight with security—God stands over you, breathing down your neck like a policeman. The closeness confines and sickens you. The nights of the unborn are cramped and lonely, and a relentless feeling of ripening fills you with anger and longing.

Fondly,
Fetus Elegante
Ex-Chairman, The Fetal Committee

I followed F. X. as he hand-delivered this letter to Isabel's house with a copy of one of her own pamphlets he found in our kitchen drawer. When we were twenty yards from Isabel's yard, we saw Mahalia descend her front steps and strike off in the opposite direction. F. X. called to her, but Mahalia either did not hear him or pretended not to. She turned up the driveway of a yellow house about a block away. She knocked on the door and waited outside.

When we reached Isabel's house, her lights were still on—I thought Isabel must be home. However, F. X. did not knock. He stuck his letter in Isabel's mail slot and skipped back down her stairs to the sidewalk.

"I'm carrying on a reverse courtship," F. X. explained to me. "I'm Isabel's secret reverse-admirer."

I felt spiteful and happy. As we walked home, tree frogs started up around us, crying "*What* are you going to do? *What* are you going to do?" I took F. X.'s hand and closed my eyes, letting him lead me along until I tripped. When I opened them, my mother and David were descending our front steps. They walked arm-in-arm together up the street. I turned around, and saw my sister knocking on the front door of a brick house two blocks away.

"I'm going to go catch up with Mahalia," I told F. X. "I have to tell her something."

"All right, devil-dog" F. X. answered, "but then come right back. It'll be dark in an hour."

I raced up the block toward my sister. She tucked something under the brick house's front door and walked back to the sidewalk. I turned sideways and ran like a crab, and then I ran backward for half a block: F. X. still stood on the sidewalk, keeping his eye on me. I looked over my shoulder until I caught up with my sister.

As soon as she saw me, she said, "Penny, go home. I have work to do." She held a sheath of pamphlets.

"What kind of work?"

"Leafleting." I felt a fleeting pity, thinking of my sister walking door to door, trying to get people to open up to her, but then Mahalia asked me condescendingly, "What do you want, Penny? Why are you pestering me right now?"

"Those women from Isabel's church group look crazy when they picket like that at the school," I answered.

"No they don't," Mahalia said. "They always follow Isabel's guidelines. They know what they're doing. Penny, I need to finish leafleting."

I fidgeted on the sidewalk: I stood on one foot and then the other, and then tried to stand on the end of just one big toe; I almost fell over. "Isabel's guidelines are nutty!" I said.

Mahalia made a dismissive gesture and counted her leaflets: I saw a series of skulls in bassinets fan out like an image repeated in adjoining mirrors.

"And Isabel is a strange fish!" I pressed.

"Penny, that's enough," Mahalia answered. "I'm not going to let you insult Isabel around me, even if you're just acting off the wall."

"She pokes in other people's mail," I said. "She read Mama's copies of Daddy's letters."

"She did not," Mahalia said curtly, but I saw that my secret, let loose finally like a rodent scuttling across the kitchen floor, had unsettled her. "Mama has letters from Daddy?"

"Isabel did too read them," I answered. "because she left one of her pointy paper clips on the one about Mama losing a baby. The letters are all in Mama's jewelry box."

"Why didn't Mama ever tell me there were letters from Daddy?" My sister said this to herself; she was no longer talking to me.

"Because they're hers!" I shouted.

"Penny, go on home," Mahalia said, turning away from me. I had not provoked the reaction from her that I wanted. She did not seem to care that Isabel had read the letters. My sister walked briskly toward the next house; it had an overgrown lawn and potholes in the driveway. A man answered, wearing shorts and no shirt, and carrying a beer in one hand. Mahalia held up a pamphlet and he shook his head and backed into his house, shutting the door. I spun around and ran home.

————

The following Saturday morning, David took my mother out to dinner in Plattsburgh, and F. X. stayed home with me, helping me build a maze for my lizards out of cardboard paper-towel tubes that terminated in shoe boxes lined with different-colored pieces of construction paper: He wanted to test whether the anoles had a preference for certain colors. We were going to see if they chose one shoe box over the others, and what color they turned if the tissue was not green or brown, but something they could not imitate, like orange. As F. X. taped Saran Wrap over the top of one of the boxes to prevent the lizards from escaping, he asked, "What if we human beings changed color according to our moods? If we could flush with sorrow or fear and not just shame? If we turned, say, green for envy and blue for grief. And hot pink for exuberant and a sickly gray for sanctimonious. . . ."

I saw Mahalia through our screen door, walking around F. X.'s Galaxie 500. She peered into the garage, as if she were making sure my mother's car was gone. She stepped onto the porch.

F. X. looked up and said, "Mahalia, come in!"

My sister pushed open the screen door. "Mama's not here, is she?" Mahalia asked.

"No," F. X. answered.

"I locked myself out of Isabel's," Mahalia explained. "She drove with Reverend Bender and Reverend Sloat and Mrs. Esselborne to Albany and won't be back until ten o'clock."

"Well, it's nice to see you, stranger," F. X. told her.

Mahalia stepped inside the kitchen. "Where did Mama and David go?" she asked.

"Out to dinner in Plattsburgh."

Mahalia made a peevish, mosquitoish noise, something like *Hnnnn!*

"When are you going back to Louisiana?" she asked F. X.

"When Tulane's fall semester starts. Why, do you want me to leave?"

"I just came by to get some things," Mahalia answered. She passed him and climbed the stairs. She rattled around in the bathroom, emerged with a flowered cosmetic bag, and then slipped into my mother's room. I started up the stairs to see what my sister was doing, but then I thought better of it; I knew she kept sanitary napkins in her cosmetic bag, and thought perhaps she had gone into my mother's room to find something that would embarrass her; I wondered if Isabel was somehow too proper to keep the kind of supplies Mahalia needed. About a half hour later, Mahalia came back down.

"I hope we can visit more together before I return to Louisiana," F. X. told her.

Mahalia sat on the edge of the couch. "Are you going to show up again at the picket?" she asked.

"If you are, I am," F. X. answered.

Mahalia looked dismayed.

"It's the only time I get to see you, honey," F. X. said half-jokingly. He added in an earnest tone, "I'm not sure you have any business being there, Mahalia. David's right—it's a public school. And those people Isabel hangs around with stand for a lot more than you think they do. It's possible they're not as harmless as they may appear to you. They—"

"I believe that I have a responsibility to fight people who kill babies," Mahalia answered loftily.

"Your mother misses you," F. X. told her. He set down the tape and sat across from Mahalia in the armchair.

Mahalia picked up a *Time* magazine and began thumbing through it. The look on her face, and the way she bent over the magazine without really reading it, unsettled me.

"Why don't you stay until your mother comes back?" F. X. asked.

"I intend to," Mahalia answered. "I have something to say to her."

F. X. raised his eyebrows and wiggled them at me; he found Mahalia amusing.

Mahalia continued to peruse the magazine. She crossed her legs and jiggled her foot, the way I always did when I had to sit still.

F. X. said carefully, watching her face, "Mahalia, sometimes when people are afraid of the devils inside themselves, they start seeing them everywhere else. Some people, like that teacher out there, look at you and say, 'What's bothering that beautiful young girl to make her hang around with the likes of those fetus-defenders—' "

"You think everything is so funny!" Mahalia interrupted him. "You make fun of what everyone else believes. But all you do is talk about blind people! It's all you ever talk about!"

F. X. pondered this statement for a full minute, as if taking it seriously, and then said, "But I come about my obsessions honestly. I was blind for years and years, blindness shaped my whole life. You, on the other hand, do not remember being in the womb. You are not an embryo now. You're fighting a battle that has nothing to do with you." F. X. waited for Mahalia to answer, but she looked away from him, toward the piano, as if she found his words too stupid to consider. F. X. ventured to ask, "Mahalia, don't you think this has gone on a little too long? I know you're mad at Marguerite. I know you had a bad year last year. And I figure it's hard for you to take in all the changes, your mother's being married, and a stepfather suddenly sharing your house, but your mother has—"

"I don't want to hear a big speech about how wonderful Mama is," Mahalia stopped him. "I'm tired of hearing about her." My sister pretended to read the magazine, but then looked up and said, "Mama's so selfish! She always puts herself at the center of everything!" F. X. cocked his head as if he detected a twistiness in her voice I could not quite make out.

"All right, Mahalia," he said quietly.

"I don't want to hear it," Mahalia said, "because I found out this morning that my own mother once had an abortion!" Mahalia pronounced these words with a layer of melodrama, and an undercurrent of something else—outrage or discomfort or satisfaction.

F. X. seemed taken off guard by her words. "Did Marguerite tell you that?" he asked.

"No," Mahalia answered. "I found out."

"If that's so," F. X. answered, "it's none of your business, Mahalia."

"Isabel told me," Mahalia said.

F. X. asked, looking genuinely confused, "How could Isabel possibly know anything about your mother?"

"Isabel read it by accident in one of Mama's old letters. In one of the old letters she keeps that Daddy wrote."

"Isabel read your mother's letters from your father?"

"Isabel wasn't going to tell me about it. She only told me because I asked if she had ever noticed any letters from Daddy when she was staying at our house. And I know it's all true because *now* I've seen the letters myself. They're *awful*."

"Mahalia—" F. X. began.

"Daddy said Mama killed her baby after she caught German measles, because she had spent all those years taking care of a blind person and didn't want to raise another person who was defective."

It was as if all the air had been sucked out of the room: No one spoke or even seemed to breathe. Mahalia continued to thumb the magazine, turning the pages mindlessly, as though she were driven to. From where I sat on the floor, I could see her half-smiling, but her eyes narrowed, giving her a worried look. Her expression made no sense at all. In the wire cage beside our maze, both of my lizards lay still, brown as dead leaves. I taped a last corner of Saran Wrap over the shoe box F. X. had been working on.

F. X. put his head in his hands and rubbed his eyes. "Christ, Mahalia," he finally said. "You're too young, far too young to have any idea what you're talking about."

But Mahalia did not stop there. She set down her magazine, circled F. X., put her hands on the back of his armchair, and leaned forward as if someone were pushing her from behind. "F. X., you of all people must understand how terrible it was for Mama to kill her baby because it was going to be a burden to her."

F. X turned to look at her; his face was pale olive. And then he leaned back in his chair and closed his eyes. He sat still for so long that I was afraid he planned to remain like that until Mahalia left. But instead, when Mahalia finally stepped away from his chair and headed for the door, F. X. rose and planted himself in front of her.

"Take back what you said," he told her. "Take back every single one of your words. If you don't, you'll live to cringe every time you remember them."

Mahalia colored, but she did not comply.

"Mahalia," F. X. said. "Not once. Not once did your mother ever make me feel I was a burden to her. I think that's heroic." He walked to the front door, opened it, and said, "Let's get some air, Penny." I slipped past Mahalia.

Right before he stepped outside, F. X. turned around. "Mahalia," he said. "That is the ugliest thing anyone has ever said to me in my entire life."

I followed F. X. to the Galaxie 500 and slid beside him on the front seat. The car nosed like a great whale into the twilight in the direction of town. "Penny," he asked. "Did you understand any of that?

"Probably," I answered.

"I'll tell you right now that the worst things people ever do, they do because they believe they're fighting what's wrong. In that way, good introduces evil back into the world and the circle is complete."

I leaned against F. X. He circled the town twice, as if we were caught in a giant eddy, and then he turned onto the road to Stein Lake. "Let's go night fishing," he said. "Night fish are livelier and more reckless than day fish. That's because while figurative blindness is a metaphor for willful ignorance, true blindness is a bottomless ocean full of long-toothed luminescent fish and uncharted currents and unnamed creatures, rich with knowledge of the unknown."

He parked the Galaxie 500 beside the lake's picnic benches and retrieved a fishing pole from his trunk. "I'll bait it and then you hold it," he said. He grabbed a tackle box, and we walked out onto the dock. He baited the hook with something that even I knew made no sense at night—a fly. I heard the reel singing, and imagined the line writing itself in its own shorthand over the darkness. F. X. handed me the pole, and I sat down on the dock beside him. I watched the stars appear like fireflies flickering on, and then vanish behind the passing voids of invisible clouds. We sat quietly for a long time, a half hour or more: Maybe F. X. just wanted to be where no one could see him. I reached over, more than once, to make sure my uncle was still there—I was afraid he would sink so far into himself that he would disappear.

Of course, we caught no fish at all. Eventually, F. X. said, "Penny, shouldering up to you is like sitting beside a sack of jumping frogs. I swear you would burst out of your own body if you were forced to hold still for a full minute." He took the pole from me, and I heard the reel winding in its empty hook.

"Now we know, Penny," he told me. "Night fish are a hell of a lot smarter than day fish."

He took my hand in his massive one and led me back to the Galaxie 500. "Let's go eat at the Motor Inn. You'll think that place is a pisser."

We drove along the outskirts of town and down Dannemora Road. The Galaxie 500 passed a van that slowed as the driver argued with a woman seated beside him; a possum whose eyes lit up like tiny headlights on the road shoulder; and a state police car that had pulled over a man whose truck radio blared so loudly that I could hear the words, *"Keep me hot, baby, until—"*

F. X. parked beside the Stein Motor Inn. It was a long, low building with narrow windows that glowed dimly in the night air, and a black entrance with its door flung wide and adult voices stumbling outward from a chaotic noise within. F. X. led me inside to the bar counter and ordered me a Shirley Temple, and a grilled cheese sandwich that a cocktail waitress made specially for me in the kitchen. The sandwich had a toothpick shaped like a sword stuck through it, and the bartender put seven maraschino cherries in my drink.

Two stools down from me, a man had fallen asleep with his fork still in his hands, and beside him, a woman spun around and around on her stool like a child, calling out, "I'm Mary-go-round, I'm Mary-go-round!" while a man wearing sunglasses told her, "Hey, Mary, hey, Mary," and tried to kiss her as her face spun by. He kept missing her; I thought his sunglasses might be hampering him in the dark bar. Beside them was a man who was talking to himself, and there was a gray cat sleeping on the counter next to the cash register, and in front of the cat was a woman whose boyfriend, dressed in a prison guard's uniform, had to prop her up as he paid his tab. A Seeing Eye dog at a table next to the front door rested with his head on his paws, his eyes fixed on the cat. The floor around him was littered with peanut shells. When I felt under the counter there were so many pieces of chewing gum that it amazed me: Either the bar was very old, or an unusual number of adults who came there chewed gum. In the darkness behind me, some women were singing a country song off key, and a man was whooping. There was a large candle-lit table in the center of the darkness, where ten or twelve men in prison guard uniforms were seated, with women who must have been their wives—they were older women, with styled hair. Before the center of the table, in a high-backed chair with heavy armrests that made me think of an electric chair, was a square-shouldered man with a stubble of gray hair and a crooked smile. "To life behind bars!" he said, raising his glass. The men around him roared. I saw, off to their left in a dark corner, Mr. Canon with his cheek resting on his place mat, his closed eyes illuminated by a red flickering candle.

Out of nowhere, a woman's voice called, "Penny? Penny Daigle? Are you barhopping, Penny Daigle?"

I swiveled on my stool; it was Annie Strang, wearing a dress made entirely out of suede, and suede boots that reached halfway up her thighs. Violet eye shadow extended from the corners of her eyes to her temples, like a raccoon's mask.

"Who's this you're here with?" she asked me, winking. I disliked being winked at by adults; it was their way of saying something they did not really mean for me to understand.

"He's my uncle F. X." I answered.

She told F. X., "We've seen each other before at church and the other day at the high school." She winked at me again, and then smiled oddly, as if her smile merely faced me but was intended for F. X. She turned her back to us briefly, fished in her purse, and opened a compact. I craned my neck around her shoulder and watched her apply face powder. She motioned toward the back of the bar and said, "I just ran into Mr. Coker. He's here with a man named Mr. Petty, from that Ohio minister's church. We're all sitting together." She winked at me a third time. "Why don't you come join us instead of staying by your lonesome selves on these old stools?"

I was not sure I wanted to go with her; I was enjoying the strangeness of being alone with F. X. in a dark and noisy bar. However, as Annie Strang began walking back to her place, F. X. leaned toward me and whispered, "We can't turn down an invitation from one of Mahalia's church friends, Penny." He grinned at me and then winked four or five times, in imitation of Annie Strang, so that I cracked up. F. X. picked up his beer and my Shirley Temple and walked after Annie Strang. I carried my grilled cheese sandwich and followed him to a table in the back, where I saw Mr. Coker sitting by himself, drinking pineapple juice.

"Mr. Petty left?" Annie Strang asked, sounding disappointed.

"I guess so," Mr. Coker answered.

"That wasn't very friendly," Annie Strang said. "Anyway, this is Penny and Mahalia's uncle F. X."

"I just popped in to get Penny a healthy supper," F. X. told Mr. Coker.

I thought Mr. Coker would say little or nothing, the way he always did around us, and that F. X. would talk in circles around him like a hurricane winding itself up. However, Mr. Coker held out his hand and said, "I'm Mark." He glanced at Annie Strang and added in a disgruntled tone, "I wasn't here with Miss Strang. I was meeting with a fellow from a brother church."

"Did I scare Mr. Petty off?" Annie asked. She sat down. "They were talking about Vietnam," she told F. X. "I always excuse myself when men start talking about Vietnam."

"Were you there?" F. X. asked Mr. Coker.

Annie Strang sighed, and Mr. Coker turned slightly away from her, so that he sat at an odd angle as he talked to F. X., half-facing the darkness behind him, his knees cramped against the table leg.

"I joined up before the war started," Mr. Coker answered. "But I fell off a jeep ten days after I got to boot camp and ended up flat on my back for the rest of the year in a VA hospital. That's why I say I'm a 'Not-Vietnam vet.' That's what my old man used to call me: 'The Not-Viet-Nam vet'."

"I'm an NVN too," F. X. answered, sipping his beer.

Mr. Coker laughed low in his throat and nodded saying, "I heard from Isabel that you used to be blind."

"That's right," F. X. said. "They still won't let blind men shoot at people. It would save a lot of lives if they did." The two men laughed together, as if their common experience of physical frailty made them old friends.

Annie Strang suddenly cried, "Do you know who that is? It's that Nohilly woman—Cicely Nohilly!" Mr. Coker barely turned around; he glanced in a perfunctory way over his shoulder. "What's she doing here?" Annie Strang asked.

I looked behind her: Cicely Nohilly sat at the prison guards' table; her back had been turned toward me when I had watched them from my bar stool. She was dressed up, in a glossy turquoise blouse and matching earrings. She sat beside her grandmother, whom I recognized from Mr. Nohilly's funeral. A middle-aged woman who looked like a miserable version of Cicely sat on the other side of her grandmother; the woman twisted her napkin and stared down at her lap. I was proud to know who she was—she was the person whom Mrs. Wroblewski had said Superintendent Nohilly must have married because he stepped on her by mistake.

"I don't see how Cicely Nohilly can show her face in public," Annie Strang said.

"Most people don't think of coming here as showing their face in public," Mr. Coker answered, suppressing a smile and sipping his pineapple juice.

"She sees me staring at her. Look at her look away," Annie Strang told me, as if I were the only person who could appreciate what she had to say. "See that guy with his back to us across from her? That's her father, Warden Nohilly." I stared at the broad back of the man seated in the chair that reminded me of an electric chair, who had given the toast earlier. He leaned forward and said something to Cicely's mother, the men around him guffawed, and Cicely's mother continued to stare into her lap. Cicely's grandmother patted her shoulder. I wanted Cicely's father to turn around, now that I knew who he was: I ached to get another look at the man who had given David his hockey scar.

Mr. Coker moved his chair slightly, so that his back was to Annie Strang. He said to F. X., "When they finally operated on me at the VA hospital, they found out I had this condition called spinal stenosis and they had to give me a medical discharge." He reached behind him and touched the nape of his neck gingerly. "The doctors told me that I had had that stenosis my whole life, but I hadn't know it—it means your spinal cord is crushed up inside your backbone because the tube of air around it is too thin." He demonstrated, by rolling up his napkin into a narrow tube and then pushing a straw up through it. "No cushion of air."

Annie Strang, I saw, was not following Mr. Coker's words and did not look at his napkin. She was sipping her drink and continued to watch Cicely Nohilly intently, as if she wanted Cicely to notice her staring again.

"The doctor told me," Mr. Coker continued, "that all that time, since I was born, if I had just had a little whiplash, or got punched the wrong way, or knocked down in boot camp and landed on my neck at the right angle, I could have ended up quadriplegic. The doctor operated on my back and fixed it so that would never happen. He took a plug of bone from my hip and stuck the bone onto something in my spine." Mr. Coker lifted his beard slightly and traced a scar on his neck I had not noticed before. The scar was thin, a slight corrugated wrinkle. It looked as if his head had been carefully removed and attached back on with fine, delicate stitches.

Cicely Nohilly noticed Annie Strang watching her again and whispered something into the ear of a man seated to her left; he burst out laughing. A moment later, a waitress brought a birthday cake to Cicely's table and set it down in front of her grandmother, who clasped her hands together in delight. Cicely leaned forward to help blow out the candles. Thereafter, she ignored Annie Strang.

"Look at her, celebrating away," Annie Strang said.

"So, the army saved your life," F. X. joked with Mr. Coker.

"All that time, I could have been crippled," Mr. Coker answered, but it was not so much an answer as the statement of a man who felt compelled to say a certain specific thing as soon as possible. "I could have been crippled in any one of those fistfights you have when you're young, and all those times my dad lit into me, and the time I was thrown from a snowmobile. It creeped me out. It made me feel like I couldn't trust anything, not even my own backbone."

F. X. nodded. "That's how I felt about losing my sight when I was a boy," he said. "I wasn't sure what parts of me were really *me*, you know what I mean? What parts I could trust to always be there as part of me, and which ones were just like—oh, like clothes say, like a hat you could put on but then could lose. If you can't believe in your own eyes, why trust anything? And then, of course, once you're blind, nothing ever looks the same." Mr. Coker laughed. "You see that facts don't matter—you can't trust facts. You have to reinvent the world as you go along—"

Mr. Coker answered, "Exactly. That's why I don't listen to what other people do. I have my own farm, and I do things my way."

I realized that F. X. had somehow enticed Mr. Coker to talk more in our ten minutes together than I had heard him do in all the time since I had met him. I thought that in that moment of mutual understanding the two men genuinely liked one another. F. X. looked at ease, caught up in the tangle and chaos of another person's life—as if Mahalia were the farthest thing from his mind. I wondered whether F. X. had drawn Mr. Coker out with some hidden reporter's skill, or whether Mr. Coker was always more talkative around men—I had only seen him surrounded by women.

Cicely Nohilly appeared without warning beside our table.

She bent over and whispered loudly to Mr. Coker, "Does your girlfriend have a problem?"

"What?" Mr. Coker asked.

"Your girlfriend here keeps sending dirty looks over to our table, and I'm just wondering if she has some kind of problem. We're trying to have a birthday party for my grandmother whose husband has just died."

Mr. Coker looked at Annie Strang as if he had never seen her before. "This lady is not my girlfriend," he said.

"Lucky for you," Cicely answered. She returned to her table. Superintendent Nohilly twisted halfway around in his seat, smiled slightly at Annie Strang, and then stuck his tongue at her between his half-open lips, in a way that I sensed was meant to be dirty and humiliating. She looked away quickly. He turned back around and began slicing his mother's birthday cake.

"Why did he whirl around his stuck-out tongue like that?" I asked Annie Strang.

Annie Strang did not answer me; I would never know. She waved to an invisible person in the back of the bar. "Ronny!" she called. "Ronny! I'm coming right over."

She jumped up and left us there. I suddenly felt sorry for her, sorry for her and Cicely Nohilly both, although I was unsure why. I experienced a flutter of worry that one day I could be like them, because I would turn into what they were—women—and then, in a single moment, I understood that I was already part of the great, sorry noise of all of the people in the bar, that I was already one of them. I felt something larger than I ever had before—I felt sorry for us all, for everyone in the Stein Motor Inn and the entire town of Stein. I lay my head down on the table.

Mr. Coker said, "That Annie Strang should be home with her kids. Instead she probably left them with her mother or Isabel again, and is going to lollygark around all night taking advantage. She still hasn't figured out that a mother's place is at home with her children." Was that what Mr. Coker would tell Lucy? I wondered. Would she have to stay shut up at home with her baby all day? "Isabel's the only one with any sense out of all of them," Mr. Coker continued, "That's why I told that boy Nicky at the church to come hang out with me. Those women would drive any boy off the deep end."

"Nicky Groot?" F. X. asked.

"Yeah," Mr. Coker answered. "That boy has had the meanest childhood of any person I've met. Me included. If it wasn't for Isabel, he would have been lost a long time ago. But even Isabel knows that Nicky needs a man's influence. I just take him out, show him how to shoot a little, how to help me around the farm, that kind of thing. It's an organic farm, except for the horseradish. Nicky can't fit into anyplace around here, just like me when I was a boy. Hell, they don't even have a baseball team at that juvenile delinquent school they send him to. And no girls in his classes."

Mr. Coker asked me suddenly, "Your sister doesn't even know he exists, does she?"

"Mahalia?" I answered.

"Yeah, Nicky's hopeless when it comes to her. Girl's too pretty," Mr. Coker told F. X.

F. X. said, "It's good you can give Nicky some kind of fatherly attention—"

"Yeah," Mr. Coker agreed. "Nicky's father was a piece of work. Just like mine. I see by your accent you're from the South somewhere. Well, right after I got rejected by the military, my mother died and I ran off from here just to get away from my dad, and I landed finally in this town called Alligator, Mississippi, where I lived on a commune for a while. That's where my daughter, Lucy, was born—we didn't call a doctor or anything, my wife wanted everything natural, and then when Lucy came, she came out backward, just a foot kicking at the air and I thought I was going to die right there. They had to rush her mother to the hospital, and then after the birth her mother just up and left her hospital bed before she was even discharged and never came back, and that's when I decided I didn't fit in with those commune people any better than anywhere else, so I headed back here with Lucy a babe in arms, and me thinking I was going to have to work at the correctional facility alongside my dad, my idea of hell, but then he died and I was able to sell his house and buy some property. And now my own daughter is going to have a baby." Mr. Coker concluded the facts of his life there.

He stood abruptly and said, "There's Mr. Petty back now, so I'll have to go." Mr. Coker lifted a leather bag from beside his chair, opened it, and pulled out a jar of horseradish labeled COKER'S BITTER HERBS: **NOT** ORGANICALLY GROWN. He handed it to F. X. "It's been a pleasure meeting you," he said. "Penny, you should get on home."

I searched behind him for Mr. Petty, but in the darkness of the bar, I could not find him. Near the doorway, Annie was talking to a young man beside the coatrack; she was leaning on her left hand, which she had placed on the wall slightly to one side of his head, and he had a pinned-down look. He seemed to be trying to press himself into the wall like a shadow. When Annie Strang removed her arm to push back her hair, he slipped past her out the bar exit. Mr. Coker followed him, waving to someone in the parking lot.

I wondered whether Mr. Coker had talked so much because he spent too much time avoiding people. I was going to ask F. X. if he thought Mr. Coker got lonely, working by himself on his farm with only Lucy around, but when I turned toward my uncle, he was sitting with his eyes closed, as if, now that Mr. Coker was gone, F. X. had suddenly remembered the drama we had left behind us at the house—I was sorry myself to recall Mahalia.

"Well, Penny," F. X. said. "Mr. Coker's right. We better be heading home." He stood up, and as I followed him from the bar, he turned around once and looked back as if he were worried he had forgotten something, or as if he needed to remind himself that the dark distracting chaos of the bar would still be waiting for him when he returned. We walked through a snarl of shouts and titters and jeers, a woman cried, "See if I care!" and then the exit door swung closed behind us with a *shhhh*.

All the lights were on in the house when we arrived there. David's truck was in the driveway, and I could see him and my mother on the couch through the screen door, talking to each other.

As F. X. entered behind me, he asked, "Marguerite, was Mahalia here when you got back?"

"No," my mother answered. "Mahalia came visiting? I'm sorry I missed her. We just got home a few minutes ago."

"I'm glad you missed her," F. X. said. "She had something especially venomous to tell you."

"What is it, F. X.?" my mother asked. "You have that tone in your voice."

"Let's talk outside," F. X. answered. He walked past her into the kitchen and waited on the back steps for her to join him. She nestled beside him, and they talked for less than a minute before my mother shouted, "That snoop! That shameless snoop! No one but Joseph and I had any right to know!"

"Is something wrong?" David asked me.

"Mahalia came here and got F. X. upset," I answered, sitting down on the couch beside him.

"Ah—Mahalia," he said, with a tone of unrestrained frustration.

"She just walked in and stirred everything up," I said.

"F. X. told me that your mother never acted all hot-tempered like Mahalia when she was a teenager," David answered. "But if your mother hadn't had to take on so much so early, I bet she would have behaved just like your sister."

"I wouldn't mind making things spin around me when I'm older," I said, "but when I do I won't be mean to you and Mama and F. X. Maybe I'll be mean to Mahalia instead."

"By the time you're Mahalia's age, she'll get along fine with you," David said.

"I don't know," I answered. "Maybe she'll end up some nasty wrinkled-up lady living in an old house with Isabel, telling everybody what's wrong with them."

I heard my mother and F. X. speaking in low murmurs. A little later, my mother said something, and F. X. chuckled in return, and when I turned around, my mother was leaning against him, and he had his hand on top of her head. I was relieved that whatever might have come between them had passed.

When my mother and F. X. reentered the house and joined David in the living room, I walked upstairs, thinking I would hold my anoles. What if they changed color not according to their own moods, but the moods of other people in the house? I imagined peering in at my lizards each morning to know ahead of time what emotion would be flying around the house that day—the lizards would flash red to warn me of a fight to come, or blue to let me know F. X. was about to sink into one of his silences. If things were calm in my house, the lizards would be some unexciting color, mustard or tan.

I opened my bedroom door—and there was my sister, lying on her bed, her eyes closed. She was smiling in her sleep. Beside her was a stack of papers—carbon print on brittle-looking pages—my father's letters to my mother. Mahalia's breath tickled them as she slept, so that they moved as if slightly alive.

"Mahalia!" I said, shaking her. "What are you doing here?"

Mahalia sat up, confused: She looked around her, as if trying to remember why she was still among us.

"Are you going to sleep here? Are you moving back in?" I asked.

"No!" she answered, sitting upright. "I was just waiting for Mama to come home."

My heart sank: I dreaded another fight in the house that evening. I wanted to run downstairs and warn everyone that Mahalia was still there.

"Why are you waiting for Mama?" I asked. "Are you going to start something?"

Mahalia turned away from me and pulled on her slipper-shoes with quick tugs, looking annoyed.

This infuriated me. I told her, "I didn't say you could come in my room. You live at Isabel's now, and you can't just walk back in here anytime you want. You can only come in here if I let you." My voice rose until I shouted, "BECAUSE I CAN START SOMETHING TOO!"

I heard feet on the stairs, and my mother asking, "Who's Penny talking to?"

She pushed open the bedroom door.

"Oh!" my mother said, looking genuinely shocked, as if she had found an alligator on Mahalia's bed and not her daughter.

"I'm not staying here!" Mahalia told her. "I just got locked out of Isabel's and was waiting for her to get back home so that she can let me inside."

My mother crossed her arms and said with some restraint, "I think you owe me an apology, Mahalia, for—" My mother looked down and saw her letters lying on Mahalia's bed. "What are these? Are these my—?"

Mahalia answered, "I owe *you* an apology!"

My mother began, "Mahalia, I'm going to try as hard as I can not to lose my temper with you. I'm not going to let you push me over the edge. I just want an explanation for why you and your Miss Flood need to poke around in other people's mail!" My mother's voice flared a little, at the end of her sentence. She picked up the stack of letters, folded it in half, and smoothed the top page with her hand. "It's simply bizarre that a grown woman would read another woman's mail and then tell her daughter what it contained—"

"*Penny* found your letters," Mahalia answered primly. "Isabel only noticed them when she went to put them back after Penny left them out."

I told Mahalia, "Isabel found them first!"

Ignoring me, Mahalia told my mother, "I can't believe you killed your own baby." She spoke emphatically, but unlike my mother, Mahalia did not look as if she were trying to keep under control; she seemed almost removed from herself. Her voice held no fury, no emotion at all, just a breathless righteousness.

"For heaven's sake, Mahalia," my mother answered. "Don't talk about what you don't understand. I don't even know how to approach you right now—"

"It's God you have to face, not me," Mahalia said.

"God!" my mother answered dismissively. "What do I need God for, when I've got a daughter who looks down on us all like the Great Holy Moly from her heavenly throne! Mahalia, you're wearing people thin with all your church talk. Don't think you understand the world from hanging around with Isabel at that preacher's church." I knew that the word "preacher" would bother Mahalia. There was something seedy about it; it was the opposite of "reverend." It made me think of a whiskery old man hawking toys that fell apart as soon as you took them home.

"I saw the date on Daddy's letter," Mahalia told my mother. "You broke the law."

My mother looked at her, baffled. "The law?" My mother asked. "What law?"

"Abortion wasn't even legal in 1965!" Mahalia said.

"Oh, for God's sake," my mother answered. "Why would I have cared about the law? You can't imagine what things were like then for women."

"I know what they were like for babies," Mahalia replied.

"You're way over your head, Mahalia," my mother answered. She sat down on the corner of my sister's bed. Mahalia immediately jumped up, as if she were about to catch on fire, and moved to the far side of the room.

"Mahalia," my mother said. "You've decided to hate me and scorn your whole family because you had too much on your shoulders this year. You had to watch over Penny too much. For how long was it? A few months?" My mother continued in a low, even tone, but as her words gathered mass, they increased momentum and rose in volume. "That's what my whole girlhood was like! F. X. losing his sight and our father evaporating and our mama caught up in her sorrow and drinking herself up to an automobile accident! And there I was, when all the other girls were off having romances—I was hunched over a secretary's typewriter fending off married bosses. And I did that for *years! Years!* Until I was sucked dry! Until I felt like the husk of a girl and the only man I thought would have me was a man like your father, who I had nothing in common with. Nothing whatsoever! Until I married a man who wanted me to be a dead stump! You think you have complete control over your life, but you don't. Do you know what life is? I'll tell you. It's a boat you step onto, and it just goes off God knows where, with you standing on it wondering where in hell it will take you. You wake up one morning, and you're a wife with two children—"

"Is that," Mahalia asked haughtily, "your miserable excuse for killing your own baby?" She took a step forward as she spoke, so that by the end of her sentence she was standing near my mother, looking down on her. "I know why you really killed him! You killed him because he wasn't perfect!"

My mother stood up and said, hotly, "I don't have to make excuses to you for anything I do! And I'll tell you something else, Little Miss, your precious Isabel who snoops around everyone's love lives because she has no love life of her own, is wrong. Wrong! And conceited! It must take unbelievable conceit for a woman like her to sit in judgment on other women."

"Isabel is not conceited!" Mahalia cried. "She herself says she works every day against pride. She says she knows the greatest challenge for her is the flaw of pride, and that she fights it in herself every minute."

"Pride!" my mother answered. "Her worst problem isn't pride! Her problem is that she's ridiculous!"

My sister stepped forward, her fists clenched at her sides, and tried to squeeze past my mother.

My mother grabbed her and anchored her next to the bed. "You listen to me, Little Miss," my mother said. "What grown girls and women decide to do with their love lives and pregnancies is not up to your precious Isabel. In my case, it was up to me. And I did not care, Mahalia, whether I had a child who was perfect. My children are *not* perfect!" She let go of Mahalia, and my sister backed away from her.

"You knew it wasn't right," Mahalia answered. "That's why you were hiding in the Stein Motor Inn from Daddy!"

"Hiding?" my mother asked. "I checked into that rat hole because it was the kind of place women were forced to go to for abortions in those days! And that, Little Miss, is *my life!*" My mother rushed past Mahalia and slammed the door with such force that the screws on its upper hinge finally pulled out of the wall. Chips of plaster showered onto the floor as the door moaned and listed backward, stopping halfway at a precarious angle.

Mahalia looked through me. She half-circled my bed and then disappeared out the doorway. She ran down the stairs; I heard her feet in the kitchen, and a hush—she had stepped through the night onto the soft earth of the backyard.

When I walked downstairs, F. X. was sitting in the armchair with his head tilted back and his eyes shut. I wanted to poke him, but instead, I sat across from him on the sofa without talking. Above us, my mother's and David's voices rumbled and murmured in their bedroom.

Twenty minutes later, they returned downstairs. My mother sat beside me and said, "Penny, I'm sorry we fought in front of you like that. There you were, standing between us, and Mahalia and I went on and on as if you were a doorknob."

I put my head in her lap. "I only found those letters because I was looking for chocolate in your dresser," I told her. "But Isabel read those letters *before* I saw them. I know because she uses these pointy gold paper clips and there was one on your letter already."

"Did you find the chocolates?"

"I ate them all," I answered.

"I wonder," David told my mother, "if Isabel left her paper clip there on purpose. If she wanted you to know she'd seen the letter."

"At least she didn't steal my jewelry," my mother answered. She laughed.

"I think it's time we made Mahalia return home," David said.

"Are you a glutton for punishment?" F. X. asked, his eyes still closed. "How long would you survive in the middle of all that snarling?"

"Maybe it will be better now that you've cleared the air," David told my mother.

"I think I'll let things cool off a little," my mother said. "If I went over there right now I think I'd shoot Princess Isabel." David looked worried. "I'll tell you what I'll do, David," my mother relented, "I'll let a day or two go by, and then I'll stop there after work and have it out with Miss Flood."

"Mahalia will hate you if you do that," I said. "She'll hate you if you make her leave Isabel's."

F. X. opened his eyes and looked at me. "Let's ask Penny what she'd do," he said.

"I don't see why everyone's making such a big fuss over Mahalia," I responded. "And I don't see why anyone wants to go get her. Make her come back herself. Make her come home on bended knee."

David laughed and said, "I guess everyone could use a break from Mahalia right now. Let's all sit and think about anything else, anything at all." He leaned back on the couch with his arm around my mother, tilting his head and closing his eyes as if making fun of F. X. "Let's relish the quiet."

I closed my eyes too: There was silence for about five seconds, and then

I heard the rustlings and echoes F. X. talked about: a pulse without a source and then a needling repetition, and a faint musical sound. It was piano music. And then, a moment later, strains of other instruments—something brassy and something plaintive, mingled with it—seemed to come from our front lawn.

David walked to the front door and peered outside. "My God," he said.

We all came up behind him: On the sidewalk before the house was a piano. A boy sat on a piano bench, hunched over the keys and playing under the streetlight, and beside him were two other boys holding instruments, a trumpet and clarinet.

We descended the steps and moved across the lawn toward the piano. The seated boy continued playing, as if he always performed piano music at night on the sidewalk. Up the road, the church Jeep was parked in Isabel's driveway, and her outside light was on. She had arrived home.

F. X. asked the boy at the piano, "Who are you serenading? Is that Bill Evans? Will you take a request?"

David asked admiringly, "How did you boys get a piano out here?"

The piano player turned around—it was Ben Fisher—and said proudly, "Ed brought it in his brother's moving van!" The boy with the clarinet pointed behind F. X.'s Galaxie 500: Under the next streetlight was a white van printed with the words *Adirondack Movers.*

Ben looked toward our house and asked, "Where's Mahalia?"

"She huffed away up the street, like always," I answered.

"Why don't you boys come on inside for a soda?" my mother asked. "Let's take a look at you."

They followed my mother into the living room, and F. X., David, and I trailed after them. The boys sat down together on the couch—Ben Fisher, who wore a necktie over a tie-dyed T-shirt; the boy who had handed Mahalia the note from Ben at the school during my first picket, whose name turned out to be Rudolph, and who clutched his clarinet with nervous, damp hands and fidgeted so much on the sofa that he reminded me of myself; and Ed, who was as tall as F. X. and had wrists as thin as pencils and a pale, sunken chest and barely spoke. My mother gave them all root beers, and the boys drank them, looking awkward and peering sidelong at one another over their glasses.

Finally, Ben Fisher asked, "Is Mahalia coming home? I have to get the piano back in ninety minutes, or my parents will find out it's missing and murder me."

"Mahalia had a conniption fit about unborn babies," I said. "She got all hot in the head and picked a fight and stormed away to Isabel's."

"Isabel the Vulture Lady?" the boy named Rudolph asked. "The one who's always out there with her weird baby-murder pamphlets by the school?"

Ben grabbed Rudolph's leg and gave him a look to silence him. "Not that we mean any disrespect about your religious views—" Ben told my mother.

"Oh, those aren't *our* views," my mother answered charmingly. "My daughter's just gotten into the grips of religion and hasn't found a gracious way to get herself out."

"We're hoping temptation will trip her up," F. X. said.

David asked, "Why do you call Miss Flood the Vulture Lady?"

"Because," Ben answered, "she moves in circles around all that blood and death!"

Ed laughed: He had a deep hollow laugh like a lonely animal's. Rudolph told F. X., "Mr. Brewer, our teacher, says that she uses photographs of nine-month-old stillborn babies, instead of earlier term fetuses, who would look more like tadpoles—"

"Which would be more accurate," Ben explained, "but the Vulture Lady is trying to persuade people with inflammatory evidence. Mr. Brewer is the *only* cool teacher in the school. The rest of them are—"

"Lobotomized," Ed said; this was the only word he uttered that night.

"So, you like my stepdaughter Mahalia?" David asked.

"I'm glad you called Mahalia that," my mother told David. "I'm glad you're still able to own her as ours."

"Ben's a lost soul," Rudolph answered.

"Completely lost," Ben agreed. Ed nodded gravely.

"Well, who wouldn't be, around Mahalia?" my mother asked. "She's a beautiful girl."

"A beautiful young woman with a fiery personality," David concurred. He and F. X. exchanged looks, as if they were conspiring to convince a suitor in a fairy tale to take a girl off our hands whom we secretly knew was vain and wicked and greedy, someone whom we knew would behead her husband in his sleep.

"What I think," F. X. told Ben, "is that you should push the piano up the block to Isabel Flood's house, where Mahalia no doubt is this very minute, and you should surprise her there. Miss Flood would probably enjoy a little music herself. Mahalia will probably faint!"

All three of the boys rose, taking this as a serious suggestion. They thanked my mother for the root beer, and headed for the door. I followed them, hoping Mahalia would faint with mortification at the sound of their instruments playing outside Isabel's window. I liked the idea of women fainting, even if it was ridiculously feminine—that self-abandonment, that swoop toward earth, men jumping forward like startled frogs, set into involuntary motion by the picture of all that softness going *crack* on the pavement. David helped the boys wheel the piano back onto the van, while my mother pointed out Isabel's house to Ed, saying, "This is just what Miss Flood needs."

F. X. told Ben, "You could be like Orpheus fetching Eurydice from hell, but instead you'll be snatching Mahalia from the jaws of heaven, back into the world." The boys drove the piano up the street into Isabel's driveway. The lights in Isabel's house flickered, and then shut off and did not turn on again. The van's rear doors opened, and the piano backed down slowly as the three boys leaned against it to keep it from slipping. It leveled itself out on the sidewalk pavement, and the boys wheeled it into the darkness of Isabel's yard, toward Mahalia.

Chapter Thirteen

Picketing

$\mathcal{T}$he following Tuesday, Isabel appeared in her helmet-hat to pick me up at All Saints. "Mahalia's already busy at the high school," Isabel informed me. "She'll meet you there." Isabel gave no indication whether she knew about the conflagration at our house two days before, or that my mother had learned Isabel had pried into my father's letters. That morning, my mother had said at breakfast, "I had a dream in which I raced over to Miss Flood's house to attack her for reading my letters. In the dream, I actually pulled her hair. Mahalia was there and kept shouting, 'Hit her, Isabel! Hit her!' It was awful. I woke up all jangled. But instead of feeling mad, I thought, how embarrassing for Miss Flood, to get caught like that. God knows what goes on in that woman's head. Whatever her reason for rummaging through my private things, it's pathetic and a little sad. I guess Miss Flood sneak-peaks at other people's mail because her own life is so empty. I don't see any point in humiliating her by bringing it up—she probably already feels embarassed enough. Besides, if I go after her in front of Mahalia, my daughter will only rush to Miss Flood's side to protect her. That's what the dream was telling me."

Sitting next to Isabel in her Jeep, I did not think there was anything pathetic or embarassed about her. Before turning on the Jeep's ignition, she read over a paper, underlining part of it; her eyes narrowed in her foxy face. She tucked the paper into her brocade bag and told me, "Penny, take your socks out of your jumper pocket and put them on. You'll find it uncomfortable walking around in your sneakers with bare feet. It will give you blisters." As Isabel turned up the road toward the school, she asked me, "Penny, do you know who those boys were who were carousing on the street last night? This morning I found a package on the doorstep that contained some articles—lipstick and perfume and face powder. Is there a boy who is courting Mahalia?"

"Mahalia doesn't wear makeup," I answered. I wondered if Nicky Groot had left the package late at night, after Ben Fisher and his friends departed; it seemed like the kind of thing Nicky might do.

"Mahalia doesn't need to wear makeup," Isabel said. "She has natural beauty." And then, in a kind tone, Isabel told me, "You'll be a pretty girl too, Penny. You'll be different-looking, but striking with your brunette hair and olive complexion. You won't need makeup either."

I studied Isabel as she drove—she pursed her lips under her helmet-hat—I could not imagine Isabel wearing makeup. I tried thinking of her as the Vulture Lady, but the name made me feel a little sad for her: I did not want to picture her as a vulture.

When Isabel and I arrived at the school, a crowd was already there. Mrs. Groot and Annie Strang were carrying signs, and Lucy and Mrs. Wroblewski had seated themselves before the literature table. They were all wearing their lapel buttons that said **ABORTIONS WILL NOT LET YOU FORGET**. Mr. Coker hovered behind his daughter and handed her a cup of milk from a thermos. Reverend Bender was there, in his suit without the minister's collar, and his glittering tiepin, and beside him stood Mrs. Esselborne in the blue dress patterned with gold chains she had worn the first time I encountered her. Reverend Sloat, wearing his knapsack and his minister's collar, was engaged in a conversation with them. Behind him, parked in Stein High's driveway, was the yellow school bus with **ARMY OF LAMBS** painted on its side that I had seen at the night march many months before. Reverend Sloat smiled so that his jagged possum teeth showed, and he moved his small hands excitedly as he talked, while Mrs. Esselborne, looking uncomfortable, nodded without speaking. Behind them, Nicky Groot leaned against his tree, drinking a Coca-Cola. A small, soft beard clung to his chin.

"I know it's not that hot to a *real* person," Mrs. Wroblewski said, fanning herself and Lucy with a religious tract behind the literature table. "But when I'm this pregnant, I always feel like a roast chicken." Mahalia handed them cups of lemonade. Lucy made a sour face when she tasted it; it must have been Isabel's recipe.

"Mahalia," Mrs. Wroblewski said, "I was afraid you wouldn't be able to come. Lucy told me how your family lit into you."

I wondered what Mahalia had said to Lucy about us. Mahalia looked uneasy—I thought she was annoyed that Mrs. Wroblewski was trying to make her a topic of gossip.

"There really isn't a problem," my sister told Mrs. Wroblewski.

People began stepping out of Reverend Sloat's yellow bus. I half-expected robed figures dazzled by a myriad of lamps to exit the bus in a ceremonial progression, but instead, by the light of day, I saw that the bus's occupants were mostly women and some men, who bore the peculiar expression of tourists lighting on the soil of a new place. There was an elderly woman with silver-blue hair wearing a pink hat with a real rose pinned to it; and the cadaverous man, Mr. Petty, wearing his gray jumpsuit embossed with the yellow script that said: *Former Member of the Legion of the Unborn;* and a blond woman in a wrinkled beige dress that fell to her feet, followed by an identical woman wearing the same beige wrinkled dress—I had never seen adult identical twins before. After them came a scruffy-looking man wearing a bright orange hunting jacket and carrying *Handbook on Abortion;* a middle-aged woman in a mint-green pantsuit, with frosted hair, clinging to a lapdog that looked like a diminutive German shepherd; and a young man with ruddy cheeks and a gold beard, carrying a Bible, whom I recognized as the same one who had talked in tongues on my only visit to a Wednesday night prayer meeting—he must have left Reverend Bender's church to join Reverend Sloat's crusades. After this, a tall, long-haired woman climbed from the bus, carrying a flute and scratching her neck nape vigorously with her free hand; and last of all, a husky man in torn overalls stepped down, carrying several signs at once. Mahalia walked through the crowd, handing sour lemonade to everyone.

The man in suspenders rested the signs against the bus. They were all printed with the words:

AND HE SHALL BE FILLED WITH THE HOLY GHOST, EVEN FROM HIS MOTHER'S WOMB.

The woman with the rose in her hat and the cadaverous man named Mr. Petty, opened the bus's back door and pulled out a wooden box. They retrieved from inside a dozen or more white crosses that the others jimmied into the sweep of school lawn in front of the literature table. Mr. Petty jumped back into the bus and handed down oblong cardboard boxes wrapped in brown paper, which Reverend Sloat's other followers placed one by one in front of the crosses: They were setting up a miniature cemetery with imitation coffins and grave markers.

The woman with the flute stopped to scratch her neck again. The husky man removed an additional sign from the front of the bus and poked it into the lawn in front of the graveyard. Mr. Coker waved at Nicky Groot to come join him, and he and Nicky hammered the sign into the lawn with a large rock. This sign read:

WE SPEAK FOR THOSE WHO CANNOT SCREAM

Mrs. Groot and Annie Strang, Lucy and Mrs. Wroblewski, all gathered in front of the sign, talking and exclaiming over the exhibition. Mahalia stopped handing out lemonade and stood slightly apart, surveying the display proudly, as if she were the cause of it all.

Mr. Petty set a shallow wire cage in front of the sign. Inside was a swirly-haired reddish guinea pig. A poster attached to the top of his cage asked, *Are your children no better than me? Stop medical torturers from using fetal tissues for their heartless research.* I pulled a piece of grass from the lawn and stuck it through the mesh toward the guinea pig.

"Don't do that," the frosted-haired woman with the dog said. "Don't feed Buster grass. The lawn could have herbicide on it." Buster squealed mournfully when I pulled the grass away.

No school bell rang, but the teacher, Mr. Brewer, emerged from Stein High's front doors. He wore the same electric-green necktie he had earlier. He approached Isabel's literature table, peered in one of the oblong boxes that served as caskets, and seemed to find something there that appalled him—he made a face and asked, "Can you believe this? Jesus Christ! Are these supposed to be coffins for dismembered—?"

I left the guinea pig to look in one of the boxes, it held a doll that was missing an arm. I saw that the next box contained a doll too: All of them did. Some contained dolls without heads, and one held a pile of arms and legs.

Mr. Brewer read the writing on the side of the yellow bus. He surveyed the people who had come out of it and were now picking up their signs and assembling into a loose, slowing, whirling oval around the literature table and the graveyard. He watched Reverend Bender flashing his underbitten grin at them; and Isabel smiling her half-smile as she strolled though the graveyard toward them; and Mrs. Esselborne tripping over a grave marker in her eagerness to head off Isabel.

"I don't think Reverend Bender anticipated all this," Mrs. Esselborne said.

Reverend Sloat answered, rubbing his small hands together, "This is our first out-of-town school. Of course, we've had plenty of clinic practice."

Mr. Brewer then turned on his heel and reentered the school building. It must have been between classes, because after he vanished, no students exited the building, except for one girl, who crossed the lawn in our direction. She ran behind the backs of Isabel and Mrs. Esselborne, made a beeline for Mahalia, handed her a note, and ran off giggling. Nicky watched the girl until she disappeared back into the building.

Mahalia glanced at the note and stuffed it into her pocket.

"What is it, Mahalia?" Lucy asked. She tried to grab the note from Mahalia's pocket, and Mahalia turned away; but then she took out the note and showed it to Lucy, laughing uncomfortably.

"Why don't you go?" Lucy asked. "I wished someone would invite me to a high school dance party." She looked sad and wistful. "Someone must be crushed out on you. Nicky Groot is going to be broken up."

"Nicky Groot?" Mahalia asked.

"Yeah," Lucy said. "He's in love with you."

"That's not true," Mahalia told her.

Nicky stood only thirty feet from the rest of us, sipping his Coca-Cola, but Mahalia did not even turn around to look for him.

Mr. Brewer reemerged from the building, followed this time by a blond older man, tall with broad shoulders, wearing a lightweight jacket stitched with a picture of a sword-carrying musketeer and the words STEIN HIGH CAVALIERS. Mr. Brewer gestured at us, moving his hands animatedly, and the two men walked together up the slope toward us.

"Hello Douglas," the man wearing the school jacket told Reverend Bender.

"Hello Jim," Reverend Bender answered. "Reverend Sloat, this is the school principal, Jim Cossack."

Mr. Cossack nodded at Reverend Sloat, and then turned his back to him. The principal asked Reverend Bender, "What seems to be the problem here, Douglas?"

Before Reverend Bender could answer, Reverend Sloat said, "There's no problem."

"No," Mr. Brewer said. "You've just set up a toy holocaust on Stein High's lawn, but other than that, there's no problem."

Mahalia sidled behind Isabel and took her arm.

"Where does all this come from?" Mr. Cossack asked Reverend Bender. The principal moved his hand in a circular motion that took in the table, the graveyard, and the yellow bus. "These don't look like local people. Have you brought in a foreign army?"

"He's brought in the army of the unborn to set up a baby graveyard," Mr. Brewer answered.

Mr. Cossack held up his hand and said, "Just hold on, Martin." Again, he spoke to Reverend Bender: "Douglas, why don't you and I take a little walk and discuss this?"

"We'd be glad to discuss it," Reverend Sloat responded.

"No," Mr. Cossack said. "I'll talk with you, Douglas, but I'm not concerning myself right now with anyone who stepped off that yellow bus."

"I'm from Stein Evangelical," Mrs. Esselborne said.

"So is Miss Flood," Mahalia added. Isabel patted her hand. Mrs. Esselborne frowned.

"Fine," Mr. Cossack told them. "Let's all sit down in the trailer and talk."

Reverend Sloat nodded at Reverend Bender as if assenting to this; Reverend Bender did not seem to notice. He accompanied the principal, with Mr. Brewer and Mrs. Esselborne and Isabel in tow. Mahalia followed Isabel, and when no one shooed my sister away, I ran up beside her. She surprised me by taking my hand. I did not let go. When I turned, I saw that Mr. Petty was only a yard behind me. Mr. Coker and the women's committee watched us expectantly from beside the table.

Reverend Bender mounted the steps into the trailer, and when we all had entered, Mr. Cossack spread his arms as if inviting us to look around. There were a few chairs and shelves and a scratched and battered reading table to the right of the door. To the left were a librarian's desk with a vase of dyed cornflowers on it, beside a cloth bag full of yarn and a half-finished sweater still connected to the knitting needles; more bookshelves; a large glass display case; and on the floor, a dull muddied carpet. Mr. Petty stood inside the trailer's doorway and peered around the library with an indifferent expression. His skin had a bluish cast, and his hands were so thin that they looked as if light could shine though them.

"I'm going to give you the opportunity to back out of this gracefully," Mr. Cossack told Reverend Bender. "And you'd do well to accept. Because, Douglas, people in Stein are not going to take well to having a traveling sideshow on the front lawn of their high school."

"I couldn't agree more," Mrs. Esselborne said.

"I doubt they'd like what your teacher here is teaching their children either, if they knew about it," Reverend Bender said.

Mr. Brewer answered, "What makes you think they don't know about it?"

Mr. Cossack put a hand on Mr. Brewer's shoulder to silence him, and told Reverend Bender, "I want you to look over here at our library's display,

Douglas." We followed the principal to the glass case. Inside it was an allotment of books with the heading BANNED IN THE TWENTIETH CENTURY, AN EXHIBIT BY MR. BREWER'S ENGLISH CLASS. A book of poetry lay open to the Gwendolyn Brooks poem, "the mother." On either side of it were *Huck Finn* and a paperback by Ray Bradbury titled *Fahrenheit 451* and two books I had never heard of called *Native Son*, which I thought must be a religious story about Jesus, and *Johnny Got His Gun*, which I thought must be about a murderer or armed robber. The left side of the case was empty.

While the adults took in the display and ignored me, I stood on my tiptoes to see "the mother." I read:

> Your stilted or lovely loves, your tumults, your marriages,
>   aches, and your deaths,

Mr. Cossack jostled me, forcing me backward as he turned toward Reverend Bender.

"Here's my proposal, Douglas," Mr. Cossack said. "Remove your baby graveyard from the lawn. Put your literature in the left-hand side of the case. You can display your religious tracts in there and your medical articles, but none of the gruesome stuff or the violent stuff. That way, you can have your say. How does that sound? You know people don't want their kids picking over pictures of dismembered corpses."

"We'll consider it," Reverend Bender said.

"Fine," Mr. Cossack told him. "Now clear out your foreign army before the bell rings, or I'll get an injunction."

"No," Isabel said. "This kind of compromise is not acceptable."

Mr. Cossack looked at Isabel as if noticing her for the first time.

Mr. Petty stuck his head farther inside the doorway.

"This is the woman I spoke to you about," Mr. Brewer said. "The one with the petition. The one who believes in 'Institutional Sin.'"

"Ah," said Mr. Cossack.

"I think your proposal is a good one," Mrs. Esselborne told the principal.

Mr. Cossack extended his hand to Mrs. Esselborne and shook it. "Why don't we all meet in my office tomorrow, and we'll discuss your ideas for contributing to our display then?" He turned to Mahalia and asked, "What's a handsome girl like you doing hiding behind a sign?"

Mahalia did not flush, as I was sure she would. Instead, she took on the wrathful, majestic expression that seemed so natural to her. "I'm from Stein Evangelical," she answered.

Mr. Cossack looked down at me and asked, "Are you some kind of mascot?"

"She's one of the unborn," Reverend Bender said. He and Mr. Cossack chuckled.

Isabel placed her hand on my shoulder.

"Well, Douglas," Mr. Cossack said. "I'm sure we'll come to some kind of resolution, if we put our heads together."

"Given a little time," Reverend Bender answered, "I'm sure we can. God didn't make the world in a day." He added, "He might even take an extra eighth day if He had it to do over."

Isabel frowned.

Mr. Cossack answered, "God would never make the world now. It would be too risky. His lawyers would keep Him from doing it."

Reverend Bender laughed, and suddenly we were all following them down the trailer steps. Mr. Petty glided away from the steps and reappeared several yards ahead of us, like an escaped, unattached shadow. Mr. Brewer grinned, and Isabel looked angry. Ahead of us, Mrs. Esselborne walked between Mr. Cossack and Reverend Bender, talking with them.

"I'll see you at five o'clock tomorrow then," Mr. Cossack told her.

When we reached the table, Reverend Bender said something to Reverend Sloat, which made him signal Mr. Petty, so that he and the other people from the bus began picking up the graveyard. Isabel and Mahalia watched, talking to one another with expressions of acute concern. The young man with the yellow beard, who had once belonged to Stein Evangelical, set his Bible on top of the guinea pig Buster's cage. He scratched his beard suddenly, as if an insect had bitten him, and then picked up the cage and carried it into the bus.

"Remind the principal," Reverend Sloat told Reverend Bender with some irritation, "that we are not leaving Stein tonight. You are not pulling back your forces."

"I've already told him," Reverend Bender said. "I have him where I want him." His jaw set in its bulldog grin, Reverend Bender looked down at Reverend Sloat, who smiled back uncertainly with his jagged possum teeth and lifted his small backpack full of photographed fetuses onto his shoulders.

Isabel circled the table in order to speak to Mr. Coker. Mahalia ran over to the women's committee and talked excitedly to them, while Mrs. Wroblewski and Lucy listened, looking hot and sticky and immobile except for their arms, which waved before them languidly as they fanned themselves.

Nicky walked up behind me and asked, "You know that paper that girl handed to your sister?"

"Yeah," I answered.

"What was it for?"

"It was some note inviting her to some stupid dance party."

"She dances?" Nicky asked, slapping his leg and looking at Mahalia, where she huddled in conversation with the other church women.

"I don't know," I said. I couldn't imagine my sister dancing with boys. "She'd probably just stand around all wallflowery, wondering what to do." I snickered, assuming Nicky would too, but instead he just nodded, as if mulling over this information.

"What kind of dance?" Nicky asked. "A church thing?"

"No, something for kids from Stein High."

"Oh," Nicky answered. "A moron dance." He looked toward the high school.

Behind him, Mr. Coker asked Isabel, "What?" in a tone of surprise. He said something angrily, in a low voice, and approached the principal and Mr. Brewer, who were now talking with Reverend Bender and Mrs. Esselborne.

"Mr. Coker," the principal said.

"Isabel has just told me what this school is up to," Mr. Coker told Reverend Bender. "You know if you let them get away with this crazy plan of theirs, Mr. Brewer here is just going to hold our church and beliefs up to ridicule before the children. He's going to have them look at our literature and take it apart and induce them to laugh at it. This is what the teachers here did with my Lucy."

"Mark," Reverend Bender said. "We won't agree to anything you wouldn't approve of. I'll promise you that." Behind Mr. Coker, the last infant graves were being whisked back onto the yellow bus.

Isabel picked up her sign and began circling the table.

Mr. Cossack watched her and asked, "Is that necessary now?"

"Let her be," Reverend Bender answered. "Nothing's been decided yet."

"You bet it hasn't," Mr. Coker said. He turned away, walked over to Nicky, and commanded, "Nicky, you come with me." Mr. Coker leaned over Lucy and whispered something into her ear.

Lucy picked up her sign, but Isabel said, "No, Lucy. Not at this stage of your condition. I and the rest of the women here can handle this." All of the other women, even Mrs. Wroblewski, picked up their cardboard signs in thrilling silence, in honor of Isabel. Mahalia hesitated a moment; she looked worried. But then she lifted a sign and followed them. Her dark red hair escaped from its barrettes and uncoiled across her shoulders as she walked. I took Lucy's sign and marched in a circle with my sister. Mr. Cossack placed his hand on Mr. Brewer's shoulder and guided him toward the school. Mr. Brewer turned around once to watch our circle, shook his head, and followed Mr. Cossack inside.

Mrs. Esselborne escorted Reverend Sloat and Reverend Bender to her car; Mahalia stopped her picketing to watch them. Nicky and Mr. Coker walked toward the yellow bus. I heard Mr. Coker tell Nicky, "They aren't going to get away with this for a living minute." He and Nicky joined Mr. Petty, and the men talked together, their heads bent and their backs to us. The yellow bus departed, leaving Nicky and Mr. Coker and Mr. Petty behind.

The women's group continued to picket until the bell rang. However, no students emerged. Teenagers' yells and shouts rang in the undefined distance, and a football shot over a grassy field from behind the school, thrown by an unseen hand.

"They're not letting the children out in front," Mr. Coker said grimly. "They're preventing us from reaching them."

Nevertheless, Isabel and the rest of us continued to walk with our signs until the last shouts had dwindled to silence, and all but the last cars in the parking lot had driven from the school. Only then did Mrs. Groot say, "Izzy, I'm so sorry. We better collect our things in time for dinner." All of the women helped to pack up the literature table and carried their signs into the church Jeep. Annie Strang patted Isabel on the back and said, "They're scared of us, Izzy. We've got them running." Mrs. Wroblewski told Lucy, "You can be proud. You can tell your baby all about this when he's born." Lucy, Mrs. Groot, and Mrs. Wroblewski climbed into Annie Strang's car, and drove away. I did not see Mr. Coker or Nicky or Mr. Petty.

Mahalia and I crawled into the Jeep beside Isabel. Despite what Mrs. Groot had said, it was not near dinnertime: The late summer sun still shone mustard yellow far above the distant walls of the correctional facility. At the end of the street ahead of us, Reverend Sloat's bus turned a corner onto Dannemora Road. Mrs. Esselborne's pale blue car passed him, sailed through an amber light, and left us behind in the Jeep, motionless before a red light.

F. X. approached our intersection from a block away. He wore dark glasses and walked with a cane beside my pediatrician, Dr. Epstein, who was also wearing dark glasses and walking with a cane. Between them was a woman with a Seeing Eye dog. F. X.'s face looked joyful. He gesticulated wildly with his free hand, talking animatedly to Dr. Epstein. Dr. Epstein said something back, and the woman stopped and doubled over laughing. Mahalia spied them, but she did not wave to F. X., as I did, before Isabel stepped on the gas pedal and drove us onward.

———

After we left the school grounds, Isabel turned the Jeep onto Dannemora Road and drove directly to the church. She looked troubled and disappointed, and at one point she told Mahalia, "We need to talk to Reverend Sloat right away. You saw that he was as concerned as we are." Looking back on it now, I understand that during that ride to Stein Evangelical, Isabel puzzled out what had happened at the school and realized that her mission had to be redirected from the world at large to her own church. F. X. would summarize for me ten years later, "It's always risky for worldly men, the politicians, to delegate the causes they claim to uphold to people who really believe in them. True belief is an unruly, dangerous thing; and Isabel Flood believed absolutely in everything that she did. She would have defended her vision of the world, even if it brought the whole Republican Party to its knees and changed the face of Christianity itself." I think it was true that Isabel probably never saw herself as part of a political force joining hands with a moral majority across the country. She had a private contract with her God, and would have continued on, whether the entire universe had embraced her cause, or suddenly dropped with a hush into black oblivion.

Quite different thoughts from Isabel's must have coursed through my sister's head as we sped along the road toward Stein Evangelical. Once the security of circling with the other women wore off, Mahalia must have pondered why Reverend Bender had left us when he did, or why the principal, Mr. Cossack, had taken Mrs. Esselborne more seriously than he had Isabel. Or perhaps Mahalia was merely thinking about her invitation to a party. Whatever preoccupied her, when Isabel asked Mahalia if something was wrong, Mahalia answered, a little sadly, "Of course not."

Isabel parked the Jeep beside Stein Evangelical. The yellow bus lay at the far end of the vacant lot behind the church, and Reverend Sloat's constituents rested with their blond or brown hair or pink faces pressing against the windows: They made me think of a litter of different-colored baby mammals in a hollow. I wondered if they slept in the bus at night.

Mahalia told Isabel, "I want to stay here. I don't want to go inside."

Isabel looked surprised. She said, "I can't leave Penny behind when I go into the church. Are you sure you won't come too?"

Mahalia shook her head and turned toward the window. Her hair glowed like a ghostly fire in the glass's reflection. She must have sensed that whatever Isabel would meet in the church, it would be disastrous, or in the very least, something to which my sister did not want to bear witness.

"All right, Mahalia," Isabel said. I dismounted from the Jeep and followed her to Stein Evangelical's front steps. However, when Isabel tried the door, she discovered that it was locked.

She backtracked down the stairs and led me around the building—or, more accurately, I followed her—she seemed half-conscious that I was there. The annex's back door was open, and the low hum and grumble of men's laughter came from inside. I followed Isabel past the organ, into the hallway that joined the annex to the church. Even though Isabel was a member of the congregation, I felt there was something secretive about our entrance.

The men's voices rang loudly inside Reverend Bender's office. Isabel paused at their door, as if trying to still the irregular beating of her heart and to summon up the perfect words to guide her church's leaders to her side.

"It's quite a concession," we heard Reverend Sloat say.

"It's a foothold," Reverend Bender told him.

"Maybe—it is if you run your constituents for the school board as early as this November," Reverend Sloat answered. "Take my advice and don't wait—grab hold right away. No one puts money into school board campaigns here—we checked it out. None of the positions are paid. If we spend one thousand or twelve hundred tops on a radio campaign and fliers in November, we'll have a landslide. It will inspire our people in towns all the way to Buffalo."

"Our head of the women's committee, Mrs. Esselborne, can run for the school board," Reverend Bender said.

"Two slots are opening up. Who else do you have?" Reverend Sloat asked. "What about the woman who was there today in the trailer with her two girls?"

"Isabel Flood?" Reverend Bender asked.

"The one without any tits?" Reverend Sloat said.

"Yes, that's her," Reverend Bender answered. Both men laughed. "Mrs. Esselborne's a better choice. We'll get a man for the other slot."

Isabel clenched my hand and opened her mouth as if to speak, and then closed it. Her hand worked like a mouth in my own then, opening and closing until she pulled me abruptly away from the office door and back down the hallway to the hard ground outside. I did not understand what the men had been discussing, but I knew enough to realize that they had insulted Isabel in a low way, and that the insult had shocked her.

———

On Thursday, a heat wave descended on Stein that would last through the end of August. My mother pronounced it "New Orleans weather" and reminisced about how she had never found the sun too hot as a girl, even in the middle of summer. Air conditioners rattled on up and down our street until the wires overloaded and our block suffered a temporary blackout. The trees stood in stark stillness behind our house, as if even the wind was too prostrate to move, and under their shady limbs the insistent complaining of mosquitoes multiplied to a frenzied chorus, and tree frogs screamed in the branches.

Despite the heat, Isabel and her women's committee group picketed again the day after Stein High School's principal first bargained with Reverend Bender. The women returned on both Thursday and Friday. I learned this because I overheard David telling my mother on Saturday, as he replaced the upper hinge of my bedroom door, "They were saying at the parole office yesterday that the school is threatening to get a restraining order against Reverend Bender's people and have them arrested if they keep it up when the new school year starts. The whole thing has gotten out of hand. We should go over to Isabel's and talk to Mahalia again, and tell her in no uncertain terms—"

This time my mother agreed with him. "Maybe Miss Flood needs to be told too," my mother said from the bottom of the stairs. "She may not understand the law very well." My mother was wearing her bathing suit and packing a cooler with barbecued spare ribs for a family outing at Stein Lake.

David admired her from the top of the stairs, and then tested the door, opening and closing it on its new hinge. He answered, "Marguerite, I doubt Miss Flood is the kind who will concern herself too much with legal consequences."

"The unborn don't have any laws," F. X. concurred. "They live in a lawless country that has no jails but the womb, no police but the preternatural stirrings of their incipient consciences, no duty but the call to escape and breath the oxygen of the outer world." At the moment he said this, F. X. was dressing up as a fetus in front of the hall mirror. I had mentioned to him the painting called The Seed in Isabel's house and told him that the unborn baby it portrayed looked like a bank robber with a stocking mask. F. X. had the idea that if he stretched a stocking over his face and neck, and padded the toes with socks to enlarge his head so that it looked like an embryo's, it would all make a good future Mardi-Gras costume. I stood with him before the mirror with a stick of my mother's black eyeliner. I drew Frankenstein stitches across my forehead, and two fangs under my bottom lip, and circles around my eye sockets for skull holes.

"A telephone cord would make a perfect umbilical cord," F. X. said.

"F. X., take that thing off," my mother told him. "You look like a tadpole."

He pulled off the stocking and said, "I don't see how women can stand these things—they're hotter than hell."

"We don't wear them on our heads," my mother answered. "And on days like this, we try not to wear them at all."

All the windows in the house were open, and my mother began making David his second pitcher of iced tea that morning. My mother had been drinking root beer; she claimed too much iced tea made her too jittery, now that she could not "offset its effects with gin and vermouth." I wandered into the kitchen and took some ice from the freezer.

My mother kissed me and said, "My favorite Daughtermonster."

I tucked in my shirt, dropped the ice down my shirtfront, and lay on the coffee table under the ceiling fan.

The bedroom door slammed. I looked up the stairs: David slammed it a few more times. "God knows how often this poor door is going to be pushed to the breaking point in the future," he said. "These hinges better be prepared." He came downstairs, propped open the kitchen door to let in more of a breeze, and walked up the street to Isabel's house to speak to her and Mahalia.

My mother opened a linen closet to gather towels. "David is so persistent," she said. "I hope he isn't too badly disappointed." She rummaged in the bottom of the linen closet and said, "F. X., David has an oversized bathing suit that doesn't fit him. You can wear that one."

"Is that how you think of me?" F. X. asked. "As oversized?"

"Definitely," my mother answered absently.

F. X. remained in his pants and white shirt, while I walked upstairs to change into my suit. As I put it on, I startled myself in Mahalia's dresser mirror: I had forgotten I was wearing monster makeup. I leaned closer and wiggled my eyebrows so that my eyes danced in their sockets. When I came back downstairs, F. X. was pumping up our household's two rafts and saying, "Marguerite, you know people did not believe in letting blind children negotiate water when I was young. I swim about as well as a rhinoceros."

"Just go in far enough to cool off," my mother said, but F. X. still did not change out of his clothes.

Ten minutes later, David returned, looking hot and annoyed, and announced, "I don't think I had much effect."

"What did Mahalia say?" my mother asked.

"She said, 'It's a fine time for you and Mama to be telling me how to act.' "

My mother set down her glass of root beer. "Of course she would say that."

"Mahalia told me that the church doesn't want to do the pickets anymore, but that Miss Flood is carrying on regardless, and that some of women's committee is standing by her."

"Maybe Isabel Flood is forming her own sect," F. X. said. "The Floodites. No—the Church of Life without Birth. Or the Ninth Month Advetists, or Cult of the Wombed Martyrs, or First United Embryos of God."

"I found this package for Mahalia on Isabel's doorstep," David told my mother, handing her a shoe box. "Mahalia didn't want Isabel to see it, so I brought it here." My mother opened the box: It contained a bottle of red nail polish, a package of C batteries, and a hair curler.

"This was on their doorstep?" my mother asked.

"I think it's from this boy," I said. "This boy who's crushed out on Mahalia."

"The one called Ben, who plays the piano outside in the dark?" my mother asked.

"No, somebody else," I said.

"Is that so?" my mother mused.

"If Mahalia doesn't come home on her own steam by Friday," David told my mother, "I think you should force her to leave Isabel's." He walked up the stairs, looking irritated, and changed into his bathing suit.

When he returned downstairs, my mother told him, "I'll speak to Mahalia when she drops Penny off on Tuesday. I'll tell her she has to come back to live with us if those church women start breaking the law. If she doesn't listen, I'll command Miss Flood to send my daughter back to her rightful home."

"All right," David answered, sounding genuinely relieved. He stuck suntan lotion, sunglasses, and a paperback copy of Lord of the Flies into my mother's bag, and then carried the bag, the cooler, and a thermos of iced tea to his truck. F. X. finished pumping up our rafts, threw them into the back of the pickup, and then carried me over his head and deposited me in the truck bed.

As we drove toward the lake, F. X. and I lay in the truck bed on the rafts and watched the cloudless sky unwind over us like a bolt of blue cloth, or a blue river. Lying down like that, without landmarks to guide us, we tried to determine by the jolts and turns of the truck and the smells in the air and the noise of people and crows and barking dogs, where we were and how close we were to arriving at the lake. "Pretend," F. X. said, "that you're up and the sky is down, and that you're flying." When I did, I lost all my bearings, my stomach lurched as if I were falling, and I reached for his hand. When the pickup stopped, we were both surprised. Neither of us had calculated correctly—we had misjudged where we were by a mile.

F. X. complained that the lake was like ice and swore he would not go in, saying, "I've already walked *on* it, so why go *in* it?" He strode off down the beach in his pants and white shirt: He looked the way I imagined all reporters did.

I set my raft in the water and paddled out thirty yards, past the adult swimmers. When I turned to look at the shore, all of Stein was there, spread out like a painting. In the center were some people with folding lounge chairs and a cooler with real lobsters in it. A lady seated among them raised a blue champagne glass high in the air, as if she were queen of us all. On all sides of her, bathers seemed to spread out in some obvious but undefineable order of diminished importance. Immediately to her right were a couple with a fancy wrinkle-faced dog they called to their sides with shrieks of "Bijon! Bijon!" On the lady's left was Mr. Biedenharn, the owner of the women's clothing store, wearing a bathing suit with athletic stripes, and reading a magazine, his eyes shrouded behind sunglasses. Beyond Mr. Biedenharn were several groups of small families with small children eating sandy sandwiches. One family had brought a whole turkey. Beside them, the Presbyterian church was having a picnic—a serious-looking woman was waving a piece of corn on the cob like a baton at the minister. Opposite them, near the couple with the dog, were more clusters of small families; Mr. Brewer, his wife, Shipra, and their two children, sat together in the middle of them, on a bright orange cloth. Beyond the Brewers was a large sand castle with a moat; several black families clustered together beyond it. Apart from them sat large families with seven or more children, many of whom I recognized from All Saints. My mother and David lay among them. Behind my mother, a few lone adults had straggled down the beach and laid blue and red and green towels a polite distance from one another. High upon the sand, past the high tide watermark, on the periphery of the least crowded area, a small group of people from the blind school lounged on a green tarp, wearing dark glasses and spreading on suntan lotion. Nearby, four prison guards drinking beer gathered under an oak tree, still wearing their uniforms.

Beyond them was Mr. Canon, standing on his own towel, swaying slightly on his feet. Directly below him, past the margin of the area where the sand was still smooth and comfortable, sat the congregation of Stein Evangelical Church. Mrs. Esselborne and Reverend Bender were spreading a gigantic pink blanket on the ground, and behind them members of the congregation, clad in bathing suits, laid down a patchwork of blankets and towels. Reverend Sloat's followers had formed a chain and were passing watermelons from the yellow bus to a blanket where Mr. Petty, looking even more cadaverous and pale than usual in a baby-blue swimsuit, sliced the watermelons with an enormous knife. The bearded blond man from the yellow bus lay down on bare sand, using his Bible as a headrest and scratching his head vigorously. Reverend Sloat sat on a towel beside him, also scratching, as if in sympathy with him. Mr. Coker carried an umbrella and two ordinary chairs to the edge of the lake, where Barb Wroblewski and Lucy plunked down in maternity shorts and sleeveless shirts. After this, Mr. Coker perched by himself on a log, beyond the margins of the group.

Isabel and Mahalia walked down the beach ten yards beyond him, twenty yards from the main body of Stein Evangelical's congregants, and Isabel lowered herself onto a green towel. She did not wear a bathing suit. She had on a long-sleeved tan dress that touched her ankles, and a straw hat. Mahalia had covered her suit with a terry-cloth robe, which she tugged self-consciously over her knees after she sat down, turned slightly away from Isabel, looking uncomfortable.

I watched F. X. approach them and speak briefly to them. Even from my raft, I could see Isabel withdraw from him: She slid backward on her towel and did not speak. F. X. wandered on, pausing to talk first to Mr. Coker and then to various members of the watermelon chain from the yellow bus, one of whom gave F. X. a watermelon. He sauntered on to Mr. Petty, who began cutting it for him, and the two engaged in a lengthy conversation.

I paddled to shore. Leaving my raft on the beach, I walked toward F. X., hoping for some watermelon. As I neared him, F. X. was saying to Mr. Petty, "Justifiable homicide? Really? Why not change your slogan from 'We speak for those who cannot scream,' to 'We kill for those who cannot murder'?"

Mr. Petty snickered. He bore that odd expression of someone who has decided to disavow what he has just said, in light of his listener's reaction. When he looked at me, he started. "What are you?" he asked. "A ghoul or a skeleton or what?" I remembered that I was wearing monster make up. Mr. Petty offered me a sliver of watermelon with his bony hand.

F. X. told Mr. Petty, "So you'll all be shuffling off to Buffalo tomorrow in your yellow bus?"

Mr. Petty answered, "The bus will be leaving."

"So you won't be attending those pickets at the high school?" F. X. asked.

"Naw," Mr. Petty answered. "That's not my style."

F. X. seemed relieved to hear this. "Well, of course not," he said.

Mr. Petty handed the whole watermelon to F. X., which Mr. Petty had cut in an ingenious way, keeping the rind intact while dividing the flesh into rindless slices.

My uncle handed me four more slices and then distributed watermelon to my mother and David, to Mr. Canon and to the group of men from the blind school who were sitting up the beach. Afterward, F. X. pulled a small reporter's notebook from his shirt pocket and lay down on a blanket. I looked over his shoulder as he wrote two letters:

Dear Miss Flood,

We wish to alert you that a maverick member of our organization, Fetus Elegante, has formed a radical society, Knights of the Unborn. We have no affiliation with this society, and find its philosophies repugnant to our mission.

> *Sincerely yours,*
> *The Fetal Committee*

Dear Isabel,

I fear that the next life will offer nothing but a murkiness of right and wrong. The resonant voices of the outer world sing to me like a warning chorus, like the lullaby of sirens, and the unspoken thoughts of a million unnamed souls move together with my heart like schooling fish or black holes rubbing elbows in the void.

Birth is not the answer. The end is the beginning and the beginning is the end. There is no liberation but conception, and to that moment our forces march in reverse. We shall change the course of time.

> *Fondly,*
> *Fetus Elegante*

When he finished, F. X. stuck the letters in his shirt pocket, rolled on his back, and read a story by James Thurber on dogs. Every now and then F. X. looked up at me and commented on what he was reading as I ate my watermelon. "Do you know that bloodhounds rarely bite or attack people?" he asked me. "It's the people who unleash them that are dangerous. Bloodhounds are apparently affectionate and just like running along the ground, reveling in the smells. When they find what they're looking for, they bark with joy instead of attacking. It's their long involuntary association with questionable human beings—slaveholders and southern sheriffs and so forth—that gave them their bad name."

David and my mother swam out to the island together and stayed there until people began to collect their things and depart from the beach. The lady with the blue champagne glass packed up her towel and umbrella, and afterward the families around her gradually drifted away. The blind men left together, and the entire Presbyterian church, and finally Reverend Bender and Reverend Sloat, followed by Stein Evangelical's congregation and the yellow bus. In the end, as my mother and David began swimming back toward us in the darkening water, only Mr. Canon was left on the beach. He appeared to have passed out on the sand, wrapped in his towel.

My mother, David, F. X., and I sat on the beach together eating supper. A slight wind worried the air, and the moon disentangled itself from the trees on the far bank and fell into the water. It lay there, looking like a plate I could have eaten anything off of. While F. X. and David talked, my mother turned on a flashlight and passed around what was left of her barbecued spare ribs. Beside her, F. X.'s and David's mustaches looked like moths fluttering around a lamp.

F. X. told my mother, "These spare ribs make me think of our own mama. They give me pork déjà vu."

"My mother used to roast whole pigs in the backyard," my mother told David. "She'd set them in a pit and baste them by dipping long stalks of parsley in hot sauce and vinegar and stroking them over the pig off and on for hours."

"Do you remember that man, Mr. Leblanc, who lived on the edge of Franklin?" F. X. asked my mother. "The one who kept all the pigs?"

My mother laughed and said, "That poor old stinker."

"I could always tell where I was in our neighborhood by how forcefully his pigs' aroma wafted by. I used to orient myself by that smell."

"When I was still little, I once knocked two poles off his fence and let his pigs out," my mother told David. "They ran back and forth all night, snuffling up peoples turnips and camellias and sending all the neighborhood dogs into a barking frenzy."

David laughed and said, "So you were a hellion too."

"The pigs were impossible to round up," F. X. said. "Pigs aren't herd animals. When Mr. Leblanc ran after one, the others would scatter in every direction. You'd be walking down the middle of town and hear a pig squeal in the doorway of the dressmaker's, or nosing around at the entrance to the Catholic church, or trotting after some debutante across the lawn of one of those godawful mansions with Spanish oak spiderwebbing down from the trees. It was days and days before Mr. Leblanc got them all."

"I once supervised a parolee, Mr. Tolstoy," David said, "who stole a pig from his neighbor's yard and then tried to hide it in his bathtub. The owner heard the pig squealing and burst into Mr. Tolstoy's house, and Mr. Tolstoy thought he was a burglar and shot him. All over a pig. The pig squealed after the gun went off and, according to a neighbor, the pig sounded like a screaming woman, so the neighbor ran into the house, and there was Mr. Tolstoy waving his gun around and the pig's owner with a bullet hole in his arm, and the pig standing on the couch like a lady caught in the middle of a fight between two jealous men."

"David," my mother said. "You have a strange bunch of characters running around in your head."

I listened to the voices of David and my mother and F. X., and imagined speaking as each one of them, and then as myself as I might sound when I was older. The voices swirled inside me and joined in undifferentiated anarchy. Stars burst into being above me, and F. X. said, "Now, Penny, imagine you're flying over a black ocean, and the stars are lights of ships bobbing on the water." I clung to his hand, held my breath, and looked down.

Chapter Fourteen

Stilted and Lovely Loves

On Tuesday afternoon as I waited to be picked up at All Saints, I watched my sister approach me, by herself, on foot. She wore a long rust-colored dress, and a matching scarf tied back her hair, billowing like a battle flag as she walked. Her mustard-seed pendant glinted when the sun emerged suddenly from a cloud, so that from where I stood, she seemed to be wearing a grain of light as her sole ornament. Her feet move gracefully in her slipper-shoes, and I noted that she no longer looked even a little girlish: She was a woman, something so separate from me that I felt pierced by my sense that she could somehow never be close to me again.

When my sister entered All Saints' gates, Sister Geraldine materialized from within the school building, saying, "Don't rush off, Mahalia. I'd like to say hello to you." Sister Geraldine wore her wimple, as if she considered Mahalia a member of the world outside the school, who needed to be addressed over a serious and practical matter. "I wanted to ask if you were going to take Penny over to that picket at the public school today."

"Yes, why?" Mahalia answered. She fingered her mustard-seed pendant.

"A woman named Mrs. Esselborne from your church called me to say that she didn't think you girls should be participating in those pickets."

"Mrs. Esselborne called you?" Mahalia asked.

"Do you have any idea why she would tell me that?" Sister Geraldine responded.

"No," Mahalia said.

"Well, she just told me that she didn't want you in a situation where you'd feel later that you'd made fools of yourselves."

"Fools of ourselves?" Mahalia asked.

"Not that we don't all make fools of ourselves every day of our lives," Sister Geraldine added hastily. "Could Mrs. Esselborne have called in part because Penny's too young for what's going on over at the school?"

"Isabel would never do anything that wasn't appropriate for Penny," Mahalia answered.

"No, probably not ordinarily," Sister Geraldine said, "but sometimes when people get a little fanatical, it affects their sense of what's appropriate."

"Isabel isn't fanatical," Mahalia answered.

"Use your good judgment and be a little careful, Mahalia," Sister Geraldine concluded. She returned inside to the office.

As Mahalia led me up the road toward the high school, I asked her, "What does 'fanatical' mean?"

"Oh, who cares, Penny!" Mahalia answered.

When we arrived at the high school, the sky was gray and the air humid and oppressive. Only Mrs. Groot was there, out of Isabel's group of women. As Mrs. Groot stepped from her parked car, Isabel was already setting up the literature table. Mrs. Groot approached her and said, "Izzy? Annie said to tell you she couldn't find a sitter, and Barb said she's too close to her time and that she took Lucy home with her from the church. I almost didn't make it myself, Izzy—the special school lets out early today and I have to pick up Nicky in twenty minutes. I hope you don't feel that I've failed you, Izzy."

Isabel answered sympathetically, "I think it would be a good idea for you to go get Nicky."

Mrs. Groot thanked her distractedly, hurried back to her car, and drove away.

Isabel wore her helmet-hat and her button that said ABORTIONS WILL NOT LET YOU FORGET. Mahalia had not put on hers. Nor did she pick up a sign—she busied herself restraightening the pamphlets and books on the table while Isabel walked by herself in a circle.

In a little while, it began to drizzle. The bell rang, and students poured out of the school. By this time, they must have been jaded by the exhibition of photographs on the literature table; they marched by us without stopping, while Mahalia watched them surreptitiously. I reached for *Life or Death*, but before I could open it, Mahalia began draping the books with a plastic cover that did not quite reach the edges of the table.

"Help me, Penny," she said. "It's getting rainier. Everything's going to be ruined." Her cheeks were pink, and she looked uncomfortable. The rain was not really falling wholeheartedly yet; a light mist dusted the table. As Isabel continued around the rim of her circular path, Mahalia told her, "Maybe we should pack these up." But Isabel did not hear her; she was watching the school doors, from which the principal, Mr. Cossack, now emerged, looking hot and uncomfortable in a suit and tie. Reverend Bender was with him. It was the first time I had seen him wear a black shirt and minister's collar. His glittery pin was gone, and he held a black jacket draped over his arm.

When Mr. Cossack spotted us at our table, he said loudly to Reverend Bender, "What is this? You told me you were going to call these people off."

Reverend Bender walked up the slope toward us. He stopped in front of Isabel and said, "Miss Flood, we're dotting our *i*'s and crossing our *t*'s with the school at this very moment. The church is asking people not to picket just now, because it looks like bad faith."

Isabel ignored him—or, more accurately, she sidestepped him. She took one step to the right and continued circling.

"Isabel," Reverend Bender whispered. "This isn't working." His voice did not accommodate itself well to a whisper. He sounded as if he were growling. He had to turn in place as he followed the path of Isabel's circle—he made me think of a dog worrying the end of a rag held on its other end by a child.

"Izzy," Reverend Bender said. As she again turned toward me, I saw Isabel frown at this use of her name. "The church phone has been ringing off the hook all day. People are more upset by their kids seeing the pictures"—he gestured to the literature table—"than by that silly poem."

Isabel continued to walk, and finally, exasperated, Reverend Bender stood directly in her path and grabbed the edge of her sign so that she stopped. We all watched Isabel: Mahalia and Mr. Cossack and Reverend Bender and I. Isabel stood where she was with implacable stillness, looking straight ahead, and although Reverend Bender continued to talk, she acted as if she did not hear him. Isabel's left hand was in her pocket, and I heard the muffled jingling of one of her metal puzzles. Mahalia looked at Isabel pleadingly, but Isabel did not see her: Red spread from Mahalia's collarbones and diffused upward like strong tea into her face and neck.

"Miss Flood," Reverend Bender said. "Let's send a message to the community that we're reasonable people, but that we mean business. Look here—" He lifted his jacket and pulled from its inner pocket a thin white book with black lettering on it that said, *The Right to Live; the Right to Die, by C. Everett Koop.* "We'll put this in the library case, and several more on the shelves, where students can read them."

Isabel glanced at the book without taking it. She said, "I'm familiar with this literature, Reverend Bender. The children won't read it—it's dull. But every child in the school will be bending over that poem. They will bend over the poem and titter. They will learn that the murder of millions of children is something to laugh at."

"Isabel," Mahalia said. "It's raining." I felt only the finest drizzle.

"That's it," Mr. Cossack announced, exasperated. "I'm calling the police."

"Don't do that, Jim," Reverend Bender said. "This woman is not a criminal. She's a valued proselytizer for our church."

"Let go of my sign," Isabel told Reverend Bender. "I am aware that you are doing what you think best. I also see that you are trying to make me look foolish. Nevertheless, I know why I am here, and I believe you are misguided."

Mr. Cossack told Reverend Bender, "I didn't want to embarrass your church by calling the police, but apparently my teacher, Mr. Brewer, was right when he said that you don't have any control over these people. There's no point in negotiating with you, if your lunatic fringe just goes on doing what it's been doing." At the principal's pronouncement of the words *lunatic fringe*, Mahalia's face colored to an impossibly dark shade of red, and she looked away.

Reverend Bender held firmly to the sign, and when Isabel saw he had no intention of letting go of it, she stepped back, leaving it in his hand so that it looked as if he had been carrying it all along. Again she sidestepped him, and continued forward in her orbit, singing in her high voice:

"Take my love, my Lord, I pour
At thy feet its treasure store."

My sister raised her hands to her ears and said, "Stop it, Isabel! Stop it!" I don't think Isabel heard her; she kept singing. Mahalia walked quickly away from us all, up the school's driveway toward the road.

"Isabel," Reverend Bender said. "Come back to the church with me, and I'll explain everything to you."

Isabel continued to sing. When she turned in her orbit so that her back was to me, she must have seen Mahalia. My sister had stopped and stood hunched over at the end of the driveway, facing us and hugging herself.

Mr. Cossack told Reverend Bender, "Douglas, it was different before you brought Reverend Sloat from the outer limits. This whole thing has gotten out of hand." The principal walked back toward the school. Reverend

Bender followed him, still carrying the sign, and I trailed after them both. Isabel's voice rose as the men retreated. Reverend Bender placed a hand on Mr. Cossack's shoulder.

"Let it go, let it go, Jim," Reverend Bender said. "Do you really want a confrontation with a martyr? Just let her be until she gets tired of it. Everyone will save face."

Mr. Cossack stopped briefly and said, "She doesn't look like the tiring type, Douglas. I've already decided that I'm not letting a crazy woman parade in front of the school every day this fall when the children get out."

"Why not?" Reverend Bender asked jokingly. "It won't hurt them to see one crazy woman now. They'll see plenty when they're older."

"Because it's not safe," Mr. Cossack answered.

"She's out on a limb, and she knows it," Reverend Bender told him. He peered down at me and asked, "Where did you come from?"

The last thing Mr. Cossack said before the men entered the building was, "This is *my* school, Douglas."

I walked back up the slope to Isabel. A few drops of rain splashed the plastic cover on the table, but she did not seem to notice. "Isabel," I said, "the rain."

Once the men had entered the building, Isabel stopped singing. She completed the last arc of a final circle, however, as if fulfilling a promise she had made to herself. The rain began to fall more heavily. Beyond Isabel, Mahalia still stood watching. She was farther up the drive, on the very end where it touched the road. She pulled her scarf forward to shelter her hair.

"Mahalia!" I called, but she turned away and vanished behind a row of low trees.

Now the rain fell steadily, and Isabel said, "Help me with the booklets, Penny." She picked up the tarp and packed the literature in a white cardboard box. As I helped her fold up the table, her mouth set in a grim line. I saw then that Isabel did not feel victorious; she was miserable. She glanced briefly at the road, but Mahalia was already lost to her.

———

Isabel stopped at the Esso station on the way home and stood in the rain next to my window of the church Jeep while she telephoned Mr. Coker. "I will need a ride home," she told him. Thereafter, we drove to Stein Evangelical, where Isabel left the Jeep at the edge of the driveway, as far from the church as possible. Reverend Sloat's yellow bus was gone. However, as we approached, I saw Mr. Petty slip into the back door of the church annex; he had remained behind.

Isabel put the Jeep's ignition keys in the glove compartment, and we waited inside the vehicle while rain pattered through the twilight air onto the windshield. When Mr. Coker appeared at the end of the road in his truck, he didn't ask Isabel any questions or talk to her while he drove me home, except once when he said, "I'm sorry and furious about this, Isabel. Try not to take things too hard. I know what these school people are like. They forced me to give up my daughter to them, and then they sent her back to me like she was a damaged package of goods."

Isabel rode quietly until Mr. Coker's truck stopped in front of our house.

She told me simply, "Good-bye, Penny." She allowed Mr. Coker to take her up the block to her home. I realized that Isabel no longer had a means of transportation.

When I entered the living room, my mother was pouring herself a root beer in the kitchen, and Mahalia was sitting on the couch next to David. My sister fumbled in her pocket for a Kleenex and wiped her eyes.

"How could she?" Mahalia asked. "How could she embarrass me like that?"

David looked at her sympathetically, without answering.

"Mahalia," my mother said. "Can you tell us what happened?"

Mahalia did not respond. She covered her eyes with her fingers.

"Marguerite—" David interjected. My mother pushed me toward the stairs, saying, "Penny, come on up with me. Don't linger in the living room."

"I don't have to go to Stein Evangelical anymore," Mahalia was telling David. "The church's summer school ended on Friday, and I don't have any reason to go back there with Isabel now—is there something wrong with her? Why does she act so different from everyone else?"

That night, Mahalia stayed at our house. She did not even return to Isabel's to collect her things.

Isabel came to our door the following day with Mahalia's suitcase. F. X. and I were in the backyard, transplanting petunias into the tractor tire, while he explained to me, "The color of petunias is structural—microscopic forms and patterns in the petals reflect special frequencies of color instead of relying on pigment. Theoretically, that means you should be able to feel the color in them." I saw Isabel pass our side yard on the sidewalk, and I entered the house to open the door. I waited for a moment before answering Isabel's ringing, but Mahalia did not come downstairs in response to the bell; she must have looked out the upstairs window and seen Isabel standing on our front steps. I heard our bedroom door shut.

"Is Mahalia in?" Isabel asked. "May I speak to her?" Isabel looked pale. There were small wrinkles under her eyes as if she had not slept, and she did not carry any of her pamphlets.

"I won't be able to get her to come to the door," I said.

A flicker of anger crossed Isabel's face, but it was replaced almost immediately with something else—she looked heartbroken. She set down Mahalia's suitcase on our porch and walked back toward her house.

After Isabel left, Mahalia came outside and busied herself in her fern beds, digging at stray plants with a trowel, and hollowing out a new bed. I caught her watching us once. She lifted her head and brushed her hair from her face, leaving a smear of dirt over her mouth: She looked as if she had been kissing the ground. When she saw me watching her, she turned away.

Isabel returned again the next day, after I got home from school. She rang the bell, and I answered it before F. X. could—I did not want her to have to face my uncle right then. He was in the backyard again, experimenting with photographing petunia petals through different glass filters.

"Is Mahalia in?" Isabel asked. "Will you tell her that I just wish to speak with her briefly?" She waited on the porch while I ran upstairs.

"Isabel's at the door," I told Mahalia.

My sister was lying on her bed, pretending to read *Ferns of North America*. She made a sound of exasperation and said, "There is no limit to human possibility."

I ran back downstairs and told Isabel, "She won't come out."

"Thank you, Penny," Isabel said, picking up my hand briefly—one of the few times I remember her touching me for any reason other than to restrain me. She turned and left, and did not ring our doorbell again that week.

Over the weekend, I saw Isabel once in town, walking out of the grocery store. She seemed strange and unrelated to us, in her awkward long dress and her old helmet-hat. She traveled on foot toward the opposite end of Main Street. She moved deliberately, with her head down as if she were thinking, and her mouth moved once, as if she were urging herself forward. She removed some pamphlets from her brocade bag, pressed them against her chest, and then straightened her bag at her side, and continued on.

Sunday after supper, my mother took F. X. hiking. F. X. tried to induce Mahalia to go with them, perhaps to assure her that he harbored no ill feelings against her for her conduct toward him that summer—but Mahalia demurred; she claimed she wanted to rearrange her terrarium. She chose to act as if no conflict had ever existed between her and F. X., although she seemed generally more willing to speak to David than to either F. X. or my mother. David's integration into our family may have been inadvertently aided by the fact that he was the person Mahalia had offended least that summer. She was disinclined in any case, to seek out any of us enthusiastically: Although she had returned, she still did not accept us fully.

While my mother and F. X. were hiking, Mahalia read David's copy of *Lord of the Flies* in our room, and David played field hockey with me up and down the street, with a rotten orange. When the orange finally burst into a dozen pieces, he told me, "Penny, we've got to cut your hair short and enroll you in the Boy's Hockey League."

Behind him, a large woman appeared around the corner two blocks away. She moved slowly and painfully, as though the pavement were burning her feet through her shoes. As she reached our block, she stopped to lean once against a mailbox, resting her forehead on it as if crossing the street had exhausted her. She waited a full minute before she continued on, leaning slightly backward as if she were allowing her weight alone, and not her leg muscles, to propel her forward. She wore a blue dress and white tennis shoes, and her reddish hair was lighter at the roots than at the tips, and her stomach was enormous—it made me think of a medicine ball.

She waved to me, and even then it took me a moment to recognize her— it was Lucy Coker. She reached the edge of our yard and halted again beside David's truck. David approached her solicitously, asking, "Are you okay?"

"I feel like I'm going to pop," Lucy answered. "I walked"—she stopped in midsentence as if catching her breath—"all the way here from my dad's farm. I just wanted to see Mahalia. I'm Lucy. Mahalia's never told you about me?"

David led Lucy inside and offered her an iced tea.

"Isabel says no tea when you're pregnant," Lucy told him, accepting the tea, "but she has no idea what this heat is like in the last trimester. It's like you added ten degrees to a fever."

David called to Mahalia and said, "I'll leave you girls alone down here. I don't want you to have to walk up the stairs, Lucy."

He dragged one of the kitchen chairs outside into the backyard and sat there, drinking one of the beers he kept hidden in the garage. He had a second beer in his other hand, and he raised it and pressed it against the back of his neck to cool himself off.

"Lucy!" Mahalia cried, coming down the stairs.

"Oh, girl, am I glad to see you!" Lucy answered. "I almost died walking so far. Mark doesn't know I'm over here. Don't ever get yourself knocked up, Mahalia! After this is over, I'm going to get my tubes tied."

"You're not really, Lucy!" Mahalia answered.

"I was just joking," Lucy said, but the next minute her face was buried in her hands, and she was sobbing. In between gasps of air, she repeated, "Oh Mahalia, Mahalia, Mahalia."

My sister patted Lucy's back in a grown-up way. "You're just upset because you're at the end of your time," Mahalia said.

"No, I'm not," Lucy answered. "I'm upset because"—she broke into sobs again—"because I don't want to raise a baby!" Mahalia patted her back some more. "I keep thinking, maybe it's just some kind of thing I inherited from my mother, because she ran off when I was born, do you know that? And now, here I am, right on the edge of having this baby, and all I want to do is run away! Oh Mahalia, I envy you, I envy you so much, having your whole life to yourself, the way you're so in charge of everything and don't care what anyone thinks! I never even thought of asking myself what I think. Not until now, anyway. Now, I know what I think—I wish I'd never been born! There's no one on earth who wishes they were me, locked up by my father all day! I'm never going to have one of those lovely loves, one of those romances where some boy loses himself over me."

"You'll have your baby," Mahalia said uncertainly. "Your baby will love you."

"I don't care!" Lucy answered, pulling herself up straight and wiping her eyes. "I don't want to be loved by a baby. I want to be loved by a boy. Do you know I only did it once? I might as well be the Virgin Mary." Lucy began crying again. "Do you want to know who the father was? If I told Mark where I met him, Mark wouldn't even let me out the door. It was just some guy named Myron I passed one day on the road walking home from the bus stop. He took me over to the Motor Inn and danced with me and kissed me in his room and BOOM! I didn't even learn his last name! I just wanted to know what it was like out in the world, what everyone was talking about, and I still do. You're right to want to go to the public high school, Mahalia."

Mahalia looked quickly at me; I hadn't known this.

"I'd kill to go there myself," Lucy continued. "I'm so jealous of you, Mahalia, the way everybody revolves around you, inviting you to their parties!"

"After your baby comes, I'll have a party and invite you," Mahalia told her.

"Oh great," Lucy answered. "Boys will just be lining up to bounce my baby."

"Well, at least you get to see Nicky Groot every Sunday," my sister joked, trying to cheer Lucy up, but this only made Lucy explode.

"You shouldn't make fun of him, Mahalia! He's just the boy-opposite of me, somebody living in Nowhere Land, just like me!"

"You aren't living in Nowhere Land," Mahalia answered, although she had trouble sounding as if she believed her words.

"Oh, yes I am. I'm Lucy Nobody from Nowhere," Lucy said, laughing a little. She wiped her eyes on her sleeve. Mahalia handed her a box of Kleenex. "Did you go to that dance thing?" Lucy asked her.

"Yeah, it was just a bunch of kids playing loud music and shaking their bodies around," Mahalia answered. She had not told me that she had gone to the party.

Lucy asked, "Shaking their bodies, how?"

Mahalia demonstrated, wiggling a little. Lucy stood up and said, "Like this?" She poked out her stomach and bobbed it back and forth. She and Mahalia both laughed.

"It must have been better than one of those stupid church parties where there's no beer or anything," Lucy said. "Was that boy who plays the piano there? The one you told me about?"

Mahalia nodded and smiled in spite of herself. Then she leaned forward and half-whispered to Lucy in a conspiratorial tone, "*They call Isabel the Vulture Lady!*"

"NO!" Lucy shouted. She and Mahalia dissolved into giggles.

The doorbell rang. I got up to answer it, but I did not want to: Things were just beginning to get lively. I opened the door, and Mr. Coker stood outside.

"Lucy!" he called. "How could you have come out here all by yourself with the baby almost on the way? I told you I'd drive you into town tomorrow. I wouldn't even have known where to find you if Myra Groot hadn't seen you and called me." He stood outside the door until Lucy rose unsteadily from the couch, trod heavily onto our porch, and allowed him to take her elbow and lead her to his truck.

When I followed them outside, I saw Isabel walking up the stoop to her front door. She bent over and picked up something on the top step: It looked like a shoe box. She lifted the lid and peered inside; she seemed surprised by what she saw. I realized that she must not have told people that Mahalia had returned home, because Nicky had continued to leave his gifts for my sister at Isabel's. I imagined Isabel opening boxes week after week, finding inside them lipstick or eye shadow or dimestore jewelry, the presents of a courting boy, and wondering who was mocking her.

She turned in our direction briefly, and then looked away as if she had not seen us, and vanished inside her rooms.

Stein High's summer session ended. When the school reopened the Tuesday after Labor Day for the regular school year, Isabel arrived on the front lawn with her picket sign. There were no students attending yet that week—just teachers and administrators preparing for classes. Mr. Cossack spotted Isabel from his office, and the school obtained a restraining order against her and served it on her that evening. However, no one was there to enforce the order when Isabel returned to picket Stein High again on Friday, because a prison riot had erupted at Stein Correctional Facility that required the aid of the entire local police force as well as the police of neighboring towns. The riot had broken out because an inmate had bled to death from a minor knife wound after the local volunteer ambulance squad failed to take him from the prison to the hospital. The ambulance squad, which was comprised mostly of men who were also employed as prison guards, had refused to rush the prisoner to Saint Mary's because, the squad chief was quoted as saying in the *Stein Record;* "Prisoners at the correctional facility are not members of our town, and the ambulance squad only serves the local populace."

I remember the morning of that day vividly even now, because state troopers poured into Stein, and then the National Guard arrived. Men in SWAT suits circled the prison with megaphones and tried talking a group of thirty inmates into surrendering to Superintendent Nohilly. The inmates had killed a guard and taken over a locked cell block, a sweltering barred hallway that contained nothing but the inmates themselves, and their own collective loneliness and bottomless rage.

Rage keeps the person who feels it company. It moves into the hollows left by grief and loss, and turns inside you like a dark furred animal that grows and fills you; it kills off loneliness and takes its place. When Super-intendent Nohilly addressed the inmates with threatening promises of ne-gotiation, the men yelled taunts at him from a single square window with a double cage of iron bolted over it. The prisoners did not need him anymore, they were full of themselves, appalled by discipline and barbarism both, sated with the despair that usually gnawed them, prepared to embrace the fullness of their own deaths. By the end of the day, tear gas spun through the heating vents of the seized cell blocks, bullets sounded one after the other like fire-crackers, two more guards and seven inmates were dead, and Warden No-hilly reclaimed his territory. Because of these events, the police paid no attention to Isabel when she showed up at Stein High School, where she was joined by Mr. Coker and Nicky Groot and Mr. Petty.

That day, Isabel came first to our house and knocked on our door, but

Mahalia did not answer. She was upstairs, washing her hair. She had been in the shower for forty minutes already; F. X. had offered to take her and my mother to Albany to spend the night and pass the entire next day shopping for fall clothes, and Mahalia had told me that she had to get ready "to stare at myself in all those store mirrors. I've barely seen myself in normal clothes. All I have is years and years of Catholic school jumpers and some summer outfits." Mahalia felt self-conscious about dressing so differently from the public school students.

I looked down on Isabel from our bedroom window; from above, her helmet-hat looked like a flattened box. She rang once, stood several minutes at the door without fidgeting at all, or even ringing a second time, and then she turned up the block, in the opposite direction from her home.

I knocked on the bathroom door, but Mahalia did not hear me. She was singing to herself, a little out of key, a plaintive song about lost promises and borrowed love, and I heard it until I hit the bottom of our stairway and looked outside: Isabel was gone. I circled our yard and crossed our neighbor's yard to my tree. His dog howled at me as I climbed to the tallest limb. I looked around to see if I could spy Isabel, but she was nowhere in sight. I thought of remaining forever in those high branches. I imagined I was an animal treed there, and that to spite my pursuers I had learned to live up in the branches without ever coming down, snatching bats out of the sky for food. I imagined many dogs barking below, and then pondered bloodhounds specifically: whether it was true that they were not in themselves vicious. I saw Isabel emerge from behind a distant house, heading in a determined way along the street that intersected ours.

I swung down from the tree, and ran to our backyard and into the woods behind it. I slipped between trees and through tangled vines, my head lowered like a bloodhound's. I wanted to bay at the sky, but I held back. I ran along a narrow path until I came out in a stranger's yard, just ahead of Isabel as she trod up the street. She was walking in the direction of Stein High School. Her hands were empty, except for a small puzzle in her right hand, which she tinkered with absently.

I stepped back into the woods, and she either saw or did not see me, but she acted as if she did not. She walked on, toward the school.

I followed her at a careful, lurking distance. As she turned onto the school's driveway, I recognized Mr. Coker's truck there. He and Mr. Petty, wearing his jumpsuit, had already set the literature table on the school lawn, and they greeted Isabel warmly. Mr. Petty shook her hand by grasping her whole arm, and Mr. Coker told her, "We got the papers but we went and forgot the signs, Izzy." He lifted the cloth on the table and showed her something underneath it. I crept up behind them but Mr. Coker dropped the cloth before I could see what he was pointing at.

Mr. Petty signaled to Isabel, and she walked a dozen yards from the table to talk with him. Nicky Groot appeared from behind the trailer that housed the library, carrying a Coca-Cola can. He sauntered up to the table and stood beside Mr. Coker.

"You can still back out of this, Nicky," Mr. Coker said. "You're old enough to make your own decisions, and you don't have to go along with us."

Nicky remained where he was, and turned to gaze across the school grounds; he spotted me first. "Your sister's not coming?" he asked.

I shook my head. "She's buying some stupid dresses," I answered.

"Hey there, Penny," Mr. Coker said. "You stay over here by the table, okay?" Mr. Coker told Nicky, "Let me talk to Isabel and Mr. Petty for a minute."

As Mr. Coker bent in a huddle with Isabel and Mr. Petty, I searched for *Life or Death* on the literature table, but could not find it. I reached for *The Abortion Handbook*, but Nicky leaned toward me and whispered in my ear, "Get a look at this."

He pulled up the cloth that covered the table. There was a cooler there, filled with widemouthed juice bottles holding a dark red liquid that I mistook for some odd kind of grape or cherry juice or maybe wine.

"Pig blood," Nicky told me.

"What's it for?" I asked him.

"Blood sausage," he answered, and then snickered knowingly.

Mr. Coker joined us again, and the three of us stood before the literature table, waiting. A woman stepped down from the library trailer and crossed the slope of the front lawn into the school. A man in sweatpants appeared at the edge of Stein High's football field and bent down to touch something in the grass, walked the perimeter of the field, and departed in a red car. Mr. Brewer, wearing blue jeans and a blue jean jacket and bright orange necktie, opened the school's side exit, looked at us briefly, and reentered the building. A bell rang, and a few teachers spilled out the school's back exit into the lot behind the building. Cars motored past us along the driveway until the lot emptied.

I thought Isabel must know that I was there, but she did not come over to the table to greet me. Instead, when she stopped talking with Mr. Coker and Mr. Petty, she walked to the trailer, mounted the steps, and vanished inside.

Five minutes later, Mr. Brewer emerged again from the school's side exit, carrying a stack of textbooks. He headed toward a blue car with its motor idling at the bottom of the drive. Mr. Coker returned with Mr. Petty to the table, and the men stood beside Nicky.

Abruptly, I saw Mr. Petty's bony hand emerge from behind me and seize a handle of the cooler under the table, and then Mr. Coker's larger hand descended to grab the second handle. I backed away, and they lifted the cooler and bore it toward the trailer. I followed them, knowing that something terrible and exciting was on the brink of happening. By the time we reached the bottom of the trailer steps, I was running to keep up with them.

"Stay away from there!" Mr. Brewer shouted.

Then, we were all rushing up the steps into the trailer—Nicky, Mr. Coker, Mr. Petty, and I. We stopped at the glass case where Mr. Brewer kept his display.

Isabel stood beside the case; she had opened it so that its glass lid leaned back against the wall. On the right were the "mother" and the books that had been there before, and on the left was a single copy of *The Right to Live; the Right to Die*, by C. Everett Koop.

The men set down the cooler, and Mr. Coker uncapped one of the bottles, lifted it high above the case, and tipped it over the display. A red wave of pig blood crested and splashed over the books inside. Nicky upturned a second bottle immediately afterward. Isabel lifted a third bottle a little clumsily, so that it splashed on the floor and her slippers as she tilted it into the display case. Mr. Petty pushed beside her and held his bottle high in the air, so that when he overturned it, the pig blood coursed from it rapidly and splattered the walls behind the case. Isabel and Mr. Coker stepped back: Isabel gazed grimly at the case, and Mr. Coker looked exhilarated. Nicky lifted another bottle.

Mr. Brewer appeared at the door. "What are you doing?" he called. "Get out of here." He walked toward the display case as Mr. Petty, cradling another bottle, stepped toward him. Mr. Petty cocked the bottle backward, and then rocked it forward so that the blood inside leapt into the air and splashed Mr. Brewer.

"Jesus Christ!" Mr. Brewer yelled. "Jesus Christ!" He stepped backward toward the doorway, and all of us followed him, drawn toward him as if he were an injured animal and we were all dogs. Mr. Coker and Isabel passed me, and I turned around briefly at the top of the stairs: Mr. Petty and Nicky were emptying bottles of blood onto the trailer's carpet and back bookshelves. They shattered the glass on the display case, and then each grabbed two more bottles, brushed past me, and caught up with Mr. Coker and Isabel.

Mr. Brewer raised his jacket over his head as he ran toward the blue car in the school driveway. Mr. Petty rushed behind him and tossed the contents of one of the bottles onto Mr. Brewer, drenching him as he climbed into his car and shut and locked the door behind him.

I saw Isabel's hat mirrored in the windshield, distorted, and then a wash of blood landed on the glass, and Mr. Petty upturned his remaining bottle, letting the last drops rain down on the car. Nicky whooped behind him and emptied another bottle over the windshield. The windshield wipers turned on, fanning the blood outward and smoothing it down. Water squirted up from two spigots on the hood, and the blood thinned until I could see Mr. Brewer, and his wife in the backseat behind him, and their two terrified children beside her, all staring at us as if we were monstrous, insane. The engine roared, and the car backed away from us, did a U-turn, and fled from the parking lot.

———

When a police officer came to our door three hours after the prison riot was subdued, I was sitting in my tree again. My heart pounding, I had run home without looking back, and scaled my tree, and sat there, looking down at our neighbor's barking dog and breathing hard.

As the late afternoon sun trickled through the branches, I watched the top of our neighbor's head as he came outside and unchained his dog without noticing me above them. I saw Mahalia walk into the front yard looking for me: She tilted back her head, located me in the tree, and returned inside.

A few minutes later, Mr. Coker's pickup truck pulled in front of Isabel's house. Nicky and Mr. Petty climbed out of the truck bed, and Mr. Coker and Isabel joined them on the sidewalk. Isabel took her keys out of her brocade bag and walked up her front steps. Nicky and Mr. Coker and Mr. Petty moved together, like the points of triangle. As Isabel paused to unlock her door, Nicky and the men stopped exactly at the same time on her walkway. When she opened her door, they started up the steps in single file and followed her inside. Only a few minutes afterward, Nicky and Mr. Coker emerged from her house. Mr. Coker was carrying Isabel's kerosene lamp. He placed it in a box in the back of his truck, and Nicky climbed in beside the lamp. Mr. Coker stepped into the cab and turned on the ignition. Mr. Petty then emerged with Isabel, walking behind her and almost touching the small of her back. They paused next to the truck as he talked to her; from my tree, I could not see her expression, but there was something about her general posture that made her look hesitant or puzzled. Afterward, Mr. Petty took Isabel's elbow and helped her into the cab, a gesture that I thought must have made her uncomfortable. Then Mr. Petty climbed into the truck bed, and Mr. Coker drove them all away.

David's truck passed them going in the opposite direction. F. X. followed behind in his Galaxie 500. My mother and David exited his truck, and my mother carried a small suitcase to F. X.'s car and slid into the back seat. David opened our house's front door, called up to my sister, and then talked to her briefly on the front steps, while she glanced at my mother, who waved to her with both hands. Mahalia stepped into the yard and pointed up toward me in the tree, and David turned around, trying to locate me through the branches. Mahalia then strolled down the walkway toward the Galaxie 500, and climbed into its front seat rather than in the back beside my mother. My mother rolled down her window and kissed David, and the Galaxie 500 drove off.

David returned inside the house. I figured he would walk to the garage, fetch himself a beer, and then wander outside and tell me to get down from the tree because dark was falling. However, before he could reemerge, a police car turned the corner of Main Street, cruised up our block, and parked in our driveway. An officer stepped out.

David answered, looking surprised. Then tilting back his head, he cupped his hand over his eyes, searching the tree for me.

I considered staying where I was: I knew no adult could get me up there. I thought of my lizards in their cage in my room—I knew that prisoners were not allowed to keep pets in jail. I realized I would miss mine; tears welled in my eyes.

"Penny!" David shouted. I imagined the officer climbing the tree to try to reach me; he would never make it. He would have to call the fire department. I had seen the local firemen making spectacles of themselves, yanking down clawing cats from trees. I did not want to be at the center of such an adult commotion. I felt weak with surrender. I grabbed hold of the branch I was sitting on and swung to the one under it, and then shimmied to the ground.

As soon as my feet touched the earth, I broke down. I covered my face with my hands and cried like a woman on television whose poisoned husband has been discovered in her closet.

"What's wrong, Penny?" David asked.

"I don't want to be handcuffed," I told him.

David and the officer laughed together, and I understood that I somehow once again had escaped being jailed. David took my hand and I allowed him to lead me inside. He apparently knew the officer already, because he called him Michael, before introducing him to me as Officer Finerty. He was tall and thin, with a head too small for his body.

"How's life with Marguerite?" he asked David.

"Doing well," David answered.

"Lucky bastard," Officer Finerty said.

I crawled onto the couch beside David. Officer Finerty sat on the armchair saying, "Penny, I just wanted to see if you could help us answer some questions about what happened at the school this afternoon with Miss Flood and Mr. Coker and Nicky Groot and the fourth man. I hear you might have been there when they assaulted a teacher at the school." Officer Finerty told David, "They threw some kind of animal blood on him and all over the school library. They did thousands of dollars worth of damage."

David asked, "Penny, do you know anything about this?"

Did David expect me to tell on Isabel and Mr. Coker and Nicky? I stared at the floor, jiggling my foot. I pictured Isabel holding her brocade bag, sitting on our living-room couch months before and telling me, "I had a neighbor once who just stopped cleaning. . . ."

"Penny," David repeated. "Is it true you witnessed what happened at the school?"

What, I wondered, would they do to Nicky? Because I was grateful to Nicky—he was the only person during my whole summer with Isabel who had talked to me as if my opinion mattered. And wasn't he better than Mahalia, because he pined for her when she did not pine for him? And hadn't he stood up for Mr. Coker when I tried to make fun of his sausage? And why would the police want to bother Mr. Coker? All he had ever wanted was to be left alone, and here they were, trying to root him out.

"I don't want to send Isabel to death row," I said, finally.

"We don't need information on Miss Flood," Officer Finerty told David. "We're sure to pick up her and Mr. Coker and the boy. It's the other guy we're worried about." Officer Finerty pulled out four photographs and laid them on the table. "Do you see the other man here?" he asked me. "The man who was with Mr. Coker and Miss Flood? If we knew a little more about him, it might help everyone concerned."

I stared at the pictures: There was a man with no hair and crooked teeth and a cocky grin; and one who looked just like Mahalia's teacher, Mr. Molinari; and a third whom I recognized as one of the policemen in town who directed traffic on Main Street during parades; and the fourth was Mr. Petty. He appeared younger in the photograph, with longer hair, but was just as gaunt. Shadows pooled under his eyebrows and in the hollows of his cheeks. I lifted up his picture.

"Does he look like anyone you know?" the officer asked.

I nodded.

David bent over Mr. Petty's photograph, and then asked Officer Finerty, "Is *that* who you're looking for?"

"Have you seen him?"

"No," David answered. "I had no idea he was back in the state. I thought they transferred Mr. Combs to Leavenworth."

"Yeah, and Leavenworth transferred Hank Combs back to us, the general population."

"That's not Hank Combs," I said. "It's Mr. Petty. He belongs to Reverend Sloat's church. He chased Mr. Brewer out of the trailer and all the way to the car. He poured pig blood all over the shelves and the books. We all just followed around after him."

"Petty must be an alias, Penny," David said. I nodded, impressed with David's knowledge of criminals, and peered more closely at the photograph.

Officer Finerty told David, "The police in Buffalo already tracked down Sloat. He said he was unaware of Mr. Combs's earlier brushes with the law, and claims to have no knowledge of the plan to vandalize the school."

"Combs is probably a long way from here by now," David answered.

Officer Finerty rose, saying, "Penny might have to give some account later of what she saw."

David followed him onto our front porch and said, "A couple weeks ago when we were at the lake, my brother-in-law mentioned that a man named Petty told him something about—" David closed the front door and spoke with Officer Finerty for a few minutes.

After the policeman left, and David returned inside, he told me that Hank Combs had been arrested in Dannemora years before, for robbing a liquor store. He had been caught with a cache of guns in his trunk and sent to jail for selling illegal weapons and for armed robbery. He had used the aliases Hank Smalls and James Smawly and James Petit before but, David said, " 'Hank Petty' must be new, and don't be impressed with yourself for having rubbed elbows with an outlaw, Penny. Mr. Combs is nothing special. When you're older you'll find out that the world is crawling with men like Mr. Combs." I nodded solemnly; I was thrilled with myself.

———

Later that evening, right before I climbed in bed, the doorbell rang, and when David answered it, Mrs. Groot was standing there, ringing her hands.

"Is Nicky here?" Mrs. Groot asked.

"No," David answered. "We haven't seen him since Penny met him at the school this afternoon." He invited Mrs. Groot inside, but she stayed on the doorstep.

"The police came to my house saying something terrible happened at the school. You were there, Penny?" Mrs. Groot looked down at me.

"Nicky just went along with it," I told her, not knowing what else to say. "I don't know where he is now."

"I thought Nicky might have come here to see Mahalia," Mrs. Groot said. "I know he was sweet on her. He came over here a lot this summer."

"He did?" David asked.

"I thought it was a good sign that he was spending time with a nice girl like Mahalia," Mrs. Groot said.

"Mahalia's not here," David told her. "She left with her mother a few hours ago to spend the weekend in Albany."

"Nicky must be upset," Mrs. Groot told him. "He always likes to be by himself when he's worried. He's counted so much on Mr. Coker and Isabel." She added with bewilderment, "And now the police are looking for both of them too."

David invited Mrs. Groot in a second time, but she refused him again saying, "No, I should wait at home, in case Nicky shows up there." She turned and disappeared down our walk, her head bent as if she were following her own dim feet through the darkness.

David led me upstairs, tucked me in, and told me, "Maybe tomorrow you and I will sit down together and talk this through from beginning to end, Penny. After they pick up Isabel and the others, the police will probably come back here." He switched off my light. He paused at my door and said, "Penny, you are not under any circumstances to visit any of those people on your own, do you understand? If any of them comes to the door, even Isabel, to talk to you or Mahalia, you call me or your mother." He walked downstairs, leaving me alone. I knew sleeping would be impossible; I felt curiosity and excitement snarl inside me until they knotted in my throat. I wanted to know where Isabel and the others were; I wished I was with them, slipping through the darkness: I pictured Mr. Petty's face when he was emptying his bottles of blood, and I thought of him sitting together with Nicky and Mr. Coker, talking about what they had done in quiet, joyous voices.

When I heard David climb the stairs and shut the door to the bedroom he now shared with my mother, I pulled on pants, stuffed my nightgown into them, and put on sneakers without socks. I walked as slowly and quietly down the stairs as I could manage; I paused to make sure David had not heard me, and then I continued on, through the kitchen and out the back door. As I slipped through the side yard, ferns clutched my ankles like tentacles.

The full moon sank and surged between clouds, and stars spread out haphazardly. When my feet touched the sidewalk, I ran to Isabel's house, and then around it. My heart beat crazily and I stopped: The downstairs lights were off.

I felt drawn irresistibly to review and replay the events of the day, to breathe in the air around the school trailer, to sniff the wind to see if it held the same smells, to look for traces of what had transpired only hours before. Just walking toward the school I felt exhilarated: The early September night felt warm and heavy as fur. My shadow changed shape and stature as I scampered quickly into and out of the glow of overhead streetlights, until I reached the last stretch of road near the school.

A single light shone in Stein High's front doorway and a second one glittered outside the trailer. As I approached it, I saw that someone had set up nose cones around the trailer and roped off a section in front of the trailer's steps; a broad band of yellow tape ran across the door. I wondered if the school already had cleaned up inside.

I circled the trailer, peering up through the dark windows. I walked around the trailer a second time, pushing on the windows one by one. The last window in the back was a narrow rectangle just outside my reach. I stood on a pile of cinder blocks below it and tested the glass: It moved to the right. Balancing against the trailer, I slid the window the rest of the way open. I grabbed the sill, hooked my leg over it, and slipped inside. I fell with a jolt to the trailer floor.

I could see almost nothing: My eyes barely adjusted to the darkness, and even after they did, I had to feel my way along ghostly stacks of books, piles of paper, shelves, and a low table. My hand touched a chair's back. I instantly jerked it away: What if I felt something wet? What if the blood was everywhere around me still? I pulled out the chair, tested the seat with my hands to make sure it was dry, and sat down in darkness, my heart dancing wildly, the sound of my own blood in my own ears deafening.

I had never been so excited while sitting still in my entire life. I sat for what I thought was an impressive amount of time. I sang to myself, with no one there to hear me, songs from school music books and snatches of melodies my mother liked or that I had heard on the radio. I sang out of tune, in a raspy whisper, and then in a tone that I thought was low as a man's: I had never sung so loud by myself before. I was joyous at the sound of my own voice rising almost in music, by itself, in the dark. I sang all of the verses of "Barnacle Bill."

I stopped abruptly when I heard noises outside the trailer. At first, they seemed far off and unrelated to me: They were adult voices, and I held myself perfectly motionless, waiting for them to recede and go on about their business. I listened to men talking, one loud and laughing, another giving someone orders, and then a funny guffaw and a muffled shout.

A hand jiggled the trailer's doorknob. I sprang from my seat and felt my way to the back of the trailer until I bumped into a large desk. I circled it, my fingers passing along its rim, and I ducked behind it. The doorknob jiggled again; I felt the vibrations of feet on the outside steps. Then the feet backed away from the door, and the noises of the men receded once again. Just as they reached the edge of audibility, I heard a voice I knew, exclaiming something in a low, cautionary tone. It was different from the others', because it was a woman's voice. It was Isabel's.

I would learn not long afterward where Isabel and Mr. Coker, and Nicky and Mr. Petty had been, and what they had done, since I had last seen them: They had driven from Isabel's house to the Stein Motor Inn, where Mr. Petty had stopped to pick up some items from a room he had rented for the week. Mr. Petty had then led the others into the Motor Inn's bar, where he had ordered them all vodka tonics, even Nicky. Isabel had not touched hers, but Nicky had downed his quickly, over her protests, before he could be recognized as a minor by the waiter (who later, when interviewed by the Plattsburgh newspaper, claimed not to remember Nicky, and recalled only Mr. Petty, Mr. Coker, and Isabel). Mr. Coker had downed his drink too— at first reluctantly, because he preferred pineapple juice, and then with a sense of abandonment encouraged by his exultation over what had happened at the school. Mr. Petty drank his vodka and Isabel's, and then ordered another round for Mr. Coker.

No one who remembered the foursome later could say what Isabel acted like in their company—whether she had seemed glad to be part of the group, to be included anywhere at all now that she had lost her church and my sister, or whether Isabel had seemed unhappy and disapproving of the men. Nevertheless, after a while, the four rose as a group and left. Mr. Coker let Mr. Petty drive, because Mr. Petty claimed that the liquor had not affected him, while Mr. Coker felt it had gone to his head. He and Nicky rode in the truck bed, and Isabel sat next to Mr. Petty. They stopped at the farm of Mr. Coker, who ran inside his house, where Lucy was surprised to see him, swaying a little and stumbling as he told her, "Just wait for me here. We have business to finish. Lock the door." He emerged outside shortly afterward, carrying a kerosene lamp like

Isabel's, which he displayed to Mr. Petty and Nicky. Then, around midnight, the four journeyed back to Stein.

They drove first to the house of the teacher, Mr. Brewer, and parked in front of his driveway, blocking it. Isabel remained in the truck, but the three others jumped out. Mr. Coker lit his kerosene lamp and Mr. Petty retrieved Isabel's from the truck bed and lit it as well. Nicky walked between the two men whooping, while they entered Mr. Brewer's yard, a weird synergy spinning between the three of them and binding them together in a not-quite-mob-sized group. Mr. Coker and Mr. Petty swung the lamps so that they bobbed like buoys. Mr. Brewer's front light snapped on, he stepped onto his landing in his underwear, took one look at the men, and closed the door. Nicky picked up a rock and threw it at the door just as it shut, and he shouted an obscenity at Mr. Brewer. Mr. Petty laughed in a hollow way and Mr. Coker answered something unintelligible. Nicky threw a second rock that shattered a small windowpane beside the door. Isabel stepped from her perch in the truck and hurried toward Nicky, but just as she reached him the men snuffed their lanterns, turned around in unison, and hopped back in the truck. She climbed in beside Mr. Petty.

Mr. Petty took off in the direction of the school. Halfway there, the four could hear police sirens racing behind them in the direction of Mr. Brewer's house. The sirens' screams diminished as Mr. Petty turned down the school driveway toward the trailer.

The men and Nicky disembarked together while Isabel stayed in the truck cab. When the men found the trailer door locked, they returned to the truck, where Mr. Coker retrieved a crowbar. Nicky and Mr. Petty followed him back to the trailer, swinging their unlit lanterns. Isabel stepped down from the truck to speak to them. Mr. Coker pried the trailer door open easily. Nicky and Mr. Petty lit the lanterns and entered the trailer behind him.

I did not see Isabel, and it took me a moment before I recognized Mr. Coker, Mr. Petty, and Nicky. I hid behind my chair. Mr. Petty bent his face over his lantern, blew on the flame, and turned the lamp key, and the flame disappeared. Then Mr. Coker stepped closer with his lantern still lit, and I saw Mr. Petty lift the glass cylinder around his lantern's wick and tilt the lamp so that a stream of liquid dripped from it onto the floor. Mr. Petty walked once, all the way around the trailer, splashing the table, the rug, the bookcase, and a shelf along the wall, while Mr. Coker followed him with a lit lantern that must have half-blinded them both because they looked once straight into the darkness where I crouched, and did not see me. I recognized the smell of kerosene when they passed me. Nicky stood by the door as a lookout, and Mr. Petty moved slowly, never allowing more than a trickle to leak from the lamp he held. He and Mr. Coker walked a full circle along the row of shelves until they reached the door again. Then, Mr. Petty pulled four or five books from the shelf nearest the door, tossed them to the floor, and took Mr. Coker's lamp. The lamp turned off, I heard more kerosene slosh onto the floor, and then the sound of footsteps. At the doorway, there was a sudden burst—Mr. Petty's face flashed behind a lit match. For an instant, the match seemed to go out behind a curtain of blackness, and then the floor burst into flame, Mr. Coker's lamp somersaulted out of Mr. Petty's hands through the air and hit the fire, and Mr. Petty jumped down the steps after Mr. Coker and Nicky.

A bright web of fire spun along the shelves and around the trailer. I heard a woman's voice outside: I stood and pressed my face against a back window, and saw only blackness. I tried to unlock the window behind me, but it was jammed. I moved toward the next one. I watched smoke twist in the air above my hand, vaguely illuminated by the flames behind me. I twisted open the lock on the next window, pushed it upward, and felt it move until it was half-open, but I could not budge it beyond there. I swung my foot to the sill, and pulled myself up; I was afraid I would not fit through, but I pressed myself flat against the sill like a snake, wiggled halfway out, and could go no farther: I held still, worried that I would get stuck there.

I had never experienced panic before, and when I felt it for the first time, I had no name for it. I remember waiting there dumbly, feeling my heart lurch like a small boat smashed by a wave, and then experiencing a terrible sensation, like a weighted rope, dropping inside me. I heard a woman's voice cry, "I think there's someone in there!" I leaned sideways and fell back to the trailer floor.

The voice shouted, "I thought someone was climbing out!" I stood, and looked out the window: Isabel's face appeared dimly, slightly below me, upturned, under the window, and her hands reached for the glass and scratched against it.

I backed away. I groped along chairs and bookcases toward the other side of the trailer. My hand felt the gap where I had climbed in. I lifted my leg over the sill and pulled myself through the window. As I hung for a moment from the sill, I heard Isabel cry, "I think I saw a child in there! It was a child! Penny, is that you?" I dropped to the ground. I did not answer or turn around; instead, I took off across the grass behind the trailer toward the school's playing field. I ran until I was winded. When I heard the sound of a truck motor, I stopped; I turned and saw the trailer, wrapping itself in flames, and I smelled smoke on my clothes.

The trailer seemed to expand, to dance, to grow luminous fur, to throw parts of itself into the air. It changed color, rose like a steeple and flattened itself, grew blinding and then lightless and then bright again. From where I stood, I imagined I could hear an odd, airy roar, the sound of something swallowing air. I saw that Mr. Coker's truck was gone.

I watched mesmerized until the siren of the town's fire engine lifted itself into the air and wailed at the sight of the school library. When the fire truck stopped, I saw someone emerge from behind the burning trailer; I knew it was Isabel; she ran with her long dress trailing behind her, toward the fire truck. I turned and raced home. When I got there, I slipped up the stairs, and buried myself under the covers.

During the night, the police arrested Isabel at the trailer; she refused to leave, insisting that a child could be inside the trailer, but the firemen found no evidence that any person had been consumed in the fire and thought she was deluded. At Isabel's request, the police called my house to verify that I was there: David answered the telephone and checked on me in my room, and reported that I was. I had stashed my smoky clothes in a shoe box in the bottom of my closet, but I was relieved that he did not bend too close; he might have detected the fiery odor of my hair before I could shower in the morning.

Several hours after they brought Isabel to the police station, they arrested Mr. Coker at his farm, and charged him with assault, arson, and malicious damage; he insisted that Isabel had nothing to do with the fire, but by morning they had written up a complaint charging her with the same offenses.

Nicky and Mr. Petty were not with Mr. Coker when he was arrested. By morning, the police learned that Mr. Petty had been staying at the Motor Inn, and they searched his room there, but he had cleared out his things the day before and apparently left town after the fire. The police also returned to Mrs. Groot's house and turned it upside down methodically, searching closets in her laundry room and her basement and the back of Nicky's bedroom. They parked two patrol cars in her driveway while neighbors gathered on their lawns, trying to get a glimpse of Mrs. Groot on her living-room couch. Nicky never came home and the police found nothing of interest.

Later in the morning, the police visited the house where Isabel resided and discovered that the lock on her front door had been jimmied. They entered and found Isabel's refrigerator open and a half-eaten apple on her kitchen counter beside a glass of vodka and Coca-Cola; a wet towel thrown on the hallway floor; and Nicky curled up in Isabel's bed, her empty kerosene lamp next to him on the bedside table. Nicky was arrested, taken down to the local jail, and held for trial as an adult on charges of arson, assault, and malicious damage.

The Stein police did not track down the man I thought of as Mr. Petty. His true name, Combs, would be associated over the years with various investigations into violence toward abortion clinics in the late seventies and early eighties. That fall and winter, Combs's picture was circulated in a series of newspaper articles that F. X. clipped and sent to us with annotations. Combs was a suspect when bottles of gasoline were thrown through the window of an abortion clinic in Omaha, Nebraska, on September 18, causing $35,000 in fire damage, and again in February, when someone broke into an abortion clinic in Cleveland; all of the clinic's furniture was slashed, and phone and electrical lines were cut, and three days later, a fire burned it to the ground. According to F. X. and David, Hank Combs was never captured. His name cropped up again in 1981, when clinics were bombed in Virginia and Florida, and in 1982, when a Missouri doctor who performed abortions was kidnapped outside Saint Louis and kept in an abandoned ammunition warehouse for seven days.

Chapter Fifteen

Mites

Reverend Bender was preoccupied during the prison riot and the arrests of Isabel and Mr. Coker and Nicky Groot, because an epidemic had broken out at Stein Evangelical. During the preceding week, various members of the congregation had suffered acute attacks of itching on their arms and legs, chests and heads, and some of the members were certain that they were losing hair. Mrs. Esselborne, concerned that congregants may have been infested by lice during mission visits to the prison, sent two church members to Dr. Cope in Dannemora. He gave them a prescription for Quell, an insecticidal hair shampoo, but its users pronounced it ineffective. Wednesday night prayer meeting was canceled, and when more members complained of identical symptoms, services were temporarily suspended, all pew cushions were dry-cleaned, and the entire church was scrubbed down with a chlorine solution.

On September 12, Mr. Harkless of the *Stein Record* printed a letter to the editor, again from Dr. Epstein:

I have learned that an outbreak has occurred at the Evangelical Church, whose members have been complaining of attacks of burning, formication, and hair loss, and that symptoms have not abated following applications of the prescription drug Quell, or more common over-the-counter lice-killers such as Nix and Rid. Because none of the church's members are among my regular patients, I hope to reach them through this general appeal. It is sug-

gested that anyone suffering from the symptoms described above seek the aid of a dermatologist who can take a skin scraping to determine if scabies or some other form of mite is the cause.

> After examining one anonymous patient, it is my opinion that this variation of dermatitis may not be scabies. There are a number of mite species that do not discriminate between animal and human hosts, and it is possible that a rodent or bird mite of some kind may be at the bottom of all this. Our offices have dispatched a slide to Cornell Veterinary School. In the interim, it is notable that arachnids are hardier than lice, and ten-minute head shampoos used to kill lice are not effective against mites. A twelve-hour application of permethrin to the entire body is generally required for eradication of mites. To avoid spreading mites to Stein's general pediatric population, infected individuals should seek treatment promptly.

Dr. Epstein's advice was such a sample of beneficence twisted through with taunting joy, that my mother proclaimed she suspected F. X.'s influence after she read the letter aloud to him in the living room.

"What kind of word is this, F. X.—*formication*? Did you come up with that word?"

"It's the sensation that ants are crawling all over you," F. X. answered.

It was true that if you walked around town, you would see members of Stein Evangelical's congregation scratching themselves at store counters or running their hands through their hair to see if it was thinning—or, in the case of one man I recognized from the church, pulling over their trucks to claw their heads frantically as if visions of devils were inflicting them by whispering in their ears. The week of Isabel's arrest, F. X. drove me toward Swastika to photograph the abandoned mine near there, and I saw Mrs. Esselborne emerge from her car and hurry surreptitiously into Dr. Epstein's office.

Whether F. X. inspired Dr. Epstein to place his letter in the *Record*, or simply derived enjoyment from it, the Stein Evangelical epidemic occupied his ruminations for days.

"Mahalia appears to have parted with the church just in time," F. X. told David as we played Parcheesi together, four days after Dr. Epstein's letter was printed. "Or we would all be sitting here in our living room right now, scratching our heads."

"I can't believe you lured me into this crazy game," David answered. We were playing Parcheesi with four boards laid together in a square on the living-room floor. Mahalia was out with my mother, buying my birthday presents.

I realized that Isabel, sitting alone in her jail cell, also might have been spared the attack of mites, along with Mr. Coker and Nicky. Mr. Petty probably already had the mites, I reasoned, because he spent so much time with Reverend Sloat, and I had seen Reverend Sloat scratching himself at the beach. It was possible that the whole group of people in the yellow bus had mites or would catch them, because they passed hours every day sitting beside one another.

The telephone rang. It was Mrs. Wroblewski, asking to speak with Mahalia. "She's not here," I answered.

"I was calling to invite her to come with us to visit Izzy at the jail," Mrs. Wroblewski said.

"I'll tell her," I promised.

"Who is it?" F. X. asked.

"Mrs. Wroblewski, from the church."

"Ask her if she has mites," F. X. told me.

"Did you get mites?"

There was a brief silence on the other end, and then Mrs. Wroblewski said, "Not yet, thank God. Imagine if seven children came down with something like that all at the same time! We would never get rid of them. And my doctor told me pregnant women can't use bug spray—I don't dare drop by the church. No one in the congregation has succeeded in killing off those things yet. Even dry cleaning doesn't seem to help. They've thrown out all the pew cushions! They think bugs crawled into the cushions one night when Reverend Sloat's people got tired of the bus and slept in the church."

"What about Lucy?" I asked.

"Lucy's fine," Mrs. Wroblewski answered. "She's here with me now. She's going to stay with us and we're going to give her room and board in exchange for baby-sitting after she has her baby. Of course, my oldest girl Roberta, will be lending a helping hand too. Lucy's father has been so worried. He's going to plead guilty. He says he thinks he'll have to serve at least four years in jail. He doesn't know what they're going to do to Isabel; he says he keeps telling them she tried to talk them out of burning down the trailer. He tried to get Nicky to plead guilty, but Nicky hasn't decided what to do yet. Myra is going out of her mind."

I told Mrs. Wroblewski good-bye. I realized that I would miss her hustle and bustle, and Lucy giggling beside her; I did not think I would have much contact with them anytime soon.

After I hung up, I said, "Mrs. Wroblewski wants Mahalia to go with the women's committee to visit Isabel."

David did not answer. We all knew that Mahalia would not go.

That morning at breakfast, David had told my mother, "They've assigned Isabel one of those part-time court-appointed guys who are used to doing real estate and wills. Those church people left her high and dry."

"Why shouldn't they?" Mahalia had answered. "They aren't responsible for what she did." (It would be Mahalia's most troublesome trait later, her insistence that people should solve their own problems. In adulthood she would end a friendship of a dozen years by telling a woman who had just learned her husband had cancer, "Well, *do* something about it." Mahalia would later find the husband a specialist who would cure him, although his wife, taking my sister's words as revealing a cold and condemnatory heart, and not as concealing concern and fear, would never revive their friendship.)

My mother told Mahalia: "Isabel's church should help her because Isabel is one of theirs. A church is not supposed to turn away from its lost lambs."

None of the adults knew how close I had come to being part of the fire; I could not bring myself to tell them I had returned to the trailer that night. I sensed that if I revealed what I had done, my mother's feelings toward Isabel would be less charitable, and I wanted time to ponder my own experience of danger before handing it over to the adults for them to examine and exclaim about. Whenever my mind touched on my last minutes in the trailer, the memory veered away like a furtive animal, and within a few days, the memory felt like it had always been my secret, that its life belonged to me alone.

Mahalia answered my mother, "I don't think Isabel would accept Stein Evangelical's help now." I thought my sister sounded a little rueful when she said this, as if she felt bad for Isabel in spite of herself, that it worried Mahalia she had forsaken Isabel when she needed Mahalia most. I suspected that my sister was shocked by her discovery of her own capacity for disloyalty, that little Judas rising up in her like a jack-in-the-box, that her mind fingered her flaw and flinched away from it and returned to it again and again. However, Mahalia did not talk to me about any of this—she seemed, for the time being, humiliated by her association with Isabel, and never discussed her unless directly questioned. Mahalia preferred to act as if they had never been affiliated.

Mahalia added, "Anyway Mama, Isabel doesn't want to belong to Stein Evangelical anymore."

"Everyone has to belong somewhere," my mother said. "I can't stand to think of how lonely she must be."

A week after her arrest, David learned that Isabel had refused to let her lawyer represent her. She represented herself and pleaded guilty to assault and malicious damage without even bargaining for a short sentence. She refused to plead guilty to arson, however, and the assistant district attorney assigned to her case eventually withdrew this charge. At first the court gave Isabel a lenient sentence, because unlike Mr. Coker and Nicky, she had no criminal history and the judge regarded her as misguided rather than dangerous. She received a thousand dollar fine and five years' probation conditioned on the court's order that she remain five hundred yards from Stein High School. However, the day of her release, Isabel reappeared at the school with a card table and her literature, and carrying a picket sign. She was rearrested and resentenced to eighteen months in jail on the original charges, and an additional six months for contempt of court.

My mother felt sorry for her. She said she imagined Isabel "sitting there all forlorn in the county jail," and wrote her a letter saying that she would not have allowed me to testify against Isabel because my mother did not want to "introduce Penny to conflicting feelings of loyalty regarding someone who had been kind to her." My mother also asked to visit Isabel at the jail.

Isabel refused her in a return letter in which she wrote that they "had nothing to say to each other, because we have nothing in common," but asked whether my mother would "box up" the things in Isabel's home because she did not have the funds to continue to pay rent there, and Mrs. Groot had offered to store Isabel's possessions in her basement. (Shortly afterward, Mrs. Groot called my mother, distraught, and asked her, "Who will watch over Nicky now? No one was willing to help my son except Izzy.") Isabel also inquired whether my mother could obtain papers from the local bank allowing Isabel to "take care of all necessary expenses and to transfer whatever is left of my small account, after expenses and the court's fine, to Lucy Coker, because her father is concerned about her welfare during his absence in jail, particularly now that she intends to take night courses at the high school, and this may lessen his worries somewhat."

On the last page of her letter, Isabel wrote: "I have attached a list of foods which Penny likes and should not eat because she tends to become excitable afterward." This list included the following:

- blue and purple popsicles and chewing gum
- green Jell-O and Kool-Aid

- cherry popsicles
- red Jell-O and Kool-Aid
- all foods containing yellow dye (such as Jell-O butterscotch pudding)
- raisins, grapes, and grape juice
- oranges and orange juice (tangerines not problematic)
- Coca-Cola, Pepsi, and Mountain Dew
- Doritos, barbecue potato chips, Cheez Doodles
- white packaged bread such as Wonder bread
- hot cocoa, Oreos, Chips Ahoy, M&M's
- devil's food cake
- chocolate generally
- Campbell's soups
- canned Chef Boyardee sauces and products
- When she is older, Penny should be cautioned against consuming aspirin, tea, coffee, or alcohol in any form.

My mother read the list and said, "What in heaven?" I hoped that she would throw it away, but instead she pursed her lips, reread it, and taped it to the refrigerator with a look of amusement.

Isabel concluded her note, *I am returning Mr. Molineaux's letters here. Please tell Mr. Molineaux not to send me any further correspondence under his false names. His letters have been nonsensical.*

————

On September 24, I had a small, boisterous birthday party. F. X. was there; he would not leave until the following week. My mother and David bought me hockey skates, a hockey stick, and a puck that I would ricochet all winter back and forth across Stein Lake, through whatever games men and boys were playing on the swept areas near the shore where the hockey teams practiced.

Sister Geraldine also came to the house for cake. She entered our living room, saying, "I have a surprise for Penny and everyone else." She pulled out an award certificate with a gold stamp on it, and a check for five dollars from *The Catholic Trotskyist*. "Penny's English teacher at summer school sent her story to a children's literature contest run by a radical newspaper," Sister Geraldine told my mother, "unbeknownst to me." Everyone gathered around, admiring the certificate and reading my story, printed on the third page of *The Catholic Trotskyist*:

The Man with a Hole in His Head

by Penny Daigle

There was a future world. Their medicine was far ahead of ours. You could transplant your heart at home, without seeing a doctor. New parts were made from special plastic and monkey parts you bought at the drugstore.

A doctor found a way to make pieces of brains that were missing, or knocked out in car accidents. He put a conscience in the brain of a death row criminal. The criminal had committed a terrible murder. The man signed a paper to have the operation because they told him that if he did not, he would be electrocuted in the electric chair. "I didn't have much of a choice," he said.

When he woke up after the operation, he said, "I feel like I was color-blind before. Everything looks different." He was nice to people and never got in trouble.

He was so good, they let him go from prison. But after a while, he went back to the doctor's office and said, "Take it out. Take out the piece you weaseled into my head."

"What?" asked Doctor Christian Saint Bernard. His eyes looked big and surprised behind his thick glasses.

"I am not afraid of dying anymore," the man said. "I want the operation done backwards. I want to be the way I was before. I don't care if I'm electrocuted, as long as I'm electrocuted as myself."

"But why?" said the doctor.

The man said, "When I was evil, I thought that good people made no sense. Now that I am a good man, I see that I was right. I would rather be fried."

At the bottom of the page, an adult had scrawled in almost illegible handwriting, Ms. Daigle—We are pleased to extend to you the warmest congratulations for your fine and sophisticated story.

"Isabel Flood would not approve," F. X. said.

"Neither would the Vatican," Sister Geraldine told him.

"Do you have any news of Isabel?" David asked.

"I tried to visit her, but she wouldn't allow it," Sister Geraldine answered. "I talked to Reverend Bender and he didn't seem to know any more than I did."

"That poor woman," my mother said. I suppressed the fleeting impulse to speak to her about my night in the trailer. (When I finally did tell my mother, I was almost twenty and her response was, "Lord, Penny, it makes my heart stop to think about it," and then "I'm sure that's about half as bad as the other ten things you've decided never to tell me.")

"Do they still have mites formicating over at Stein Evangelical?" F. X. asked.

"I believe they haven't gotten rid of them yet," Sister Geraldine answered, "but they've been diagnosed. A professor at Cornell says that it's some kind of rodent mite. Reverend Bender thinks they may have been carried by a guinea pig that Revered Sloat had on his bus. Apparently they let the guinea pig roam up and down the bus aisle when they traveled."

"His name was Buster," I said, recalling his rust-red fur and his hungry look when I was not allowed to give him a blade of grass. I imagined him on a road somewhere in New York, scurrying up and down the yellow bus's aisles, searching for food and comfort. I thought of Hank Petty, also, carrying mites across the country as he fled, not even knowing what he had.

F. X. gave me a book on Morse code for my birthday, and a small ham radio, which David would later help me set up, so that I could correspond with F. X. by shortwave radio while he was doing fieldwork in Mexico. "Imagine your words, buzzing over the continent in the black air, invisible but there at the same time," F. X. told me. But I thought of the opposite: F. X.'s words barreling across the sky like meteorites. Over the next dozen years, he would send news of his discoveries, which I penciled into a notebook I still keep. He would wire me at dinnertime, or midnight or two o'clock in the morning, that "the ancient Maya raked in the gods' graves and proved them men," or that "the age of temples can be determined by the depth of bat guano on the floors," or that "the Maya were both more civilized and more barbaric than the Daigles."

In 1985, he would wire me, "I have fallen in love with a blind simultaneous interpreter fifteen years my senior named Antonita Stanatoupoulous, and feel at home in the world." Two months later, Antonita would call my mother and frantically ask her for help with F. X.: He was drinking too much.

My mother and David would fly to New Orleans and cart F. X. off to a hospital, and he would tell them, "We have returned in our orbits to our meeting place." He and Antonita would come visit us a year later. She was tall and stark, and used green eye shadow, despite her blindness, and wore her hair in a gray braid thicker than her arm. She would talk a mile a minute in a high, tittery voice that made her seem as if she had stepped right out of the radio's shortwaves into Stein. It was she, and not my mother, who would take me by bus to a Plattsburgh doctor's office, in order to get my first diaphragm the summer before I started college. Afterward, Antonita would request in payment that I swim across Stein Lake with her, because F. X. did not swim well enough to accompany her. "He won't go over his head," she told me as I struggled to keep up with her sidestroke. "He sinks after two strokes. It's good that you can swim. Study Greek in college," she advised me further. "Greek and mathematics and ancient Spanish literature." I closed my eyes as I swam, turning occasionally to peek at Antonita or the far shore, and I realized only then that F. X. must have been terrified when he crossed Stein Lake alone and at night to fetch my mother, because he had known with certainty that he would drown if he fell through the ice.

———

Three days before F. X. departed in September of 1977, my mother drove to Isabel's landlord's to pick up her keys, and afterward took a carload of empty boxes to her home. While my mother packed the dishes and glasses, she enlisted me in rolling up Isabel's scanty silverware in newspapers. Aside from her five pieces of furniture and her painting, all of Isabel's possessions in the rooms she had inhabited for nine years fit into thirteen boxes. When my mother opened the bedroom closet, she said, "six dresses, my lord!" She wrapped each dress in tissue as if it were made of silk or fine linen. She found dozens of puzzles on the floor and the top shelf of the closet. The puzzles were tucked into Isabel's slipper-shoes, wrapped in her winter hats, piled inside cardboard boxes at the back of the closet, and stuffed into the pockets of her coats and sweaters.

When my mother finished boxing the puzzles, she tried the extra door in the back of Isabel's bedroom, but it was locked. My mother returned to the kitchen for the house keys, but none of them fit the closet. Then, as if my mother understood the workings of privacy too well, she felt under Isabel's bedside table, under her bathroom sink, under her lampshade, and behind her painting, and finally thought to check in the back of Isabel's underwear drawer, where a yellowed envelope held a single key.

The bedroom's extra door led to a storage room about twenty by twenty feet, cramped, with a slanted ceiling. The room was almost inaccessible—as my mother touched the interior light switch, a tower of cedar chests rose in front of us like a brick wall: The chests were old and heavy, with metal clasps. When my mother struggled to pull one down, she almost toppled over from the weight, and jumped away as the chest crashed to the floor.

"Penny, watch out!" she called, but I had stepped back in time, and now stood examining the contents that had spilled out. They were new clothes, the tags still on them: pretty flowered blouses and dainty slips and a red patent-leather purse on a delicate gold chain. My mother pulled the chest upright. Inside it were ten more red purses, identical in color and style, with receipts of purchase stapled together and clipped to the strap of one of them. Under them were more blouses—thirty or forty—all of the same style and size, but in different colors, and under these as an envelope filled with more receipts, and a sheet listing the dates of purchase. At the bottom of the chest were various clothing catalogs whose pages had been clipped with Isabel's gold paper clips.

"She bought these blouses every month, for a period of four years," my mother said as she puzzled out the handwriting. "Maybe they were for people the church helped out." My mother shook out a blouse and held it up so that it seemed like Isabel's own flowered skin, or her colorful shadow: It was exactly her dimensions, too tall and narrow for most women. "No," my mother said. "She bought them for herself. They belong to her." My mother looked at a second pile of blouses that lay under the first and counted the tags. "There are forty-eight," my mother said. "She bought forty-eight blouses of exactly the same style."

My mother brought down the next chest more carefully, letting one end balance on the floor before she eased down the opposite end. She opened the chest and peered inside: It contained more catalogs and shirts, and under these, slips, tan and apricot and dark brown, cream and white and navy blue, with scalloped lace at the tops and along the hem, and miniature lace roses at the centers of the bodices. "There must be over a hundred of these," my mother said. My mother lifted some blue tissue. Another envelope lay underneath, containing another paper and more receipts, and when my mother turned the paper over and read the entry at the bottom, she said, "One hundred and twenty-four. There are one hundred and twenty-four slips here." My mother wrinkled her forehead and said, "If she lived to be a hundred she couldn't have worn all of these."

The third trunk, the one that had lain under the other two, contained new shoes unlike the shoes I had always seen on Isabel. These had heels—

not the highest kind shaped like horned animals, like my mother sometimes wore, but high enough to evoke an image of someone who was not Isabel. The shoes were narrow like Isabel's feet, with gentle slopes that made me think of the shoulders of horses, and they were in every shade of color—brown and black and sky blue and lime green and pearl gray—as if she had owned so many gowns that she had found it necessary to purchase shoes in every color ever imagined.

"I think I'll have to come back here tomorrow to finish this up," my mother said. I looked at the other trunks. "I guess we'll have to get the men to help us load these chests onto David's truck."

I was disappointed. I wanted to know what was in the rest of the chests. We loaded Isabel's painting and the cardboard boxes from her bedroom and living room into the pickup and drove to Mrs. Groot's house. When we arrived, Mrs. Groot's front door was wide open, and she was sitting on her couch, looking griefstricken and huddled into herself.

My mother knocked in a perfunctory way on the door frame, and leaned inside, asking, "Myra Groot? We've come with some of Isabel's things."

Mrs. Groot answered without rising, "Oh, Mrs. Daigle! Nicky's agreed to accept a five-year sentence. Five years, until he's eighteen!" She looked at us, her mouth half-open and her eyes wide, as if stunned by her own words.

My mother sat down beside her and took her hand; I felt uncomfortable and retreated to the front steps. I listened to Mrs. Groot's voice stagger upward in wails and then collapse suddenly, vanishing in an inward take of air, a shock of sorrow, before staggering upward again. The evening crept down the sky, and the first planet flickered on over the rim of the world, exactly at my eye level, as if it belonged to me.

My mother stepped outside and said, "Let's help Myra put Isabel's things away."

When we had finished carrying in our few boxes, my mother told Mrs. Groot about the chests of clothes, and Mrs. Groot said, "Oh my, who would think?" and then, "There's plenty of room for them in the basement. Isabel must have bought those things with that settlement she got when that priest ran over her."

"She was run over by a priest?" my mother asked, suppressing a smile.

Mrs. Groot answered, "In a drunk driving accident. A priest ran into her, and his parish paid her something—she told me it was several thousand dollars and she wasn't sure what to do with it. I think she bought all that food and those baby clothes she took to people when she went on her missions. Well, I'm glad she bought something for Isabel Flood too. She sent me a check for five hundred dollars to put in the bank for Nicky when he gets out, you know." Mrs. Groot leaned toward my mother and whispered, *"She blames herself for Nicky setting the fire."*

My mother lifted Isabel's painting from the pickup, and Mrs. Groot said, "Oh that!" in a tone of dismay and then added, "Maybe we can store Izzy's picture in Nicky's room. He told me he liked it once. He said it made him think of an ocean cruise. I don't know why."

I opened Nicky's door for them as they carried in the painting. His bed was unmade, and a stack of records had fallen and stretched across the floor. All of the lightbulbs in his lamps were blue lights; they made the dirty socks on his floor glow like sapphires. "He never liked me to come in here," Mrs. Groot told my mother. "I had to pick it up a little after the police came and turned everything upside down, but I tried not to do too much." She looked around uncertainly, and then pulled the painting sideways and lowered it onto Nicky's bed. I wondered if she would leave his room just like it was for five years, cluttered and disorderly, in honor of him.

My mother told Mrs. Groot we would return with the rest of the boxes the following day. As she drove home, my mother was so lost in her own thoughts that she forgot to talk to me. Ahead of us, the September sky had deepened to pitch black, and tree frogs shrilled like police whistles high overhead.

That night, while I lay in bed, I heard my mother tell David and F. X., "Do you know what I'm going to do? I'm going to clean out all my closets and my attic this weekend. The things people can find out about you from what you possess! When I die, I'm not going to leave one hint or clue about anything."

"What do you have to hide that we don't already know?" David answered.

"God knows you've seen enough of it," my mother told him.

"Maybe this is what it all means," F. X. said. "All those frilly clothes. Maybe what they mean is that Isabel is a closet woman."

David guffawed.

"Maybe she secretly, secretly, wished that—"

But my mother cut F. X. off and said, "That's mean-spirited, F. X. It makes me sad, sadder than I can even explain. Lon Chaney may have carried off my daughter, but I got her back, so I don't care. And what would we have done if Isabel hadn't been here to watch the girls all summer? How many people could have dealt with Penny so well for so long?"

After a while, my mother came upstairs to tell us good night and asked, "Penny, are you awake?"

I heard Mahalia turn under her covers beside me, and I pretended to be asleep. My mother sat down on Mahalia's bed.

"Are you excited about your new school?" my mother asked her.

My sister answered, "I'm terrified." She laughed, and my mother joined her: They weren't really friends yet, but my sister got along with her for brief moments like this.

"It's nice that you're trying a new school," my mother answered. "It will be an adventure." She rose to go, but then she turned at the door and sat on the edge of my bed. She pulled up my covers and leaned down to make sure that I was sleeping.

"Mahalia," she said, "I'm going to tell you about that baby I lost, all right?"

My sister did not answer—perhaps she had counted more than she realized on my mother's love of privacy.

"I'm going to tell you," my mother continued, "because you're getting to be a young woman, and maybe that's why you have questions about these things. You're going to have to deal with them yourself one day soon."

I half-expected Mahalia to sit up and answer with a passionate argument that my mother would find infuriating. Instead, my sister just turned over under her covers—I could not see if she was turning away, to avoid listening, or turning toward my mother to receive something. "You're going to tell me right now?" Mahalia asked—and the tone in her voice was clear—she really did not want to know.

"No," my mother said. "I wrote it down for you, so that you can pick the time yourself. I tried to recall as much about it all as I could, because it seemed so important to you." My mother's backlit figure raised a black rectangle—an envelope—and set it on the bedside table. "But it's not something I would have chosen to have you know about, and I wasn't sure how much you cared to hear."

As soon as my mother left the bedroom, my sister picked up the envelope. She did not turn on the bedside table lamp to read. Instead, she switched on a flashlight under her covers, as if she did not want anyone to know she was interested in what my mother had to say. When Mahalia finished reading, she got up, and put the envelope inside her dresser drawer. She stepped out of our bedroom and into the bathroom. I could hear her washing her face. I jumped up, turned on the flashlight, and opened her drawer: I saw an envelope, and the mustard-seed pendant Isabel had given her, laid out neatly in a small cardboard box. Mahalia shut off the water, and I snatched the envelope, switched off the light and got back into bed. Mahalia must have gazed at herself in the mirror for a while, because whole minutes passed before she came back into our room.

She brushed by my bed and climbed under her covers. Whatever my mother had written did not appear to keep Mahalia awake: Perhaps my sister had never deeply cared about my mother's secrets at all—Mahalia had only wanted some of her own. I listened for Mahalia to stop shifting under her covers, and shortly afterward, her breath came evenly. I got up quickly and carried the envelope to the bathroom.

"Penny?" my sister asked.

"What?" I answered, the envelope clamped under my arm.

"What are you doing?"

"I'm going to the bathroom, just like you!" I said.

"Don't forget to turn off the bathroom light," she answered. "You always forget to turn it off."

I closed the bathroom door, locked it, switched on the light, and sat on the edge of the bathtub to read the envelope's contents. I would read what my mother had written a few more times, over the years, and I did not begin to make sense of most of it until I was around Mahalia's age. However, the night my mother gave the envelope to my sister, I felt left out, as well as curious—why should Mahalia be the only one my mother told, when Mahalia was the person who had given my mother such a hard time, and for so long?

My mother wrote her letter in shorthand, as if, while she had determined to reveal part of her past, she intended to give it only to people who understood her language. (When shorthand disappeared years later, her letter, oddly, would become a relic as indecipherable to most people as a scroll of Mayan hieroglyphics). Her account launched immediately into detail:

I was over at the house of a little girl, Lottie, who was your friend then, Mahalia. You won't remember her because her family moved away the next summer, and you only played together a few times. I had just found out I was pregnant a few weeks before. It was too early for me to let myself get excited. Your father was excited. I wanted to wait until I was farther along because at that stage you think, well anything can happen. But I was feeling happy in spite of myself, sitting out in Lottie's backyard with her mother Pauline.

We were drinking iced tea. And then Pauline looked down at Lottie, who was sitting in her lap, and lifted Lottie's hair and said, "What's this on her neck? A rash?" She felt Lottie's forehead and said she thought she had a fever. Lottie's face was bright red, I remember, so we picked both of you girls up, and I took you home, and Pauline called me and said Lottie had a rash in her mouth. She had taken her to Dr. Epstein, who told her that Lottie had German measles.

When Pauline told me, we both cried. I called my doctor, who in those days was Dr. Cope in Dannemora. He told me the symptoms to watch out for, and I watched you, but you never seemed to get them. Three weeks later, after I thought the danger was past, I got them. I woke up one morning and saw spots on the roof of my mouth, and I knew by the way my heart stopped when I saw it, what I had. I lay in bed all day, although the whole thing was no worse than a flu—my throat hurt a little, my joints hurt, a rash you could barely see crept from my face down my arms to my legs. I just lay in bed and watched it, knowing what it meant. I had seen German measles before as a girl. My mother used to take me over to the houses of children sick with it, to make me catch it while I was still young, but I never did.

The next day, the rash was gone. I left you at Pauline's, Mahalia, and I made an appointment with Dr. Cope and told him that I was sure I had had German measles, and he told me, simply, that I had not. I thought I just hadn't described my symptoms right, so I told them to him again, and he accused me of making them up to get him to connive with me to get rid of the baby. My mouth fell open. Well, I had no proof at all except my own word! And I saw that my own doctor was not going to take me at my own word. And at the same time, it hit me: German measles must be even worse for an unborn baby than I thought, or he wouldn't be making such a crazy accusation.

I left his office like a person in a trance, and I drove to the library in Plattsburgh and looked up German measles there in a medical textbook. I almost fainted when I read it: It said that if the baby did not miscarry or die stillborn, there was a good chance it would be born with cataracts and a tiny head or abnormal brain, or a bad heart, and that it could develop a worse form of the disease itself as a teenager where its muscles and mind deteriorated. I had been ten weeks pregnant at the time I was with Lottie, the worst time, it said, for me to have been exposed. I don't expect you to understand how this all made me feel, Mahalia. What I felt mostly was used up. I knew this would be much worse than anything F. X. and I had ever gone through together, and when I reached into my heart to try to see how I would face this, what I found there was nothing: I did not have it in me to watch such suffering forced on my own child.

At first, it didn't even occur to me to get an abortion illegally—the idea was terrifying to any woman, back then. I just drove home and went back to taking care of you, and every day I became more and more frightened. I would have these panic attacks where my heart would beat too fast and my skin would cover itself with hives and I would find myself thinking, "Maybe this will kill the baby. Maybe if I had a heart attack, the baby would die even if they could save me." I did not know where to turn—your father thought Dr. Cope knew best, and your father had his own compunctions about breaking the law, and about abortion too. I almost gave in, gave in to him and Dr. Cope. But then Pauline called me and told me about someone right here in Stein, who performed abortions at the Motor Inn.

I called the number. I remember the worst thing was that I had to wait three weeks—by that time, I was almost four months gone. I was afraid I wouldn't survive the procedure. I hocked my engagement ring and drove to the Motor Inn with more money than I'd ever held in my hand at one time. I checked into the Motor Inn, and I knew as soon as I paid for the room that the clerk knew what I was there for—he gave me this wolfish, sneery look and handed me the key to a back room. I walked over to a door with the number fifty-two on it—I still remember that number. Parked right outside the door was a station wagon with five children sitting in it, looking dumb and scared and worried and quiet, and inside the room with the number fifty-two on it, I could hear a woman moaning.

No one answered when I knocked—I found a chambermaid and asked her to open the door for me. We both heard the woman crying when we stepped in—the room looked like the inside of a barn, and lying on the floor by the bathroom was a woman pale as death, and under her was a dark red slick that it took me the shock of a second to see was her own blood. There was blood soaking her skirt, and on the bed and a chair beside it, and running in a stream across the floor, more blood than I knew we had in us. I think my whole life changed after that second, because I had never really known that kind of horror before.

She moaned, and the chambermaid, who was just a girl, barely older than you, just stood there, scared and stuck to the floor, asking, "What's wrong? What happened? What's wrong?" I did not know what to do—I could not believe that this was something that was happening in my own life. I felt so shook up—and even in the middle of all this, Mahalia, I found myself think-

ing, maybe the shock of this will make me miscarry, so I won't have to have the baby.

I backed out of the room and found myself outside, staring at the car full of the woman's children. I walked right past them, to a pay phone outside the motel. I called an ambulance and waited there until the ambulance came and the ambulance men carried the woman out of the building and the children jumped out of the car shrieking, while the chambermaid and I tried to calm them down and the ambulance men stood there, wondering what to do with all of the children, until they gave me the woman's name and I called their home and their father came to get them. He looked like a dead man when he arrived, and I did not ask him if he knew whether his wife was all right because I myself was so numb I could hardly talk.

I called your father and crawled back into my car and curled up in a ball on the front seat until your father came and found me. I told him what had happened. Your father called his minister at the Baptist church, and he called a Baptist minister who worked out of a church in Greenwich Village in New York City, and he gave us the name of a doctor who was willing to lie for us and say that the pregnancy endangered my life.

I was four and a half months gone by then. Your father drove me down to the city. A regular doctor performed the abortion in his office. The nurse who was with him kept shouting, "It's a boy! It's a boy!" I could have slapped her. Afterward, the doctor told us that he thought the baby's head was deformed, but he wasn't certain. It was easier to tell, he said, later on.

My mother's account ended there, abruptly, without further appeal, or even a conclusion, which might have revealed a deeper sense of her own emotions or judgments at the time.

I felt alarmed by the details of the letter, and puzzled, and awed in that way peculiar to children when they see the breadth and length of a parent's life as a territory that predated them and invented itself without need of them. I folded the letter and returned it to its envelope. I thought of leaving on the light, just to nettle Mahalia, but when I heard talking, I turned the light off to make myself unobtrusive. I hid the envelope under my nightgown and opened the bathroom door. At first, I thought Mahalia was muttering in her sleep, but as I stepped into the hall, I saw my mother sitting on the foot of my sister's bed.

Mahalia was asking her, "*Daddy* helped you?"

"I told your father I would leave him if he didn't," my mother answered. "But in the end, Mahalia, I don't think I had to. I think he just wanted to do what was right in his own mind, but he wasn't sure what was right. It was hard for him. It made me love him more, but I think it made him love me a little less."

Mahalia was quiet for a minute: I sensed that my sister wanted to choose what further facts my mother would reveal. My sister—who, as far as I knew, had never prodded my mother with a single question about her experience at The Place, or about how hard she might be continuing to struggle now—asked, "Don't you ever wonder what it would have been like if the baby had come. If he was here now?"

"Sometimes," my mother answered. "But not the way you might think—it doesn't drive me crazy like some telltale heart under the floorboards—I think of it the way you do all the things in your life that might have gone in one direction instead of another. What would my father be like if I knew him now? Or my mother, if she'd lived to be old? What if F. X. had never lost his sight, or never gotten it back? What if your father hadn't died, or I hadn't even married him to begin with? What if I didn't know David?"

"You don't wonder sometimes what it would have been like to have a boy?"

"If I'd had that baby, I might not have gone on to have another, or I would have had a different baby, who wasn't Penny. I would never have known Penny, and I can't imagine that. I can't imagine my life without either you or Penny. This is the life I ended up with. It's *my life*."

The envelope rustled under my nightgown. I pinned it to my ribs with my arm, stepped forward, and slipped into the bedroom and under my blankets. My mother stood, pulled up my covers, and patted my leg through the bedspread.

She lingered for a moment in the doorway. "Considering how little control I've had over my life," she said, "It's ended up pretty good."

―――――

The following morning, F. X. and David returned with us to Isabel's to load her furniture and cedar chests into David's pickup. The men could not fit all the chests in the truck, and while my mother and I waited in Isabel's bare kitchen for them to return from their first trip to the Groots', our curiosity got the better of us both and we reentered the storeroom to look in the trunks that were left. In the first one, we found a dozen brocade bags exactly like the one I had always seen Isabel carry; and a furniture catalog that featured cedar chests; and three more in which Isabel had circled various items of clothing.

I remember that there was nothing of great value in the remaining chests either: no jewelry or money, for example, although the clothes the trunks contained my mother pronounced to be of good quality. One chest was full of stockings, and another a rasher of linen skirts, lined with satin, laid on each other as closely as strips of bacon. There was a small trunk that contained only puzzles, so many that when I ran my hands through them I had the sensation of dipping into a treasure chest. There was a trunk that contained satin undergarments that my mother pulled me away from, saying, "We can't do that—it's too much of a violation of her privacy," so that I ached to look through it.

Isabel had no personal letters or relics. Only one chest contained any biographical documents: a birth certificate dated 1941 that gave her mother's name as "Lily," and no father's name; a record from Saint Anne's Home for Girls, which noted that Isabel had come there when she was two years of age; and a high school diploma from Andalusia, Ohio. "Lord, I had no idea Isabel was raised in a home," my mother said. "Did you know that about her?" I nodded, and my mother folded the documents neatly and replaced them in the chest. Isabel had in her possession no childhood photographs, or pictures of friends or caretakers or people who might have been close to her at one time. The letters she had received from Ohio were all impersonal, mimeographed correspondence and religious pamphlets from right-to-lifers allied with a priest named Father Griese in Dayton, or with Reverend Sloat in Cincinnati.

My mother paged through some of the right-to-life pamphlets from Ohio, and said, "It's so odd. None of the pictures show any mothers. There's not one body drawn around any of the wombs—it's all disconnected wombs with babies curled up inside. You'd think unborn babies lived free-floating, bobbing around in the air."

Mahalia did not accompany us to Isabel's house. She did not attend Stein Evangelical anymore, or wear her mustard-seed pendant or her long skirts and dresses or her slipper-shoes, and she spent long hours fixing her dark red hair. Once, she looked up at me while transplanting some of her ferns behind the house and asked, "Penny, do you think I'm timid and insist on things being predictable?" I shrugged my shoulders; I'd never thought about it. And once, in the fall, I walked in on Mahalia standing stark naked before the mirror, looking over her right shoulder to admire her body's profile: She was so breathtaking, with her new breasts and her hipbones like fish breaking the surface of water, that even I could understand why that image of herself arrested and astonished her. At night, I would hear her tossing and turning under her covers, and once she asked me in a dreamy voice whether I thought Isabel had ever been in love or understood what it was.

———

Mrs. Wroblewski gave birth on October first. She named the baby Isabel. The following week, Mrs. Wroblewski called us from the hospital to tell us that after thirty-six hours of labor, Lucy had given birth to a boy she had named Myron. Ten days later, Mrs. Wroblewski came to our doorstep dressed in a housecoat and slippers, looking exhausted, and pressing her own new-born against her shoulder. I could see her husband sitting in an old station wagon behind her, the motor still running as he balanced a second baby in the crook of his arm. Mrs. Wroblewski told Mahalia that Lucy had run away with the Wroblewskis' oldest daughter Roberta.

"Have you seen them, Mahalia?" Mrs. Wroblewski asked. "They left a note saying they were tired of caring for babies and were going to New York City! Do you think they're telling the truth? Have they been by here at all? My daughter never said a thing to me about it. And Lucy—Roberta's eighteen, but Lucy isn't even old enough to get a job. How can they be serious?"

Mahalia told Mrs. Wroblewski she had not talked to Lucy since the baby had come home from the hospital.

"She just left her baby with us," Mrs. Wroblewski said in a baffled tone. "I don't have any idea where we're supposed to go from here. Do we just let him stay until Mark Coker gets out of jail, or tell the police, or what? Myra Groot says not to tell Mark yet—it will just upset him, and maybe Lucy will come back, who knows? Lucy didn't take all the money Isabel put in the bank for her, so she must be coming back, don't you think?"

Mr. Wroblewski honked, and Mrs. Wroblewski returned to the car. Her husband handed her the second baby. She clutched him next to her new daughter as if holding an unwieldy stack of firewood, and they all drove off.

By the end of October, the Wroblewskis had posted a notice with the police for both of the girls. All fall you would see Lucy's baby Myron being pushed around town stores by Mrs. Wroblewski, in a twin carriage, beside Mrs. Wroblewski's little girl. He had a lot of brown hair, and eyes the dark gray of magnets, and a lipless frown like a bitter old man's. Sometimes Mrs. Groot would take over and spell Mrs. Wroblewski, and you'd see Mrs. Groot strolling with the babies, especially after Nicky had been transferred from Stein to a detention facility near Buffalo.

On November third, Mrs. Esselborne, and an additional member of Stein

Evangelical named Mr. Floater, won two places on the school board. A week later, four constituents of Stein Evangelical filed a lawsuit against the school district superintendent, five high school teachers, and Stein High's Mr. Cossack, demanding that Stein's children not be taught about "pagan holidays, especially Halloween, or instructed on other subjects with religious content including but not limited to numerology, Egyptian tombs, the Hindu gods of India, Earth Day, and human sacrifices conducted by the Mexican Aztecs." During settlement negotiations in the spring, Gwendolyn Brooks's poem, "the mother," would be eliminated from the English curriculum, and Mr. Brewer would resign in protest. However, by this time, Isabel would be hundreds of miles south, serving her sentence at Bedford Hills Correctional Facility in Westchester County, and would have long since stopped communicating with Stein Evangelical. She wrote brief letters to Mrs. Wroblewski and Mrs. Groot, but never inquired about Reverend Bender or the church.

When David learned in mid-November that Isabel was being transferred from our county jail to the state's women's prison, my mother asked Mahalia if she would visit Isabel before she left Stein. Mahalia agreed dutifully and reluctantly, and when we arrived at Stein's county jail, she did not want to enter the visitors' room alone. She made my mother and me accompany her and sit by her side when Isabel came out to greet her. Their meeting was stilted and little conversation passed between them.

Isabel looked no different than she ever had. She wore a narrow dress and her slipper-shoes, and her hair pinned back to her head; her ordinary habits needed little adjustment to fit life in jail. When she greeted me, I was surprised that I missed her, surprised by how large a piece she had come to be in our lives in so short a period, and I felt sad to leave her there.

She told my sister, "I was at fault, Mahalia. I allowed prideful ambition and my own unexamined feelings to cloud my vision, so that I allied myself with someone when I should not have." I found Isabel's statement cryptic and still do: Was she blaming herself for leaving her solitude, or just for choosing the wrong ally?

Mahalia did not ask Isabel what her unexamined feelings were. Our departure was uncomfortable, and Mahalia's face revealed a mixture of guilt and gratitude that it was time to go. We drove home through a cool dusk—November's purples arched high above us and the first stars snapped on like the lights of distant houses less important than ours. When we parked in our driveway, no frogs sang in the heavens above us; no cicadas catcalled; not even the busy delicate voices of gnats gossiped in the air; winter was approaching, with its hush. That night I barely held myself awake while I listened to Mahalia cast about in the dark, trying to find a place to hook onto sleep. I knew my sister wrestled with what had happened between her and Isabel, that Mahalia was still trying to figure out whether she had betrayed Isabel or Isabel had betrayed her, that my sister was embarrassed and remorseful and relieved all at once. Mahalia was lucky to have us then, lucky to be able to return to our loving darkness, the prodigal good daughter received back into our electrified welcoming chaos.

A NOTE ON THE AUTHOR

Paula Sharp is the author of the critically acclaimed *Crows Over a Wheatfield*, two previous novels, *The Woman Who Was Not All There*, and *Lost in Jersey City;* and the short-story collection, *The Imposter*. She is a translator of Latin American contemporary fiction, including Antonio Skármeta's novel *The Insurrection*. A graduate of Columbia Law School, she lives in New York State.